Bone to

the Bone

Bone to the Bone

A NOVEL

Nathan Shaham

Translated from the Hebrew by Dalya Bilu

Grove Press
New York

Library of Congress Cataloging-in-Publication Data

Shaham, Nathan.
  ['Etsem el 'atsmo. English]
  Bone to the bone: a novel / by Nathan Shaham; translated by
Dalya Bilu.—1st ed.
  ISBN 0-8021-1001-0
  I. Title.
PJ5054.S3E7713   1993
892.4'36—dc20   92-38330

Manufactured in the United States of America

FIRST AMERICAN EDITION 1993
10 9 8 7 6 5 4 3 2 1

Introduction

I sit and write in a small, utterly quiet room, by a desk which is all mine, by the window, the white sand, and the sea. I write as if someone were breathing down my neck and I had to fill a quota.

You can hear the stillness and my pen scratching the paper. My writing is small and crooked, as though a fly had dipped its legs in ink and crawled over the paper.

What am I writing?

It's not for me to define the genre. I write down whatever comes and insists on being written.

I've tried my hand at writing three times in my life. It was always something. . . . Each time it was something different but each time it was the same thing. Testimony, summing up, the moral of my story, bits of history, reflection, an indictment of the people who distorted the revolution—all the same.

I came here with nothing: empty hands. My wife had burned "The History of the Commune of Via Nova" for fear of the police. "Black Snow" had been seized by the NKVD. I had destroyed the draft of "The Classless Society." Years of work down the drain.

I bought this notebook while waiting for the plane at the airport in Vienna. Thick with a hard cover, it is like the notebook where my father kept the accounts of his wretched shop in Rashov. I fell on it as soon as I bought it. I took a sensual pleasure in inscribing the words on the smooth white paper. A boy running into the sea, jumping over the shallow waves with his knees raised, and his feet kicking out sideways.

I was done with the underground. Finished with the straitjacket of communicating by code. I could write down everything that came into my head. No more crouching in a dark corner so my cellmates wouldn't see. There was no need to secrete scraps of paper in a hollow tree trunk or scratch signs on onion skins with a sharpened twig.

I could write, erase, make mistakes. Tell insignificant stories.

On a bit of rag hidden in your anus you write nothing superfluous. There's no room for anything but a scream. And what about the riches of life between one scream and the next?

And yet, I feel a certain disappointment. Nobody needs the treasures I smuggled out in my memory. My secrets have been broadcast to the world in the newspapers. They are no longer news. The Iron Curtain did not silence the voices. But I can't help myself, I have to rake it all up again. It's like scratching a rash in spite of yourself.

At first I thought of writing my autobiography, but I soon discovered that three pages would be enough. I'll stick them at the beginning of this notebook, as a kind of introduction to the characters. I found that I could not write my biography from beginning to end for a few reasons. First, my memory needs a stimulus. It doesn't work to order. Second, if I begin with the past, I may never reach the present. And then the sequence is wrong. All the times are present. And there are things I didn't know about until many years later, when they no longer existed. I'll begin with the here and now, I said. Whatever comes up in my memory means that its time has come.

Even this confusion is one of the freedoms a man can enjoy in a country where policemen read books to pass the time of day, not to expose traitors.

I write Russian, that's my language. I know a few other languages, Hebrew too. But my mind is full of Russian images. My thoughts fall into place to the sound of Russian. When I speak or write in Hebrew, it comes out clumsy and pompous and that is precisely what I want to avoid. I desperately want the details to be accurate: facts, evaluations, even descriptions of moods.

Writing gives me enormous satisfaction but no little pain, too. It is hard for me to choose the words but not because my thoughts falter. Many words in Russian, like magnetic pins, drag behind them the slogans in which they were imprisoned. We must count the Russian language among the victims of our dreadful times. If I write in the prisoners' argot, I will have to add a glossary.

Whom am I doing this for?

A Western writer I once met in Moscow said literature is a letter to a bosom friend you have not met. Why print it? Because you don't know his address. You scatter your letter to the winds in the hope that a copy will reach him.

My case is different.

I am writing to people I know. I don't know where they are. I don't know if they're alive. But I need them to know that the last word has not been said yet.

We had harsh, bitter arguments which are not yet over. There were terrible silences. In our lives in Russia, in those days, words left unsaid could do great harm too.

Whenever I sit down to write now I remember Slutzki.

Slutzki was the proofreader of *Der Emes,* the Yiddish-language newspaper of the Jewish Section of the Soviet Communist Party. Young but old for his age, lanky, balding, and silent. The editors, writers, and poets who crowded the editorial offices were fond of him. He was the only one who seemed to know his place. He never buttonholed great poets to show his verses, never pretended to know a better joke than the one just told by somebody else.

He was not a Party member and he never took part in arguments about political programs or the significance of current events. "I'm not an active type," he would say to the Party members who tried to press him into their service. He would stoop over the galley sheets on his rickety table, scribble his corrections on them, and place them before me with an apologetic smile. He was sorry for giving a printer, a real proletarian like me, extra work.

One day he opened his mouth and spoke.

I was busy mending the old printing press. Slutzki was on his way to the samovar. He had a glass in his hand with a teaspoon and a bag with tea leaves. There was a cube of sugar between his teeth. When he passed me, he stopped. For a moment he stared mesmerized at the new press piling up sheets of print. Suddenly he spat the sugar cube into the palm of his free hand and said, "One day we'll be buried under this . . ."

I kept quiet. A man with a screwdriver and a highly developed class consciousness has no time to listen, in the middle of his work, to the philosophical ramblings of a clever Talmudist. But he did not take the hint.

"Our children and our children's children will have to waste years of their lives to find one word of truth in this pile of rubbish."

I raised my head. His eyes were burning. I thought I'd better warn him: "Careful, Slutzki. You'll be hauled in for despising your brother writers." Slutzki put the sugar cube into his dirty pocket and got ready to talk, like a starving man who has come upon a loaf of bread. He had visited the Lenin Library, he said. He had looked at the catalogue, browsed in the basements. Long tiers of shelves from floor to ceiling. So many books! And most of them printed recently, official books by official writers. Stuff and nonsense and deliberate lies. "What about the generations to come?" he shouted. It would take years of work to sift the lies from the truth. This thought gave him no peace. He was an accomplice. And every day the pile grew higher. Soon it would be impossible to rescue a single word of truth from it. If only we could be sure that it was all lies, perhaps we would be able to burn the lot and begin again from the beginning. But in a barely decipherable code there were true, painful things written there too. Job and Lamentations and Ecclesiastes. And what would happen to these reams of print in the hour of truth? Every book that was written then would have to refute a book that already existed. Every word would have to cancel another.

Whenever I pick up my pen, I think of what Slutzki said. Each word will have to cancel another. I feel weak when I think of it. The library has an iron door and an army of academic guards.

I would like Slutzki to read what I am writing now.

Where is he? For thirty-five years I longed for a chance meeting, but it never took place. Perhaps he was murdered. I would very much like him to know that it wasn't I who informed on him. The newspaper office was crawling with spies and opportunists who would do anything to get ahead. But sometimes even the greatest cowards are seized by an insane courage. What did Slutzki think when he was arrested? What was it that got him? Was it cowardice? Selfishness, malice, stupidity? Or historical inevitability?

I write with a passion. Sometimes I fill five or even ten pages in one evening. Whatever comes into my head. Sometimes I have to force myself to overcome my weakness to remember something. I hate straining my memory. I haven't the patience to reconstruct chapters of my life history. I even feel an inner resistance to making the effort.

I've had to write my résumé so many times, and in such maddening detail.

Was there anyone who didn't ask for it? The residents' committee, the Party cell, the registrar of the university, the police, the interrogators, the trade union. Never mind who it was who asked for it, all the documents ended up in the same interminable file. And when they got there they were checked by an official who compared every detail to make sure that no attempt had been made to mislead the authorities. He would pounce on any mistake, omission, discrepancy with previous documents, and report it.

Whenever they needed to, they could prove that you were an inveterate liar.

You needed a rare memory to survive in that country.

After being beaten, starved, and humiliated, it's hard to remember your replies to the idiotic questions some official asked you ten years ago, when different policies held sway. Forgetfulness is exile and memory redemption, said the Baal

Shem Tov. In Russia, this beautiful metaphor was the literal truth.

At the beginning I wrote almost every day, although I had my moments of dejection then, too. When we meet sometimes, a group of Jewish exiles in the land of the Jews, we tell each other stories which are amazingly similar. They sound like one long monologue in which the names of people and places, as in the ramblings of a senile old man, are interchangeable. At times like these, I lose all desire to bequeath my own self-justifications to the generations to come. But as soon as I get home to my room the urge to make love to my notebooks overcomes me again.

A few months ago, when I was still living in my daughter's house, my son-in-law came into my room when I was writing.

He glanced at the notebook with the contemptuous look in his eye reserved by practical men of the world for loafers.

"What are you writing?"

I was confused. I had no answer ready. Without thinking, I said quickly, "Diary."

"Really? I thought you were making amendments to the *Short Course*," he said sarcastically, referring to the official Bolshevik history.

He hates the Soviet Union from the bottom of his heart. And when I listen to his superficial lectures on events over there, I feel the wish to defend the people of that country from the shallow and facile criticism of men like him, who have no idea of what really goes on there.

Later on, I overheard him talking to my daughter.

"I caught him red-handed. Writing." "So what?" "You're going to have your work cut out for you." "What work?" "He's writing in Russian." "That's the language he knows best." "Take it from me, he's going to ask you to translate it from Russian into Hebrew or English." "Why should he?"

He did not answer her, but only said: "He must be writing his autobiography. Mark my words: people with something to hide always write their memoirs."

I thought about his words without anger. I felt: They're

willing to take me back to the bosom of the happy family that was immune to the revolutionary germ, on the condition that I give up any claim to being an honest man. I have to accept it. And there is some justice in his words. People at peace with themselves do not usually write their memoirs.

But sit two Russians down with a bottle of vodka and they immediately feel the need to confess. The Russian security police did us a favor by planting informers in our cells and weaning us from this dangerous habit. The moment they began confessing, the rest of us knew it was time to be careful.

Sometimes we write in order to include people close to us in the things we experienced without them. Our lives in the present seem insubstantial without those past experiences. This is the meaning of love.

In our first year of marriage, before we had a room of our own, even in someone else's apartment, my wife and I used to roam the parks and kiss in the dark entrances to movie theaters. Bit by bit we created our own map of Moscow, each place with the thrill of its hasty, enthusiastic embraces. And then my wife grew jealous of all the places I had been without her. We had a feeling that our love would not be complete until she became acquainted with Rushkov, Odessa, Tel Yosef, and Hebron.

That's what I'm doing now: drawing a map of the places where we were separated from each other.

This letter is addressed to her, too.

To a friend who asked me what I was writing, I replied: a Jewish family history.

You have to understand the story of my life to understand the irony in my reply. A résumé, in short, of the kind I used to copy out neatly over and over again in the old days, like a kind of detailed identity card, this time of my own free will and unexpurged:

I was born in Rushkov in the Ukraine, at the beginning of the century. The fourth of seven. Today one of two. My sister, as far as I know, is in the U.S.A. I don't know where exactly.

My father was a shoemaker and a Talmudic scholar with a

voracious appetite for public affairs. He tried to set up a local branch of Tzairei Zion without success. His workshop was shut most of the time. I don't know what we lived on. My mother worked all day and half the night, washing, sewing, knitting, cooking. We were wretchedly poor, but when I had to write my résumé for all and sundry in Russia they did not allow me the privilege of claiming proletarian origins. I had to write "bourgeois origins" because my father sold old shoes and had a workshop.

I went to heder, yeshiva, and spent one year at a gymnasium. At the start of the First World War I had already acquired a number of substitutes for the faith of my forefathers. Our home was destroyed during the war. My eldest brother, a Ukrainian officer, a patriot, was killed by his own soldiers. The second was killed when the Bolsheviks conquered our town. We moved from one town to another: Mogilev, Odessa, Moscow. The whole of Russia seemed populated by my aunts, each poorer than her sister. My mother died during our wanderings, and the family scattered in all directions. I was in Moscow during the revolution. For a while I stayed with family and afterward I joined the pioneer Zionist youth movement Hehalutz and worked on an agricultural training farm near the city. During the civil war I was in the street, wherever shots were being fired.

In 1920 I made my way to Odessa and from there to Palestine. I worked on building the Migdal-Tiberias road and on Kibbutz Ramat Rachel; I was a member of the Joseph Trumpeldor Battalion of the Labor Brigade, at Ein Harod and Tel Yosef. I was a farmhand, a shepherd, a building worker, a cowboy, and a maintenance man. I was involved in every fight of the Labor Brigade with the fanaticism typical of my generation. For a while I was also a member of the militant underground, one of the true believers who could be relied on to shout at the top of his voice and also keep his mouth shut.

I was on the left. In 1926 I took one step further and secretly joined the Hebrew Workers Socialist Party, but it got out and I was forced to leave the Labor Brigade. Ideology has played an important role in my life.

I had a girlfriend in Tel Yosef. When I was thrown out of the Brigade in 1927, she was pregnant. Nobody thought the one had anything to do with the other, and neither did I—personal affairs took a backseat when public issues were at stake. Our son was born a few months after my expulsion and I wasn't allowed to see him. People were quite ruthless and fanatical in those days. I myself would have despised a man who was prepared to back down in an argument for the sake of living with a woman or bringing up a child.

For almost three years I worked for the Communist Party of Palestine. Since I had learned Arabic when I was a shepherd, I was employed as a liaison between the Jews and the Arabs. I was arrested twice, and since I was already well known to the authorities and of no further use to the Party, they let me go back to Russia.

For a few months I was a member of Via Nova, the Jewish commune of ex–Labor Brigade members in the Crimea. I threw myself passionately into physical labor. This is my life, I said to myself. But after a few months I went to Moscow to visit my father in the hospital and fell in love with a girl there, the daughter of a Polish Communist, and she followed me to the commune. We only stayed a few months. We had a baby daughter who caught a disease they didn't know how to treat. She was transferred to a hospital in Moscow and we followed her there and never went back to Via Nova. I worked as a printer and studied at the Technical Institute, but I never graduated.

I was a Party member until 1936, when I was expelled for deviations dating back to my Palestine period. In 1937, I was arrested for the first time. I was in the Vladimir Prison for a few months and after that I wandered from camp to camp. I worked in a road gang, in the coal mines, and as a lumberjack in the forests. I became an expert miner and was in charge of a whole mining region for a while.

After the outbreak of the war, which we called the Great Patriotic War, I received a conditional release and volunteered for the Red Army. I served in the engineering corps, where I laid railway lines and dismantled mines on the southern front up to

1943 and on the western front to the end of 1944. I was decorated twice. At the beginning of 1945, I was arrested again, for hostile propaganda. Pro-German sympathies they called it, when I had tried to stop looting in a little town conquered by one army after another. At my trial, I made a sarcastic speech and got ten years. In the mining region where I had been a prisoner before, they welcomed me back with open arms. I was released seven years later and then rearrested for leaving my place of exile. In 1957, I was released for the third time. I entered Moscow illegally to look for my wife and daughter. There, for the first time, I met a son I had fathered with a woman who was my mistress before my first arrest, but he was leaving Moscow. For a time I wandered around the city with nothing to do, hungry and destitute, looking for people who were all dead and gone. In 1958, I was expelled from Moscow and spent a few years in the zone where ex-prisoners were allowed to live, until I obtained a permit to take up residence in the city in 1963. I earned my living doing various odd jobs, and for short periods I was allowed to work at my trade. The revolutionary mosquito kept buzzing in my brain, and once I had settled down and found a steady job, I began printing forbidden books on a typewriter. I was arrested for the fourth time, but released shortly afterward.

One day a distant relative of mine arrived in Moscow from the United States. He brought me news of my family in Israel, and soon afterward the first letters arrived. These, by the way, were signed by people I did not know. It was only after I had written giving exact information about myself that I received letters directly from my family. The first one came from Vera. She sent a photograph of my son's family—him and his wife and their three children. She did not send a picture of herself. She wrote that she knew my daughter and her family, and that I would be hearing from her soon, too. A month later I received a letter from my daughter. It was short and cautious, as if she was afraid of the censor. She did not mention her mother. She also sent a photograph: a man and a woman with a boy and a little girl. I spent a couple of hours looking at it through a magnifying glass. I applied for an emigration permit within days and was fired from my job two weeks later.

In a thin but steady trickle, the correspondence continued for about a year. The letters carried no warmth or emotion. It seemed they had been written on the assumption that the police would read them. Two or three old friends sent me letters like articles in an official newspaper. I wrote little about myself—I could say nothing important and it was hard to write empty phrases. Suddenly, without warning, I was given forty-eight hours to leave the Soviet Union. I packed my few things and left.

In general, I can say this about myself: I have few needs and some modest interests. I like to play chess and design engineering projects, even if I know they will never be realized. I like listening to music, especially Russian folk songs. I also like to look at the faces of passersby. I think this hobby would annoy them if they knew what I was looking for. I try to guess how they would behave under stress, in conditions of hunger or torture. This is a bitter and unpleasant habit which I cannot break. (N.B.: These pages were written later when I had been in Israel for about ten months and was living in a place of my own. I added them to the first notebook as an introduction, to give the reader some background. They are like an author's apology of the kind customary in the days when people felt the need to apologize for any act which was not productive and whose purpose was not clear. The account continues in more or less chronological order, dealing with events and the memories they evoke. Most of it was written in the notebooks as things came into my mind; other parts were written on bits of paper and inserted into the notebooks after corrections. The first pages were written on the train to Austria and at the airport in Vienna on the way to Israel. I saw no point in specifying dates. Whole chapters are about the past, and I doubt if there is any importance to the particular day on which the memory came to life.)

First Notebook: Second Coming

We crossed the frontier between Czechoslovakia and Austria. There was the same scenery on both sides—the same gentle hills, farmers' houses, and vegetable beds. Only the policemen's uniforms were different, and the gleam in the passengers' eyes.

It was as if they couldn't be sure up to the last minute that they would really be allowed to leave. Perhaps the train would stop before the border and policemen would get on with gloating faces and say, "Get off please. This will only take a few minutes, a mere formality," like a cat's paw finally descending on its prey.

I sat next to the window with mixed feelings. I thought about everything I was leaving behind, never to see again. I felt homesick. I ordered myself to be happy; hadn't I always managed extreme changes in my life? As long as I chose the change in direction myself.

The confusion in my soul sought release, but there was no one to talk to. Most of the passengers were from Georgia and didn't seem eager to talk to me.

Writing was a release then. I felt the need to capture the moment, and began to write, like a Japanese tourist with his camera. Later when he gets home, he can look at the pictures.

"Home" was a loaded word for me, loaded with the irony of fate. In 1929 when I left Palestine to return to Russia, I used the same word. But then I still had a father, a brother, two sisters, and a group of friends at Via Nova waiting to welcome me.

I had a family in Israel, too, but we didn't know one another.

I wrote about things which may have had no particular

value or significance, but were perhaps symbols of the place and the time. I was under no obligation to connect every detail to the principle in which it is imprisoned. Out of the corner of my eye, I watched the Georgian passenger sitting next to me. His left hand tightly gripped the opening of his sack, while the fingers of his right hand felt the objects protruding from its sides. He seemed to be making sure that nothing escaped on the way. His concern for his property gave his face a profoundly reflective expression.

Did I learn anything from watching him? Did I learn that acquisitiveness is second nature to us? That our minds are mostly occupied by trivialities and only rarely by thought? Perhaps I learned nothing and wrote about the Georgian as a kind of declaration of spiritual freedom. We are under no obligation to draw useful conclusions from everything we see. The right of these things to exist is inherent in the fact of their existence, in the fullness of being which they radiate and in their trueness to themselves.

People without rights are constantly troubled by questions about rights, and seek legitimization for everything they do, even for loving and hating. We are never sure if we are free to enjoy the view or whether there is room for pure enjoyment.

The Georgian, Mr. Avramshvili, felt no brotherly love for me. Our names will both appear in the statistics, but he felt no curiosity about that, either. Our common fate did not concern him. We traveled to the same destination, but our reasons were different. He talked to me without enthusiasm and was not inclined to share his secrets. Crossing the border did not unlock his tongue either. He had managed to obtain a certain measure of freedom in the Soviet Union too. I am free only when I can call things by their names. He is free whenever he can keep his property. No one can prevent him from whispering his prayers. He answered my questions with obvious unwillingness, yes and no. What an old nuisance! He did not bother to disguise his suspicions—people like me are nothing but trouble.

In the restroom at the airport, with its soft music and syn-

thetic smells, I looked at my face in the mirror and my spirits fell.
I saw myself through other people's eyes and could not imagine
that this man wanted to make a fresh start. My face was tired,
tense; my eyes were bloodshot, and bags of wrinkled skin hung
beneath them. I had an unhealthy flush and brown blotches on
my cheeks, with cracked, white lips. I looked like an old man
going to the Holy Land to die, so he would be there ready for the
resurrection of the dead. A man should avoid unexpected meetings after the age of seventy. They produce a stirring in your
breast, like bursting bubbles.

I was the only one who didn't seem to care about the plane
being late; I wanted to put off arriving as long as possible.

There was a sour, middle-aged reporter traveling with us,
the only Israeli who wasn't from the Jewish Agency. Stuck with
his boring, upbeat assignment, he was looking for something
juicy, dramatic, even shocking. He cursed his luck, having missed
a hijacked plane.

I avoided him for the second day running and listened to
him interviewing other passengers from a safe distance. I
watched him pick people up and drop them with charm and
ease. I didn't think this experienced sensation hunter would
waste his ammunition on small fry. His shoes shone and his eyes
glittered. He listened to people's stories with a patronizing
smile. He reminded me of one of the better Cheka interrogators.
He would look at you in the same way, with a mocking smile. You
couldn't pull the wool over his eyes. He knew who was inventing
things to make a strong impression. He would find what he was
looking for, even if it was a needle in a haystack.

It was a foretaste of what we could expect: he pitied us. He
thought we were cripples; we had been imprisoned in a dark box,
8.6 million square miles big, and our eyes were still blinking as
we emerged into the light. He represented enlightenment and
democracy; he had no idea that he too was the prisoner of his
prejudices. I had heard him scolding a family from Riga who had
sent their sons on ahead to the U.S.A. People who only looked
out for themselves made him sick, he had said. The basic demo-

cratic right of the individual to live where he liked didn't apply to Jews, apparently. The moment the Jewish question had come up, this man had stopped being the objective reporter. The Western liberal had disappeared in the blinking of an eye and the Zionist commissar had appeared, responsible for the education of the people.

Eventually, he noticed me. He had completed his first round of interviews and I was the only one left. While I was writing he approached me, a jovial twinkle in his eye.

"Writing, eh?" There was a hesitant note in his voice. Who knew, maybe I was a colleague, to be treated with respect. He spoke Russian with an acquired accent and addressed me in the formal second person:

"What are you writing?"

I answered him in Hebrew, using the ceremonious third person.

"What did the gentleman ask?"

The conversation was a comedy of errors. He explained to me politely that nobody in Israel used the third person. He was delighted at having this opportunity to compare the two cultures. On the one hand, Israel was an open society with private enterprise and no pretense of equality. Nevertheless, people spoke plainly and wore open-necked shirts. On the other hand, Russia was supposedly a classless society, simple and unaffected, but there I was with my outmoded manners and standoffish reserve. Then he asked me how I knew Hebrew, and when I replied with a private joke—"This isn't my first immigration but my second; my first was in the Third"—he didn't understand what I was talking about. He thought I was having trouble with Hebrew and suggested we speak in Russian. I said, as a joke, that I had vowed to speak nothing but Hebrew from now on, and he wrote down this nonsense with a pleased look on his face. Then he asked me if I had any interesting stories to tell, or if I could remember meeting any important people. I told him that in 1937 I had met Elkind, but he said Elkind wasn't famous enough. Then he asked me what I did for a living and if I had any plans and if I had family waiting for me in Israel. I was loath to tell him about my family, or perhaps I should say my families—a story as complex and convoluted as a molecule of organic matter—because I didn't want him to lay his slimy hands on us and write about us in an article which would be as stupid and shallow as he was. I was afraid that my family, some of whom I didn't even know, would be angry with me for boasting of connections I didn't deserve. I preferred to say that I had no family at all.

This reply put an effective end to the interview. He seemed to feel a complete, impersonal resentment toward me as the representative of a type: the egoist without conscience who took advantage of Israel and didn't give a damn that he would be a burden on the economy of a poor country. The professionals who could make a contribution went to America. Senile old men, former members of the Yevsektsia, the Jewish section of the Russian Communist Party, came to eat the fruits of the labor of those Zionists whom they had fought as long as they had the strength to do so. He had no interest in an old man whose youth had been devoted to the dreams of strangers.

I thought this was an unfortunate beginning. I hadn't set foot in Israel but I had already been obliged to lie twice. I had not vowed to speak only Hebrew, and of course I had a family. The nature of my family relations was another question.

It was true that I had taken a vow, but not the one I had spoken about. My vow now seemed absurd, from this side of the border.

I had always needed lies to survive. I had thought that now I would be able to do without them. The moment of truth, so to say, had arrived. Perhaps the word "vow" was too strong for what I had promised myself. It was more like a naive assumption about life in the West than a solemn undertaking. I had thought of falsehood and truth as abstract values or warring worlds. Surely, I had said to myself, freedom implied the right to choose when to tell the truth.

But nevertheless I felt uneasy. When a man has lied to save

his life, he looks down with contempt on a man who lies to improve his standard of living, to get rid of a nuisance, or to make himself look better. He feels as though he has used a cannon to kill a fly. I think it was Turgenev who said that the Russians are a nation of liars who spend their lives yearning for the absolute truth.

In this respect, I am a true Russian.

When the plane approached Israel I was engulfed by a wave of emotion. I was troubled by memories which came at me chaotically. My mind spewed out unconnected items of information like a malfunctioning computer. I remember my first journey to Palestine in 1920. The sea was gray and sullen. We all lay exhausted on the decks and even the arguments between Poalei Zion and Hapoel Hatzair on the question of the class struggle ground to a halt. The Orient did not look at all like the picture postcard from the Holy Land: sunny palms and prickly pears and Bedouin on camels. Jaffa, appearing and disappearing in the fog, looked like any other Mediterranean port. Only the mosque rising above the hill gave the view an Oriental air. The ship idled for a long time before anchoring. A few tugboats detached themselves from the shore and approached the ship, rising and falling terrifyingly on the waves. My few precious belongings, a bag with a few books, things I had brought all the way with me, were swept away and lost in the sea. There was no mistaking the smiles of the Arab sailors rowing the boats to the shore: in their eyes we were ridiculous and contemptible. I grieved for my lost books and the family possessions I had brought in my bag (in a moment of weakness I had taken the mezuzah my father had taken from our home in Rashkov; I had promised him to give it to a God-fearing Jew working the holy land). I regretted arriving at the land of my forefathers with the wrong spirit. Swaying like a drunk and ashamed of the fear showing on my face, I trailed behind the Poalei Zion representative who had come to receive new immigrants. On the first night I couldn't sleep for a stomachache. The next day I vomited everything I ate.

This time the sun shone fiercely and from time to time there was a quick flash from the windows of the skyscrapers by the sea. Tel Aviv rushed past beneath us and in a few minutes there was a dull thud from the bottom of the plane and a loud explosion of air from the engines. I was swept up in the stream and allowed the Jewish Agency officials to direct me. I would not give way to disturbing emotions. I had felt a kind of emptiness from the first step on the burning asphalt and I was afraid of a dangerous acceleration in my heartbeat. I had been ordered to avoid excitement, tension, or sudden anger. At the end of my life I had been sentenced to stoicism after years of living with passion. I said to myself, History repeats itself and comes full circle, but I remembered saying the same thing when I got off the ship at Odessa.

I trailed from counter to counter, detesting the bureaucracy with all my heart but submitting to it meekly. I felt alienated from myself and from everything around me. "Whom can I call? To whom can I express my sorrowful joy at being still alive?" I said the lines in my head. (In the spring of 1919 I had haunted the poets' cafes, a barefoot pioneer in love with meter and rhyme. Once I even rushed to help the drunken Yesenin, who was beating up a supercilious young man who had made fun of the new poetry.) I looked away from the glass partition where families were waiting. There was no chance that I would recognize anyone there.

I clung to the superstitious belief that if only I kept my head down and expected nothing and was prepared for every possible disappointment, I would be rewarded by chance (which compensates us for not anticipating the Messiah and expecting miracles). All my lost family, including my wife, would be waiting for me at the end of the road. We would meet in silence, careful not to hurt each other. We would avoid strong emotion, and allow our feelings to ripen gradually in the dark. Perhaps my eyes would be able to say what my mouth could not: Here I am, a bankrupt Party member, a father who betrayed his trust, an old pioneer whose world is in ruins. The only thing is this family which I do not know. I have no claims whatsoever. The only thing

I ask is that you let me stay with you, at a certain distance, reconciled to my fate and gathering crumbs from your table. I need nothing but a roof over my head, a bowl of soup, a table, a bed, and the right to watch your happiness.

There was a faint hope in my heart: Nina, my wife, was still alive and perhaps, with great caution, we could restore the family. True, she hadn't written, but I gave a romantic interpretation to her silence: she was ill and she didn't want to upset me. They didn't know me: I was ready to walk around her sickbed on tiptoe; I would put up with the caprices of a sick old woman who had no reason to think well of me.

A middle-aged man with burning eyes, gray hair, and an arrogant air stared at me after I presented my papers at the counter. "So you're Berkov," he said, as if he knew who I was. "We've been waiting for you. We got your telegram."

I'd wasted my paternal feelings on him. He wasn't my son. He was a representative of the office in charge of looking after immigrants from the Soviet Union. In 1957 he had been attached to the Israeli Embassy in Moscow and had met Epstein, who told him about me. For a time he had tried to arrange a meeting with me at the request of friends from Tel Yosef, but I had been expelled from Moscow before he could trace me. One of the mysterious letters I had received had been signed by him.

"At first you'll be staying with your daughter, until we can make suitable arrangements for you," he said, as if he was apologizing for not unrolling a red carpet. I was surprised. I didn't think I had any rights to speak of. It astonished me that he should think it necessary to apologize. But an experienced Soviet citizen doesn't ask provocative questions when he's offered privileged treatment.

The man put my things onto a metal baggage cart and told me to follow him. He showed my papers to a policeman and took me out onto the pavement next to the Arrivals hall. As we stood there waiting, a large green American car came slowly and hesitantly toward us. My escort waved at the woman with short golden hair behind the wheel and the car drew up next to us.

"Here he is," he said to the woman as she got out of the car. She nodded her head without looking at me and went around the car to open the trunk. Only after my things were stored away did she offer me her hand, except for two fingers which were holding a bunch of keys.

When I remember that moment, I cannot reconstruct feelings, sensations, thoughts, or pictures. Perhaps they will leap out of my memory in a few months. Now I can remember standing on the pavement, the man with the cart ahead of me and my daughter facing me, from the other side of the car. The man's look of eager anticipation (the emotional scene he would now witness—a father meeting his daughter after thirty-three years of separation) paralyzed me and I looked at my daughter like a man who had stopped feeling anything.

The cells in my body had been replaced four times since I last saw her. I remembered a little girl in a pink nightgown holding a doll with a broken head. There was nothing left of that man, a chaotic heap of facts, figures, prejudices, fading attachments to men and women, miseries which had congealed, and neglected wounds under his skin. The Soviet authorities and I had succeeded in thoroughly repressing his well-known sentimentality over a period of many years. My sharpening vision isolated the woman from the crowd, a strange and unfamiliar creature. We had nothing in common.

I didn't dare look her straight in the eye. The first thing I noticed were sandals with narrow straps and slender ankles, like Nina's in her youth. And suddenly stupid tears welled up and overflowed.

What happened after that is a blur, and a second look wiped out first impressions. My mother's tears bathed my eyes. The man put his hand on my shoulder and contradicted himself. "Now, now, no need to upset yourself. . . . Tears are good for you, they wash your soul . . ."

My daughter stood apart. She was afraid to approach and embarrassed, perhaps even a little annoyed. My tears didn't appeal to her. We belong to different cultures, I thought. Where I come from, people are emotional and passionate. Over here, people are repressed and controlled: they don't burst into other people's lives or fall into each other's arms; they don't draw near one another except in response to the subtlest of hints.

In a few minutes we were inside the car, with the deafening noise of a landing plane giving us a good excuse for silence.

My daughter drove without confidence and she didn't glance in my direction. Her eyes were fixed on the road. She was a bad driver. Big trucks cut off the view. We made small talk. I told her that in Russia only members of the Politburo could afford cars like hers. She thought I was criticizing her extravagance and explained that the car belonged to a commercial company and the expenses were tax-deductible. She asked about the flight and I spoke like a fool about the queues next to the lavatories. Her eyes were glassily frozen like a sign saying "Trespassers will be prosecuted." Keep cool, I ordered myself. Don't push, don't stir things up, don't fall on her. The girl with the long thin arms protecting a doll with a broken head from a secret agent trying to take it away from her is now a grown-up woman. She has no place for me in her memories and perhaps doesn't remember the incident as traumatic. In the end nobody managed to take the doll away from her; the senior interrogator rebuked the young policeman for his obstinacy: "All we need now is a baby crying." She went back to bed pleased with her victory and fell asleep before the search was over. Perhaps it was days before she noticed that her father was missing—he usually came home late at night. I stopped myself from mentioning the incident, although I had often promised myself that if I ever saw my daughter again I would tell her that her stubborn defense of her doll had saved a garrulous poet from the police. Inside the doll, in the hollow arm attached to the body with loose elastic, was a piece of paper with a caustic rhyme on it, bad verses, real rubbish, but under those conditions the quality of the verse didn't matter. There was value in the courage it took to write that rubbish. In any case, we related to poetry with profound solemnity in those days—all of us, poets, printers, and the police—and when the man in question was arrested for some trivial offense I hid the incriminating evidence. It never occurred to me that I could destroy a literary creation.

We were silent for what seemed like ages. I said it was hot. She said that it was hotter than usual this autumn. She suggested that I take off my jacket. I thought that I might allow myself to see this as a sign of thawing emotions. But when I looked out of the window I saw that very few people in the street were wearing jackets. Even people driving expensive cars were sitting at the wheels in open-necked shirts. In other words, the people who wore open necks and shirtsleeves were not necessarily class-conscious workers who believed in simplicity and modest dress on principle, but the bourgeoisie too. This pleased me. It was another point in favor of the country I was coming back to. I had a heavy heart and many doubts, but I was eager and it was my sincere intention to credit it with whatever I could discover. In Russia, nothing was left of comradely simplicity. The children and grandchildren of the revolutionaries wore smart foreign suits and assumed impeccable bourgeois manners. Modest living was something they palmed off on the poor. Academics did not dirty their hands. Anyone praising frugality was suspected of ulterior motives. Dialectics had become a way to purge impurity without needing the minimum of proof.

The silence was oppressive. When we are alone with our thoughts the chasm is enormous. Dialectics had probably never entered my daughter's head. I started to chatter. I said that the streets had changed beyond recognition. My daughter said that she was sometimes amazed at the changes too. New neighborhoods sprang up overnight. I asked her about the political situation and she said: Nothing special. She asked if I had any other luggage besides my suitcases. I said I had sent a few crates by mail, mainly books. She asked if I was hungry and I said no. I asked if we still had a long way to go and she said: We've arrived.

We were driving through a quiet suburb, one- or two-storied houses with tiled roofs in a street shaded by an avenue of ficus trees. At the end of the street we turned off into an unpaved path and stopped by a stone wall in front of a garage. She drove up to the doors and they opened by remote control. Then she drove backward into the garage. She did everything automatically, accustomed to life's luxuries. But I could see that it was all new—the garage, the remote control, the paint on the doors, the lawn mower standing in the corner. I wasn't thrilled by the handsome Spanish-style house, an obvious sign of success which should have impressed me, and I saw disappointment in her eyes. I suspected that years of poverty had made her into the kind of person capable of deriving real happiness from possessions.

We went through the garage into a kitchen and from there to a living room. I offered a few words of praise for the room, although it seemed overcrowded to me. There was an ostentatious show of affluence not to my taste.

I had once seen a dacha like this on the Black Sea. It had belonged to a newspaper editor. I was there as the electrician's mate. I had been stunned by the editor's wealth, without taste. Furniture, ornaments, paintings, and carpets were indiscriminately piled up like an antique shop. It was a triumph of internationalism: the porcelain was from China, the carpets from Uzbekistan, the furniture was Spanish and Scandinavian, the copper Persian, the icons from Greece. All the gilded rubbish which the bourgeoisie had inherited from the impoverished aristocracy had been placed at the disposal of the Party bureaucracy. Here too, the pioneers had despised possessions and their children were scraping their knees on superfluous furniture.

While she put my things down, locked the door, and hurried to the telephone, I wandered around the room. There was a cabinet of china statuettes—dolls, glass, little bottles, souvenirs, bronze jars, electric clocks, pipes—but very few books, and more in English than in Hebrew. I had to bite my tongue to stop myself asking a provocative question about the scribbles that hung on the walls. Perhaps I just couldn't understand these innovations of the twentieth century. Anyway, wasn't this the reason that I had come here to live in a country where the artist could use his brush however he wanted?

I had a question on the tip of my tongue but I couldn't bring myself to ask it. When my daughter had finished her long conversation on the phone I could not restrain myself. I spoke in Hebrew to give legitimacy to my stammer. I asked the question indirectly, inquiring if my telegram had come in time for her to tell the rest of the family. She said that Walter was out of town and couldn't come. Who was Walter? She hadn't mentioned him in her letters. Walter was Evyatar, her husband, whose old friends still called him by his previous name. Something cunning gleamed in her eyes. She knew very well that I wasn't asking about her husband. Of course I wasn't expecting a red carpet, I joked. A man knows what he has a right to expect. But my heart had missed a beat when I had seen her there alone. I was afraid that perhaps something was wrong. No, she reassured me, nothing was wrong, everyone was all right. But she didn't say who these people were. She pretended that she had only just understood what I wanted to know: Nimrod was in Sinai, he couldn't get back in time. He had intended to meet me. And the others? I asked. She said that her son was in the army and her daughter was with friends and would come later. But she didn't look me in the eye so I couldn't read any hidden signals of the kind we send when words fail to express what we want to say. Perhaps sign language was impossible for us, in the absence of shared memories. It seemed to me that she even failed to understand why I was speaking Hebrew. I wanted to give her an advantage: me with my clumsy speech and her with her fluency. But she thought I was trying to make an impression. You can talk Russian, she suggested, it will be easier for you. As if it was lack of words that made me stammer. I can't deny that my Hebrew was broken. I lacked the words for subtle, hidden, elusive things. All I had was the language I had learned in the yeshiva. For years I only had one book, Heine's poems, and the translation had nourished me. I would discover how outmoded my language was when I got hold of newspapers, bank statements, a book in memory of the Bialystok Jews. My daughter could not hide her smile when I said I had not wished to be welcomed with trumpets. Nobody talks like that anymore. In the end I despaired of the idea that I might be able to tell her what was weighing on me without words. When she took me upstairs to the room she had prepared for me, I surprised her with a direct question.

"And your mother?"

The gleam in her eyes went out like a light.

"We have to talk," she said.

As if we hadn't been doing that for the past hour.

She pushed me into the room, gently but firmly, ignoring my "What do we have to talk about?"

"Rest now, calm down, and we'll talk later," she said.

There was a resolute, uncompromising expression on her face. I sensed that I would be no match for her stubbornness.

"Just tell me one thing," I begged. "Is she alive?"

"She's alive," she said and pursed her mouth.

"Here in the country?"

"Here in the country."

And she refused to say any more.

"We've got plenty of time," she said, "to talk about everything."

She immediately began to talk about practical things again. The shower was here, the towels were there, and the taps were turned on this way, the hot water on the right and the cold on the left. If I needed anything she was downstairs, in the kitchen, and I mustn't be shy about asking, I must make myself at home, and she hoped that I liked the room, it was quiet and airy, and I could open the window if I liked, and it would be a good idea to take a nap now and recover from the journey. Flying was exhausting even for people younger than me with more experience. In two or three hours the rest of the household would come home and a guest or two as well, and there would be quite a noise, she said and went away.

She shut the door in my face with a movement which reminded me of other doors closing in other places, and I turned on my heel, this too a practiced movement, to look over the place in which I was to spend the coming days, puzzling over a ques-

tion which had remained unanswered. The play was familiar. But the setting had changed beyond recognition.

Here are a few words about the room. Only someone who has never had a place of his own can understand the feelings of warmth you can have for a door which you can close whenever you like.

The room was far from spacious. It had actually been built as a kind of annex to the house. Its construction had given Walter Sheffer, my son-in-law, the weekend exercise his doctors recommended. He used to play tennis, but his poor childhood had trained him to apply his energy to more productive things. The room had been added to the garage roof and had spoiled the facade of the house for a long time. Recently the work had been completed and the whole house repainted. Walter had been assisted by an Arab builder, a friend, who had supplied the materials for next to nothing and worked alongside him without pay. Walter liked boasting that if he had done the work by himself, it would have cost much more. The room's purpose was unclear; the house had been large enough for a family of four. Walter had a floor of offices in a Tel Aviv high-rise building. His bedroom was big enough to hold the entire Jewish sector of the Communist Party in the twenties; his salon (which he for some reason referred to in English as the living room) would have held a hundred guests, standing and sitting, if not for the furniture, which took up every inch of space. His house had another two rooms for his children, one of whom didn't live there any more and didn't intend coming back, either; there was a garage, a storeroom, and a basement for the washing machine and the drying machine and the Ping-Pong table. But according to Walter, he lacked "a room where he could just throw things and come across them in a few years' time." My daughter had not taken the hint. He did not like her domestic arrangements or the exaggerated neatness and hysterical fear of dust. For this reason he had decided to set aside a private area away from her, a place where he could do whatever he wanted. The day he retired from

business, he announced, he would spend most of his time in this room. He would read all the books he had missed, perhaps he would go into politics as a kind of hobby.

The room's finish would not have passed the test of a professional eye. The alcove in the wall did not fit the window frame, the left half of the window could only be opened one third of the way, and the least wind made the whole thing rattle. (One day I would fix it. In the meantime, I shoved a folded piece of paper into the gap.) The paint job, too, was not smooth enough and the putty was already cracked in several places.

The room was five paces long and its breadth from the window to the door, four paces. In the winter you could heat it with your breath. But it was sufficient for my needs. For me, it was enough that the window was at waist level. I needed no more than a bed, a table, and a window. And here there was much more: a bookcase (which had evidently been removed from the living room), a rocking chair of superior quality and also an upholstered chair which turned on its pivot, and a table lamp which cast a clear, soft light on my words. And through the window, covered with a lace curtain as delicate as a bride's veil, through the filtering foliage of the casuarina tree, hints of other people's lives, rooms in houses like this one, standing apart from each other, not too close and not too far. As if some humanistic engineer had calculated the exact living space required by the family cell in order to enjoy its autonomy without secluding itself from the community.

The first time I stepped into it, despite the nagging question occupying my mind, the room immediately infected me with its tranquility. It was love at first sight. I knew right away I would like to spend the rest of my life in this room. This may sound melodramatic—and it is melodrama which I want to avoid above all—but this is how the thought formulated itself in my mind: I would like to die in this room. Exactly so. I would lay my head on this embroidered pillow in the expectation of sweet sleep after toil. Never mind if I woke up in this world or the one to come, I would rest in peace.

Only a man who had never had a dream of his own could feel as I felt. And I never even had a desk of my own. In my parents' home there were seven of us in two rooms. In my aunt's house in Odessa we were four to a room. In Lefortovo, on the Hehalutz training farm, there were six boys and three girls living in one room. In the "haunted house" next to Hebron we lived three to a room. In Tel Yosef we were three to a tent. After one of us committed suicide, there were two. My neighbors' groans were my dreams at night. In Haifa we were four. In Via Nova, five. In Moscow, my wife and our daughter and I lived behind a wooden partition in her parents' apartment, in a room containing four other people. Her father and mother on the other side of the partition listened to the passionate panting of a daughter who had been brought up to place her feelings at the service of a more noble goal then the sexual appetites of a poor boy from Palestine. Later on—in a flat with two more families. Even in my prison cell I had been persecuted by the transparent tricks of an amateur informer trying to improve his status at the expense of my indiscretions. In the camps, we lived in crowds—like cattle.

Now for the first time I could shut the door and luxuriate in a private corner of my own.

When I think about it, I come to the conclusion that I never had a private life at all. Wherever I went it was with the eager enthusiasm (my own or that of others who felt they had the right to decide my fate) to obey some historical command.

That was how I went to Palestine, that was why I came back to Russia. There is no doubt that my experiences in the eastern part of the continent belong to the history of our times more than they do to my own life story. Even in my return to Israel I was being borne on the back of a wave. A gesture of utter despair, which professional Zionists interpret as the revival of hope.

Only my death would really be mine. And in the meantime, the only signs were a numbness in my foot, pains in my anus, and high blood pressure. I remember a certain young man, about thirty-six years old, an outstanding student at the Polytechnic

Institute, a married man with a daughter, who regarded even his petty betrayals of his wife as stemming from an ideological revolt. His adulteries reached a peak precisely during the period when his (purely opportunistic) application for Party membership was being considered—in the belief that his disgraceful behavior was somehow undermining the virtuous regime. The pathetic revenge of a disillusioned idealist. And was anyone different in those days?

Even my children aren't mine.

And suddenly I have been gathered into an inviting private domain, as into a compassionate womb. A flicker of hope.

The official had said to my daughter: "We'll be very glad if you can keep him for a while until we can find suitable accommodations for him." He stressed the word "suitable" as if I had some special rights due to me. (Presumably they had an exaggerated idea here of the role I played in the Jewish emigration movement, whereas I was not at all sure that I had any right to impose an obligation on the homeland of the Jews, on "rootless people"—an expression beloved of the Zionists who had learned to say a few phrases in Hebrew. I knew that many of them would prefer to take advantage of the opportunity to disappear into America and have nothing more to do with the Jewish fate.) He told my daughter that most of the apartments in Tel Aviv and its environs were occupied, but there was "a solution in the offing." She said: "We can keep him here as long as necessary." I was a little hurt.

When I closed the door of the room behind me, I knew that from now on I would do whatever I could to stay here as long as possible. What could I do? You can never tell. Human life is full of all kinds of tricks. The mind of a Soviet citizen never stops scheming. Which is only natural for people whose every act is determined by a comprehensive plan.

Moreover, that night I felt a kind of secret current flowing inside me, a current which the body can hear only in utter silence, when the soul is ready to listen to the weeping of a disconsolate animal on the distant plains. I felt an agreeable prickling all over as the realization grew in me that as long as I could find rest and repose in this room, in the great serenity shining from its white walls, as long as I could go on sitting at this table, within the circle of light falling onto the white page, waiting patiently for memory to awaken in my mind, I would be able to vanquish the plot being hatched inside my body, beneath the contaminated tissues, and suspend the sentence which has been passed on to me. I believe that within the complicated mechanism of the body, composed of millions of hard-working agents connected to each other by a sophisticated but unreliable network of communications, there is a backward, clumsy bureaucracy, careless and benighted, and that if we know how to exploit its weaknesses we will be able to escape our punishment.

It's not only a door that I'm closing behind me. I feel as if there's a slow sunset taking place inside me. As if I could withdraw into a kind of willing exile inside my own skin, live the rest of my life outside history, which up to now hasn't left me to my own devices for a minute.

Why shouldn't I live from now on without its wrath, without its hectoring demands? I shall forget about where I came from and where I'm going to end up, where I will have to give an account of myself. I shall breathe the passing seconds deeply into myself. I shall concentrate on the rehabilitation of my neglected body. Partake of the necessary nutrients with scientific circumspection—calories, vitamins, carbohydrates, fats, sugars, minerals, all in exactly the right degrees and amounts. Take care to evacuate my bowels regularly. I shall sink into a life of quiet contemplation and allow my memories to clarify in my mind like jelly.

And lest I forget: I shall take care to be happy. By force, if necessary. By the skin of my teeth. I can be as stubborn as an ox if I have to.

I tend to accept a theory I once heard in the thirties. The body is chemistry and so is the soul, they said. The body may not always obey us but with the soul we can manage.

Scientists have established that anger and tension and fear influence the chemistry of our bodies. They influence it so much that a dog can smell fear from a distance; even the interrogators, whose noses are less sensitive, can smell it. And if such clear processes can take place in us for ill, then why not for good? Well? Surely it must be easier for our bodies to build up damaged tissues when we are happy, calm, and composed? In other words, he who is content with his lot is not only wealthy, as the old saying has it, but also healthy. All you have to do is cast off sorrow and anger, and you will be sure of a long life. Like a snail retiring into its shell and shutting its ears even to the sound of the sea.

I heard this theory from a forgotten Yiddish poet, but then I didn't grasp the point. I accepted it literally. I was told that he had succeeded in curing himself of cancer by the proper control of his feelings. He had learned to drip happy thoughts into his brain whenever gloom got the upper hand, like a chemist adding the elements whose lack has disturbed the delicate balance of a solution. Later on I understood what he had been trying to tell us in a carefully concealed code: times are coming when only those who have learned to greet the horrors with a foolish smile of happiness will survive. The others will perish.

But here, in this sunny land, in the company of my family who will grow accustomed to my existence, remote from history, perhaps I will really be able to heal my body by peace of mind and concentration on simple kinds of happiness. Every passing moment without grief and anger expels an unhealthy element and liberates a healthy one.

*T*he first evening. Voices rose from the living room. I put on my best clothes—the new gray suit and the reddish tie with the golden stars—and went down. I appeared to have dressed too formally. The others had not dressed for dinner at all, even though they were entertaining guests. Perlmutter, the official from the Absorption Ministry, was there, a young woman who was a friend of my daughter's, and two girls who were either well-developed twelve-year-olds or childish fourteen-year-olds, and one of whom, the one who was trying to put as much distance as she could between us, appeared to be my grand-daughter. All of them were dressed as if they had just come in from working in the garden. Walter, a middle-aged man, hairy and paunchy, did not seem to see anything wrong in appearing in short trousers and an undershirt in front of a strange woman. There was no dinner in the sense of an occasion when the family sat around the dinner table with their guests. Olga, my daughter, fried eggs and the visitor, Rachel—"a name which holds the gentleness of consolation" in the words of the poet Mandel-stam—made a salad. Everyone took a plate and ate wherever he wanted: one in front of the television set, another standing next to the fridge. Walter sat at the kitchen table and stuffed himself with huge quantities of salad. My daughter's friend ate only an apple, as if she was afraid that anything more would kill her. Me they seated in an armchair, the guest of honor, an elegant figure who seemed to have wandered in from a different opera, and they took care that nothing was missing on the low table they placed by my side. They all came up and introduced themselves. Walter pulled up a stool and came to polish off what was left of his salad next to me. We exchanged a few words on meaningless subjects and then he left me to go and make coffee. Perlmutter too stood next to me for a few minutes, promising again that he would see to it that a suitable "arrangement" was found for me. A surprising conversation developed with Olga's friend Rachel. She had a kind of natural curiosity which charmed me. She was really and truly interested in me and my affairs, and I was tempted to hold forth at length. Underneath the makeup and the puffy hair style I saw in her face the face of a Russian woman of the twenties. I could see her in my imagination in the famine years: a sad-eyed, eager attendant at lecture courses, in a patched dress and high-buttoned boots, full of lofty ideas, ready to give her all without asking anything in return, one who would not withhold her sad breasts from a poet.

A few years before she had written a seminar paper on the Labor Brigade and now she wanted to write about Elkind and his group of left-wing Zionists who went back to the Soviet Union in the twenties to establish a commune in the Crimea. So my return had not been in vain, at least from the point of view of one learned young woman. My memories were likely to improve her grades.

In the prevailing commotion there was no chance of elucidating the mystery. Where was Nina? Why didn't anybody tell me anything?

The guests stayed late and discussed the security situation. Perlmutter held forth like a man with connections in political circles and Walter mocked him subtly. The girls went to Nira's, my granddaughter's, room, but came back shortly to watch a television program. For a while there was an argument about the volume, but it was clear from the outset that the younger generation would win. Rachel asked if in Russia parents were afraid of their children too, and Walter took it upon himself to reply for me: "In Russia parents are afraid that their children will inform on them." Although I had criticized the regime in the Soviet Union very harshly myself, I found this kind of shallow spitefulness disagreeable. I wanted to express my reservations and put things into perspective, but I refrained. First, perhaps it was a kind of humor which escaped me. And second, I didn't want to get into an argument with the person who held the key to the room upstairs.

Later that night I had another chance to put my question. The visitors went home and my granddaughter went to sleep at her friend's house and Walter and I were left alone in the living room. Even before I managed to formulate the right sentence in my mind—I was looking for an indirect approach, but my Hebrew obeyed me only when I wanted to say something direct and to the point—the telephone rang and Walter entered into a long conversation with the anonymous person on the other end of the line. As soon as he put the phone down Olga came in, and for a while the two of them conducted an exciting conversation as if I wasn't there. Neither of them took the trouble to explain what it was all about to me, and I kept my vow not to interfere in things that were none of my business. Afterward they led me upstairs to my room and said good night to me at the door without stopping, and the unanswered question was put off to the next day.

When I woke up in the morning I was alone in the house, except for a German shepherd dog, snarling and sullen, who barked at me furiously when I wanted to go out into the garden. And when Olga came home at noon she had Rachel with her. They prepared the meal together. I tried to get into a conversation with my daughter, but she said it wasn't something that could be spoken about in a few words, or a subject she wanted to discuss in front of strangers. I couldn't understand what all the mystery was about, but I respected her wishes. In the evening, too, I couldn't get her alone. Rachel was worried about something and Olga invited her to sleep over in order to distract her from her worries.

Only after a quick lunch the next day, after which Rachel went home and my granddaughter went to her room, did I find myself face to face with my daughter. This time she couldn't get away.

I said: "Maybe now? I don't understand all this mystery."
Olga said: "Nina is married."
I said: "Ah."
And then there was a silence. And then I asked: "When?"
And she said: "Twenty years, maybe more."
I should say something about Nina.
On the eve of Rosh Hashanah in the year 1930 I disembarked from the ship in Odessa. I was twenty-nine years old, disappointed and disillusioned but ready and willing to make one more effort. All my life was still in front of me. I was returning to the motherland of workers and peasants, whose language I understood and whose poetry was music to my ears. And strife between brothers was behind me. Tomorrow I would go to Via

Nova. I would be a happy and contented worker on the land, close to nature, close to his comrades and to himself. I would be free of political duties and responsibilities—I wasn't cut out for them. The admission of failure in this respect did not cause me any pain. I had long ago accepted the fact that I was not molded of the clay fitted for movement leaders and party secretaries. Moreover, this nation of 150 million, building the society of the future, needed people like me—people willing to devote themselves to a simple job of work and be content with their lot. I had no aspirations to lead the herd and win titles of honor. In Russia, I said to myself, a man can plant beets in season and bring redemption to the world, and I felt a great sense of relief. In Eretz Israel there wasn't enough air to breathe; we were painfully few, and each of us was obliged to serve at several altars at once.

I had renounced political office, but not my political ideals. I was certainly not prepared to say God had failed.

In Tel Yosef a child was growing up for whose education I had taken no responsibility at all. It wasn't my fault. My comrades had expelled me because of my opinions. Should I have betrayed my dreams because his mother refused to give him up?

I tried to cut the grief out of my heart. I blamed Vera, which was my girlfriend's name, for trying to force me into a family life which held no attractions for me—without warmth, without love, without the hope of happiness. I wished the boy a long life of physical and spiritual health. The total absence of a father, I comforted myself, was preferable to rare, sporadic appearances which would only unsettle him. I believed that the revolution would conquer the world within a few years and that we would be able to meet again. He would understand that in leaving him to live by my principles I had bequeathed him a courageous spirit. I forgave Vera, who did not know how to appreciate my nobility. I was sure that a man who slept with a famished woman he did not desire should be thanked for his generosity, and I couldn't understand why she was angry with me when her pregnancy did not seem to me a sufficient cause for compromising with my conscience.

Ideology is not vanity and vexation of spirit, I said to myself, but "politics," even if it is a necessary evil, is better off without amateurs. They do more harm than good. In Via Nova all my positive qualities would come to the fore, I thought. There I would not have to take part in power struggles, intrigues, dirty tricks, false friendships with repellant characters just because they were political allies. My experiences in the Labor Brigade had left a deep scar. Although I still had a hidden desire for underground activities (the dark allure of cunning and deceit, the permission to lie in order to bring the coming of the Messiah closer), the bitter hatred of the members of the Brigade, who felt themselves betrayed by my actions, taught me that I was not endowed with the heroic spirit necessary for deciding what was good for others and imposing it on them. It was enough for me that I did myself what I demanded of others.

There was nobody waiting for me in Odessa. The letter announcing my arrival was presumably lying in a mailbag in the bowels of the ship I had come on. For three days I was obliged to scratch fleas, resigned to my fate, in a detention cell in a police station, until it transpired that I was not an imperialist agent, a counterrevolutionary, a Zionist propagandist, or simply a spy from some hostile, anonymous agency. I chatted with my interrogators with gay insouciance, astonished that they could even imagine that so charming a fellow could be a spy, but I soon realized that I was only making them more suspicious. There is no limit to the number of masks an enemy of the people can don, as a bored agent, in whom my attempts to make friends gave rise to a deep loathing, explained to me. In the end I signed a declaration that I had "washed my hands" of the Zionists, and they let me go.

Odessa was not welcoming either. Many streets were completely deserted. Friends of my youth had scattered in all directions, the market square had lost its cheerful bustle, the shopkeepers were sullen and when they told you they didn't have something, you could almost hear the gloating in their voices. Jewish institutions bursting with vitality in the past were now shut up and deserted. My aunt's apartment was occupied by an official from the Interior Ministry. To all my questions he replied: "I don't know." As if he were guarding secrets of state. Only when I got up to go did he agree to disclose one of them to me. My aunt had gone to Tashkent and she never came back. About the rest of the family he had heard nothing.

The next day I was on my way to the Crimea. As far as Yevpatoria by train, and from there—on a cart drawn by a pair of mules—a half day's journey to the commune of Via Nova.

There I was welcomed like a lost lamb returned to the fold. They fell on my neck with hugs and kisses. Ephraim, my younger brother, stood apart, embarrassed. We spoke later, in the room we shared with three other boys. After my mother's death, he told me, the family had scattered. Our father remained in Rashkov alone. He had aged greatly and become sickly. After Ephraim left home too, my father left Rashkov and went to relatives in Moscow. Our father was not happy, he said, because he was dependent on the charity of strangers and was without means of livelihood.

We sat silently and shed a few tears. And what could I say to him: Why did you abandon our father? Ephraim had only followed in my own footsteps. . . . We wrote him a letter, on either side of one sheet of paper. We hoped he would be glad that at least two of us were living under one roof. After the terrible deaths of our brothers—one at the hands of the Ukrainians and another at those of the Bolsheviks—the only thing he could say was "Look after each other . . . ," and now it was as if we were keeping that old promise; not only that, we had also reached safe harbors at last. We even played with the attractive idea that one day when the commune was able to bear the expense, we would invite him to come and live with us. Gradually—if fate was good to us—we would assemble all the lost members of our family.

That evening they improvised a party in my honor—black bread dipped in milk and one bottle of spirits for the whole tribe—and Elkind, the chairman of the commune, made a speech of welcome. The next day, at dawn, in order not to postpone the coming of the Messiah for one single day, I went out to work in the cowshed.

Life in Via Nova was very much to my taste. Everything was amazingly similar to Tel Yosef in the idyllic days before political controversy embittered relations between comrades. Even the institutions were modeled on those of the kibbutz in Eretz Israel. We had a communal dining hall, children's house, laundry, bakery, clothing pool. The comrades spoke to each other in Hebrew and the jokes about our poverty were reminiscent of the jokes that had been popular in the Labor Brigade. Even our clothes, which wore out without being replaced, were from there. And so were our talks on the long winter nights. "You live with one foot here and one in Palestine," the district secretary would reproach us. Some spoke nostalgically about the past. And they never stopped fishing in those troubled waters: Why had they been obliged to leave? And whose fault was it? Of the leaders they spoke with great anger, but the rank and file were remembered with affection: "Subjectively—wonderful chaps; objectively—capitalist lackeys."

Although the poverty was grinding, a certain process of refinement had taken place. The boorishness for its own sake had disappeared. They had stopped pretending not to open a book. The charge of isolationism leveled against the group by the district secretary drew them together. Only the style of the speeches hadn't changed. Elkind, who was then in the middle of applying for Party membership (he even wrote to the Palestine Communist Party and asked them to recommend him—Hadn't he done great things for them? Hadn't he denounced the Labor Zionist settlements? Hadn't he brought a large group of comrades with him to Russia?). He would make programmatic speeches and lay down the line: The Via Nova commune was the correct realization of the Hehalutz idea; for it was only here, in the Soviet Union, that the conditions existed for the establishment of the true commune, the prototype of the society of the future; only where "construction was subservient to instruction" was it possible to build socialism; in Palestine the commune was a tool for the repression of the masses of Arab workers. When the spirit came on him he would denounce the Labor Brigade derisively. A dangerous illusion! It was impossible to establish an egalitarian society without a bureaucracy and socialism without a strong central government; only Christians believed that it was possible to found human relations on kindness and mercy; our century knew that you couldn't rely on philanthropy; justice had to be enforced by physical strength; and so on and so forth, harsh truths which gained him the admiration of all.

The conflicts with the district authorities were not long in appearing. The authorities demanded that the Jewish commune open its membership to other nationalities. In one place they arrested the chairman of a commune. There was an ominous feeling in the air.

And nevertheless I felt a certain serenity. I enjoyed the work and delighted in the sweat of my brow. Work purifies, I said to myself. It purges you of memories of the past. I want to be like a peasant who worships his God with his ox and his plough. And for the Jew, labor is a double blessing. It atones for the sins of a nation which consists mainly of shopkeepers and usurers. The anti-Semitic poison had seeped into our blood too.

For seven months I never left the commune. I refused to accept any duties which meant traveling to the provincial capital. From the day the First World War broke out I had been uprooted eleven times. It was time to put down roots. At the end of the year, I promised myself, I would go and visit my father, whose reply to our letter, which arrived after three months, was: "If you are happy—I am content."

My father died on the eve of the festival of Shavuot.

Hooligans set upon him in the street. A few days later he went to his world. I use the Hebrew expression, "went to his world," because I am sure that this world of ours always seemed strange and alien to him.

At the moment he was giving up the ghost, Ephraim and I were on the train to Moscow.

A few words about my father.

I'm not sure that I knew him. There can be no greater estrangement than that between the members of his generation and mine. I was fifteen when I left home for the first time; when I was seventeen I returned, and when I was eighteen I left again, never to return.

Mother was closer to us. She was a practical woman, overflowing with useful advice, and she ran the house with an iron hand. Father was rather lazy, although he was a first-rate craftsman. A studious cobbler, a pious Zionist who never imposed his religious observance on the rest of the family. He was a man with a truly liberal mind, although he did not know it. He simply interpreted the Jewish religion according to his own lights. The rabbi of our town, as far as I remember, did not enjoy our father's regard. He said that he was self-seeking, money-grubbing, a chatterbox, and also, although he didn't like saying it, rather ignorant. He had only one dream: to give his children the education he himself had never received.

The war put an end to his plans. Of all his sons only the eldest received a high school education. And after he became infected by the virus of Ukrainian nationalism, my father was no longer so sure of the benefits of higher education. Our brother, who was an officer in the Ukrainian army, was murdered by rioting soldiers. They chopped off his feet and dragged him along the ground tied to a galloping horse.

I met my father a year after this happened. He gasped for breath when he spoke and there was a strange gleam in his eyes. Only his letters remained as lucid as before. He even tried to introduce a little humor into them. The letters were written in Hebrew, even though we spoke Yiddish at home. Letter writing, in his opinion, was an act of worship to be performed in the holy tongue. Secular matters were conducted in a Yiddish full of Russian words.

When I became curious about him, the letters were no longer in my possession. The letters to Odessa, from the days of my youth, had been lost during the revolution. The letters he wrote to Eretz Israel had been confiscated by the British police, who did not take the trouble to return them. I had nothing to remember him by.

Ephraim went back to Via Nova immediately after we buried our father. I stayed on in Moscow for a few days at the request of the chairman of the commune. He had an acquaintance with some standing in the Ministry of Agriculture, and he believed that if we explained our position to him, Via Nova would be allowed to retain its special character.

I stayed for a few days with our relations. I was there long enough to understand just how miserable my father must have been in their company. They weren't complete strangers to me. I had visited them about ten years before when I joined the Hehalutz training farm in Lefortovo. And they had sickened me then. Even though I was hungry I hardly ever went to visit them. They always had sausages, and fruit too, and once I even ate roast goose there in the middle of the famine. They were assimilated Jews who spoke only Russian. I suspected them of knowing Yiddish too, but they despised the language of the people from the bottom of their hearts. My "uncle" was a shrewd businessman whom the revolution did not succeed in bankrupting and my "aunt" was a well-known piano teacher. They lived in their own apartment while other families were crowded two and three to a flat. Inside their apartment they tried to preserve an aristocratic way of life. As if their airs and graces had some magic power to keep the evil at bay. My filthy shoes and black nails horrified them. Sometimes, just to shock them, I would swear obscenely.

The man Elkind had sent me to see kept putting me off and I was already on the point of leaving Moscow without seeing him, when one day my aunt fell ill and one of her promising pupils came to the house for her lesson.

That was how I met Nina.

I stayed in Moscow for another week, grateful to the official in the Agriculture Ministry for postponing our meeting again.

When we parted at the railway station, Nina promised to love me forever. For four months we exchanged letters full of quotations from the poets of our generation. The final examinations of the conservatory took place at the end of summer. I didn't believe that she would come to Via Nova. She was a delicate girl, refined, artistic, not used to hard work. I began to find fault with the commune, with my comrades, even with Elkind's ideological directives. I was preparing myself to leave for respectable reasons, which would be a credit to the leaver. But one day Nina arrived at the Yevpatoria station with two large suitcases in her hands.

Her parents had seen her off at the Moscow station as if they were loading a political prisoner into exile. Their feelings betrayed their principles.

Her father was one of the leaders of the Polish Communist Party and he had spent a number of years in jail under the old regime. He had been invited to come to Russia two years before. For some mysterious reason he had managed to evade the fate of the other Party leaders who were arrested and condemned to death. Perhaps he wasn't important enough. Perhaps they needed him in order to convict the others. In those days I tried not to think about this possibility, although his attitude toward me did nothing to make me feel particularly sympathetic toward him. He made no attempt to hide the fact that he considered me unworthy of his daughter. In any case, behaving as if it were some kind of comedown to volunteer to build socialism in a backward area was certainly not compatible with the principles he preached in the articles he wrote in Polish.

Her mother attributed diabolical powers to me. She could find no other way in which to explain the fact that a simple, self-educated fellow like me with a bent for technical subjects, who spouted a lot of nonsense about physical labor purifying the soul and a simple life in the bosom of nature, could have led her daughter astray from her chosen path in life.

The physical labor was harder for Nina than she was ready to admit. Making love in the haystacks enchanted her at first, but after the first flush of enthusiasm she was overcome by exhaustion. The comrades did not believe that she would last long in Via Nova—she was too pampered, they said. But she really and truly wanted to be part of the commune. She missed her piano sometimes, but the commune intended buying an old piano and putting it in the kindergarten.

The mysterious skin disease that infected her in the third month of her stay at the commune would probably be attributed today to some inner resistance to a way of life she could not endure, but I was convinced that the dirt, and especially the old leather shoes we picked up at the municipal rubbish dumps, were to blame. The letters from Moscow grew more and more aggressive. Her mother was prepared to bring the full force of the authority of her contacts in the Central Committee to bear to extricate her daughter from the "rural existence" that was endangering her health. Her emotional letters seeking to save the daughter of a man who had been prepared to give his life for socialism must have reminded the people in the Cheka that they had been negligent in the purge of the Polish Communist Party. The letters reappeared in the trial of a group of anti-Party Poles at a later date. The mills of justice grind slowly. In the meantime, Nina gave birth to a baby girl in the commune. The district doctor, who seemed to like experimenting with the children of the wretched kolkhozniks, was reluctant to treat an anemic baby who had influential relatives in Moscow, so he recommended taking her to a city hospital. Since her father was still in favor at this time, Nina was accepted for treatment at a special hospital for Party members where, after a rather lengthy stay, both the ailments of the mother and the birth defects of the child disappeared.

Since the treatment took so long, I too was sent to Moscow. I lived with Nina's parents, who did not make me very welcome. In order not to idle the time away I found myself a job as a typesetter at *Der Emes*. I brushed shoulders with some of the best Jewish writers of the period. On Elkind's advice, in view of the glorious future he prophesied for the commune, I registered for an engineering course so that one day I would be able to act as the director of the agricultural-industrial *combinat* at Via Nova.

With the useful connections of Nina's father, Minkovsky, I was accepted as a regular student at the Polytechnic Institute. If I may say so without boasting, I was a good student.

Ten months passed before Nina and Olga were completely recovered—you must remember that the nutrition available in those days didn't help to speed recovery—and for all that time we went on discussing our return to Via Nova with complete seriousness. But at the end of a year, when it transpired that the knowledge I had acquired in one year of study was not enough to design even the simplest machine, we stopped talking about it. The letters from Via Nova, which testified to a mood of growing despondency, did not encourage us to burn our bridges in Moscow. Nina enrolled in the Dental School and in the meantime we obtained a room of our own in a three-room flat, which we shared with two doctoral students and their families. Life in Moscow seemed to us reasonable—settled and organized, a fitting conclusion to a period of storm and strife, the last station on the road of a wandering Jewish revolutionary, a decent reward for a man who had served the revolution in foreign lands and who had also made a modest contribution to the renewal of Soviet agriculture. Since Nina was working in the evenings as a cashier in the Little Theater we received free tickets to most of the season's plays. Olga, a rosy-cheeked baby, rather nervous and cautious, spent part of the day at a crèche and the rest with her parents, either at the printer's or at the theater box office. Like many inexperienced parents, we competed for her love, and we kept reminding each other of the declarations we had made at Via Nova that we would never bring children into the world before the commune was well established and able to provide them with a decent standard of living. Nina would sometimes play the piano—with touching enthusiasm—at the kindergarten celebrations, and her mother consoled herself with the thought that children were a wonderful audience and that the lives of concert pianists were full of tension and their family lives suffered. In 1933 it was still possible to believe that we had peaceful and productive lives in front of us, during the course of which we would gradually accumulate knowledge and a modest amount of property.

I enjoyed working at the printing press. I may have preferred work with strong, obedient animals in the open fields, but my technical aptitudes now came into their own. I introduced certain improvements in the press, and was rewarded by the praise from my colleagues. I enjoyed the atmosphere of feverish activity and the comradeship between the printing workers and the editorial board who tried to honor the principle of equality between mental and manual labor. I was emboldened to express my own opinions on questions of Jewish culture. At the paper I met with friends from Eretz Israel. We had common memories and understood each other implicitly. Personalities from the period of the underground made themselves known to me by their real names, listened politely to my criticisms, and corrected my ideological errors patiently and without being insulting. And for a time, I was content with my lot and almost happy. The Eretz Israeli adventure was regarded as an enriching experience. At our cell meetings I denounced the utopianism of the left in the Labor Brigade and the anarchism of Hashomer Hatzair. I was praised for my dialectical perception of reality as if it were some inborn gift, and I basked in the recognition. I even allowed myself to suggest some stylistic corrections in the name of "popular common sense" to a sensitive and subtle writer called Zlotnik, whose pessimism offended Party officials, and he felt obliged to agree to the "uncompromising demands of the toiling masses."

When a year had passed, I wondered how I could ever have lived anywhere but Moscow, the metropolis of the world. In addition to my engineering studies I participated in various courses and study circles. I even took part in a music circle, so that Nina's interests would not be alien to me. I went to concerts and lectures and sat in the audience with all the dignity of an educated proletariat devoting his leisure hours to the superstructure. I saw myself as a young man preparing to take his place in the elite of society, where public affairs were more important than private ones. I was in complete harmony with myself and my friends. The Party was for me a kind of Divine Providence keeping an account of my good deeds and grieving over my deviations. I did not doubt the correctness of its decisions. The ideas I had entertained on my way to Via Nova—strict, abstemious ideas from the period of the Labor Brigade—I put behind me. Nobody was under any obligation to abstain from the development of his talents. A loyal Communist served the public with all his qualities and not only with the work of his hands.

I completed my first year of studies with distinction. I studied engineering with all the enthusiasm of a yeshiva scholar sacrificing himself on the altar of the Torah in order to expedite the coming of the Messiah.

Nina went back to her piano playing, this time for her own enjoyment. She and a number of friends from the Dental School organized a chamber orchestra and played for workers at factories. We saw ourselves as an active, happy, positive couple modestly accumulating friends, correct acts, and commendations. A couple bringing up a cute little citizen of the world of the future with patience and according to reliable theoretical principles.

Party membership brought clear advantages. I would willingly have forfeited the material benefits, but I did not dare criticize the leadership. Building socialism in a nation of over 150 million souls, where hostile and backward elements abounded, was no small matter. If every soldier took it upon himself to criticize the decisions of the general staff, it would be chaos. The cell meetings were boring and our resolutions shallow and sycophantic. But I realized that there was no place for squeamishness in a revolutionary period. In my heart I criticized Nina's mother and the brazen way she exploited her privileges as a Party member, but I said nothing, not even to Nina, both in order to preserve domestic harmony and because I realized that it was impossible to outstrip historical conditions. The conditions, presumably, were "not yet ripe." The distortions would disappear only in my daughter's generation, when the new men would serve the public without expecting any reward for it.

The second year resembled the first. But there were some disturbing signs. The group that had coalesced around the paper split up. The hint of a change in the Party line made people clam up. Petty squabbles were rife. Even the literary criticism became more aggressive. Any deviation from official policy was harshly condemned. Jewish jokes were described as the rotten fruit of perverted souls. The editors became haughty and arrogant. There were frequent telephone conversations with mysterious callers. At the cell meetings my long speeches were received with demonstrative impatience. Exhortations against materialism were overnight proclaimed left-wing deviations. I was reminded of my Zionist period as evidence of my instability. I withdrew into silence. "Shoemaker, stick to thy last" became my motto. I concentrated on finishing my studies without quarreling with anyone. I sought firm, mathematically precise values to cling to, set my sights on becoming an engineer who took pride in his work and his honesty, a Jew building bridges and dams in the motherland of all humanity.

In the third year, I was attached to a planning team of senior engineers as their assistant. They were not Party members, and I was supposed to keep an eye on them. It was an unforgettable experience. They did their work without expectation of advancement or recognition. Their lives were their reward. They had the humility of true professionals. I did not believe that people whose lives hung by a thread could be capable of sabotage, and they, who were sure at first that I had been sent to pick their brains so that they could be discarded, showed friendship and affection for me when they realized that I had no other motive than eagerness to learn. In days to come, this was to be held against me.

Olga grew up like a pale flower in the shade. She was a weak-willed and weepy child. Nina showered guilty love on her. She thought that our ambitions were depriving her of her due. I told her that children grow up happy in homes where the parents are content with their lot. This was our only disagreement. Our love was complete. Our bodies were satisfied and so were our souls. We were both incurable romantics. In the spring we made love under the bushes in the park. Discreet advances by dentists were humorously rebuffed. Even the mutual dislike between Nina's parents did not cast a shadow over our happiness. Until one day a letter came from Vera to say that our son was dangerously ill with pneumonia. Nina's reaction was extreme. She accused me of betraying her trust, of ruining our lives. The fact that I could have kept something so important from her shocked her deeply. She pretended to forgive me, but she kept on raking it up.

In the meantime, however, certain events occurred which forced our private affairs to take a back seat to more important matters, In 1937 I was summoned to the Interior Ministry for a talk. A talk which cast its shadow over all the years to come.

A wreath of flowers on the grave of Via Nova.

Once I tried to document its history, now I can no longer remember the sequence of events. One thing sticks in my mind. Not an important event. But perhaps it has a place here.

I remember a heavy wooden table with clumsy legs and patches of peeling paint. On the table a telephone, a pile of papers, files, a folded newspaper with red pencil marks on it. On the wall: Lenin, Stalin, a mountain view, a diploma. A letter signed by Stalin in a gold frame. A medal.

The district party secretary polished his spectacles. He said nothing as long as the Tatar in the shabby gown and thick socks was in the room. The Tatar was carrying a tray with two glasses of tea and a saucer full of shining white sugar cubes on it. He put the tray down on the table, bowed humbly, and went out of the room, shuffling his feet. His socks made a soft squeaking noise, as if they were polishing the floor.

The secretary took off his spectacles to polish them and for a moment there was a cruel, frightening expression in his eyes. But then he put them back on again and his eyes resumed their twinkle.

"Help yourself."

"Thank you."

It was a wide table and I had to lean over it to reach the glass, I didn't dare pull the saucer of sugar to the middle of the table. I took one cube and sat down. I pretended to put the sugar in my mouth and dropped it secretly into my pocket, feeling it with my fingers to make sure it didn't have a hole in it. A pain in the big toe of my right foot marred the pleasure I felt at having a piece of sugar to give Nina. I was wearing two right-foot shoes which I had found in a heap of rubbish. I didn't want to go in to see the secretary barefoot, as if I was boasting of my poverty.

He spoke and I listened. I prayed for him to go on so that I could sip my tea slowly and deliberately and make it last long enough to take another cube of sugar.

He spoke of the duties of the Jewish commune toward the indigenous peoples of the Soviet Union, and I thought of my sick daughter. I remembered how once, when we were cutting stones on the Tiberas-Migdal road, one of the cart drivers transporting the stones had brought his little daughter with him. I couldn't take my eyes off her. She was a beautiful, golden-haired child, as cuddly as a teddy bear. She sat next to her father and played with the whip which was too heavy for her fragile arms to life. Suddenly I had a revelation: only those who were prepared to bring up their children here were entitled to speak of holding on to the motherland.

I thought of poor little Olga and saw myself as a socialist hero. Here I was endangering the life of my baby daughter in order to hold on to a wretched commune in a godforsaken province. This thought emboldened me to take another cube of sugar from the saucer. I put this one too in my pocket.

Yefremov spoke like a true party secretary.

"Is this what you came back from Palestine for? To set up an advanced post of international Jewry here on Soviet land? Can't trust the Tatars? Lazy, are they? What of it? They'll get paid according to what they produce and they'll learn to work. Against your principles, is it? That's not how things work on a true commune. Tell me, why do you have to be better than everyone else? It only makes people envious. They hate you anyway. Internationalism, comrade, is not something that can be created from nothing by the fist of the authorities. It's a principle that has to be worked at every day, every hour. And if the Jews, who have no motherland, don't show an example—who will? A hypocritical Zionist chauvinist? No. A man with firm principles, like you. Well? Between the two of us, if you refuse to take in these crooks, who never imbibed revolutionary principles with their mother's milk, who's going to teach them how to build a commune?"

When he had finished he said: "That's enough for the meantime. Take it as a warning, and now—give me your hand."

When he shook my hand I felt a hard lump in my palm. Gently Yefremov closed my fingers around two cubes of sugar.

"Take! You have a wife and child too."

His eyes twinkled: "And just so you won't say we're bad people here, I promise you that no one will ever know that you were caught stealing sugar . . ."

After I left Via Nova I never went back. I wanted to go a few times, to visit my brother and my friends, for whom I felt a love full of guilt, but I put it off from day to day. Both because of circumstances, and because I wanted to wait until their hostility toward me had faded.

My brother Ephraim was a member of the commune to the last. During the war he volunteered for the Red Army ("to fight the fascist beast," as he wrote to me in a letter which arrived sixteen years later). He left his wife and small children and went to the front.

When he returned, Via Nova no longer existed. An old Tatar led him to the old well into which they had thrown the bodies of the women and children murdered by the Germans. The indigenous peoples—Tatars, Ukrainians, and the rest—who had been taken into the commune for the sake of the principle of internationalism, had informed on the Jews.

My brother Ephraim committed suicide. He put a bullet

through his head on the steps of the District Committee offices in Yevpatoria. It happened on the twenty-second of June, 1945. But I only found out about it in 1957, one week before his enthusiastic letter reached me at last.

$\mathcal{T}$he next day, very briefly, in disjointed sentences, with obvious unwillingness, like a person submitting to a painful but necessary ordeal, Olga finally spoke to me about her mother.

She didn't remember much. They had traveled from Moscow to the Urals. They stayed there for a while, for a few months, maybe a year. Maybe more, maybe less. When the danger was past they went back to Moscow. For a time they lived with Nina's parents. What year was Minkovsky arrested? She couldn't remember. When was he executed? She didn't know. They kept it a secret from her. She knew that something was going on, but she didn't know exactly what. People cried often, she didn't ask why. Perhaps she wasn't curious. Perhaps she was afraid to hear the answers. Children are able to be completely indifferent. Like a camera snapping photographs that are never developed. For a time they shifted from place to place, and she rather liked it. New places, new people. Surprises. And then Poland. Warsaw. They stayed there for a while. She didn't go to school because she didn't know Polish. By the time she had learned the language and made a few friends they were off again. Zakopane. Kosice. Taking mountain paths. On foot. And then Prague. Karlovy Vary. And then on foot again. To Germany. First Eschwege, and then Munich. They waited for American visas which never came. Then the immigrant ship to the shores of Naharia. In Israel her mother married the man she met in Kosice. First they lived in Bnei Brak, then in Jerusalem. And now she was here.

There was a long silence. I refrained from asking questions. But there was one, at least, that I had to ask.

"Does she know I'm here?"

"Yes."

"And can I see her?"

"I suppose so."

And then she found it necessary to add: "He doesn't know."

"Are you keeping it a secret from him?"

"Yes," sighed Olga.

"And how long do you think you can go on sweeping me under the carpet?"

The smile on my lips upset her.

"It isn't funny."

"Of course not," I quickly agreed.

The world war had created situations that were even more complicated. And it had also solved them. People came back from captivity, from Siberia, and found their wives married to others. Life solved the problems. Presumably there must have been terrible dramas and tragedies too. But not at the age of seventy. I wasn't about to claim any rights. I wasn't going to break into the protected life of a woman I hardly knew anymore. The woman living with an anonymous man in Jerusalem was not the Nina I had remembered, for good and for ill. The idea of meeting her in secret, like a pair of conspirators, without her husband's knowledge, was ludicrous. More important, things had been hidden and come to light in the years that had passed.

"But in the end he will have to be told."

"I don't know."

"But really it's—"

Olga interrupted me.

"Let's leave it up to her."

Just like that.

"If my questions upset you, please tell me."

Olga softened.

"No it's not the questions. It's the whole thing. It's all so complicated. So strange. I don't know myself . . ."

"It would have been better if I'd stayed there. Right?"

"I'm glad you came . . ."

The tone was false. But I forgave her. Patience, I said to myself. They don't know you here. You can't expect them to love you. You must let time take its course. They'll get use to your existence. And after that—perhaps. If there's a spark. Perhaps.

"The Soviet Union is a bigger country than this. And nevertheless you can't keep a secret there. If there's an accident in Novosibirsk, people whisper about it in Leningrad. And here? This whole country is like a single suburb in Moscow. And in one family yet . . ." I wondered.

She surprised me: it was more than possible. Precisely in this little country, there was an iron curtain. People moved in closed circles and they didn't mix with others. Like the ultra-Orthodox.

They didn't eat at people's tables, they didn't read newspapers, they didn't watch television. They were completely cut off. And so it was possible, if nothing unexpected happened, that the other man, who hardly ever left his closed kingdom except to go to America to collect money for his congregation, would never know that a ghost had come back to haunt the secular branch of the family from which he had cut himself off completely.

"You mother must be frightened out of her wits," I said.

"Maybe she is."

I let it go at that. I could see that the conversation was difficult for her. My questions remained unanswered. Their time would come. Anyone who has undergone police interrogation knows: patience is the ointment you smear on the wound to draw out the pus.

Words ran through my mind. But no picture came. On no account could I "see" Nina inside the frame I remembered from the days of my youth. I could only remember an unruly curl falling on a pure forehead, eyes blue with a trembling radiance, a slender delicate hand stretched out to . . . I mustn't let my imagination run wild. . . . An old woman sitting in the women's gallery in a Jerusalem synagogue, her finger in her prayerbook, her lips muttering. A wrinkled neck, dim, watery eyes, glad perhaps that they could weep at last, for no special, painful reason, but simply because the time for weeping had come, because the cantor was raising his voice on a high, quavering note. And the man in her thoughts was not me. Not "the burden of the memories of love." Not a virile man in his prime "too much for the strength of a working woman," breathing on her neck "like a fierce mountain engine"—the quotations are hers and Anna Akhmatova's, whose poems she loved reading in a voice trembling with emotion—but a stale piece of bread overlooked in the Passover cleaning, discovered too late and thrown out with feelings of guilt. A spoiled celebration. She sits there with her thoughts straying. Tormenting herself. Should she tell him or not? Either way, she is in the wrong, a sinful woman. Does she herself believe in her sin?

"Look, there's nothing to worry about. We're not barbarians. There must be some way out. What one rabbi forbids, another permits. And I certainly won't put forward any claims. You can tell her that. Let her do whatever suits her best. And I'll accept it without arguments. Whatever she wants."

But Olga refused to talk about it. She gave me to understand that she would not be drawn into a discussion she did not want. She only nodded her head without looking at me.

She was more willing to talk about her half-brother. He was on the Suez Canal, commanding a stronghold north of Quneitra. He had volunteered, in spite of his age, to set an example to others in his capacity, as a father of young soldiers. When the telegram arrived they couldn't locate him at first. It was two days before they could make contact. He said: "I'll come as soon as I can, but not now: in ten days the unit will be replaced. I can't take off on my own."

Olga's gray eyes rested on me with a quiet, level gaze. There was no complaint in her voice. Nor was there any malice. A meeting had been delayed for so long, another ten days didn't make any difference. He wasn't the kind of person to ask for special favors. His daddy had come home from abroad: the daddy of a forty-five-year-old soldier. A sad joke. No hard feelings: I couldn't expect him to drop everything and run to meet me with outstretched arms. In any case there would be a long period of cautious testing, like a lone wolf on the edge of the territory of a homogenous pack: would they bite him or take him in?

I asked her when she had first found out that she had a brother. What was their first meeting like? And so on. But she evaded my questions. Do you have to know everything on your first day here? You're not going away tomorrow.

I don't need much time to catch on to the local mores. There's no point in expecting the kind of emotion we were used to at home. They treated me with exemplary decency. But not an inch beyond that. Honor thy father. But not with open arms and shining eyes. Each of us encapsuled in his own space suit.

I had hoped to be encircled by radiant faces, kisses until it hurt, bone-crushing hugs, and afterward—all night long, until dawn broke—questions, stories, filling in the missing details, eagerly fitting the broken pieces together, as if we were busy reconstructing a broken jar.

And instead: my daughter tight-lipped, laconic. Nina far away. And Nimrod? Who was interested in an old ghost?

Ghost—go away!

"I promised Vera we would manage without you on Saturday," said Olga suddenly.

Was it my imagination or did I really hear irony in her voice when she said "manage without you"?

"How will I get there?"

"Don't worry. Vera's taken care of everything."

That same day she called. There was a slight tremor in her voice but it was strong and clear. She must have been shouting into the phone. She spoke for a long time. Forty-five years like yesterday. She didn't ask if I would come, only when. She thought she heard a note of hesitation in my voice and said reproachfully, "You needn't worry. It's all ancient history now." Apparently quite a few people still remembered me, and there were no ill feelings. In spite of everything. The law of limitations applied. And I didn't have to worry about transport either. There was no need to harness a horse to the cart. If I was ready to come on Friday they would send a car from the kibbutz to fetch me from my own doorstep, like an important guest.

Then she asked if I had seen Nimrod. She was indignant: he should have come. She would have told him a thing or two if she had succeeded in getting hold of him. They could manage there without him for a day or two.

I said that if he didn't come then presumably he couldn't make it. He wasn't a free agent. And I added that it was of no importance at all, I didn't mind waiting a few days, as long as he didn't have to ask for special treatment on my account.

I forgot my golden rule: never try to be clever on the telephone. You say something, in all innocence, something in the nature of a private joke, smiling agreeably into the receiver, and years later you discover that the person on the other end of the line has been deeply offended and bears you a grudge.

I said one thing, Vera heard another. She suspected that I was trying to play things down, belittle the importance of the occasion, and secure myself against disappointment. She hinted that this was a cowardly way to behave. A real man would behave differently. Why keep on pretending and putting on an act? She was telling me frankly that they were looking forward to seeing me, glad that I had come, curious to see what I looked like after all these years and hear what I had to tell. And the sooner the better.

And in a voice which was suddenly slower and resonant with richly expressive chords that even the telephone could not flatten, she said that she was sure Nimrod must be excited too, looking forward curiously and impatiently to meeting me. And perhaps he was glad to have the meeting postponed for a few days, to give him time to get used to the idea.

I tried several times to put an end to the conversation, which went on and on. I wanted to spare her or the kibbutz the expense. A long-distance call in the middle of the day! I was afraid they would be angry with her for chattering at length at the expense of the common purse. The mental habits of a pauper. But she refused to take the hint. She didn't want to put the telephone down until everything was quite clear: what time to wait for the car to fetch me; whom to inform if, God forbid, I should suddenly fall ill; and what to wear and what to bring with me. And what was completely unnecessary—"Sheets and towels you don't have to bring. I have plenty"—and what was necessary and indispensable.

In this Vera had not changed at all. Her busyness was like a dybbuk. Busy hands shifting things ceaselessly from place to place, and a mind that never stopped planning for a minute. There was never a moment to be wasted. The general meeting was devoted to knitting, and while she was waiting for the train she learned her lines for the Passover play. Even a romantic walk in the hills was used as an opportunity to catch up on her education: what did they say yesterday, in the debate on the economic situation, when she had to take a woman in labor to the hospital?

Long afterward I thought about the telephone conversation. Vera's voice rang clearly in my ears. There wasn't even a hint of resentment in it. As if someone had been obliged to go away, and through no fault of his own he hadn't been able to write, and now that he was back again he would be welcomed warmly and gladly. I've known more than one person in my life who nursed resentment against me, or even harbored dark and lifelong hostility, for words I never said and things I never did. Very occasionally I succeeded in unraveling a tangled knot of grievances or in gaining a pardon for a sin I had not committed. But Vera!

From the day I first applied for an emigration permit I had been thinking of the meeting awaiting me with my nearest and farthest, whom I had taught myself to blot out of my mind. Most of my thoughts were devoted to Nina. I tried to guess what she would look like. A doctor, a family friend who assisted at Olga's birth, once said that she was one of those people upon whom time does not leave its marks, but to whom it adds layer upon layer. I saw her in my dreams as I remembered her from our last meeting, only a little heavier, like her mother, who had kept her figure even at the age of fifty-one (which seemed to me then a ripe old age). Olga and Nimrod I had seen in the snapshots they had sent me as soon as the correspondence was renewed. But Vera, who had hastened to write to me but omitted to enclose a photograph in her letter, I could not remember as a real, flesh-and-blood figure. What came into my mind instead whenever I thought of her was the Hebrew expression: a reminder of wrong-doing.

I try to wean myself of the awful Russian habit of wallowing in guilt like a drunk in his vomit. But even if I try to detach myself for a moment and regard my actions in those days from the point of view of some coolly objective historian, prepared to under-stand and forgive, seeing individual actions as stemming from the ferment that infected everyone in those stormy days, I cannot avoid the conclusion that at least toward one person I am right to feel guilty. And that person is Vera. I sinned against her. Those who love me will no doubt find excuses even for what I did to her. But how many of them are there? I'm not even sure anymore that I myself am one of them.

A few words of apology.

First: the times.

Efrati, the ideologist of the right, would say: "The birth pangs of the Messiah"; "an apocalyptic period." One of the signs of the time will probably seem ridiculous to young people today, who know what they want and can accept their feelings simply and directly: we needed permission even for our loves from that all-devouring Moloch. Even for our sexual instincts. As if a cer-tain organ was not permitted to stiffen without ideological justi-fication. There was one girl in the Brigade, a pretty, lazy girl who had landed among us by accident. She thought: a romantic life, horses, tents, bold boys, walks in "nature." But she soon discov-ered her mistake: hard work, boredom, ideological debates that lasted all night long, and quarrels about political platforms, our own and others'. She stayed with us for a few weeks. All the boys tried to rub against her when we danced. *But nobody dared to love her.* They probably had many a lewd dream about her, but they did not dare to befriend her, for fear of betraying their princi-ples. The girls we were supposed to love were hard-working, strong, devoted, loyal to the idea of the commune, and capable of leading a hard life. A firm and attractive body did not, of course, do any harm. But it was considered reprehensible to set store by external appearances.

Perhaps they weren't all like that. It may be that those addicted to the drug of ideology were in a minority. In any case, a young man like me, who blushed with happiness whenever Elkind addressed him—and how much more so if he actually asked my opinion on any serious subject, such as the question of the Jews and the revolution—would have been deeply ashamed, like a pious Jew caught red-handed in sin, if there had been any grounds for suspecting that I preferred beauty to the capacity for hard work.

Second: the place.

You must remember the bare hillside, the smoke out of the burning thorns, the sweat pouring down the red-hot faces in the tent smelling so strongly of disinfectant, and the gnats. And the sleepless nights under torn mosquito nets, and the ugly fights against flies and mosquitoes, and the snakes and scorpions, and the sooty kerosene lamp, and the heavy eyelids, and the watery jam with dead wasps floating in it, and the tasteless soup, gritty with stones, and the boils that never healed, and the hurting hands and dirty blisters, and the grinding poverty and petty squabbles.

All of which, perhaps, makes the need for feminine softness understandable. The light touch of a caressing hand. The warm breath on your shoulder. The silent acquiescence in the movement of your loins.

Softness may not be the right word. Responsiveness, perhaps. In any event, not a weak, submissive feminine softness, tired and wounded. Not the softness of a weak woman, leaning on you so as not to fall, but the softness of a strong woman, hard and courageous, coupling with you without shrinking in fear, without feminine anxieties, without demanding rights. With steadfast devotion, ready to build a home on this cruel soil and bring up a child among the vipers and asps.

I wonder if anyone who wasn't there himself can really understand what I'm talking about.

In that place, at that time, you were grateful to anyone who wasn't afraid of the future.

Vera wasn't pretty. Many of her features were actually ugly. But she had tremendous vitality. She had a passion for organizing things: work, celebrations, her own affairs, the affairs of others. A busy bee producing honey twenty-four hours a day. And when she loved she loved with all her heart. With wonder, with utter devotion, uncalculatingly. With total exposure, as if the name of the man she loved were written on her forehead.

How insulted she was—and presumably scornful too, but the alchemy of love transformed the scorn to pity, which only added more coals to the fire—when I asked her to keep our relations a secret from the others and not make them public until "our love matured" and we were "quite sure." She saw these doubts as the vestiges of educational backwardness, and she laughed at my fears.

"If you get tired of me, you're free to leave me. I won't hold you against your will. If you want to go—you can always go. Even if we have a child."

I took her words literally.

But other, weightier matters intervened. On the face of it, I didn't make a single decision regarding Vera completely on my own. Events took their own course. And the break was inevitable. But later on, at the time when our ideology disappointed us so bitterly, I would reflect on what had happened between Vera and myself in a spirit of ruthless self-condemnation, and say to myself that despite the profound seriousness with which we took political, national, and international problems, it is quite possible that ideology was often nothing but an excuse for our own selfishness. A justification for simple lusts and shallow feelings. It is certainly possible that even if the revolution had not come between myself and Vera, I would not have lasted long in her tent. Simply because I didn't love her. For all my eagerness to save the world, immediately if possible, I was not the man to sacrifice myself on the altar of happiness of others. Even others who deserved it from every point of view.

*S*tanding at the marble-topped table in the kitchen, with her back to me, cutting vegetables and throwing them dexterously into the soup pot, her head lowered and her eyes on her busy hands, Olga answered my questions.

Nimrod was Vera's only son. Had she remarried? Olga didn't know. For a time she had lived with someone. She probably hadn't married him. But it didn't make any difference on the kibbutz if you were married or not. In any case, there were no other children. But she might not know all there was to know. She hardly ever saw Vera. Sometimes years went by without their meeting. There had to be some family affair for them to meet. They had hardly ever spoken about me. Occasionally Vera would say something about Nimrod and add, "Just like his father." But Olga never asked how, in what way, "like" him? She was sure that we would never meet. Had loneliness left marks on her? She supposed so. But Vera was not a depressed or bitter woman. She was always busy and practical. During the War of Independence she had been in charge of a home for wounded soldiers. Later on she worked as an instructor on new immigrant farms. She taught them Hebrew. She had kicked up a big fuss and claimed that nobody understood their difficulties. She had no time to complain about loneliness. Maybe now it was different.

I could sense that my questions annoyed Olga. Once she even raised her voice in protest: How on earth could she, a stranger, know why Vera never married again? The kibbutz was a small place and if you didn't get married in time you were liable to remain single. If staying on the kibbutz was a principle for you, you had to pay the price.

In the evening, Olga's soldier son arrived. A sturdy lad with an honest face. I avoid the term "grandson." A person who was a total stranger to me stuck a hard hand into mine and kept his

sharp eyes fixed on a point somewhere above my head. I felt that
if he could have made me disappear by waving a magic wand, he
would have done so without a moment's hesitation. He announced his name, Gil, without enthusiasm and withdrew his
hand. And before the warmth faded from his palm he was already talking to his father about something else.

That night we sat in the living room watching television. His
sister teased Gil. He amused himself with her for a while, until
he lost patience. Olga and Walter told her to leave him alone.
They spoke to each other, exchanging comments, laughter,
reacting to what they saw on the screen. This went on for a long
time. In the end I couldn't stand it anymore. I got up and went
upstairs to my room.

Olga followed me. She knocked hesitantly on the door.
Then she opened it quietly and looked into the room.

"Is anything wrong?"

"No, why?"

"Why did you leave the room like that?"

"What do you mean, like that?"

"Suddenly, without saying goodnight?"

"I did say it. You didn't hear me."

"Did we say anything to offend you?"

"No, nothing."

Even the maid who came to clean the house three times a week
stalked past me expressionlessly. She was a woman of about
thirty, full-fleshed with a broad, sensuous face and a timid look.
At first I tried to get into conversation with her—an ally from the
working class—asking her how much they paid her and how they
treated her, and trying to convey by the tone of my voice that I
was on her side, that I was aware of the way she lived—in her own
house, far away from this luxurious suburb, she had left three
small children, the oldest of them only five, in the care of her
mother-in-law who was eighty years old and blind—and moved
by her poverty, but she appeared startled and taken aback. A
sudden look of hostility flashed through her eyes and she walked

past me in silence, taking care not to brush up against me with her big breasts in the narrow passage.

When I told Olga about it she smiled. She said that Nadya must have thought I was trying to seduce her. She couldn't imagine that a man of my age, of my position (what was my position?) would get into conversation with a woman like her unless he wanted to seduce her. Especially since I began by asking her intimate questions right away. When Olga was there she was not afraid of me and she was prepared to talk. Not very willingly. She couldn't bring herself to admit that I could take a real interest in her and her fate. She was well paid, she was well treated, she lacked for nothing, thank God. Once I even succeeded in making her smile. My accent amused her, especially the way I pronounced her name: Aflalo.

The only one who never ignored me was the dog. A German shepherd whose good nature belied his terrifying appearance. He fawned on all their visitors and kept his barks for me.

I scolded him: Don't you know that Jews are afraid of dogs?

Only Olga smiled. Walter took the occasion to explain, quite seriously, that the Jews here were not the same as the Jews elsewhere in the world.

Walter is not an easy man to understand. He doesn't say much, but whatever he does say is conclusive. He is used to being obeyed, even by Olga. Only his children refuse to submit to his authority and he blames Olga for it: she has failed to bring them up properly. He, presumably, was too busy to educate them himself. When they were small he was an officer in the regular army. Now he is in an export-import business of some sort, the exact nature of which I have not yet grasped. He provides for his family with an abundance of which he is as proud as if he earned his money by the sweat of his brow. Whereas in fact he receives commissions, among other things, for transactions between governments, such as arms deals and the sale of military equipment. But I don't know enough about it to judge. And in any case, a guest should not set himself up in judgment over his hosts.

He treated me with a kind of irony, the reason for which is

not yet clear to me. Perhaps it was the patronizing attitude of someone who had made a success of everything he did toward someone whose life was a failure. Perhaps it was the arrogance of an active man who had nothing to say to old-age pensioners, and considered the act of communication with them a gesture of goodwill that had nothing to do with the serious business of life and was in any case unfruitful. And perhaps it was the hostile pity of someone who had never had any ideology of his own toward people like me, whose beliefs have made them lose their senses and ruined their lives.

From my own experience I can testify that it is precisely those people who claim to have no ideology who are the most opinionated. Sometimes they are more fanatical about their lack of belief than the ideologues are about their beliefs. People who believe that the status quo is the natural state of affairs cannot be budged from their opinions by any logical argument.

In any case, he is a Zionist, although he argues that his Zionism is a purely emotional matter. He is a firm and aggressive Zionist, in whom doubts about the justice of the Zionist cause give rise to profound revulsion. I wonder how a man who calls himself a liberal can think that the opinions of those who disagree with him must stem from some dark and evil source.

I envy him his self-satisfaction and conviction that he is on the right road. He has no doubt that Israel is the one and only answer to the Jewish question and any Jew who does not acknowledge this simple truth must be perverted. He is sure that Israel is strong enough to conquer Libya and Saudi Arabia, and only refrains from doing so for "political" reasons.

I am careful not to tell him what I really think. I know very little of the facts—my access to foreign newspapers has been severely limited—but nevertheless I am full of the gravest doubts.

At the Ovir office in Moscow, while stamping my passport with the exit permit, the clerk permitted himself a personal remark. He asked me if I really wanted to emigrate to Israel—the last place on earth where Jews were killed because they were Jews.

I was tempted to make some heroic reply, along the lines of "But they die proudly" or "with guns in their hands," etc. But since the man was not trying to be provocative there was no call for heroic gestures. "I have family there," I replied.

I am afraid that if I express my doubts to Walter he will be angry and say: In that case, why did you come here? And I don't think I could bring myself to make the same reply to him.

I refrain from discussing the matter, but I cannot understand how Walter can be so confident of the ability of a tiny Jewish state to survive for long in the jaws of a volcano, or to go on bearing the cost of its military needs for any length of time. He is sure that the Soviet Union is a dog whose bark is worse than its bite. The naiveté of a practical man of affairs like himself, an arms merchant what's more, astounds me. But I cannot allow myself to listen to him with the ironical expression with which he listens to me. I haven't the impudence. My desire for confrontation too seems to have weakened over the past few years.

Let no one imagine that the two of us indulged in long talks about current affairs, or anything else. Not at all. He hardly spoke to me. Everything I have said here is based on mere snatches of conversation, hints, the expression on his face when he listens to me, and information gleaned from Olga.

Walter talked with me at length only once. He came home from work early and found me alone in the house. He offered me imported vodka. He was surprised to hear that I don't drink. My image as a Russian suffered a setback in his eyes. In the end I agreed to take a drop, for the sake of the ritual. He filled his own glass with whiskey and soda, sat down in the armchair opposite me, stretched out his legs, and looked at me with the beaming face of a man about to do a good deed. He asked me about my plans for the future, if I had any, and how I saw things in general. A very vague question, which I could interpret as I wished. In other words, if I was thick-skinned enough I could pretend not to understand that he wanted to know how long I intended staying in his house.

I said that I still hadn't recovered from the shock of the first encounter with the country and I still did not dare wish for things I did not know if I was entitled to expect. I was ready to go wherever they sent me, if they gave me the opportunity to work at my trade. He asked me what my profession was and I told him I was a mining engineer.

Walter is a man who knows how to sigh and smile at the same time.

"You should have brought a few mines with you, if that's all you know how to do," he said.

The price of copper had dropped, and the few mines that existed in this poor country had been closed down, he explained.

The question which had really interested him was left in the air. I wondered if he was going to ask again. When I saw that he was too polite to press me, I offered the answer of my own accord.

I told him what I myself had been told: I would be informed as soon as suitable arrangements had been made for me. I don't know why I should be so lucky, I confessed, but I don't want to presume upon my luck. I shall just have to wait patiently until a solution is found.

I stole a glance at his face when I said the word "patiently." But Walter is a man in control of his reactions. He only said that he thought it would be difficult to find work in my profession, put his glass down on the glass-topped table, and rose to leave the room.

I stopped him.

"I don't want to be a burden on you," I said. "If they can find a temporary accommodation for me, I'll take it. Never mind if it's far from Tel Aviv."

He breathed an inward sigh of relief. But his face betrayed nothing.

"What's the matter? Aren't you comfortable here?"

"Very comfortable indeed."

"Then why this talk of temporary arrangements?"

I was only too familiar with his brand of heavy-handed humor, the humor of people accustomed to getting their own way.

I told him that when I read about the problems of the

Russian immigrants in the newspapers, my gorge rose. I was not prepared to be placed in that category. I was an independent individual, and I had no demands which stemmed from the expectations of people accustomed to having the authorities organize their lives for them, for better or for worse. My only problem was that I was seventy years old. And presumably I would have a hard time proving I was still a strong man.

Walter nodded his head understandingly, but the ironical expression did not leave his eyes.

That was all very well, he said, but old men were supposed to make way for the young. And I should be satisfied with a national security pension and the occasional odd job.

He crushed my hopes together with the cigarette stub he ground into the ashtray with his thumb.

The disappointment must have been evident in my face, for he asked me what was troubling me.

I told him that I had to work. Any work, never mind what.

"We'll try to help you. But I can't promise anything," he said and hurried out of the room.

It will be a sin again at the spirit in which these lines are written if I hide a certain fact. Walter asked me what my profession was and the answer I gave him was true enough. But I didn't tell him the whole truth.

I never graduated from my course. I stopped in the middle of the fourth year. When I arrived at the mining district in Kuznetsk I passed myself off as a certified engineer. The camp commandant didn't bother to check. He needed the signature of an engineer in order to obtain the materials he sold on the black market. When I arrived at Norilsk it was already written in my file that my diploma had been lost. In the chaos prevailing during the war even documents stamped with the express instruction "To be kept forever" were lost. The most pedantic bureaucracy made mistakes. So when I was arrested during the war, I was already registered as a certified engineer. The sharp eyes of the interrogators, which always caught me out in deviations from statements I had made in previous interrogations, apparently never found it necessary to subject official statements about me to close scrutiny. No one noticed that the date of my graduation, as it appeared on the documents signed by the camp commandant in Norilsk, was later than the date of my first arrest.

I never studied mining engineering in my life. Nevertheless, I worked as a mining engineer responsible for an entire *combinat.* I found a book in the camp library and learned it by heart. I had a few pangs of conscience, if I can dignify my fears and hesitations by this name, before taking on so heavy a responsibility. But they never gave me any time for scruples. I lied in order to save myself and help my brigade, which was composed of people no longer capable of hard labor. At the beginning I thought I would get an easier job—engineer's assistant, storekeeper, or something similar—which would provide an extra plate of soup as well as the chance to lend a helping hand to my fellow unfortunates. But just at that time the chief engineer who specialized in mining died, and none of the other engineers in the camp, some of them men of wide experience, were prepared to state that they had any special knowledge of mining.

I will never know how many victims I have on my conscience. There was no way of ascertaining if the collapse in the northern wing was due to error in planning or to thievery and corruption. Even if the planning had been faultless, the materials were flawed. The cement we received was sand with a few gray crumbs sprayed over it. We had to do our jobs and hold our tongues. I am not trying to make excuses for myself. I really don't know. In any case, surprisingly enough, no one was punished. The camp commandant decided it was sabotage. The list of saboteurs was identical with the list of the names of the victims killed in the collapse. Any impartial commission of inquiry would have torn his report to bits. But the commission of inquiry was headed by the gentleman who was on the receiving end of the surplus steel we never used. Cry, the wretched country. . . .

In any case, when I left the camp I was an experienced mining engineer. No one could cast doubt on my skill. Today I don't need certificates, my deeds speak for themselves. I don't think I'll be cheating anyone if I use a dubious document. Experience is the best qualification, after all.

I built a bridge, too. Quite a large one, in fact. And when the tanks went over it and it shook slightly but showed no signs of collapsing (I didn't even trust the huge steel tracks that came on the army train), there were tears in my eyes. Anyone who has never built a bridge in his life will probably have difficulty in understanding that there can be moments of sublime happiness even in Hell.

And there is another little lesson to be learned from my story: lies have great power. You cast them upon the waters, and in the fullness of time you find that they have become truth.

> *My poems will not be required here this time,*
> *And perhaps I myself am not required either.*

These lines of Yesenin's in "Soviet Russia" kept buzzing in my head, like a dentist's drill probing to the root of the pain.

Could it perhaps have been a mistake, from beginning to end, this second aliyah of mine, dragging the bones of an old man whom nobody wants to a country that doesn't need him, like the pious Jews who believe that dying in the Holy Land will save them the trouble of rolling there underground when the Messiah comes? But I can't force myself to believe in what I do not believe just because the sleep of believers is sweet.

And perhaps I fought with my friends in the democratic movement for nothing. They said: When you Jews say all we want is the right of repatriation, you are turning your backs on the struggle for the right of emigration for all. I said: We're tired of fighting for the good of humanity at large. Isn't it time we did something for ourselves? And it seemed to me that they reconciled themselves to the idea that we had the right to be weary in the twilight of our lives. We—that is, I and others like me. But they had no sympathy with the young "refuseniks." They said: You're fanning the flames of anti-Semitism. When you say that only the Jews should have the right to choose, you are making enemies precisely among those who were your firmest friends.

And now I sometimes find myself succumbing to despondency. I am from there and that is where I should have fought my battles. The battle for the soul of that vast country which will decide the fate of the world. Perhaps I had no chance of achieving anything. I am not speaking of victory here. Perhaps I would have been arrested for a third time, and perhaps they would have locked me away in a lunatic asylum. But there I would have fallen, if I may be permitted to borrow a lofty phrase from the past, on my sword. Here I count for nothing. My opinions are of no importance and the lesson of my life means nothing to anyone. They knew it long before I learned it the long, hard way. Here I am an old man with a rubbed-out face, buttonholing people to tell them a cautionary tale they have no need of. I shall die here of a miserable old age. A useless old man, a burden on the state whose right to exist I denied.

At moments like these I am not thinking of my family. But their lives too, it seems to me, without putting it too strongly, were more comfortable and respectable before I intruded on them like a drop of pitch in a barrel of wine. I am not talking about Nina, for whom my return is quite simply a catastrophe. I'm talking about Olga, Walter, and the children. It is their self-respect I have endangered here, by the very fact of my existence. Previously they saw themselves, as others saw them, as generous and kindly people, and now they must be wondering what is the matter with them that the presence of a poor relation disturbs them so much.

And Nimrod. He, too, does not seem eager to meet me. Even supposing that he couldn't come for reasons I have no way of knowing, I don't imagine that he is sitting there biting his nails in impatience to meet me. What need has a forty-five-year-old man of a father he never knew in his childhood? To see what he himself will look like in twenty-five years' time? To see how certain common characteristics, the kind that are passed from father to son, grow dominant as the years go by? I certainly cannot expect him to regard me as a model, and I have no right to expect love either. At the most, he will be prepared to tolerate my existence as an inescapable part of the Jewish fate, a legacy of suffering the members of our race cannot avoid. Even when they were sure that they were the first generation of a redeemed era, the Holocaust of European Jewry came and resurrected from their graves the ghosts of the fathers they had abandoned to their fates.

Only Vera, perhaps, is really glad to welcome me back. Like the correction of a historic mistake. But the meeting with her fills me with uneasiness. Does that long-suffering woman actually believe that we can renew our youth and begin all over again? I fear that more than anything.

How ironic that the one who welcomed me most gladly and wholeheartedly was Rachel, the friend who lives down the road. I have already described her. I can add only that she is a native-born Israeli, the same age as Olga; it seems to me that they even served in the army together. Although from many points of view typical of the local girls with their radiant self-confidence, their ringing voices—slightly hoarse, either because of the climate or from competition for attention in their early years—she seems to me to have been lifted out of my own youth and transported just as she was, but in far less modest garb, to the present time. All the other qualities are there: the curiosity, the wondering look, the ability to switch from wholehearted admiration to sharp dismissal in the twinkling of an eye, the passion for fine phrases and poetic allusions, the predisposition to trust everyone and to suffer disappointment as if the whole world had collapsed, the desire to hoard tidbits of knowledge like a magpie and then display them like a peacock.

She invited me home and bustled about me as if I was an honored guest, and she plied me with questions about the Labor Brigade, the Communist Fraktzia, and Via Nova. From her leading questions I realized that she knew more than I did. I remember only what I remember, and sometimes all I have to hang on to is the thread leading into a labyrinth guarded by others. And there must be many facts which I have either forgotten or which have undergone a process of refinement and idealization in my memory. She had studied a vast amount of material, including confidential documents which had been kept under wraps for many years, and recently she had also interviewed many people and verified their testimony by comparing one with another. Nevertheless, she attached "great importance," as she solemnly announced, her eyes shining with happiness, to what I had to say, since I—so she said—was one of the few people who had been involved in the political struggles between left and right in the Labor Brigade, had left the country with Elkind and his group, had lived in Via Nova, and had come back.

In other words, I was useful and necessary to someone here—which was some small comfort.

However, I was obliged to disappoint her to a certain extent. For I did not return to Russia with the group organized by Elkind and I could not give her any firsthand information about the first days of Via Nova. I told her that I was one of the people expelled from the Battalion in Tel Yosef a long time before that, and I could tell her as much as she liked about the years I spent in what was then called the "Arab street."

She said the time for that would certainly come, but for now she was mainly interested in Elkind and his group. Elkind, a bundle of whose photographs was lying on her table in a file made of a hard plastic material, inflamed her imagination. She wanted to know when I had seen him for the last time. When I told her that I had seen him in 1936, she was beside herself with excitement. She had not yet met anyone who had met him after 1933.

"You're a gift from Heaven!" she cried, her eyes shining like the eyes of a gazelle in the zoo when it sees the keeper coming with a bunch of greens in his hand.

She sat down on the sofa opposite me like an attentive pupil, with her knees together and the material of her blue dress flowing to her feet, her right hand reaching for the small tape recorder on the arm of the sofa.

"Can't we do without that?" I asked.

"Why?"

I didn't know why. The machine frightened me. I might be ready to confide in an intelligent woman some things I was not necessarily prepared to broadcast to the world.

"Go on," she said, "I'm listening."

Our last meeting was in '36. A strange, sad meeting, full of secret hints, many of which I suppose I must have interpreted wrongly, according to my mood at the time. I was walking down Zubovski Avenue when suddenly I saw Elkind and Krochmalnik opposite me. There was a moment of exhilaration—hugs and kisses and hearty slaps on the back—but it all died down abruptly. As long as the conversation turned on family and children our enthusiasm did not desert us. But the moment I asked about Via Nova a light went out in Elkind's eyes. He muttered something: a simple magic formula which if memory serves me may be summarized as follows: The autonomous Jewish commune had been ahead of its time. In other words, conditions were not yet ripe. And perhaps he said something even worse, namely that it was an attempt to swim against the tide of history: isolationism, when the general tendency was in the direction of international solidarity, etc., etc. He quoted Marx and Lenin. His voice was monotonous, boring, joyless, which was unusual for him (speech for Elkind usually involved passionate emotion: his eyes would flash, his head would be thrown back, his chest would swell like an opera singer about to sing a popular aria). Perhaps that voice, sad and downcast, was a sign. Perhaps it was trying to convey something his words could not. Perhaps it was even trying to contradict them. He asked me again about what I was doing with myself, and it was only as he listened attentively to things that made no difference one way or the other that the old flash of intelligent alertness returned to his eyes. He listened to my words as tensely as if they called for some immediate aid, some vital counsel not to be withheld from a comrade. His delicate face was illuminated by his radiant smile, twisted by the crooked teeth which had been warped by malnutrition. But whenever I tried to turn the conversation to the issues of the day, he closed up and a dejected look came down like a gray curtain over his eyes. At first I thought he didn't want to talk in front of Krochmalnik. Indeed, he quoted passages from the early Marx which were not then in favor and which could have exposed him to criticism, but he could have relied on the ignorance of Krochmalnik, whose "Marxism" did not amount to much more than the notion that it was somehow more "manly" than reformism. However, when Elkind left us, I was no longer so sure. When he took his leave, he avoided giving his address, saying that he did not yet have a permanent place to live, and Krochmalnik later hinted that he knew that this was not the case. I was a little hurt, but Elkind promised he would come and see me at the printer's to give me his permanent address the moment he had one. I forgave him. Agitated and excited, I remained with Krochmalnik in the street. For a while I stood watching Elkind's stooped figure walking away with a slow, heavy tread—a young man suddenly grown old before his time. Until Krochmalnik began to talk.

What Krochmalnik told me upset me ever more. He told me about the conversation they had had before I arrived. I was astounded to hear that Elkind had said things to this unreliable fellow which he had been careful not to say to me. Did he really trust him more than me? I may as well admit that I was jealous. In our youth, in the Brigade, we had courted Elkind like starstruck girls, trying to attach ourselves to him and get into his good graces. The friendship he had shown me then had made me glad and proud. And now he preferred this loutish fellow who lacked the subtlety and discrimination to understand him.

The things that Elkind had told Krochmalnik were the kinds of things a man confided only in his closest friend. In the Moscow of those days it was like putting your fate into someone else's hands. According to Krochmalnik, Elkind had acted like a shattered man. He said that Russia had disappointed him and the Party had murdered his soul. The bureaucracy was full of mean, cowardly men who had to get rid if the idealists as quickly as

possibly. Pure-souled people like us, he said, were a danger to
the bureaucracy. And the bureaucrats were not giving up all the
power they had accumulated to satisfy the innocents. And then
he had reproached himself and expressed regret for what he had
done to the Brigade. He had dragged people after him without
telling them the whole truth. Although he had done it for ideological reasons, today he wasn't sure that he had not actually
acted out of fear. He said that in the beginning he had believed,
like all the others, that it might prove impossible to build socialism without cruelty. Today he feared that it was the cruelty which
would destroy the socialism. In any case, it would be a socialism
which had no place for the Jews. The Jews needed a socialism of
their own, a humane, compassionate socialism.

I refused to believe what Krochmalnik told me. I knew him
to be a man who liked dramatizing things and who would have
no scruples about inventing exciting stories simply in order to be
the center of attention for a while. I didn't believe that Elkind,
who knew Krochmalnik well and had once even given him the
nickname "actor," would pour out his heart to him of all people.
Everybody knew that Krochmalnik was a chatterbox and an exag-
gerator. And yet I was upset by what I heard. There were some
things that Krochmalnik wouldn't have been capable of inventing himself. The style was not his. And yet . . .

I couldn't stop myself from getting a dig in at him: Had
Elkind really said all those things without fear of a little bird
carrying them further? But Krochmalnik did not take offense.
He gave a straight answer to a provocative question. "He must
have thought of it," he said, "because he didn't forget to add: 'It
won't do you any good to inform on me, Krochmalnik. You may
be rewarded for your pains, but your rein will get shorter, not
longer. Don't forget it.' "

Krochmalnik even showed a certain delicacy—making me
regret all my bad thoughts about him—when he said to me in
parting, to console me: "You know, people don't say to two
people what they say to one. Two people can say what they like
to each other. Get drunk and spill out their guts through their

mouths. But with three, it's something else again. Three people and it is already a secret meeting." And then he added that when Elkind had told him it wouldn't do him any good to inform on him, he was insulted. What decent person wouldn't have been? He had said to Elkind: "If there was any risk of my informing on you, why did you talk to me in the first place?" And Elkind, with his wonderful smile, had said: "Haven't you ever felt the need to squeeze the pus out of a pimple, despite the danger of infection?" And I said to him: "You see, Elkind really should have been careful. A few minutes ago he told you his deepest secrets, and you go tell them to the first person you meet in the street." The astonishment on Krochmalnik's face amused me vastly. He bit his tongue and an expression of mounting anxiety spread over his anguished features.

Of course, I had no intention of informing on either Elkind or Krochmalnik. But for a moment I suspected that Krochmalnik might hurry to get in first. It was certainly reckless of me to have frightened him. A dangerous joke. The man had trusted me utterly, and I had tormented him. I hoped that my friendly slap on the back and accompanying smile had reassured him. At any rate, the incident continued to worry me for a while—I wouldn't have chosen a man like Krochmalnik, a man with the theater in his blood, to confide in. His urge to participate in some heroic drama might put all three of us in danger. But apparently in this case too Elkind proved my superior: he trusted Krochmalnik and his trust was not misplaced. He had, without even speaking to me, succeeded in making my own loyalty to the Party suspect, too. My silence—covering up for him and Krochmalnik—was disloyal. The ideals of duty and honor of those days called on a man to give warning of danger. The disillusionment of a man like Elkind could spread like wildfire among his admirers. And yet I said nothing. My loyalty to my friends was apparently stronger than my loyalty to the Party.

The meeting with Elkind upset me, as I say, but not for long. I told Nina I had met him and that I had not invited him home.

I didn't tell her any details, in order not to burden her unnecessarily (caution was already in our blood), but I think I used an expression popular in those days: He has fallen off the galloping chariot. To this day, I am filled with shame when I remember how I preened myself on my friend's disgrace. With what pride I spoke of his fall! In other words: Look at me! Don't I see what Elkind saw? Of course I do. But Elkind now sees the trees while I see the woods. Doesn't he know that when you chop down trees the chips fly? The death throes of the old world will of necessity be accompanied by ugly convulsions, and so on and so forth. All of this thinking was meant to place me in the ranks of the strong and resolute, those devoted to the revolutionary cause. As if I was lamenting Elkind's weakness. Nina was more human. She couldn't understand why the fact that Elkind was sad should be a reason for not inviting him to our home. After all, that's when friends needed each other—when they were in trouble. I had to promise her that if I ever met him again, I would invite him. And Nina put her arms around my positive hero's neck and kissed me. "You have to encourage him," she said. "We all have our moments of weakness."

So remote am I from the man I was in those days that I can speak of Elkind with complete objectivity, as if I were speaking of a stranger and one, moreover, for whom I had no particular respect. The Soviet classics were my bible—Gorky and Ostrovsky—and also the pulp magazines of proletarian culture. In my youth I had been attracted, like all the members of my generation, to the Imagists, the Acmeists and Futurists, and all the others who regarded Soviet life as a kind of giant laboratory for all kinds of innovative artistic experiments. But the hot winds of the Jordan Valley had blown away the last traces of my "decadence," and I had come back to Russia determined to "reconstruct myself" from top to bottom—calling consciousness, behavior, and even passions to order to conform to the model of the positive Soviet hero in a fourth-rate novel. Ostensibly, I should have concluded that man (me!) was nothing but a peg in the chariot ("the galloping chariot"), and that he (I) was acted upon by immense historical forces beyond his (my) control, in which case he (I) had nothing to do but obey and be silent. But the positive hero, nevertheless, had a wide scope for his activities. Everything was foreseen, but freedom of choice was given—to work harder than others, to strengthen the weak, to encourage the depressed. An ordinary worker does his work. I worked twice as hard by day, and in the evenings I went to hang up slogans in the club. A weak-willed citizen is content if he has a job and a roof over his head and an education for his children and if things are going more or less in the right direction (that of "a better future for all humanity"), but I wanted Russia to be proud of her sons (me!) and to this end I never missed a single one of the study circles open to us, and went to sing in the choir as well. I was a hoarse singer who sang with all his might and main, eyes fixed reverentially on the conductor's baton. I received commendations with becoming modesty. I did not need them in order to feel superior to my comrades, but was nevertheless obliged to accept them, because of the shirkers who would not do their duty without rewards. The latter, who would not do a decent job of work unless they were compensated for it, had to see that the outstanding received recognition and gratitude. I would have preferred these gold and silver and bronze medals to be given not to the outstanding, but rather to the weaklings who made an effort to overcome their weakness. Devotion rather than excellence should be rewarded, I thought. But I told myself that our leaders knew what they were doing. We saw only a fraction of the giant mosaic whereas they saw the whole picture. Even my language in those days was copied from a fourth-rate Soviet novel. It was absolutely free of obscenity and unnecessary slangish expressions and full of verbs derived from the initials of institutions, five-year plans, and so on. I was an exemplary Soviet citizen: a Party member serving the aims of the Party with all his might and main, free to understand the official interpretation of historical necessity and to obey it gladly; a man who behaved as if his every act was being watched and judged from above, even when there was nobody there to see him.

Last night I had a dream which I have already had several times before. I am running up a sandy hill, my legs are heavy, and two vicious dogs are chasing me. My feet sink into the treacherous sand, and the dogs come closer. I wake up at the moment when their teeth sink into the flesh of my thigh, in the place where a piece of shrapnel from the explosion of a grenade in the war is still embedded.

Such things have never happened to me. I had once seen a manhunt in an old movie and the sequence must have left a profound impression on me. None of the things people did to me in closed rooms ever came into my dreams, but the dream of the dogs came back on the eve of every interrogation.

When we spoke among ourselves, the painful subject was avoided. Everyone kept the moments of his humiliation and disappointment in himself locked away in his heart. Only one of my friends, Epstein, liked talking about it. We never knew if the horrifying stories he told had happened to himself or others. His appearance, with its prominently Jewish features—the sharp face, the big, clever eyes, the hooked nose, the thin, fragile hands, the short legs with turned-out feet, the stooped back, the long neck with the huge Adam's apple—were a provocation to a sadist (our picture of the world became simpler day by day, leaving room for an equation with no unknown factors: every sadist was an anti-Semite, every anti-Semite a sadist). He took a morbid interest in the subject and seemed to be investigating it with some practical purpose in mind—perhaps he thought that he might be able to fit the arbitrary cruelty of our tormentors into some systematic format from which he would then be able to derive simple rules of behavior. Perhaps he was collecting the "material" because that was the way of a scholar. The day he stopped believing this erudition somewhat capable of protecting us, he would be lost.

He told us about a certain German Communist, whose name I have forgotten, who had gone through hell at the hands of the Gestapo and the NKVD one after the other, and had made comparisons. He wasn't trying to discover which were the most vicious. There were sadists everywhere (and the Jews weren't free of it either, said Epstein—in their passion to excel in everything they were sometimes better at it than others). The German was able to point out one basic difference. The Germans had tortured him to make him tell them something they needed to know. He had borne his suffering with pride, for he knew that he was protecting people and ideas. When the suffering became unbearable, he would invent some lie and gain a breathing space. In the meantime his comrades would have time to change their address and cover up their tracks. He was sure that he would die in the end, and the bodily pain and spiritual humiliation were a calvary which he undertook to suffer heroically. He would live as long as he could and die a hero's death in the name of the proletarian revolution. In Russia, they tortured him to *make* him lie. He was obliged to withstand the torture in order to defend his own life (nobody is executed in Soviet Russia unless they confess to their crimes. An invention of genius: the prisoner himself delivers his own death sentence, and the hands of the court are clean). But his own life—after the proletarian revolution had betrayed him and a "member of the Russian working class" had found it necessary to urinate into his mouth in order to degrade him and make it clear to him that he had nothing more to do with the historical process for whose sake he was willing to sacrifice his life—was no longer so important to him. Self-respect was dead. All that was left was a rudimentary urge to survive. And he was ready to confess to any imaginary charge which did not carry the penalty of the death sentence. The interrogation of the German had not been accompanied by any particularly cruel torture. Generally speaking, he received the common treatment: a hard bunk, sleepless nights, lights shining into his eyes, and insulting abuse—until he was delivered into the hands of a perceptive interrogator who found out his sensitive points. He was the one who urinated into his mouth, who forced him to march like a soldier in boots full of feces, to wallow in his own vomit, to wipe his glasses on a blood-soaked rag, and such inventions of a sick mind—until he was ready to confess to any imaginary crime as long as they let him wash his face and eyes. That day the NKVD files filled up with the names of German Communists who had deserted to Russia. Everyone knew. And the ones he had forgotten he supplied the following day. His conscience bothered him, but he consoled himself with the thought that his action might be the means of saving them all. He believed that Stalin knew nothing and he hoped that the sudden mass of German prisoners would attract attention in high places.

What they had done to Epstein himself he did not say. And nobody expected him to. If he was still alive, a weakling like him, he must have given his interrogators satisfaction in some way or other. And presumably he must have given them names too. Perhaps he had fallen into the hands of a clever or educated interrogator who had summed him up at a glance as his own most severe judge. His own conscience would torment him more than any hard labor they could impose on him. On the contrary: as long as he could stand he did the work without complaint as a punishment he deserved, not because he had sinned against the socialist motherland, but because he had sinned against the nameless men he had betrayed. It was only when he no longer had the strength to chop down trees that he resorted to the use of contemptible tricks in order to survive.

(And perhaps he is still punishing himself. Why did he refuse to apply for an emigration permit? "What right have we got to live at the expense of Jews who built themselves a state? What was our contribution? They need soldiers there, not old Marxists who know how to thread a bear through the eye of a needle," he said. The generation of the wilderness. . . .)

I think that I must put down a few things about myself here, too. The details aren't important. No, I'm not trying to hide anything. There were no dramatic incidents. They even succeeded in making suffering boring. One day perhaps I shall write a practical manual for the tortured. Describe a few archetypes of interrogators and explain how to behave with each one of them. My own interrogations were conducted legally, if it is possible to define the permissible and the prohibited in this context. Some say physical violence is prohibited; the prisoner must be returned unscathed to the bosom of society which spewed him out when he was the rotten apple in the barrel. Which is ridiculous. They do you violence the minute they slam the door behind you. They crush your testicles and you emerge unscathed (if they don't make too good a job of it as they did with Colonel K.), even if you haven't a future. In Russia they believe that prison makes you strong. If you don't go mad your spirit is tempered. That you don't come out as whole as you went in should be obvious to everyone. The exact nature of the damage cannot be known. In any case, a few muscles are strengthened. And the mind is a little blunted and a little sharpened, too. A draw.

In any event, I was relatively gently treated. At first they slapped me a around a bit because I refused to confess that I was a British spy. I was defending my life. The moment they accused me of Zionism, I confessed willingly. Unlike others, I was not forced to confess to imaginary crimes. For five years I believed in Zionism. "If coming to my senses is a crime, I am prepared to take my punishment," I said. For this witticism I paid dearly: a week in solitary. I was cold, wet, and bored. Especially bored. To death. Metaphors take on a literary meaning in extreme conditions. Humiliation literally means crawling. The expression "Hold your head high" in these conditions describes a simple movement of the head.

For two weeks they questioned me and I wasn't obliged to lie even once. My information didn't hurt anyone. All the members of the Communist Party in Eretz Israel had already been arrested before me. Their confessions were already in the file before I was even arrested. Epstein told us about a certain Trotskyite who said defiantly to his interrogators: The walls aren't thick enough to silence the scream that will rise up from here. I didn't scream and the walls were thick enough. I didn't inform on Nina's father, either. I told them: I wasn't found worthy of his confidence; to a man like me he speaks only from a platform. I don't know if these remarks helped or harmed him.

After my release, I was full of silly pride. Only a man who has had lights shone into his eyes has the right to express an opinion about the experience of our times, I said. And for a while I even amused myself with the idea that we should wear a red badge on our jackets and take pride in the historical right which had fallen to our lot—we knew human experience from all sides.

"All Shakespeare's tragedies can't compare with the life of a single Soviet citizen," Larissa Verchinsky wrote me—from one exile to another—and I set myself to discover the hidden meaning in this sentence. (We kept up a correspondence for a long time after they separated us. Ostensibly we were exchanging views about literature, but in fact we succeeded in sending each other simple information by means of characters from Russian literature. Oblomov, for example, was the Man with the Mustache. We could revel in spiritual masturbation, and any letters that fell into the hands of the authorities did not give us away. To the uninitiated reader they seemed like silly love letters written by a pair of bookworms. This is not to say that there was no love between Larissa and myself. But we saw no point in putting something which had no chance into words.)

In any case, in the letter in which she invaded the territory of English literature, with which she was not as familiar as the Russian, she meant what she said quite literally. Shakespeare's heroes would not have survived the opening scene of a Russian tragedy. Jealousy, for example—a princely, heroic jealousy. Or rage—a sacred, idiotic rage. What wouldn't I have given for the luxury of wallowing in a simple, ordinary emotion of that kind! I knew that the camp commandant went to bed with Larissa in exchange for allowing the doctor to inject her with the insulin she needed to survive. And I prayed for his health, for fear he would get syphilis and infect Larissa. A consignment of prostitutes had arrived at the camp, and it was no secret that he did not abstain from their favors, either.

Later on, when I asked myself what I had done to deserve so

relatively mild an interrogation, I could find no satisfactory answer. I could not accept the view that it was all a matter of chance. As an explanation this would have contradicted my view of the world. I assumed that in a time of chaos, men's baser instincts came to the fore and for this reason interrogation in the early years had been savage and cruel and lawless. The year 1937, the period when the bureaucracy ran wild—which many people saw as a kind of second revolution without fighting in the streets, without any conspicuous changes on the surface—was also a year of chaos, but the regime did everything in its power to control and regulate the upheaval, and from this point of view the hands of even the most brutal interrogators were tied. They could not employ the more vicious means of interrogation unless they received permission in advance from their superiors. And applying for such permission was tantamount to an admission of failure. Their colleagues in the room next door managed to extract their daily measure without bothering higher authorities or trying to share responsibility with others. I could imagine a social meeting between interrogators in some executioners' club, where they drank tea together and exchanged impressions, and one of them, whose professional proficiency was generally acknowledged, boasting to his colleagues: "Today I managed to break a tough customer, who came to me determined not to talk if he was beaten within an inch of his life, by offering a cup of tea and a cigarette at the right psychological moment." I, at any rate, went into interrogation determined to learn as much as I could about the man sitting opposite me and to conduct the interrogation in my own way (yes indeed, the prisoner can "conduct" his own interrogation by giving vague or ambivalent replies, which oblige the interrogator to disclose his "method"; a battle of minds takes place in which the prisoner who is able to keep a clear head even when insulted and demeaned can pull the wool over his interrogator's eyes and steer the interrogation in the desired direction). Never for a single moment did I forget that the man sitting opposite me was an ordinary mortal, a fellow with habits and weaknesses and a family to support, and maybe a son who played the violin, and athlete's foot, and a girlfriend whom he needed to love him, and a few friends whose respect was important to him, and maybe a vague fear of his bosses, and professional anxieties lest others were proven better at his job than he. I always remembered that I myself, weak and helpless and completely at his mercy as I was, could determine his success or failure by my own behavior. In one way or another, in the unfortunate circumstances of the times, we were tied to one another by unbreakable bonds, and a human relationship existed between us which was far from simple; and perhaps for this reason it was important to me to get to the bottom of the stranger sitting opposite me, and this same human curiosity, which I could not and did not wish to hide, infected him too. There must have been something about the way I looked at them, too, a penetrating but not unfriendly look in which the gleam of understanding flashed from time to time, which was presumably not calculated to awaken in the heart of a loyal member of the security services—unless it was a particularly vengeful and vicious one—the desire to cause unnecessary pain to someone who had lost his way. Sadists are usually like dogs: they bite those who fear them first. (When Epstein spoke about the way a person's insight is sharpened in moments of extreme tension, I could not help imagining him presenting himself before some red-necked interrogator with cruel, cold pig's eyes—his knees quaking with fear, his imagination making him into his own worst enemy, his Jewish appearance arousing latent anti-Semitic instincts . . . how on earth did he emerge from it alive?

Nineteen thirty-seven was a revolutionary year for me, too. However paradoxical it may seem, it was precisely my interrogation which sharpened my ability to see individuals rather then abstractions. I stopped seeing dust and began to see each grain separately. A process which was the opposite of the one that had begun in Ertez Israel in the twenties. I remember how fascinated I was by Daniel's way of looking at things. It was he who "opened my eyes" and made me see individuals as members of general categories. People were no longer themselves but the representatives of the views of classes, ideas, historical processes. When Daniel analyzed Berl Katznelson—who for a time made a profound impression on us with his eloquence, his common touch, and his ability to listen attentively to opinions with which he disagreed, and which Daniel believed stemmed from the fears of a Jewish boy from the Pale of Settlement who was unable to see the buds sprouting beneath the snow and the positive aspect of controlled violence—I see myself as having stood above the uncrowned leader of Ahdut haAvodah. I felt that I myself had grown a head taller thanks to this ability to observe myself from the outside. Even my own modest movements, from Rashkov to Odessa and from there to Moscow and then to Jaffa and the Migdal Road and Tel Yosef, took on a kind of historical significance (the Messianic convulsions of the Jewish people, unable to read the stirring signs of the times and drawn to Zion like a moth to the flame). But in prison, of all places (or, to be more precise, the interrogation chambers; my cellmate I ignored, certain that he had been planted there to make me talk), I stopped seeing the uniformed figure confronting me as the representative of forces with which I would never be able to contend; if I had, I would have been broken at the outset. I would never have stood a chance. But as long as I was able to see him as a family man hoping (at my expense) for success, a unique individual upon whose intelligence and quick wits my own cunning would be sharpened, I could get through the waiting for some verdict as a kind of Gorkyan university, where my only chance of graduating lay in learning the laws of the jungle. In order to defend my life, I had to know who the man before me was. I studied his character, his virtues, his weaknesses, his language, his self-esteem, his aspirations, and if I could have I would have tried to find out what he was like at home with his wife, his children, and his cat or dog. It was necessary to me that he stop being the representative of something abstract (the interrogation, the authorities, the Party) and return to his unique individuality. I remember the relief I felt when they took me up to the third floor of the building. I even developed feelings of intimacy toward the interrogation room. It ceased to be a threatening entity and became an ordinary room with a window overlooking the street, a curtain neither clean nor new, a table, chairs, a telephone, and a picture of a snowy mountain and a lake, like many other rooms in office buildings in Moscow (the very idea of the "Cheka dungeons" was enough to turn your blood to water and deprive you of your means of defense even before you entered them. Since I was not taken downstairs but up, I felt a marvelous sense of relief. The interrogation was going to be conducted like a normal clarification. If I didn't interrupt them, if I answered them correctly and accurately, I would be recognized as the loyal, obedient, thrifty, and useful citizen I was). Ostensibly, I was the one under interrogation (there were more than one of *them,* of course; they would change places, like different figures from different folktales who would appear in different places, but each of them became for an hour a friend-enemy, and correct reading of his mentality could save my life), but actually, it was my own mind that was busy putting forth questions all the time. In an effort to understand what was going on inside the skull of the man confronting me—the secret of his stupidity, his stubbornness, his wickedness, his diligence, his cunning—I could distract my thoughts from all kinds of small sufferings (the pain in my groin, the glare of the lights, the hunger, the exhaustion), like a soldier in the heat of battle who is surprised, on coming home, to find the fresh wound or scratch he did not even notice before. I would think of him (them) on my way to and from my interrogations, on my bed in my cell, during my meals, like a man obsessed with a single idea. I would listen to the conversations of the other prisoners in the hope of acquiring crumbs of information that would enable me to complete the mosaic of my private battle plan.

I should have been grateful to Stalin's henchmen. They gave me back a correct picture of the world in which there is room for little people trying somehow to survive. If I had not been personally affected, I might to this day have remained one of those world reformers who see people as forces of production and as classic representatives of global political factors, and who pride themselves on treating even those closest to them with exemplary objectivity: they see only the goal, and as far as they are concerned, everything that crops up on the way is only an obstacle or simply dirt. Cold shivers run down my spine when I remember things that I myself said in those years of passionate enthusiasm: "Is it really permissible for a stupid mob of greedy kulaks to hold back the galloping chariot of history?" And that was enough to make me indifferent to the fate of millions.

Second Notebook: The Magnetic North

$\mathcal{A}$ soldier and a young girl were sitting in the car. They were so deep in conversation that they didn't even notice me getting in. The driver, a vigorous man of about forty or forty-five with thick arms and a sunburned face, looked like a cossack with his handlebar mustache and piercing eyes, but genial, without malice or cunning. A man to put on the cover of an illustrated Soviet magazine: the classical type of a Russian peasant.

The man laughed. Neither a Russian nor a peasant. In his early youth he had made the mistake of agreeing to be a teacher. As if he were volunteering for a life sentence. Now he was in the movement's education department. Drawing up school curricula, organizing seminars, talking hot air. But his handshake— "Baruch Bashan, glad to meet you"—was the handshake of a peasant, strong and honest.

He joked with me and with the two youngsters As if he felt it was his duty—as the representative of the middle generation— to bring the extremes together. But his efforts were in vain. They listened to his witticisms without smiling and resumed their conversation. I laughed with all my heart. After a while the four of us were driving in two closed, impenetrable spaces. Them and us.

A man after my own heart: open-faced, eager to please, courteous, friendly. He was surprised that I understood his jokes. He couldn't believe that someone from there was capable of understanding local humor. Altogether, he had imagined that Russians lacked a sense of humor. They liked loud jokes, clownish tricks, but anything more subtle "didn't get through to them."

Where did he know the Russians from? He had "grown up among them, was reared at their knees, fell asleep to the sound of their speeches." A friend of his had visited Russia, gone there to take part in some congress. When he came home he said: Our parents didn't invent anything new. They simply transplanted everything they brought with them from the old country—and added some bullshit of their own."

Baruch said that he wasn't driving straight home. He had to drop in on a couple of places around Tiberias on the way. If I liked, he would let me off at the bus stop in Afula. If I preferred, I could come with him. He would arrive in Tel Yosef in the early afternoon.

I would be glad for the chance of a drive through the countryside, I said. Especially in the Galilee.

"Vera will wait," he said and laughed. "I promised to deliver you safe and sound. But I didn't say when. . . ."

There was no need for me to introduce myself. He knew everything about me. The history of my life, where I came from and where I was going. He knew Nimrod too. From the army in Tel Yosef. They had met there shortly before Nimrod left.

"Why did he leave?"

"There was a split."

"What about?"

"Ostensibly, for ideological reasons, but they weren't serious." Political splits obey laws of their own. Immediately he corrected himself: "The reasons, I mean. Nimrod was serious enough. Sometimes too much so." I made him laugh when I asked him what was too much and who would decide. It was only an expression, he said.

The gentle lines of the limestone hills on the coastal plain had been ripped apart. Modern asphalt roads cut indifferently through their curves. I could barely tell where we were. Before, acacia hedges had encircled the citrus groves. Then even the earth had seemed foreign to me, hostile. I remembered it as being sandier, poor, and dry. The last time I had traveled from Tel Aviv to the north it was on an Arab bus. On a different road, and slowly. The bus stopped for everyone: peasants with their sacks and squawking chickens; a British policeman with pink knees . . .

The two youngsters got off in Afula. At the toll Baruch took on two others. A taciturn young man and an old farmer with his arm in a plaster cast who knew everything there was to know. How and why and when, what the harvests were like, how so-and-so was keeping, and if he was still as quarrelsome as ever. A talkative old man. By the time he got off, he and the young man were already fast friends.

We drove down to the Jordan Valley by a new road, north of Arbel. The blue of the Kinneret hit me in the face like an electric shock Its beauty, its tranquility. My memories. Like a damp cloth collecting crumbs from a table. I remembered the sight as if I had last seen it only yesterday. The narrow shore, strewn with big basalt rocks, the cultivated fields reaching all the way to the water line. The steep cliff of the valley of Arbel. The trapeze of the "horns of Hittim." Kafr Hareb. Susita. The mouth of the Jordan River.

A tractor crawled slowly over a field, a white train of dust in its wake like a long, pointed, fragile shell. A patient cycle of life, without beginning or end. If only I was young! To land here again. To begin again from the beginning. What peace of mind I would find here, sitting on the tractor, going back and forth, back and forth, leaving a long brown furrow behind me. Where others might be bored, I would welcome the tortoise pace of time joyfully. And the fine dust settling on my arms. A man of the land.

Had he ever heard of the Labor Brigade? What a question! Endless lectures. Stories of the founding fathers, interpretations, contradictory opinions, ideas, ancient quarrels. "If your soul thirsts to know the well from which your brothers drank . . ." he declaimed. And left the quotation unfinished. Assuming that a man of my generation would have read Bialik. These were the sources on which they educated the youth. But if you asked him—the infantile diseases of the proletariat. A lot of dust had gathered. And now they were painting it pink. As if no one had been hurt. You could even hear the battle cries of the class struggle on festive occasions, such as the First of May. And you could still sometimes hear an ardent speech in the old style in the general meeting of the kibbutz. A style that no longer applies. Today's style is different—cool, practical, efficient. Wise men don't waste words.

With me it's the opposite. Then, I was cold and chilly, dissecting with a surgeon's scalpel. Today, I tend to get emotional. Then my eyes were always dry. Today my tears are ready to flow. My mother's tears, which dried up before their time, gush from my eyes. Even the Kinneret. Today it shines into my soul. As if my very guts were drowning in that jubilant blue. Then, I came here because I couldn't find work anywhere else. I immunized myself against enthusiasm. I saw myself as a man with both feet planted firmly on the ground. I issued grim warnings: all those ardent dancers till dawn—they'll be driven away by the first cloud of flies. Hysteria doesn't build roads.

The Migdal junction. How many layers of asphalt have been put down on the stones I laid here. If I close my eyes I can wipe out all the buildings. And here I am, on a cart, a young pioneer in a gray cloth cap and a dirty white shirt, all his possessions tied up in a bundle on his knees.

The cart trundled along the dirt track next to the road in the process of being built. The sky was blue as glittering steel. The water was the color of emeralds. The people sitting next to the piles of stones in their dusty clothes and dark cloth caps looked from a distance like flies on cones of sugar. The cart driver cracked his whip but the weary horse did not respond. "Here it is," he said, and I attached a profound meaning to his words. Like a man reaching the end of the road. The final station.

At the side of the road, in the shade of a eucalyptus, one of the Crimeans—the *tsarskoye familia* or "royal family" they called them—a sturdy, handsome lad, stood drinking water from a narrow-necked clay jar which he held high above his head. Next to him stood a girl in a long white dress with her head bowed in a kind of meek expectancy. Was she in love? Thirsty? I'll never be like them, I thought. The work was too much for me—it drained all my physical and mental powers. This is your last chance, I said to myself. With all my heart I longed to join this band of happy youths, breaking stones with economical movements and glorying in their achievements. Some accomplished more and some less, it made no difference—the payment for the contract labor was given to the group as a whole. A man who respected himself tried to be among those who made a decent contribution.

This was a motive no less powerful than the threatening pressure exerted by a group of convict laborers: there you knew that if you were one of those who reduced the bread ration earned by the group, your comrades would leave you to die in the snow without lifting a finger to help you—but if your capacity for work was higher than average they would save your life and even carry you on their backs for miles, however exhausted they were.

Among the Crimeans it was a different story. The worst that could happen to a poor worker there was that his disgrace would enhance the status of his comrades. At that time I was naively convinced that the part of the world they came from produced strength, joie de vivre, and mental health.

At first I had only one friend there, a native of Kiev called Fineman. Our origins brought us together. He tried to pretend that he was a match for the rest of them in ardent enthusiasm, singing until he was hoarse and dancing till dawn. But one Saturday, when we were going for a walk in Capernaum and peeped into the monastery where a few monks were to be seen going reverentially about their business, he made a remark that was both related and unrelated to what we had been talking about: "As long as you enjoy your suffering you'll never be a real worker—a real worker does everything in his power to avoid hard labor and liberate his children from his own fate." This was a blasphemy my mind could not digest. I said to him, "Fineman, you must be feverish, you can't possibly mean what you're saying." And then I added spitefully, "You'll never be a real worker because you can't stand the smell of your own sweat. You have to wash yourself three times a day." He said that Jews were incapable of being monks and that Judaism had never demanded it of them. I said that frugality was not monasticism. Monks retired from the world in order to save their souls. We, on the other hand, abstained from the vanities of this world in order to conquer the world. People said things like that then without feeling presumptuous. In the end he admitted that he was in love with a certain girl and that he dreamed of a little house with a cow and a goat. I ridiculed him: "You're a petit bourgeois with trivial, petit bourgeois dreams. I'll forget what you've just said, for your own good." In the course of time he became the secretary of the Jerusalem Workers Council. Without a cow or a goat.

From time to time Baruch Bashan left me in the car and went out to do whatever he had to do. I got out of the car and wandered around. Having a look. Nobody asked me what I wanted. In one kibbutz we had lunch. Then he went to the secretariat for a short discussion. I went down to the lake. Narrow paths, lawns, tall ficus trees, palms, cypresses, casuarinas, all jumbled up together. Magnificent communal buildings. The members' apartments were modest, and different from each other. Some in a rustic style: red-tiled roofs, a garden surrounded with pruned myrtle bushes. Others like a suburban housing estate: two-story buildings, brick roofs, a road, a lawn, a garden enclosed by the houses around it.

In the area of the workshops, a hive of activity: the racket of machines, a noisy tractor sweeping everything before it, a huge truck unloading its freight. In the residential area, peace and quiet. As if its inhabitants had all abandoned it. The noise of the work reaches here dimly, like the murmur of the sea. Among the bushes and the buildings a bit of the lake is visible. Shining, glittering. Quiet waters. Waves lower than the grass lap the black basalt boulders. Between one wave and the next—an eternity. Without a sound.

The houses face the lake. In the gardens—deck chairs, hammocks, children's swings. Metal rusted by the winds from the lake.

I sat down on a boulder in a still eucalyptus glade and looked at the lake. The silence was as deep as the trees were high. A door opened behind me. I looked around. A woman was sitting on a bench on the porch of her house and idly pulling off her boots. When she saw me she drew her dress down over her bare knees. She stood and looked at me for a while and then vanished behind the door.

A green door.

Pictures from the past come in pairs.

Then too I asked myself: Why not stop now, here, and stay for the rest of my life? Here under these trees. With the water opposite me. And the mountains all around.

This was after I was freed for the first time. I was free to live in another town. I wasn't allowed to go west. But nevertheless I took the risk and stowed away on the train. Three days later they found me. But they didn't hand me over to the militia. At an isolated siding next to a junction they threw me off the train. Spite? Generosity? I don't know. I found myself somewhere in the Urals. Without money, without papers. I walked along the railway tracks in the deep creek between two steep slopes. Suddenly I saw a clear lake in a secluded valley, with poplars on the opposite bank reflected in the water. The water was black and gleaming as ebony. Forests climbed the slopes on either side, exuding pungent forest smells. A milky mist was suspended over the heads of the fir trees. And on the banks of the lake, a little township: tiny white houses, like a child's toys. I took my life in my hands and approached. Suddenly I said to myself: Why not here? Now? What more does a man need than a forest and a mountain, a lake and the peace of the poor. Far from Moscow. And an end to wandering.

At that moment a tall woman dressed in black emerged from the green-painted door of a wretched hut. Her body was full and strong, her cheekbones prominent, and there was an enchanting wildness in her big round eyes. She looked at me for a moment as if she was debating with herself. I said to myself: If she calls me, I'll follow her. I'll shut that green wooden door behind me and sever the thread connecting me to my life history forever. In this woman's arms I'll find perfect happiness and peace of mind. No one will come looking for Avigdor Berkov who was released from prison and lost in the Siberian wastes. The woman inspected me from top to toe with a frank, shameless look, and in the end she bent down, picked up a pail, and went down to the banks of the lake to draw water.

I didn't stop there after all. I couldn't find a job. I went on walking until I reached Klyuchi, a biggish, well-organized town in the middle of a hilly plain. There were two or three small industrial plants there, an old manor house that had been taken over by the militia, an ancient castle divided up between local artists and the Party institutions, and a woman who was willing to take me into her home. She wasn't beautiful like the woman on the lake or wild like her. She never missed a single one of the performances of the local amateur dramatic society, and at concerts she wept with emotion. She soon wearied me with her provincial enthusiasm for the insipid verses of the local bard and her loud sniffs in the concert hall I felt no strong desire to go to ground in Klyuchi and open a new page in my life. I discovered the local post office and with the first pennies I earned at work I bought note paper and stamps. At the first opportunity I stowed away on the train traveling west. I didn't reach Moscow, because I was stopped on the way. But I didn't go back to Klyuchi either. I spent a few more years wandering in various places until I arrived at a place which was about a day's train journey from Moscow. I would slip into the city from time to time without a permit—every trip a celebration and an exhilarating adventure—and from these trips, and especially from the inspiration I received from them, I learned that I was not molded from the clay of those who are capable of escaping from themselves to an enchanted lake in the heart of the country. I belong in the metropolis, where your anonymity is reflected back to you from the suspicious eyes of millions of strangers passing you by in absolute indifference to your existence. I would have no peace of mind until I was sitting in a smoke-filled room, among comrades and informers, debating the theory which would lead us to a new, more successful experiment that would guarantee us our daily bread in happiness and dignity without pain and electricity, without losing our human image.

In 1921 I went by foot from Migdal to Beitanya. People said that there was a group of peculiar, upper-class pioneers there. The boys were cultured, the girls refined. Some of our boys had stolen there one night to eavesdrop on their debates. They came back splitting their sides with laughter. The things they said! The soul-searching! They behaved as if they were conducting direct negotiations with Almighty God. My curiosity was aroused.

Spring was running riot in the fields and I made my way through thorns taller than a man. I had a keffiyeh on my head and a dagger in my belt. There was a couple sitting on a rock, outside the camp, and when they saw me they were overcome with terror. I felt sorry for the boy, who looked as if he had seen a ghost and picked up a stone in his trembling hand. "A friend!" I called. The way their faces lit up!

The girl was pretty and delicate. Her Hebrew was poor. The boy was indeed highly educated and full of fashionable ideas. There wasn't a book which had been popular with the younger generation over the past decade that he didn't know by heart.

We sat and talked for hours. Later we were joined by others. I spoke about the class struggle, they of the salvation of the soul. I spoke about the Arab question, they about Western civilization. A dialogue of the deaf.

I was touched by their enlightened, intellectual poses. I was a year or two older than them, and to myself I seemed as old as the hills. They were a kindhearted crew and believed in all innocence that it would be possible for Jews to settle the land without any opposition from the Arabs. Their weakness was their charm. Who would want to hurt such nice people? They were incapable of harming a fly.

Later on we became allies for a time. I was always astonished by their faith in their ability to establish a little kingdom of righteousness on two hundred dunams of irrigated land and one thousand dunams of unirrigated land. And in Russia I was amazed to hear that they of all people had established a Marxist party in Eretz Israel. The ways of God are wonderful indeed.

Their settlements, Baruch Bashan told me, were very successful and well organized. "But if you ask me, all the kibbutzim are the same, however much they differ."

He himself had not been born on a kibbutz, he told me. He was a youth-movement graduate from Tel Aviv. He had joined the kibbutz after serving in the Jewish Brigade during the war. For his wife's sake. He was well aware of all the imperfections of the kibbutz. And nevertheless he had chosen to live there. It was preferable to any other way of life he knew. He told me about his childhood in Tel Aviv. A happy childhood. He hadn't even known that his parents were poor. He spoke of them fondly. Modest, simple, bookish people. His mother worked in the Histadrut Sick Fund dispensary and read a lot of scientific articles. Every time she read a new one she would change the family diet. One month they lived on raw vegetables, the next month boiled, and the one after steamed. His father worked for the Histadrut too, in the dues collection department. From time to time he wrote an article for the *Young Worker:* "Are We Living in Sodom?" "Are Things Really as Bad as They Seem?" "On the Question of Jewish Labor." "Further Reflections on the Problem of the New Immigrants."

Bashan was the name he had taken when he was sent on a movement mission abroad, he said. The family name was originally Besskind. There was no connection. Bashan was the name of a cheese. And a border area in biblical times. He had always dreamed of settling on the frontier. As far as possible from the center of the country.

"You lived on Ben Zakkai Street in Tel Aviv. A two-story house with a garden. On the first floor. The side entrance," I said.

He was astounded. Overcome with confusion. "You knew my parents?"

"A little."

"And you remember the address, even the entrance to the apartment! You must have a phenomenal memory," he exclaimed in admiration.

"You can never know why your mind chooses to preserve certain details, facts, numbers. Sometimes it seems like a rubbish heap. A storeroom of information that nobody needs. I remember other insignificant details too: a garden, a mulberry tree, a washing line, an ironing board on the back porch. And more: a child's shirt. White, flapping sleeves. One cuff buttoned, the other loose," I added to amaze him.

"Incredible."

"Sometimes I strain every fiber of my being to recall some important detail—and I can't."

"But you remember things as if you were a frequent visitor."

"Not exactly. I met your father once. And I only caught a glimpse of your mother. She was standing and ironing. I asked her if your father was home and she said 'Yes,' and that was all."

"It's hard to believe."

"By the way, who did the shirt belong to? You were still a baby crying in the bedroom."

"It was my brother's shirt. He's four years older than me." He couldn't get over it. "You amaze me. You only visited my parents once and you remember all those details!"

"It's a fact."

"You're sure it was only once?"

"Absolutely. But it's a small world, and you never know in what circumstances you'll meet again." An association from another compartment of my memory. Words said by a prisoner to his interrogator, meant as a threat. And they did meet again, a few years later, in Kolyma. And the prisoner took his revenge.

Baruch Bashan refused to believe that I couldn't remember the reason why I came to his parents' house. And he was right.

It was only a little white lie. Perhaps if I'd known him longer I wouldn't have minded telling him the truth.

I went to see Besskind on a mission from the Party. But

under the cover, as it were, of a movement for promoting friendship between Arabs and Jews. We came to induce him to do what he was unwilling to do.

The Executive Committee of the Histadrut, the Jewish Labor Federation, had decided to expel the members of the Communist Fraktzia. We were fighting for our lives. Not only were we about to lose our means of livelihood but we were also facing the threat of deportation. The British authorities used the Histadrut expulsions as a means of identifying Communists, whom they subsequently deported from the country.

We couldn't hold protest demonstrations. We were more or less underground. A public meeting could endanger our very existence. We decided to bring out a petition and get signatures from people outside our ranks. Public figures, intellectuals, writers, poets, and ordinary people who had earned themselves a reputation for fair-mindedness in the narrow circles of the Jewish Yishuv.

The task of getting signatures on the petition was far from easy. Many people were afraid of being tarred by our brush. Others were afraid of exposing themselves to the public eye because they didn't have papers. Some hated us passionately and they couldn't have cared less if we were deported. After all, the gates of the Soviet "Paradise" were open to us.

It wasn't my idea to go to Besskind, a member of Hapoel Hatzair, an unassuming, upright worker in the dues department of the Histadrut, whom no one could possibly suspect of being a Communist and whose articles were always full of the sayings of the sages. It took someone shrewder than me to think of him. Efros was the "Talmudist" among us. He was the one who could pay back our religious opponents in their own coin. He was endowed with the quality which sets a leader apart from the rank and file. He was quick to note another man's weaknesses and he never hesitated to exploit them. Although he had never set eyes on Besskind in his life, he had read his articles. He judged, correctly, that he would not be able to withstand moral pressure. A man as passionately committed to liberal ideas as Besskind should fight for the right of others to disagree with his opinions.

My weaknesses too were well known to Efros. Which ones? Empty arrogance, conceit, the pose of a professional revolutionary. He let me talk first, and I felt the sweat pouring down my neck. I took a liking to Besskind from the moment I set eyes on him. He stood in his little room surrounded by books—in the cupboards, on the table, on the bed, the floor—and looked at us from behind his thick glasses with a stricken expression. He seemed to guess who we were and sense that he would not be able to send us away empty-handed. We had seized him by his principles like a cat by the nape of its neck. I wanted to run away. I remembered the woman ironing on the porch, I thought about their happiness, the baby crying in the other room, the little boy who had probably gone to nursery school. I assumed that Besskind's signature on our petition would upset the tranquility of this cozy little nest. I said to myself that I was presumably not made of the stuff of a true revolutionary.

Besskind behaved exactly as Efros had assumed he would. He said that everything we did and said and stood for was wrong in his eyes and that Russia was the Kingdom of Evil and the Communists in Eretz Israel were cutting off the branch they were sitting on with their own hands, but that he would sign the petition nevertheless. Since it was unthinkable to allow a foreign power to deport Jews from Eretz Israel. I was sorry that he found it necessary to actually repeat the classic liberal phrase—"I'll fight for your right to express our opinions however much I disagree with them"—and thereby play into Efros's hands and give him a chance to congratulate himself on the acuteness of his own perceptions.

I was right to be concerned about what would happen to Besskind. For things turned out exactly as Efros had expected. There was a scandal and an outcry and the workers' papers denounced the signatories on the petition. Besskind defended his action, and was brutally attacked—with insinuations about as subtle as a sledgehammer. One day he was arrested and questioned by the police and later released. Perhaps the episode left a mark on his life forever.

I was sorry for him. I thought we had done him a wrong. Our petition didn't change anything. Perhaps it brought a few of the people who had signed it closer to our camp. Perhaps they said to themselves: If liberals aren't tolerant either, what advantage have they got over radicals? In any case, Besskind lost on all counts. The *Poel Hatzair* stopped publishing his articles. Only a letter to the editor in *Davar* appeared from time to time. A voice crying in the wilderness. He acquired a reputation for being a fool and a bleeding heart.

One day I talked to Efros about it. I said that I regretted what we had done. All we had accomplished was to destroy a naive man without doing ourselves any good. Efros was furious. "What did we do to him? Did anyone harm a hair on his head? Poor Arab peasants are evicted from their land and nobody sheds a tear. The world won't come to an end if Besskind's idiotic articles don't appear in print. You and I have made greater sacrifices for the revolution. Rest assured that Besskind isn't bemoaning your fate. On the contrary: with the help of Besskind we exposed the true faces of his hypocritical, self-righteous friends. As long as you agree with them everything's fine. But look out if you dare to have an opinion of your own!"

Then he patted my shoulder. "You've still got a lot to learn, my lad."

On the way Baruch Bashan pointed out Nimrod's kibbutz, a settlement climbing up a gently sloping hill so drowned in greenery you could hardly see the houses. Far from the road, isolated, keeping all its goodness to itself, I thought. Presumably the dusty trees would have seemed more welcoming if Nimrod was at home. But I had a certain feeling of belonging anyway. As if I had a house there, only it was hidden by the trees.

"And those fields, the fish ponds, the citrus groves—that's Tel Yosef."

In the first year I didn't miss anything, except for the snow. And when I say "snow" I see a picture.

A child of seven or eight standing next to the fence of his house on the outskirts of the little town and looking out. In front of him an expanse of spotless snow. Untouched. At the edge of the picture—a few bare trees standing like signposts next to a bluish forest, and the edge of a village. A thin column of smoke rising into the air and dissolving into the white sky. A strong wind whirls the snowflakes around the laden branches of the firs. On the border of the forest, in the distance, a sleigh drawn by three horses cleaves a new path through the snow and disappears into the mist rising from the valley.

My mother calls but I don't hear her voice.

As if I had been granted a revelation. But I don't know what it was that was revealed.

Looking back: the borders of my world. Perhaps a bitter lesson: my motherland, however miserable I was in it. A man is the mold of the landscape of his motherland. Wherever I go I shall take that picture, that yearning, with me.

Whenever I remember it, I imagine I can hear the sound of a soft bell and the crackle of the ice breaking under the sleigh and the horses' hooves.

The first meeting with the Jezreel Valley—"Nuris block" we called it then—was stunning. It was summer, everything was parched and dry, the earth was cracked, sparse bushes spread a sickly yellow over the roadside, and an ominous whisper passed through the standing grain, like the despairing sigh of ten thousand insects. The stalks of wheat were measly looking, yellow-gray and meager. Field mice had left ugly, pale-brown, bald patches, and the barley drooped broken-headed. And the few thorn trees were swarming with wasps, depriving the weary wayfarer of the bit of shade he longed for.

I dragged my legs, swooning with thirst and fatigue, unable to comprehend why our comrades should fight for this piece of land.

The winter was no less discouraging. We trudged through

the mud and shivered with cold in our tattered tents, exposed to every wind. It was a filthy winter, our boots crowned with layer upon layer of curly mud. Heavy rains whipping through the tents splashed mud onto our coarse woolen blankets. And there was no hope of a little wintry consolation: to get up in the morning and see the whole world covered with pure white snow. White and silent from horizon to horizon with a glory not of this world.

I left Tel Yosef on a rainy day in the winter of '27 intending never to return. I stood at the railway station determined not to look back.

I did steal back once, a few months later, but that was at night. And I never saw anything except for a few lights twinkling and trees looming suddenly out of the dark. If I had been caught, I would have been thrown out in disgrace. They might even have beaten me up. We never lacked for hotheads.

I spent four years in Nuris block—a base from which I would depart to perform the historical tasks of my generation, and to which I would return. Those years left their mark on my life forever. Whatever came afterward was measured in their terms.

Nothing remained of what I remembered. Only the contours of the road, the railway tracks, a little wood at the bottom of Mount Gilboa, and the skyline. But even that was broken here and there. There were a few houses on the summit of the mountain on the east. And the village of Mazar had been wiped off the face of the earth. On the summit of the mountain, where the village had once stood like a kind of castle in the sky, there was nothing now but a few solitary trees. Even the southern slope of the mountain had changed beyond recognition. A forest of trees. As if they had taken it upon themselves to prove that the return to Zion had lifted the biblical curse.

The kibbutz itself belonged completely to here and now. To discover my traces here I would apparently have to dig up concrete and asphalt. Not a single tree for my memories to attach themselves to. Never mind a building.

Only Vera belonged to the past. I don't know if she walked

past the parking lot the moment we arrived by chance or if she had been waiting for us there for hours. If she had changed as little as the expression on her face—a mute appeal: "Tell the truth, but try not to hurt"—she was capable of it.

I would have known her even if I met her in the street, among strangers, far from home. Women who have never been beautiful grow old gracefully. They don't suspect time of betraying them with their younger sisters.

Vera was highly excited and bustled about without stopping. She seized my bag and ran into her room and ran out again to thank Baruch Bashan. She kept up a steady stream of chatter interspersed with promises to herself and me that we would talk properly later. When we finally stood facing each other in the room I was led almost by force to the bathroom "to wash my face and hands." On the assumption, evidently, that a man of my age would have to answer the call of nature after a three-hour drive. I came out of the bathroom with my hands wet and asked her to take the towel I had brought with me out of my bag. Vera was indignant: "I wouldn't be surprised if you've brought sheets and cans of food too!" Had I really forgotten what a kibbutz meant? We almost had a quarrel over this nonsense and Vera leaped into the bathroom and fetched two towels and thrust them into my hands with a lavishness that seemed to me misplaced. "Why shouldn't I use my own towel?" I said. "It's a shame to send a towel that's only been used once or twice to the laundry." Vera explained that the kibbutz laundry was no longer done in cauldrons heated over coals. Then she held forth at length about the marvels of their new "automatic" or "electronic" laundry. She was as proud as a Komsomol member showing a tourist from abroad a Soviet factory. In this too Vera had not changed. She had always been blessed with a mighty will to be happy and gay, but she had never had a sense of humor. Perhaps this was one of the signs of the times or perhaps it was something inherent in her own personality. Idealists are afraid of frivolity and ugly women only feel comfortable in the presence of serious men.

Afterward we had tea and cake and spoke about everything

under the sun except for what it was really important for us to know. I, because it was convenient for me that way. The only thing I really wanted to ask about was my son, but I chose not to in order to avoid striking a note of intimacy. And she perhaps shrank from speaking of anything serious because I was trying too hard to be clever. I expect that she too said to herself that I had not changed. I was still the same enigmatic boy, throwing out ambivalent remarks in order to demonstrate my intellectual superiority. Which was the accusation she had leveled at me before we parted.

In the early evening we went out for a walk in the kibbutz grounds. I tried to identify the place where my tent had been pitched. But the gentle contour of the hill seemed to have been flattened by bulldozers. We walked along a pretty avenue of palms leading from the center of the old yard to the hill of Kumi and looked at the valley: the old Tel Yosef, Heftziba, and Beit Alfa, and the overpowering wall of the Gilboa—the sight I used to see every morning when I sat on the low stool at the opening of my tent with my oiled boots in my hand. In the old Nuris block, white houses were scattered over the shoulder of the mountain. The quarry, it seemed, had not widened its wound. Somewhere up there, during the pageant we put on at Passover, parodying the traditional sources as befitting a band of heretics, I once hid among the rocks to speak the word of God in a rolling bass voice thundering across the valley.

The peace of mind I felt at the sight of the tranquil green valley was somewhat disrupted when Vera informed me in a would-be casual tone of voice that she had invited a number of friends to drop in after supper. They would be expecting me to say a few words. What did they expect me to do? Beat my breast and beg them to forgive me?

And how could I refuse? She had given her promise and how could I let her down? I said yes, although I looked forward to the meeting with heavy misgivings.

Sitting in Vera's room and observing her closely when she wasn't looking, I saw her strong arms with their gnarled veins and I thought: a Jewish woman who made up her mind to turn herself into a peasant and succeeded.

God was kind to her when he gave her her beautiful eyes. They attracted our attention and asked us not to look down at her body. She had lost a lot of weight over the years but she was still as dumpy as ever, and when she bustled about on her thin little legs, her enormous bosom taking up half her body, it was impossible not to be reminded of the cruelly apt nickname given her by one of the Crimeans who had settled at Migdal. He called her "Beetle," and since it suited her the name stuck. "If all a man wants is to settle down," he said, "at least he'll be well padded." And since he was a good-looking, successful lad, an excellent worker, a good shot and a heartbreaker—we all ate out of his hand. No one dared to fall in love with Vera. I'm not exactly filled with admiration for myself when I remember the tricks I resorted to in order to conceal the fact that there was anything between me and the "Beetle." I contradicted Remez and Ben-Gurion, I insulted Berl Katznelson in public, but I didn't have the courage to face the ridicule of a successful fornicator, even though I felt true affection for Vera and enjoyed her company immensely.

By the way, the desire to settle down wasn't considered anything to be proud of either.

Vera avoided looking into my eyes, she kept getting up and sitting down again for no reason, filling my plate with cookies, straightening pictures on the wall, and looking for things to do so that she could skip from one subject to another and direct our conversation into byways lacking in any significance.

I remembered her as a girl who believed in what she believed in with the fanaticism of the ignorant. Her principles were a rod to beat those of little faith with. She worked with passionate diligence, as if she wanted to lose herself in a life of labor (she was one of the few individuals who came to the Labor Brigade from Hapoel Hatzair, steeped in the lore of A.D. Gordon's "religion of labor"), and looked down with profound contempt on anyone who sought out easy work or a refuge in the shade. And she didn't restrict herself to looking, either. She didn't spare her rebukes, although she never preached or moralized. She always spoke with profound pain. As if she was mourning the decline in values, or coming to the defense of an orphan child.

Now there was a gentle, cautious note in her voice. The words seemed to slip out of her mouth of their own accord, and there was a sense of an attempt to load them with heavy meanings. How careful she was not to say anything that might sadden or anger me! I was not called upon to confess my sins, bewail my wasted life, envy the horn of plenty or the restful repose of herself and her comrades. She did not hint that this plenty and peace could have been my own lot if I had not gone chasing after illusions. She even allowed me to understand that not everything was perfect. There was much to be thankful for—but something important was missing.

Her room testified to the changes that had taken place in her. The rooms we live in tell all our secrets. I have always felt that I could learn something about a person from looking into his room, even rooms that contain almost nothing.

There wasn't much furniture. A couch, two armchairs, a table, chairs, a bookcase, and a cabinet with the radio and television on it—all in a rustic style. It was all quite austere but for the many handmade cushions and colorful rag dolls (it was of these objects that we mainly spoke: how she made them and from what materials and how much work she put into each and every one of the decorative articles she made for herself and others with a lavish and unstinting hand)—exquisite handiwork into which she wove the loneliness increasingly closing in on her. Challenges demanding patience and distracting her from superfluous thoughts, scraps of material and bits of wool, things into which she could pour her need to organize things and keep them clean and tidy. During all these years, it seemed, she had not become a prey to greed or envy or acquisitiveness.

Only a longing for color seemed to have awakened in her with old age. But perhaps it was not her own taste but simply poverty which had dictated her penchant for the browns and whites and grays of former years.

The word "acquisitiveness" rose to the surface of my memory at the moment when I would have been most happy to have forgotten it.

After that first night she came and sat down beside me in the dining room. She didn't speak to me or drop any hints, but her face was radiant with a quiet happiness. She put the spoon into her mouth but her eyes weren't on her food. They were fixed on a mysterious point somewhere on the ceiling of the hut, as if she was reliving the night before minute by minute.

I couldn't stand this complacency. Didn't she know how to distinguish between hunger and love? And did we have to announce our feelings in public?

The next day I went to Kibbutz Ramat Rachel. I stayed with the Jerusalem "company" for a month. (On duty. Ostensibly to instruct them in stonecutting but actually, in self-defense: I taught the young men to shoot a revolver.) Afterward I fell ill with malaria and spent some time in Hebron, in the haunted house. There too I had a short, insignificant affair. Women appear to possess a highly developed sense of smell: the minute one of them falls in love with you it immediately arouses the curiosity of her sisters. After that I went to the Histadrut council, and from there to Kfar Giladi. There too on Haganah business. I got back to Tel Yosef after three months. I arrived at night—hungry, exhausted, worried, full of anger against myself. Miriam, a beautiful girl for whom I had felt tremendous respect and also presumably a secret love, without ever allowing myself to approach her, had responded to the advances of one of the other boys, a fellow who in my opinion was not worthy of her in any respect. I bumped into Vera by accident. I had no intention at all of seeking her out. She dragged me to the kitchen, made me something to eat, and then took me by the hand and led me to the same place as before on the edge of the olive grove. Nothing was said. I was full of pity for myself and for the sad treats she showered on me, and she, again, was overjoyed. When she came to my tent early in the evening I asked her not to come again. She was insulted: "Are you ashamed of me?"

And it was then that I spoke to her so harshly. I'm in favor of free love, I said. Not that anyone could call what was between us love. I didn't want her to think that because of one or two nights she had some kind of claim on me. And I didn't want her coming to sit next to me in the dining room full of the pride of possession, as if I belonged to her or something.

She didn't deserve it. The lust for possessions, which we all scorned, was never one of her failings. She hadn't come from Russia as a penniless refugee. Her parents were well off and they had succeeded in smuggling a large part of their fortune into Germany. She had an aunt with means in Petah Tikva and a cousin in the Anglo-Palestine Bank. If she had been acquisitive, she wouldn't have shared our property with us. In other words, the things I said to her were not only insulting but also unfair.

The walk through the kibbutz grounds was full of symbols. Some of them she didn't shrink from naming. And the rest I was supposed to guess from the tall trees, the well-tended lawns, the neat, attractive houses, the healthy children playing with their parents—the life of a Jewish village where "four generations of Jews live in the shade of the same tree," as Efrati said to me afterward. The evening of a full life, continuing from generation to generation. We walked through the grounds like a sad triumphal procession: they were right and I was wrong. Every now and then she permitted herself to correct my Hebrew. A simple symbol: my rootlessness, her rootedness.

The tired tread of our feet was loaded with meanings. But only the members of my generation could have understood that sentimental journey: in their eyes I was not a visitor but a prodigal son, returning penitent to the fold. All the youngsters we encountered on our walk probably saw was an elderly couple taking the evening air. A little ridiculous and perhaps a little irritating, too, as if they didn't have a mirror in their room and didn't realize how ill-suited they were for romance.

We went for a long walk. I saw the dining hall, the cultural club, the children's houses, the playgrounds, the Sturman Mu-

seum, and the musical education workshop. We looked over at
Ein Harod, too. The harsh rivalry of the old days was now a thing
of the past. I wasn't surprised to hear that there were two Ein
Harods now, one on the right and one on the left. I had forseen
it in '27. The big, open kibbutz, a kibbutz for every Tom, Dick,
and Harry, was a utopia, just like the "general commune of the
workers of Eretz Israel." "People who hate each other's dreams
with all their hearts can't be expected to eat from the same dish,"
I argued then. "Mutual suspicions will corrode every achievement. Scarcity can be shared and shared alike, but you can't
impose your debts on a man who has no desire to mortgage his
dreams of the future for you. A man may even be willing to
burden himself with a few parasites who don't contribute anything to the common good, on condition that they not cast
stones into the well they drink from. But if they pray from a
different prayerbook, he'll demand one of two things: either
work hard or get out."

My foot, which was suffering from a mysterious infection,
hurt a little, but I went on walking in order not to disappoint
Vera. There was still a lot I had to see: a big workshop which they
called a factory, Joseph Trumpeldor House, agricultural ma-
chinery. And I wanted to linger in the metal workshop—a rather
messy area which Vera wanted to hurry past. There, in the piles
of junk, I came across a few old acquaintances: a rusty plow, an
old harrow, and a wooden wheel with iron spokes (I caught a
glimpse of another wheel close to my heart in the shape of the
battered remnants of an old enamel basin in the garden of one
of the members' houses: a modern statue). All the old familiar
landscape was covered with lawns, roads, concrete paths.

Somewhere here, I thought, under these lawns and concrete
surfaces, a few remembered objects must be buried: rusty nails,
wire, enamel dishes with blue rims, aluminum mugs with narrow
chains attached to them (even in the days of utter trust, before
we fell out on the question of the world revolution, the aluminum mugs were firmly attached to the wooden lid of the cold-
water jug with chains). A funny thought occurred to me: my eyes

were busy with the work of demolition. Probing under the buildings and roads to dig up junk.

Vera's eyes were calm and shining. I knew what she was thinking and some of it she said aloud: "We've built a model farm here. There were hard times and bitter disappointments. But in recent years there's been a terrific push forward. And we have our children and grandchildren with us here. Not mine and yours, specifically, but that doesn't matter. What matters is that the younger generation are on the kibbutz, following in my footsteps, not yours. In other words, our labors have been rewarded. Everything we sacrificed on the altar of national revival and intensive farming was not in vain. We sowed our seeds and had faith in the future."

Other thoughts were racing through my brain. How long would it take for a unit of tanks to turn this place into a pile of rubble?

We walked for a while in the fields to the east. The road, it seemed, was the same one along which I had returned in the evenings with the sheep in the old days. Only the color was different. A dirt road churned up by tractor wheels and trucks and cars does not resemble a dirt road churned up by hooves. So many years had passed and yet I still remembered that grayish shade which as far as I was concerned was always the color of Eretz Israel.

During the Second World War, when I was serving in the army, I heard speeches by political commissars. They spoke not of the revolution but of the motherland. And I remembered then the few years during which I had called Eretz Israel my motherland. Abstract words need simple pictures to make them real. The picture that appeared in my mind was this: a young man with a mustache waxed with butter into points, wearing a voluminous abaya and a striped tunic in black and white, his arms hanging carelessly over the shepherd's staff lying across his shoulders, walking in front of the sheep kicking up a cloud of white dust. That boy was me.

Of all the roles I played in my life—those who never dream

dreams or try to realize them probably succeed in being themselves all their lives long, but dreamers play the many parts they envisage in their dreams—this one was the best: the role of a young man in love with the loneliness of a shepherd, delighting in his filth and trying to make noises like a Bedouin, full of the belief that by walking like this with his staff over his shoulders he was becoming one with nature and the landscape and the sheep and the flies, a god to a few dozen goats and sheep and one sheepdog. It was a peculiar combination of cossack and nomad. When I came back to the camp in the evening I was the happiest man in the world. With what modest pride I would enter the big tent and join my washed and combed companions with the oil lamp casting a pale light on my clothes as floury as a baker's with the white dust, ready to modestly accept their admiration. You have to remember: taking the sheep out to graze involved real danger then. In those days the men who worked in the fields did not look down on the shepherds and nobody said that only confirmed loafers and idlers born and bred would be capable of spending hours every day in the company of dumb animals.

I was faithful to that role for a long time. I even abstained from reading during working hours. I wanted to be a real shepherd and nothing else. But a Jewish boy can't do without books forever.

In the end I could no longer restrain myself and I asked about Nimrod.

A question without real substance. For what could she say? What did I actually want to know? What kind of a man he was? What did he have in him of me? But I was afraid that if I didn't ask she would be hurt. As if I took no interest in my offspring. What's more, she would be reinforced in all her prejudices about me: that I was a heartless, unfeeling man. A cripple. A lost soul. A link without a chain. A puff of smoke. A man without a father and without a son.

I know that this is what she thought, although she never wrote it to me. From a distance of thousands of miles I guessed her thoughts. Even after the connection was broken and the letters stopped coming, I knew what she felt.

Many people might think it strange. Although I had abandoned her when she was with child, she bore me no grudge. At any event, not openly. She clung to the belief that I had been thrown out and had not left of my own free will. Which is both correct and incorrect. And when I went to Russia, she shared the responsibility for the separation with me. She would never have returned to Russia. Perhaps she said to herself that if I had called for her to come and live with me in Tel Aviv or Jerusalem she might have renounced one lofty ideal and gone to succor the man she loved. An honorable compromise at which even the most orthodox of the movement disciples would have winked an eye. But in returning to the Diaspora I betrayed a principle which was more important to her than the family itself.

This was how she saw things. In the saga of her life, I was cast in the role of a lost soul. On no account did she see me as an unprincipled scoundrel exploiting the innocence of a woman hungry for life and then running away from the scene of his crime.

A great soul in a sad body.

We corresponded for a few years. The letters to Via Nova were full of facts about the child. His weight, his health, his cute tricks. About herself she wrote nothing. Nor about the comrades and the farm. As if she had set herself a limit: the rights of a father were still valid but the rights of a comrade had been forfeited. In her letters to Moscow there was a suppressed note of rebuke. Why hadn't I written and told her that I'd married? What was it, a secret? And then the comrades suddenly appeared: "Everyone wishes you happiness and good luck." I felt that up to then she had still hoped that I would come back, for the sake of the child. After her hopes had been dashed, a note of bitterness crept into her letters. She hoped that my wife would enjoy what she had not enjoyed: love, loyalty. Once she even shot an overt barb in my direction. In the past I had made an effort to be a worker. In that at least I had been serious. And now in

Russia of all places, the motherland of the workers and peasants, I was abandoning labor and going to work in an office. I sent her a reply which in my opinion was irrefutable: the Soviet Union is a classless society and therefore it makes no difference what work a man does, over here the engineer is a worker too, and without his contribution society could not exist.

Vera was not without weaknesses. Sometimes she took her revenge on me in touching ways. One day she wrote that Nimrod had caught pneumonia. Afterward she wrote again and made no mention of the illness. I dashed off an urgent note: How is the boy? And then she replied, If you really cared about the child you would come to see what he looks like, at least. I replied: How can I? The British Intelligence have a file on me: if I come they'll arrest me and deport me before I manage to set foot in Tel Yosef. And the comrades, I asked, will they all be so glad to see me? Her answer was long and apologetic; she asked me to forgive her for losing control of herself.

Vera said that Nimrod was a serious person. Baruch Bashan had said the same. She added only, "You'll get to know him and see for yourself." Her blue eyes, which looked as if a whitish liquid had been poured into them, suddenly cleared and she said, "I can't wait for you to meet each other."

"I'd prefer the first meeting to be in private," I said.

She made a slight movement with her shoulders and then she said it in words: "Better not. You'll both swallow your tongues if we leave you alone. Better for me to be there at first, and after things warm up you can go on by yourselves."

Vera really hadn't changed.

*I*t will be remembered that I kept my correspondence with Vera a secret from Nina. Why? It's hard to explain. Obviously, I wasn't afraid she would suspect me of being in love with a woman in another country. And I didn't tell her about Nimrod either. But it wasn't the fear of hurting her that motivated me.

You have to understand the atmosphere of those days. Those of us who went back to Russia were convinced that emigrating to Eretz Israel in the first place was wrong, and we tried to correct our mistake by rubbing it out. Like crossing out an unnecessary word. It wasn't hard to erect a barrier between the present and the past. It was plain that the hostility was increasing. You didn't have to be a political genius to realize that the wall between Russia and Eretz Israel was going to grow higher. Here a new world was being created—and over there they were the agents of imperialism. Any common fate between them and us was out of the question.

Nina was a frail, refined woman and in those days sickly too. I made every effort to spare her pain, anger, or perplexity. I did not approach things from the point of view of true or false. The dialectics we believed in gave me the tools to paint my behavior in rosy colors. I believed that I was protecting Nina when I tore years of trial and error out of my life like pages out of a book. The past was dead and the life ahead of me belonged to me and to Nina exclusively. Vera and her son had nothing to do with Nina's life. I could find no fault in keeping her ignorant of their existence.

When Nina found out about Nimrod her anger astonished me. How could this fact cast a shadow on our happiness? And when we made our peace she said that the thing which had shocked her was the fact that I had lied to her.

"I didn't lie," I put the record straight. "All I did was to keep certain facts that had no bearing on your life from you. What happened in Eretz Israel is over and done with. There's no way back. And the child who was born from that unfortunate episode will have a life of his own, without any connection to the man who fathered him."

An orphan of the period, I said to someone else, at a different time. The First World War had filled the world with orphans. One heard the most appalling stories. Even in my own family terrible things had happened. The case of a boy in Eretz Israel who had been parted from his father as a result of circumstances did not seem to me something about which it was legitimate to be shocked. But in Nina's eyes the marriage union was an irrevocable vow in which the partners undertook never to conceal anything from each other. Not even the slightest fluctuations of feeling. She even demanded that I describe my childhood and youth to her without leaving anything out, as if I was betraying her with every picture that escaped my memory.

I hated it. It did not diminish my love for her, but I sometimes grew sick and tired of this passion for intimate soul searching. There are anxieties in a man's heart which he should not reveal even to his wife. A passing sigh is inflated to huge proportions the moment you have to explain the reasons for it. And she wanted to know everything. What was happening inside my mind. And every word which tried to describe some faint, subtle feeling only succeeded in turning it into a monster.

On a number of occasions she gave me gratuitous pain when she found it necessary, faithful to her vows, to tell me things that no woman should say to her husband. Momentary weaknesses which would have been better passed over in silence and forgotten. Did we ever receive a promise from our bodies that they would never betray us? But she was not a woman to feel something and keep it to herself. She had a theory, too, which she had picked up somewhere: things which are born in our brains and never see the light of day are like stillborn babies.

In any case, after the incident in question, Nina too learned to keep some things to herself. Vera's letter was never mentioned again and she never asked about Nimrod. Shortly afterward the correspondence came to an end anyway, as a result of circumstances beyond our control. And not long after that I was arrested. And the few letters we wrote to each other after that concealed more than they revealed.

The affair was only spoken about once again.

In 1942, as I have already mentioned, I was permitted to volunteer for the Red Army. Although I was already profoundly disillusioned by then, I believed that the war against Germany would cleanse Russia of its ills. People who had mistreated their fellows so shockingly—the old Party members, the kulaks, the national minorities, the Jews, the deviationists, the vast numbers who were slaughtered on political battlefields without knowing how or why—would not be able to revert to their evil ways when they saw how the people they had let down so badly were prepared to sacrifice themselves for the motherland.

The journey took two weeks and the train only stopped in Moscow for four hours. I arrived at the house and Nina wasn't there. I ran like a madman to the dental clinic where she was doing her apprenticeship. They let her go out with me for two hours. I wanted to go to bed with her there and then, on the laboratory floor, but she rushed me to the crèche to see Olga. Olga was not in the least affected to see me and took no notice of me at all. I was driven wild by the thought of the poison they must be dripping into her mind: enemy of the people, traitor. I resigned myself to my fate and only regretted having come to see her without having prepared her in advance. But when we tried to say goodbye to her she wouldn't let us go. She complained of imaginary pains and cried hysterically. We had two versions of why she did it. Nina said that Olga didn't want to part from me. I thought things were simpler. Olga believed what she had been told about me and she was afraid of entrusting her mother to my hands. She was already old enough to understand why I was so keen to get her mother away from there. I was impatient and angry. Nina thought that a quick, frustrating union of the kind which united us for a moment, standing up, covered by my soldier's overcoat, behind a public lavatory, was not worth the harm done to the child (faithful to her marriage vows, as usual, she was completely truthful and told me right there, whispering into my sweating neck, that it gave her no pleasure at all, only pain).

Then an ugly quarrel broke out. Nina said that I was a hard-hearted man without paternal feelings. And she reminded me of the letter from Vera. This time she offered another version. It was not my lie that bothered her. She was shocked by my indifference to the child's illness.

She said it with her body too: her pale face, her heaving bosom, her vexed flesh beneath the crumpled dress.

In the end we made up. We cried like children, and she was sorry for what she had said. But what could she do—that was what she had felt at the moment she had said it.

When the train moved out of the station I was upset and angry. I was going to be killed, I said to myself, and my daughter would be an orphan. And her mother would not have to be ashamed of the hard-hearted father and enemy of the people anymore. She would be able to be proud of the fallen soldier.

*I*n the evening the meeting took place. At first Vera had intended holding it in her room, but so many people expressed the wish to take part that in the end they transferred it to the kibbutz "club."

An institution unfamiliar to me. In my day all members' meetings took place in the dining room—a big tent from British Army surplus supplies, which was the living heart of the kibbutz during almost all the hours of the day and night. The kibbutz club was a kind of cafe where people met to read newspapers and pass the time of day. In the days of poverty the big frying pan in the kitchen served the same purpose. The night owls would gather around it, wipe up the dregs of the oil with thick slabs of bread, and gossip to their hearts' content.

I was not all keen to make a speech in front of an audience. There was an abyss yawning between me and the kibbutz members, and it could not be bridged by words. And how much the more so in a language I was not fluent in. They suggested that I speak in Russian but I refused. I preferred stammering in Hebrew. Furthermore, if I spoke in Russian only the members of my own generation would come and I would feel like a Party member forced to criticize himself at a cell meeting. In any case, since I had already, in a moment of weakness, agreed, I could not go back on my word.

Efrati opened. He had aged greatly; his shoulders were

stooped, and only his mane of white hair—the hair of a poet, even though to his mind poetry distracted people from seeing things clearly and simply—was as heavy as ever. As if the snows of his youth had come to crown his head in his old age. His opening remarks, full of witticisms, were astonishingly similar to the kinds of speeches I had heard him make forty-five years before. He remembered that our last meeting had taken place in the isolation ward in the Beit Alfa hospital, when I was ill with a bad bout of malaria. This memory gave him a good excuse to jump straight into our own times. The metamorphosis of a word: in the Soviet Union the "isolation" wing was the wing reserved for political prisoners in the jails. I was obliged to agree with a nod of my head, for everyone looked at me inquiringly. Unintentionally an atmosphere of confrontation had been created. It became clear that I was going to be required to beat my breast, recant, confess: Who was right? Who was wrong? Who was at the gates of Hell? And who at the gates of Heaven?

Let there be no mistake: there was no rudeness, no insistent demands or sarcastic questions. On the contrary, Efrati was very polite and tried not to give offense to a visitor. But the expectation in the eyes of his audience was stronger than the rebuke in the eyes of a frowning cell secretary. They had good reason to feel hatred and anger. Soviet arms were threatening their sons and grandsons. They did not pour their wrath out on my head. They simply waited for poetic justice to be done.

I had been asked to speak about the Soviet Union, but my head was spinning with thoughts of another time. The days of the Labor Brigade had come back to life in me. The bald heads gleaming in front of me sprouted mops of boyish curls and time took a great leap backward. What I had previously tried to forget, I now tried to remember.

Had they forgiven me for what I said on parting? "Subjectively each of you is a poor laborer, but objectively you are the servants of the bourgeoisie—poverty excuses nothing. Every bloated capitalist has a flunky to sweep the dirt off the floor in front of him."

* * *

I was not a skeptic. On the contrary. I tried to cling to certainties.
I was prepared to entrust my soul to anyone who promised me
a codex of laws, a secular Talmud. How happy I would have been
if it had been granted me to abandon my body to the current
flowing down to the great sea. I would have been willing to follow
anyone who gave me a guarantee that from now on not a single
moment of my life would be wasted. That all my acts added up.
Even a soccer game was not an empty amusement. It gave me a
healthy mind in a healthy body. Every drop of sweat poured oil
onto the great bonfire.

The idea of the Labor Brigade captivated me. I submitted
to its principles with the fanatical zeal of a Jewish monk, faithful
to the general commune of workers in Eretz Israel, a soldier in
the army of labor, ready to be sent wherever he was needed. The
conquest of labor was no empty phrase to me. And it meant not
only conquering the labor market for the Jewish worker but also
conquering ourselves for labor. Although I did not suffer from
physical weakness, I found the work exhausting. For a long time
I tormented myself with the question: Was my escape to the
sheep as blameless as it seemed? Perhaps I found it so idyllic
because I was actually bone-idle? And when we were building the
road I had tried to get myself attached to the cart drivers who
received a daily wage, rather than the stone breakers who were
paid according to the amount of work they did. I punished
myself for this backsliding, and when the foreman discovered
that I had a talent for organization and put me in charge of a
section of the road, I sentenced myself to hard labor and did all
the hardest jobs myself.

Looking back: the Labor Brigade was a good place to sow
one's wild oats. A tumbledown, wide-open house where everyone was welcome. A home for a young man trying to put off
deciding who and what he was, who did not want to settle down
yet in a home of his own. Any loafer or ne'er-do-well could join
for a time, live like a parasite, learn a trade, and take off at the
first opportunity that offered. How we scorned those who went

to Tel Aviv and built themselves a hut and bought themselves a table and chair and candles for the Sabbath. The mother party, Ahdut haAvodah, did not get off scot-free either. Worrying about the needs of town dwellers, occasional workers with petit bourgeois souls! Imagining that it would build a political force on their shoulders!

The commotion, the disorder, the anarchy—all these were to my liking. I didn't join the party. In the elections for the Histadrut convention I voted for the left-wing list. I believed that the commune would do away with the need for a political party. An enthusiastic mass movement had no need of steering committees and secretariats. The faithful would carry the slowpokes along with them. The wise would teach the foolish. The conscientious would shame the scoundrels. In the language of those days—a workers' economy would be more successful and cheaper even in the present system. I was one of the faithful. I volunteered for every hard job. I chastised the wastrels. I gave back every penny not spent on fares to the common kitty. I was a soldier in the Jewish revolution. Sentenced to hard labor for life to atone for the sins of the shopkeepers and peddlers. Content that the sweat and dust had peeled the skin of the Diaspora from my body and soul. Even malaria was a welcome guest, an emissary from the Messiah. I submitted myself to loving the dry earth, the flies, the snakes, everything that was part and parcel of the nature of the place. Suffering purifies, as everyone knows, and all our tears are collected in God's pouch. Only by renouncing himself and his freedom can a man make himself free. "Only what I have lost is mine forever." An end to splashing in the shallow waters of some imaginary weltschmertz, I harangued myself soundlessly in moments of gloom and low spirits. The iron discipline of the commune is the definitive answer to the Jewish fate.

I was even able to overcome the boredom. I forgave the licentious their license and the cursers their foul language. The empty-headed braggarts who boasted of their lack of culture were heroes in my eyes if only they knew how to hit a nail on the head with a hammer. At night I too was swept into the hysteria of the dancing, which kept doubt at bay for a few hours.

Disillusionment is not something which is visited on you like a sudden eclipse of the sun. It is more like candles going out one by one. I was personally offended by the deficit of the first year. How could it be possible? After all that effort? All that passionate devotion? Was it possible that the commune could not compete with the private economy? Was the idea false? Or were the comrades themselves to blame? Or perhaps there was no hope for the commune except when it was the ally of the regime?

The comrades were indeed a disappointment. First of all—the loafers, who did not understand the full weight of the responsibility that had fallen to their lot: to show the world that the sense of comradeship was a greater spur to effort than the acquisitive instinct. Then the scoundrels, the exploiters who came to learn a trade for nothing and had no scruples about pretending that they were with us heart and soul. And last—the poor in spirit, who spent a few days in Tel Aviv and saw little houses with clean rooms and a Sabbath loaf, a child playing the violin and a well-dressed woman, theaters and dances and parties—and lost heart.

The commune itself was a disappointment too. At first it was supposed to exempt us from the need for intermediaries, swollen-headed little bosses living like parasites on the productive labor of others. And now a new bureaucracy had grown up around our necks, inexperienced, incompetent, full of cant and power-greedy.

And over and above all these, like a menacing shadow: the Arab question.

In Tel Aviv you could walk from one sunny street to the other, in a merry group of children playing barefoot in the soft, hot sand and shouting in Hebrew—and ignore it. You could believe that Jaffa was inhabited by savages incapable of understanding the pure intentions of the Jews. In Tel Yosef that was not possible.

I remember one picture: a blazing noon, the sheep like a

huge ball of fleecy wool next to Harod's spring. A wind passed through the thorns with a husky whisper. In the distance the mountains of Gilead looked like a shimmering mass of bluish vapors. The delicate smoke rising in a spiral above the hill of Kumi seemed the only certainty, lingering on from ancient times. All the rest—a mirage. I sat under a tree and read a letter from a friend in Russia. World-shaking events were taking place there, he wrote. And what was I doing, I thought to myself—lying in the shade, chewing a straw, waiting for evening to fall, waiting for morning to come. Suddenly, as if he had materialized out of my own fears, an Arab lad in an old army uniform and army boots without laces emerged from the wadi. With one look he appraised my strength and agility and immediately unloosed a volley of the kinds of oaths which I tried in vain to imitate. The sheep scattered in all directions, as if a bomb had exploded in their midst. I chased after him, cursing him roundly with all the Arab curses that I knew. The boy eluded me in his loose boots and laughed. For a while I stood and shouted, but my voice sounded artificial, alien, false. And then, while the sheep were trampling the scanty wheat growing next to the spring, I said to myself: He's from here, and I'm not.

After that incident I abandoned the sheep. I looked for harder and more manly work. I went to Tel Aviv to learn the building trade. In the meantime I enlisted in the military underground. Shochat took me into his confidence. I learned to use arms. I taught others. I drowned my doubts in feverish activity. The day was devoted to work and the night to self-defense. We had big ideas. We spoke of a navy and an air force. Deputations were sent abroad. I too was considered as a candidate for one of these delegations. My doubts seemed to me the scruples of a Jewish adolescent. The lives of grown men were a struggle for survival, not for justice.

Who knows how my life would have turned out if the attempts of Shochat and his friends to set up an independent militia in the Labor Brigade had not been nipped in the bud? In any case, when the Kibbutz—the name of that underground within an underground—was disbanded, I was at a loose end.

Our own people were beaten and the opponents of the "general commune" were gaining the upper hand. It was then that my meeting with Daniel took place.

Daniel did not speak loudly or passionately. He seemed the reverse of the usual political propagandist. He spoke gently, in a soft, musical voice and with quiet confidence. His arguments were strong and convincing, but he never pressed me to admit that he was right. He allowed me to part from him as if our argument had ended in a draw. At night the doubts he had sown in me grew like mine. His criticism of the Labor Brigade was moderate, constructive. It was a noble experiment, he said, but hopeless. A general commune of workers in a semifeudal country ruled by an imperialist power was a dangerous illusion. A small group of workers with good intentions and revolutionary fervor could tramp the country from end to end without accomplishing anything, except to arouse the Arabs who would suspect—and rightly so—that we were trying to deprive them of their means of earning a living. The Jewish labor leaders had discredited themselves. Intelligent, enlightened, humane people who nevertheless permitted themselves to relate to the members of another nation as if they were some kind of natural disaster—like the khamains or the snakes. At the most they were prepared to regard them as ungrateful savages. Offered civilization, they did not say "Thank you." And if anyone ventured to suggest that things might not be so simple, they were immediately ready to cast stones at him as the agent of a foreign power.

He did not ask me to join the Party. He only encouraged me to participate in a common organization of Jewish and Arab workers. He introduced me, in secret, to members of the Arab intelligentsia, and waited.

The secrecy of the meetings bothered me. But Daniel justified it on the grounds that it was for my sake that these meetings took place underground. The leadership of the Histadrut was hysterical and if they knew that I was talking to an enemy of Israel like him, I would be doomed. Even if I didn't agree with his ideas, my fate would be sealed.

Perhaps it was all simply a question of technique. A craftsman who had perfected his tools. But it made a great impression on me. Bitter and acrimonious debates were then raging in the Brigade. People were raising their voices at each other and sometimes their hands too. And lo and behold, precisely the revolution which was out to subvert the entire order of creation, spoke in the gentle tone of a Jewish scholar.

It was Daniel's language that enchanted me. It did not have the niggardly dryness of Marxist jargon. He talked Marxism in the language of the Prophets. A strange mixture of sociological jargon with Talmudic sayings and Russian symbols. He spoke of our "tortured century" with affection and sorrow as if he were speaking of a mentally unbalanced mother, and of "cataclysmic movements of populations" and "apocalyptic visions" in the same breath as "the birth pangs of the Messiah," "the stirrings of redemption," and the "breaking of the vessels."

I repeated his words to various friends, and discovered that they too were tortured by doubts. This was not the birth we had been praying for. It was impossible to make a revolution in these tiny, measured steps. In Soviet Russia a mighty torrent was raging, and what about us? A little brook, no more, shallow waters, a failed spring; we would dry up long before we reached the mighty torrent. Perhaps Jewish nationalism was a grave mistake. The solution to the Jewish question would have to be found on a worldwide scale. And only revolution would solve the acute problem. Eretz Israel was nothing but a refuge for the persecuted. And perhaps we should not upset the inhabitants of the country by exaggerated demands. We would only bring down a catastrophe on the heads of refugees from the sword who had fled here for their lives. We would give birth to anti-Semitism in a place where it had previously been unknown.

From here it was no more than one step out of the Zionist camp. If the revolution could solve the Jewish problem, we should devote our efforts to furthering it. Its triumph was far from certain. It was surrounded by enemies, hounded by foes. In all conscience, the comparison was inescapable: just as the individual was called upon to renounce his egoism to build the commune, so the little national group must renounce its self-ishness for the sake of building the new world. When you are for yourself alone—what are you? When you are part of the whole—you are the place, the time, you are history.

(In 1933, in *Der Emes* press, I often met Daniel. He would smile and greet me like an old friend. But he never spoke to me about the Eretz Israel period. After he was arrested I thought that he had kept quiet out of caution. In those days a man who held his tongue with his friend was doing him a great favor. Although sometimes I wondered if it might not have been something else entirely: he did not know how far we had taken his teachings and whether he could safely show us how much he regretted the past. In any case, the thought that he was suffering pangs of conscience for leading me by the nose pleased me. It was not a desire for revenge which made me want to believe this. On the contrary: I loved him and this was why I did not want to entertain the thought that he had been manipulating me in ways he had learned in a course for Party propagandists.)

My way into the Communist Party seemed perfectly natural to me. A step which was dictated by my own character. The same impatience which had led me into the ranks of the Labor Brigade thrust me into the "Union of Jewish and Arab Workers" and after that into the Fraktzia. All that time I continued as one of the left-wing activists in the Brigade. Nobody gave me any instructions on how to behave. My instincts told me how far to reveal my true opinions. I did not see myself as a subversive in the ranks. Although I had no objections to that role either. I saw myself as waiting for the right conditions to ripen: a minority converting souls to its creed without trying to hasten the coming of the Messiah. My garbled quotations from the words of Daniel, which were sometimes beyond my comprehension, served the shrewder men among my elders as a clear proof that what the younger generation needed was a lucid, homogenous ideology. A whole loaf, not a collection of crumbs.

We adored mysteries. We had left Russia before the denunciation of "revolutionary romanticism." We were in love with it.

An underground within an underground was nothing new to us. I have already spoken here of the Kibbutz. The experienced veterans of Hashomer, like Shochat, did not put too much faith in the Histadrut officials who had taken "security matters" upon themselves. They saw fit to set up a defense organization along the lines of a revolutionary party. When we kept the secrets of the Kibbutz from our friends who had not been called to its ranks, we did not think of ourselves as deceiving them. We believed that we had shouldered a responsibility they were not yet ready to bear. We were proud of ourselves. Everyone had placed their necks in one yoke—we in two. When the day came we would open the secret arms caches to them and save them from disaster. I felt the same about hiding my Communist affiliations from my friends. When the day came, the others too would be invited into the inner circle. There were some people who woke up and saw the light immediately and others who did so little by little (like Borya, my tentmate, who woke up in the morning in stages: he yawned, stretched, groaned, lay down again, pulled the blanket up to his chin, and curled up like a fetus, but then his conscience pricked him and he threw the blanket off, abandoning his body to the cruel cold, sat up, muttered something, got dressed with his eyes closed, and fell back into bed fully dressed for a few more seconds. I would get up, get dressed, and go outside). In those days, after the crushing victory of the Bolsheviks in Russia, it was possible to believe that a little group of people who knew what they wanted and read the signs of the times correctly could suddenly emerge from the seclusion of their smoke-filled rooms and decide the fate of the world. The thought that it was permissible to lose a generation in the wilderness on the way to the Promised Land was not alien to us either.

I did not get all my ideas from Daniel. I had a few aphorisms of my own, metaphors with concealed political messages such as: "Gravel is necessary too, but roads are built with rocks," or "A tributary which does not join the mainstream only creates a swamp," or "When you're busy raising a heavy beam you can't stop in the middle to scratch yourself," or "You can't make half a revolution on half a dunam of land." And so forth. Before it came out that I was on the farthest fringes of the left, Berl asked me to write something for the *Kontres*, something about daily life in the Brigade, or simply reflections. And he flattered me too: "They say you've got a gift with words. Articulate men are at a premium among us." After I joined the left-wing list, he decided to do without my services.

The underground was also a shield against boredom. A life without flavor—every day the same as the one before—suddenly took on a new fascination. Your most insignificant acts were only the reflections of more serious matters. You could work in the kitchen without feeling inferior to the laborers in the fields. The man next to you was scrubbing pots and so were you, but there was a world of difference between you. The boring work that you were doing was only a cover; you were preparing a revolution, and you had the patience, the cunning, and the ability to keep your mouth shut of a revolutionary.

But not for long. After the split I couldn't take it anymore. We were no longer people waiting for their hour to come. We were identified and our freedom of action restricted. I had already spoken my mind ("We are inverting the Jewish pyramid on the backs of the Arab peasants") and made myself enemies. We were about to be expelled from the Histadrut. Political arguments ended in blows. I couldn't decide whether to abandon the fight or allow the members of the right and center to expose their "true faces" and eject me from the Brigade by force. In the meantime Vera became pregnant and announced that she intended to have the child and bring it up with me or without me. And then relations between myself and the others became so strained that it was quite clear there was no longer any place for me on the kibbutz or in the Labor Brigade.

In Vladimir I spent some time in the same cell as an Englishman who had spied for Russia and come fully expecting to reap his just reward. He was sure that his arrest was a kind of trick, to confuse the intelligence agencies of the West. "These things are very complicated," he explained to me, "and the brains of your top bureaucrats work at dictation speed. It will take them a little time to sort things out." In a moment of truth, perceiving my curiosity—What had made a man like him, well off and well educated, put himself at such a risk?—he said with a smile, "Pirate ships are full of nice boys who run away from home and family life." I understood that the same applied to me. But we really and truly believed in what we believed, and we believed that a man has to live according to his beliefs, and ideology for us was very far from idle chatter, a substitute for the yeshivas we had abandoned in our youth. I thought about Vera. I didn't run away from her. I didn't push things to extremes in order to be expelled from Tel Yosef. Political splits are subject to laws of their own. But I had to admit to myself that "these things" too are sometimes "very complicated." My expulsion from the Labor Brigade cut through a very complex knot with one stroke of the sword.

I have never regretted the things I didn't say, but I've often regretted things I did say. And even more—enthusiasm that went to waste.

There are about thirty people sitting in the kibbutz club. Most of them were from my own generation. There was only one young girl there. She stood behind the counter and served hot drinks and cake to anyone who asked for them. When she wasn't busy she sat on a stool and read a newspaper—working, not participating in the meeting.

I glanced around me. I knew eight people by name and another five or six by appearance. I could understand why no young people had come. But where were the fifty-year-olds? I found some merit in it. All those soul searchings and inner agonies would die with my generation. Other generations never had such grandiose dreams and so they would have no painful disillusionments on waking. I did not know what to say to them. There were a thousand and one tales I could dredge up from my memory. The speaker bears witness not only to himself but also

to his audience—whether he wishes it or not, what he says and
how he says it reveal what he thinks of them. Anecdotes and
stories are for those who want to enjoy themselves in this world;
to those who wish to reform it, one speaks a different language.
But were they still interested in the poor man's wisdom here?
Prohodnik kept nodding off. His deaf wife kept blinking her
eyes. Others stared at me with weary indifference. They only
woke up a little when I said something they didn't like. Signaling
their displeasure with cold eyes: the leopard hadn't changed his
spots.

("It's a question of character rather than ideology," Avrunin would say. What character? He didn't say. It was clear that he
meant some kind of psychological perversion which was pecu-
liarly Jewish. A curse afflicting a miserable nation. The burden
of inherited suffering. He didn't realize that he was talking like
an anti-Semite. "How many more people have to be killed before
the Yevsektsia sees the error of its ways?" he would ask.)

I spoke a little about the democratic movement in Russia.
About the setbacks it had suffered over the past year. From the
expressions on their faces I could see that most of the facts were
already known to them. Who was in jail, who in a mental hospital. The Western press was apparently extremely well informed.
I described some of the personalities I knew personally. I sensed
that a number of my listeners were displeased that I hadn't given
them halos. Not all of them were heroes, as people thought here,
but ordinary, decent people with principles who in any other
place would do their jobs without cheating anyone or devote
themselves to bringing up a backward child without expecting
any praise for it. None of them had decided to declare war on the
regime. Each of them had probably reacted to some piece of
arbitrary injustice or some too blatant lie. When he was hauled
over the coals he was angry, and refused to confess the error of
his ways. For this crime he was punished even more severely than
before, and his defiance increased in proportion to the punishment. Thus, step by step, he found himself at odds with the
regime as a whole, and he had no choice but to make his quarrel

with the authorities public or disappear somewhere in the snows of the north. Once he had become a "public figure" they were obliged to beat him with padded sticks. And from then on no one would believe me when I said that he was a modest, unassuming fellow who had no desire to seek the limelight and who would have been willing to compromise at a much earlier stage if, for example, they had agreed to give the Ukrainian poets the honor due to them.

Afterward I said a few words about Zionist activities, the national revival among the youth, and the underground Hebrew lessons. (I had given Hebrew lessons for a long time myself. I remembered the grammar well enough and knew a few poems by Bialik and Tchernihovsky and Shneur by heart. A friend who had once corresponded with Shlonsky had entrusted me with more recent poems. Quite possibly, it was due to this activity that Perlmutter and his friends thought I deserved special treatment. The truth is that I was not one of those who shouted from the rooftops. The state of my health forbade me to go back to jail. I restricted myself to things that could be done in secret, without exposing myself. After I received a permit to live in Moscow, I disappeared almost completely from sight.)

The questions they asked me in the kibbutz club were about life in general: how much a worker earned and how much consumer goods cost. For a few moments there was a certain unpleasantness. Avrunin requested permission to ask a question about the Jewish writers. And then he answered his own question. He was unmoved by their fate. On the contrary, he seemed to take a certain spiteful pleasure in their downfall. People who ran after will-o'-the-wisps could expect to be devoured by wolves in the end. They had declared war on the Hebrew language, Jewish schools, and Hehalutz. The Soviet system had put an end to literature, he concluded. Books were printed there but no literature. And the illustrious tradition of the great, humane Russian literature had come to an end.

He made me feel very bitter. How could I come to the defense of these unfortunates? Only a writer could understand the plight of his brothers who had no chance of seeing one word in print unless they prettified reality a little. An ordinary man might say, perhaps with justice: Keep your self-respect and turn your hand to some other trade where you won't have to compromise your integrity. Easy to say. Anyone who has never been forced to wallow in his own excrement by three elegantly uniformed young stalwarts smelling of expensive shaving lotion has no right to judge those who compromised their integrity with a broken heart (even Osip Mandelstam, a great poet not endowed with excessive physical courage, who in a moment of insane bravado wrote a poem about the man with the fat fingers, also wrote a poem in praise of the White Canal where hundreds of thousands perished). I said only this: There are scoundrels who lie brazenly and flatter the powers that be (and sometimes the power is in the hands of the masses) shamelessly in order to obtain important posts and dachas on the Black Sea. But Russian literature is alive and kicking, and not only in the samizdat. Except that Russian literature is written between the lines. Even the lines themselves are written in code. And the need to write in code sometimes makes for an extra-special brilliance. And those who are not endowed with sharp eyes and ears neither hear nor see. In Russia, I said, even children's fairytales are full of dynamite. As an example I quoted the ostensibly naive stories about birds and beasts by a certain poetess who had emigrated to Israel in the meantime. Here, I had heard, for some reason she had stopped writing. Could it be because there was no need here for parables and fables in order to criticize the government? Not only that—here she would feel that she was being devious if she chose to hide behind stories about tigers and giraffes instead of writing a logical article that would be exposed to countercriticism in its turn. At that moment I thought: Perhaps we Russians are no longer capable of taking any interest in books written in the West where everything is permitted. In Russian books, on the other hand, even those that contain a few little white lies to pull the wool over the eyes of the censor, we find a feast full of flavor. No outsider could understand.

All of a sudden I felt a heavy lethargy. Like the heaviness that would come down on me in the period after my return to Russia when I was asked to lecture about Palestine at meetings of Jewish workers. With hindsight the problems of Eretz Israel seemed more complex to me. I remembered my opponents of yesterday without anger. I tried to get under their skins, explain their motives, the "roots of their errors." But my listeners did not want to listen. They knew better than I what was happening over there. They only wanted to hear it from my lips because I had been there. The king's witness.

And it was the same with Avrunin, with Yekutieli, with Efrati (maybe I'm wrong about Efrati—an intelligent, broad-minded man, he thought that his friends' eyes had dulled and were no longer able to perceive any shades between black and white). They knew better than I did what was actually happening in Russia; they saw things in "perspective." From close up a man could see nothing but his own finger. Since the authorities had crushed my fingers, I had been able to understand something at least. But the whole picture could only be grasped by someone who had not been blinded by the red-hot sword dangling before his eyes.

They knew that there was no truth or freedom in Russia. Everyone lied to everyone else in order to protect themselves from police informers. And everything was dark and bleak; there was no honesty, no joy. People walked on tiptoe, hugging the walls, looking over their shoulders. You never knew what was permitted and what was forbidden. You never knew who would be punished, or for what crime. The walls were full of ears. A man could not trust his wife, a father his son. The perfect, positive hero, the example to the Komsomol, was the boy who informed on his parents—it was a fact; there was a monument in his honor. Poets were forbidden to weep and writers to joke. Painters were forbidden to make a blot on their canvases.

I wanted to say to them: Ordinary bourgeois politeness is also a little white lie. Politeness makes life more pleasant. You tell a fat woman that she's looking wonderful, and you won't go to Hell and your lie won't make her any fatter than before. You're a kindhearted man and no one will criticize you for it. With us in Russia, everything is on a bigger scale, grand and tragic. Over there a lie is the charity that saves from death. When you lie to your friend you save him from trouble. For example, you're sitting with your pals, having a drink or two, swearing and telling off-color jokes, and you feel like making a heartfelt gesture, something to show them how much you love them. Will you confess that you loathe the Man with the Mustache? That you are revolted by the cult of the personality which turns you into a deaf idiot obliged to nod like a donkey whenever he mouths some new inanity? Let's say you do. What will you have actually done? If they inform on you, they'll hate themselves. If they say nothing, they'll live in fear. Someone else may inform and they will be arrested. Who knows—you yourself might hand over the list of those who heard you blaspheme and did nothing about it. In either case, you've lost your friends. They'll be furious with you, and rightly so. What made you behave so foolishly? You found a worm in your hand and threw into the lap of your friend. Can't you keep your mouth shut? Dig yourself a deep hole and whisper inside it what everybody knows anyway? In the future they'll stay clear of you. You're a dangerous man and you don't know how to be a friend. Certainly no one will ever open a bottle of vodka in your company again. And the opposite: when you sit in the company of scholars and express your admiration for Stalin's brilliant essay "On Language," you're doing them a great favor. You said it; they didn't have to. You know and they know that language was not "created in order to." You know and they know that the essay is a piece of shallow, pretentious nonsense. And nevertheless they'll love you for it. You are a true friend. You have saved them from agonies of embarrassment. The essay has just been published and it can't be ignored. They'll be grateful to you for volunteering for the role of court jester. After the official ceremony is over and the ritual has been correctly performed, the guests can descend on the refreshments and begin to enjoy themselves. No one will suspect for a moment that you really believe in what you said. The musical Russian language has now been enhanced by an additional range of subtle notes which enable its speakers secretly to mock words mouthed in utter solemnity. Human relations have been enriched by subtleties impenetrable to a foreign ear. In the course of time you stop noticing your lies. You wear your agreeable mask as naturally as a bald man wears his wig. Just as a respectable citizen never goes out of his house without a tie and jacket, you never venture out without it. This mask protects you and your friends from disaster. True generosity beams from your pleasant lies. You bear their burden as lightly and gracefully as an athlete. Everyone seeks your company.

I wanted to say all this—but I didn't. Was I there to defend liars and advocate falsity? I felt disappointed in myself for not having been able to make my description a little livelier. I spoke as if I was giving a sociology lecture, and something basic was lacking. Perhaps I should have said to them: Russia is a place where human beings live. Millions of people live there in all innocence, doing their jobs as best they can, trying to win the approval of those they love. Some are keen to win prizes, others are careful to avoid punishment. Pretty girls who play games and have love affairs cherish feelings under the surface of their honeyed skins that the secret police would have no idea how to classify. In the springtime, behind the bushes in the public parks, in the rowboats, love blossoms. Its ancient pain is pure, and innocent of meaning. The factories are full of young men who can play the harmonica and dance and who take pride in the quality of the goods they produce. They are faithful to their wives and friends and they love their children with an enchanting, bearlike love. The thieves and rascals and smugglers have their own solidarity, stronger than all the fraternal alliances we are familiar with, right under the noses of the police. The audiences cheer at soccer matches, wipe away a tear at the theater, listen to music reverently, and eat sausages on the lawns to the strains of a military band. Boys and girls learn their lessons with solemn reverence for the written word, and doctoral students burn the midnight oil in single-minded pursuit of the degree that will set them apart from the toiling masses forever. In philosophy departments, earnest young men, as familiar with Marxist literature as yeshiva students are with the Talmud, engage in learned debates about the history of the concept of God.

The seminarist from the Kremlin who persecuted clericalists with relentless fury was not averse to the ancient symbol, torn from its source, serving secular goals with a meaning adapted to the needs of the times. Since the word existed in the Russian language, he thought it should be invested with a new content. Otherwise the old meaning would crop up and with it all the old narcotic values. It was legitimate to say about music that it was divine, and also about his own virtues that they were not of this world.

One day a young woman met a famous poet at a party in a friend's house. The next day she wrote to a bosom friend, "Last night I met God." They wanted to arrest her and charge her with clericalism. The affair came to Stalin's notice. He called in his advisers. He asked them: Is the man really so great? They said: A genius. He said: Pardon her. Geniuses may be described in the lexicon of the past, not permitted to ordinary mortals. Presumably he was thinking of himself. Only God allows Himself to raze a city because of its sons. And if there is a God, there are also ministering angels. And a celestial choir of poets as well. In other words, the metaphor was legitimate. There was no reason to suspect the foolish girl of criminal tendencies to bring back the old regime. But when the poet—who had in the meantime become the girl's lover—was disrespectful to the sun, then the girl was punished. In the belief that a discerning poet would understand the hint, the young idol worshiper was taken away by polite men in blue uniforms and sent to Taishet to be reeducated. Her case was heard in a Soviet court—the most fascinating of all the theaters of the absurd of our generation. Solemn judges and investigators, full of reverence for the letters of the law which gave them their dignity and daily bread, humorless as the heroes of a classical tragedy, recited her sins to each other with narrowed eyes and passed sentence on her. The poet, like a caged lion in his dacha, sent urgent letters full of indignation to his influential acquaintances. The girl, in the depths of Siberia, came to know the people the poet loved from a safe distance at close quarters, too close for comfort. When she returned, crushed and worn, full of raw folk wisdom, the poet took her to his bosom and built her a temple in his verses. His lawful wife, to whom the glory and the honor were rightfully due, fumed and made scenes in public. The Man with the Mustache smiled to see the havoc reigning in the rival God's harem.

Efrati was not pleased when I expressed the opinion that the Soviet system was not in danger of imminent collapse. The regime was stable, I told them, even though it was founded on violence and lies. People who lived in small countries did not understand the law of large numbers. The people had bread, work, and culture, the latter in abundance: books, plays, concerts, dances, for next to nothing. They did not lack national pride. Who cared if the members of the "free" professions lacked the freedom of their colleagues in the West? In any case the people envied them a little and hated them a little (and how much the more so the Jews, who enjoyed the fat of the land and laid their eggs in strange nests). And the rulers were experienced and sharp-witted foxes. In Russia, an opportunist cannot be a fool. He must have all his wits about him and know how to use his elbows to get to the top. And when he reaches it, at the age of discrimination, he is already adept in the uses of the strap. The intelligentsia are privileged but they are also more severely punished. Academic education makes wiser but not sadder men. Dialectics has done away with the confrontation between good and evil, truth and falsehood, forever. And for the weak-minded there is always anti-Semitism. Like the illicit hooch which it is illegal to brew but legal to drink.

    The language made things difficult too. In Russian I could probably have expressed my thoughts more clearly. But it was precisely my Hebrew which everyone admired. And it was to praise of my Hebrew that Efrati devoted his closing remarks, although he also found it necessary to say snidely, "Some of us may feel that not all of our questions have been answered, but. . . ." When he finished speaking they all got up and walked away, the ones who had slept through everything I said finding it necessary to come and shake my hand before going to bed. I was left alone with Vera and the girl in charge of the refreshments. The two of them cleared away the cups and plates and cake crumbs from the tables and refused to allow me to help them. I glanced through the movement newspapers and waited for them to finish washing the dishes.

I looked forward to a sleepless night. I'll never learn to speak spontaneously and naturally in public. Others talk their heads off without doing any harm to anyone. But I have to pour my whole soul into every word I utter and excite myself, and sweat, and afterward I can't fall asleep.

The kibbutz grounds were dark and rustling as a forest. Vera walked ahead, shining a small flashlight onto the path and pausing from time to time to make sure that I was behind her. I sensed the dejection radiating from her as one senses the presence of an animal in the darkness. Before we set out from the club she said to me: "If you still keep faith with them, why did you ever leave?" She spoke in an offended tone of voice, as if she had been personally insulted. "Is that how my words were understood?" I asked. "I don't know how others understood them. I only know what I understood." I laughed without really meaning to. And then she exclaimed indignantly: "If that's the way you feel you should have said it straight out and not beaten around the bush." I tried not to be angry with her. You can't blame a person for the limitations of her understanding. "I spoke as simply as I could," I said to her. "I don't understand irony or see quotation marks unless they're actually written down," she said.

We went to her room to get my suitcase.

"We've been talking about everything under the sun and we still haven't said anything about Nimrod," I said.

"What is there to say?" she asked and sat down.

I sat down too.

She said, "You haven't said much about yourself either."

We sat there for an hour and a half. She told me her story and I told her mine. Mine was longer than hers. Counting off the stations on the way was a lengthy business in itself. She couldn't understand how a man who had nothing he could call his own, not even a family, could speak about the hardships of his life like some collector showing off his treasures. She spoke about her own life as of something that was drawing to a close. She had married very late in life. Her husband was a widower, a Holocaust survivor, who had come from Germany after the war. A few years later he died. She had brought up his two children, a boy and a girl. Both of them had married and moved away.

"Would you like to see a photograph?"

She showed me a boy and a girl who resembled each other and had reserved, withdrawn expressions. At the same time she pulled out a number of photos of Nimrod. A baby, a child, a boy, and a man. I looked for similarities to myself. I couldn't look for long, since Vera was staring at me curiously and I imagined she was waiting to see signs of an emotion which failed to manifest itself. I asked how Nimrod had reacted when she got married. She laughed. Nimrod was twenty-two years old when she married. And the War of Independence broke out almost immediately. He was glad that she had something else to occupy her attention and distract her from worrying about him.

I understood what she was trying to say. She had brought Nimrod up alone, without a father. She had no other children. Now she had three grandchildren. Suddenly I understood her previous anger. The Soviet Union was supplying arms to the enemy shooting at Nimrod on the Suez Canal. She had wanted to hear me denouncing it in no uncertain terms. And I had scrupulously painted in shades and nuances.

"We've always been close," she said, holding Nimrod's photo up to the light. "During all these years."

And as if she could read my thoughts she added, "After he left us he came to visit. Twice a week, sometimes more."

Then she recalled something that made her smile.

"First he came on foot, then on a horse, later in a jeep, and lastly in a truck."

I asked her tactfully, not wanting to offend her, why he had gone to another kibbutz. Vera sighed. There was a split, and he had gone with his friends. Only a few of his peer group had remained on Tel Yosef. And his wife had tugged him in the same direction.

She couldn't remember exactly what the argument had been about. The party had interfered. After the split in Mapai and the merger of Ahdut haAvodah with Mapam, the split in the kibbutz had become inevitable.

She chuckled. "And it didn't take long, no more than a year, before there was a split in Mapam too."

After the first split, Elkind had predicted that one split would lead to another. Fanatics were incapable of compromise. Maybe the next generation, which would have roots in the fields where they took their first stumbling steps, would be able to live with people without having to agree with them in every single respect, so the milder souls among us said then. We liked imagining the future: our children would be children of nature, simple, healthy, without complexes. They would be able to hold their own on horseback with the children of the Bedouin, know how to win with enthusiasm and lose with dignity, and do their duty as if it was the simplest and most natural thing in the world. Without big words. Without philosophy and dialectics. They wouldn't split into factions ready to kill each other with their tongues because of the dot on an *i*. And lo and behold—less than a quarter of a century later the same ideological conflicts were tearing them limb from limb again. There were no mass arrests, no labor camps, but nevertheless . . .

It was late and I got up to go to my room. Vera rose heavily to her feet and led the way. Only when we were nearly there did she tell me that I was going to sleep in Borya's room.

"Do you remember Borya?"

"What a question! We lived in the same tent."

"I remember," she said. "But I wasn't sure that you did."

Her voice dropped and took on a mysterious note, as if there was some kind of surprise in store for me. But she waited until we were inside the room and she had shut the blinds and drawn the heavy curtains—I marveled at the way she did everything in the dark without bumping into the furniture—before switching on the light and telling me that Borya had died the week before. Standing at the door she told me the story of his life. As briefly and dryly as a page from an archive. He had remained a bachelor for many years—"You must remember how crazy he was about Zina Shaverin"—and then he married a girl who came on an illegal immigrant ship before the war. They had a son and a daughter. The son died of a snakebite. The wife got sick and died. The daughter married a painter who took her to Jerusalem and committed suicide. She was killed in a road accident after her son, a boy of thirteen, was murdered by terrorists. The history of a Jewish family.

Borya died suddenly. He wasn't ill. The room was exactly as Borya had left it. Nobody knew what to do with his things. She had only cleaned it a little and made up the bed with her own sheets. The towel in the bathroom was clean too. Hers.

Suddenly she said, "But if you feel uncomfortable about it, come back and sleep at my place. In the other room."

I said, "I don't believe in ghosts."

She apologized. It was just a thought. Perhaps I had grown more sensitive to these things over the years. You could never know. She herself would not have been able to sleep here. Not until some time had passed.

"I've already lain next to a dying man and waited for him to die so that I could take the boots off his feet," I said. "I hardly believe in life before death . . ."

On the table I saw three photographs of children. I took one of them and held it up to the light. "Who's this?" I asked. "The son or the grandson?"

Vera smiled. "It's Nimrod. When he was ten years old."

I didn't ask, but she told me anyway. When Nimrod was

growing up in the kibbutz yard, Borya was in charge of the garage there. And that's where the boy spent all his spare time. Borya taught him to drive a tractor, a car, to dismantle engines, to weld. And when he grew up Nimrod shared the responsibility for the arms stores with him.

There was a warm glow in her eyes as she said, "Maybe it's because of that that he's alive today."

After the War of Independence there were only two men from his entire group left alive, she said. One who was abroad at the time and Nimrod, who spent the war first as an armorer and then in command of the workshop which built the first armored cars. And perhaps it was due to this, she added, that he had felt the need to volunteer for active service now, although he hadn't been called up. He always had the feeling that he owed some debt. His friends had been killed one after the other while he sat in a safe place repairing weapons. And not only that, in the Sinai campaign he was abroad. And during the Six Day War he had been sick with measles. She remembered how angry he had been with her then, for taking such good care of him when he was small that he never caught the common childhood diseases.

I passed a restless night, beset by a nervous, painful wakefulness. The stillness of the night seemed full of unfamiliar noises. The hot-water heater in the shower made a soft, whistling sound, like a train in the distance. I could even hear the sheets wrinkling under me as I tossed and turned. Through the slits in the blinds I heard the rustle of leaves outside, the mooing of a cow, the neighing of a horse, and an airplane in the distance. But it wasn't the noises that kept me awake.

There was a heavy smell in the room. The smell of dust and old age. The smell of an unhappy life. Smells were the only ghosts whose existence I could not deny. I had always been particularly sensitive to smells, and all the vile smells which had assailed my nose had not succeeded in dulling it. In Kuznetsk, before I obtained a privileged position and a certain amount of privacy, I always tried to occupy the lowest bunk. As the stench—a revolting mixture of excrement, vomit, pus, disinfectant, and rotting limbs—grew denser it would rise into the increasingly hot air and thicken under the ceiling like a fetid miasma. On the bottom bunk I could isolate my private stench and crawl inside it like my own exclusive space. I would shut my eyes, abandon myself to my pain, and insulate myself. In a new place I could never fall asleep until my nose had identified all the new smells.

So Borya had departed this world the very week I arrived—as if the country was too small to hold the two of us. And Vera still asked me if I remembered him!

We lived in the same tent. And there was a difficult, demanding, discontented kind of friendship between us. I wearied of his gloomy seriousness and he regarded me as a sly, frivolous person whose character needed improving. When I left the Brigade he boasted of having predicted it when I was still a popular fellow for whom people had high hopes. He was a taciturn, withdrawn man who never wasted his words. If he opened his mouth he did so to protest against wrongs, to warn of dangers. He was one of those who got up early to go to work and came home late. Everything he did was full of a suppressed passion. He never cut the wheat like anyone else—he saved the crop from disaster at the very last minute. He never installed a tap in the kitchen—he saved the girls from untold hardship. And if he beat an Arab shepherd boy who strayed onto our fields by mistake— he was saving the honor of the Jewish people.

Our tent was surrounded by small whitewashed stones, which continued in a narrow path to the kibbutz yard, where they turned gray and disappeared. Our oil lamp was polished until it shone. Borya would work away at it with a bit of newspaper and a handful of earth. He always got there before me. By the time I noticed a bit of soot on it—it was already clean. He never missed the chance to catch my eye when I discovered that it had been cleaned already even when it was my turn to clean it. I've met a lot of unfortunate people in my life, but not many of them would have been able to compete with Borya in the production of sad, reproachful looks—the look of a kindhearted man unfairly taken advantage of. He even made my bed sometimes, to punish me. Sometimes I would tell a dirty joke to embarrass him. He would raise his eyes from his book—the lamp was usually closer to my bed than his, so that he had to read in a poor, dim light—and give me a hurt look. My humor did not fool him. He knew that in my heart of hearts I was a serious person. I was a devoted worker and therefore he forgave me everything.

Sometimes he took me into his confidence: he did not trust the motives of some of the people who were joining the Brigade; it upset him to see intelligent girls falling in love with fools; some of our leaders were unworthy of their positions—loafers who took up public activity to get out of doing a hard day's work. He expected me to reciprocate in kind, but I said nothing. My secrets were not my own property. They were the secrets of the Haganah. And my love affairs were no secret.

One day Shochat put his hand on my shoulder and said, "I want to have a few words with you, my lad."

It was the happiest day of my life. I guessed immediately what he wanted to talk to me about. At night the yard was full of mysterious noises. Clanging metal, loud whispers, and busy footsteps. Sometimes a mysterious car would turn up and unload its freight in secret. Even the chatterboxes kept their counsel. Security was one subject we all treated with a respect bordering on reverence.

Shochat led me silently out of the yard, his hand still on my shoulder. When we reached the railway tracks he removed his hand and went on walking. And I walked behind him. We walked some way into the fields before he began talking. He spoke in a whisper, as if there were people listening, and his whisper held a note of firm authority.

He had been observing me for some time, he said, wanting to make quite sure that I could be trusted before he approached me.

The Haganah was in the doldrums. The Arabs were busy

arming themselves and our people were playing with pistols. The
Histadrut had entrusted the Haganah to a crowd of schoolchil-
dren. They didn't know the Arabs and they didn't have the first
idea of how to purchase arms. The leaders of our political parties
didn't understand that no Jewish force would be capable of
emerging here unless it was in the interests of the revolution.
They believed that Great Britain would help us, but reality would
soon disabuse them of this notion. Great days were in the offing
and we would not be ready for them. They spoke of a mass army,
and that was their mistake. Normal states could organize armies.
The Jewish people could not afford the luxury of drill parades.
We had to work underground, like a revolutionary movement,
and an underground could not take in a rabble of unemployed.
What we required was a strong, clandestine, narrowly based organization. Only people who knew how to keep a secret would
be recruited, and I'd better remember it. The question was political too. There was a left and a right—no need to say any
more. . . .

I announced that I knew how to keep a secret, and that I
would do my best to be worthy of his trust.

A few days later I was sworn in. They called me in the middle
of supper, led me to the stable, saddled a horse, showed me a
point of light at the foot of the Gilboa, and told me to gallop.

Many years have passed since, but I still remember the
sensation of freedom I felt then, and the warm steam rising from
the wild horse's coat. And the wind in my hair and the suppressed cries on the point of breaking out of my throat.

On the edge of a wood at the bottom of the mountain a man
wearing a hat was sitting behind a table. Next to the oil lamp lay
a book and a revolver. I wasn't lying then when I swore that I
would never give away the secrets of the organization, even
under torture. But the task they imposed on me was harder: I was
told to get Borya out of the tent on some pretext or other. He
was not to know that they were going to hide a consignment of
arms under my bed.

What excuse could I possibly find for keeping Borya out of

his bed the whole night long? There was only one that would work: a lovers' tryst. He agreed to voluntary exile. We were friends, weren't we? He only wanted to know who the girl was. It wasn't much to ask in return for his generosity. I said, "Zina Shaverin." Why Zina Shaverin? Because his question had taken me by surprise and hers was the first name that popped into my head. The day before, during supper, I had had an argument with her about an article in *Kontres*.

How could I have known that Borya had chosen precisely that time to fall in love with Zina Shaverin? And characteristically—with all his heart and soul, painfully, worshipfully. When he disappeared in the morning and didn't show up for work, I guessed what the matter was. When we went out to look for him I already knew that the whole exercise was only a test. The barrel we had buried was empty. And Borya was a member of the underground himself—but they hadn't let him in on it, in order to make things more complicated. I was worried because Borya was the kind of person to do something drastic. Zina Shaverin was an intelligent, serious, modest girl. Borya must have concluded that if she was capable of casual fornication, he would never be able to trust a woman again. I galloped toward a rock on the Gilboa where we used to sometimes sit and look out over the valley. And there I found him, his eyes wild and staring and a loaded revolver in his hand. I took the gun away from him and apologized. It was only a joke, a lie I had to tell him because of a security exercise. If I'd known it would hurt him, I would have invented some other name. I swore by everything precious to me that I had never touched Zina Shaverin, not even with my little finger. Borya agreed to go on living. But our friendship was spoiled.

(A few words about Zina Shaverin: a flower on the grave of a slender pioneer. After she returned to Russia she joined a commune called Tel Hai. When the commune broke up and the man she had followed there was killed by a mule kick, she moved to Kiev, where she had relatives. She joined a clandestine group of former Socialist Revolutionary Party members and edited their paper. When she was arrested they gave her a show trial. They accused her of treason but they only sentenced her to life imprisonment. She died on the train to Siberia. She got off at some isolated station and joined the queue for hot water next to the lavatory. She was too refined to stand up for her rights and stronger, coarser women kept on pushing in front of her. When her turn came the train began to move. She was afraid they would shoot her for trying to escape if she remained behind and she ran after the moving train. One of the guards played a cruel trick on her. He held out his hand and pulled her into a men's compartment. The eyewitness who told me about it wasn't sure if she died before they had finished with her or afterward. Looking back: the truth is that I was a little in love with Zina Shaverin myself. But at that time I was capable of falling in love for a few days with any girl in whom I suddenly discovered some grace, charm, or generosity—sometimes even good humor was enough. I remember this too: when the man who had been an eyewitness to the rape of Zina Shaverin (another Jew from Eretz Israel) told me about it—I felt sorry for him, not her. In those days I was unable to weep for the dead. One by one close and beloved friends disappeared or were shot, and my heart grew hardened to the dead. But not yet to the living. I could guess how he felt. He would never be able to forget how he sat there in the train compartment and didn't dare defend her for fear the non-politicals would put out his eyes. Did she scream? Cry? Beg for mercy? I could understand his despair. And I myself, if I had been in his place, would I have risked my life to save her from the animals who fell on her with savage yells? Or would I have shut my eyes tight and listened to my soul being murdered inside me?)

At two o'clock in the morning I switched on the bedside lamp. I found a few week-old newspapers and they seemed even older to me than the *Book of the Third Aliyah* in which I absorbed myself in the end. With great interest I read articles by the people I had once known, but I was left with a feeling of dissatisfaction at what

I had read. There were no blatant lies, like the lies in Soviet historiography, and presumably everything written in them was true, but nevertheless something important was missing. Perhaps it was the style which stood between the words on the page and what had actually taken place. Perhaps it was the contempt for details which seemed unimportant to the authors of the articles. In any case I had the feeling that I was looking at events through a glass darkly. For example: the Kibbutz. There were a few hints about the Haganah and the crisis in its relations with the members of Hashomer. But it was all wrapped up in secrecy as if some kind of internal censorship was at work here. Perhaps they didn't want to damage old friends? In any case, I thought, if Borya had written his own story, in plain language, it would have been possible to learn something which the articles in the book did not tell.

Suddenly I found myself grieving for Borya. I was sorry that he had died before we met, before I had heard his own version of the facts from his own mouth. Perhaps Borya had understood our relationship from either side of that eternally polished lamp completely differently.

It seemed amazing to me that after I left the country we had become unconsciously closer to each other. I wondered if Vera had chosen him for the father of our orphaned child running wild in the kibbutz yard. Was it his own virtues which had drawn the child to him, or the machines which had surrendered to the touch of his hand? In any case, this man who was my son had very little of me in him—certain hidden characteristics perhaps, an immunity to a hereditary disease—and a lot of Borya. Borya had shown him little miracles with a wrench and opened his eyes to the marvel of metal turning white-hot and softening. Perhaps he had also shown him how a man could work bent over all day long and still stand tall at the end of it. According to the Talmud, the father is not the man who sires the child but the one who rears him. And Borya must have seen me in the child he reared. And perhaps he was fighting my hidden influence all the time in order to make him into a man. And until I disappeared completely he couldn't make him into his son. Perhaps Borya was taking his sweet revenge.

A fine, floury dust covered the books in the bookcase. They hadn't been opened in a long time. Vera's eyes must have dimmed if she hadn't noticed the dust when she got Borya's room ready for me. The furniture was simple, square, monkish. The curtains colorless, worn, like old sacking. Only the television and the armchair by its side were in another style. The intrusions of the new into his secluded life. In the other room, which contained a narrow bed and books, there were also two paintings which did not seem to belong to Borya's spiritual world. A picture of a man riding on a unicorn and holding a naked woman on his hand, in purple, and a black painting with mysterious shapes in gold and brown and crimson on it. Perhaps these were the works of his artist son-in-law whose talents the kibbutz had refused to recognize. I wondered if Borya had really liked them, since he had put them in the other room where nobody could see them. Or perhaps he had mellowed and grown tolerant in his old age? If some young man exerted himself to produce paintings which he, Borya, did not understand, and if other people claimed to enjoy them, what right did he, an old pioneer whose days were numbered, have to turn up his nose?

At this hour of night I would gladly had made up with the old comrades who had dozed through my lecture and also with those who had been angry with me for not saying what they wished to hear. After all, I had no other friends besides them. We spoke in tongues in the same tongue, although we prophesied different things. They too, like me, addressed History in the second person and saw themselves as entitled to interpret her signs. They would never shoot anyone who disagreed with them, but they had methods of their own of excommunicating you. And there was no chance that they would ever see me as one of them again. In a place where there was no punishment, there was no pardon either.

I fell asleep at dawn and woke late in the morning. The room was unbearably stuffy. I got up and opened the window and the view of the Valley of Jezreel burst into the room: Mount Gilboa opposite, Beit Alfa and Heftziba like stones that had rolled down the mountainside, and at its feet cotton fields, the dark color of plowed land, glittering fish ponds.

Vera had pushed a note under the door: "I didn't want to wake you up." And she added instructions about how to find the way to her room. She was waiting for me, sitting and reading the literary supplement of the Friday paper. On the table were a bowl of fruit, an apple pie, and a teapot. "The tea's cold," she apologized. She went into the kitchenette to put on water to boil, asked if I had slept well, and offered to peel me an apple. We didn't say much. Everything was very domesticated, as if it were all part of a familiar routine.

In the afternoon I returned to Borya's room and wrote. At five o'clock Efrati came to invite me to his room. The room of a Jewish scholar. Books from wall to wall, and piles of journals, dictionaries, encyclopedias on the table. Most of his time was devoted to a history of the communes in the United States, where he had been sent as a movement emissary on the eve of the Second World War. He had an amazing collection of Hebrew books: novels, volumes of poetry with dedications from the authors. He knew six languages fluently and was also an expert on botany and the physiology of plants. I suppose he would have been indignant if he had known my thoughts. A man like him wasting himself here. If he hadn't been infected with the Zionist germ he would have been able to play a role of great significance in the Comintern. His life might have been shorter, but it would have been full of interest and fascination, like those of Yankelevitz, Trapper, "the Worrier." Even his familiarity with Russian affairs astonished me.

He spoke to me as if he and I together could close some kind of circle. There was one thing that bothered him to this day: What had happened in Russia during the visit of the delegation from the Brigade? What, in fact, did Shochat really want of the Russians? Did he really believe that they would agree to train

Jewish pilots from Eretz Israel? Was it true that the three of them
had been welcomed with great honor and afterward arrested? It
was well known that they had offered Mochonai a chance to
study at a technical college and the temptation had been too
much for him and he had abandoned the delegation. But what
about Shochat? What did they say to him? And how had they
threatened Elkind, if they had? There were rumors, he told me,
that Shochat had been accused of the fact that his wife had shot
a Russian. And Efrati's strong face, to which age had added a
winning nobility, took on an expression of profound contempt—Manya Shochat had shot a secret agent of the tsar years
before the revolution. Shochat returned from the visit deeply
shocked. He dismantled the Kibbutz without giving any reason
and sentenced himself to total silence. He took the secret with
him to the grave. And perhaps he never even told it to Manya.
But the essential mystery was what they had done to Elkind. What
had they accused him of? Had they tortured him? Or simply
terrorized him? When he came back to Eretz Israel was he already a Soviet agent, with orders to cause moral damage to the
Zionist movement? Or had things simply unfolded of their own
accord, according to the "dynamic of controversy" pushing the
opposing sides to extremes?

He was disappointed that I didn't know the answers. I told
him that in '26 I wasn't yet a Party member. I think he didn't
believe me. I told him that when Shochat announced the
breakup of the Kibbutz I was very indignant, like many of my
friends. But we didn't connect it to his visit to Russia. On the
contrary, we were sure that he had given in to Ben-Gurion and
Golomb. We saw it as a takeover by the bureaucrats. I told him
about my meeting with Elkind and Krochmalnik. If Elkind had
already confessed to the *actior* and told him all the things he
subsequently told me, then the business of the arrest had not
been mentioned. Because it had never taken place or because he
never considered it important enough to mention? Or because
he didn't trust Krochmalnik? I don't know. I told Efrati this too,
that in the circles of the Fraktzia a different story had gone the

rounds. At the beginning, Shochat had made a great impression on the Soviet officials he met. The idea of setting up an anti-imperialist underground in Eretz Israel captured the imagination of the more enterprising members of the Comintern. It was decided to send a delegation to Eretz Israel to examine matters at firsthand. The latter, who presented themselves as the commercial attaché from Constantinople and his wife, were astonished that anyone would have taken "that fantasist" seriously. They wrote a report to Moscow recommending breaking off all relations with Shochat. A dreamer and not a serious person, they said.

Efrati sank into thought. He too had said similar things in his time, and now he was sorry for them. "He was a great man," he said sadly, "and we never knew how to value him at his true worth. He may have taken a few steps ahead of us. Perhaps if he hadn't been so striking to look at he might have avoided certain fateful mistakes."

We sat together for hours and missed supper in the dining room. Efrati's wife gave us sandwiches and drinks, tea and coffee, and alcohol by turn, and late that night we were like two young boys who have discovered friendship. We spoke at length about the last days of the Brigade, and Efrati was willing to hear, without losing his temper, that if they hadn't persecuted the members of the Fraktzia so ruthlessly, many of them might have recovered from their tragic love of the revolution, and Eretz Israel would not have lost men of inspiration with a passionate desire to perform great deeds. Unwillingly, he listened to the thesis which I put forward, that more than a few of those who had carried on an open struggle against the Zionist movement believed in all innocence that they were saving the Jews from disaster. They were warning the nation against a political adventure in a land whose population would enjoy the support of hundreds of millions of Moslems.

We got carried away into a philosophical argument. Did the dividing line between good and evil pass between one man and his fellow or did it cut through our own hearts? Did ideology make us crueler than we really were? Was the belief in a God or the moral code of our fathers likely to make us better people? Hadn't those who believed passionately in the faith of their fathers murdered millions? Was there a way back? And other questions in the same vein which reminded me of the debates on the training farm in Moscow when I was nineteen years old. Except that now there were pictures haunting us; every issue conjured up countless stories, which we simply did not have the time to tell each other, to enforce our arguments. The more we talked the more compelled I felt to write everything down. Even if it would make it plain to everyone that we were nothing but dangerous fools in our passion to make history with every tool that fell into our hands, whether it was a hoe, a gun, or a pen—it would all be written down and recorded as a warning to future generations not to follow in our path. (Our paths, to be precise. And yet, although we went in different directions, we did it with the same fanaticism and the same loyalty to a detailed master plan, as if history had entrusted us with a blueprint which would enable us to build a magnificent mansion if only we followed its instructions to the letter.)

We spoke of Borya, too. I told Efrati about my feelings when I found myself in his room opposite the picture of my son. Efrati sang his praises: people like Borya were getting rarer all the time—strong, honest, loyal. I surprised him by expressing some doubt as to whether loyalty was really such an important value. People who raise loyalty to the status of a supreme value exempt themselves from the obligation of subjecting their leaders to any kind of criticism or control. They would obey any order, even if it was immoral. Efrati said that Borya was loyal to the idea, not to individual leaders. Then he had second thoughts and said that perhaps the only one Borya followed blindly was Ben-Gurion. "Simple people need to believe that there is someone above them who is infallible," he went on as if reflecting aloud. I hoped that he would say something about my son. But he hardly knew him. Nimrod was a boy when he went off to join the Palmach. And when he came back he immediately left again to join a different kibbutz. Efrati remembered only that he was a strong, quiet, athletic boy. And then he immediately added, "But that's a description that could fit almost any of the lads." After rummaging through his memory he came up with the remark that Nimrod was a "heartbreaker." Every time he came home on leave during the War of Independence he appeared with a different girl, each one prettier than the last. But this too did not distinguish him from the other young men. Nor the girls in his company from their sisters. In times when young people are being killed in droves, all girls seem a little more beautiful.

Efrati deserves to have his portrait sketched here. Among the other Crimeans he stood out. They gloried in their muscles; he, in his weakness. They boasted of imaginary conquests, even though the girls who pretended to believe in free love were not nearly as bold as they seemed: he made much of his modesty, although his women pursued him all over the country. Next to the touching efforts of the poet in the group to resemble his fellows, going out of his way to use tastelessly coarse language and crack empty-headed jokes, the isolation of Efrati, resolute in his determination not to betray his vocation as an intellectual, was conspicuous. In return for a certain surrender of dignity— he was prepared to do all the jobs generally regarded as not masculine—he was allowed to maintain the traditional posture of the man of the book among the people of the book. He read fiction too, and with all the passion of a true Russian intellectual. He read Dostoevsky and plunged into gloom. Dipped into Tolstoy and recovered. Opened Chekhov and sank into reflection. Secluded himself with Turgenev and filled with love. Herzen's diary was like balm to his soul.

The philosophical works he read were the teachings of the socialist fathers. He began with the first—Thomas More, Robert Owen, Fourier—and for a time he was also an orthodox Marxist and didn't skip a single word by Marx, Engels, Lenin, or Trotsky, and ended with the last: Bernstein, Kautsky, and their followers. He didn't read books the way others did—simply in order to increase his knowledge. He studied and questioned them and debated with their authors. Every time he agreed with one it was like an oath of allegiance and a sacred obligation to follow behind the pillar of fire that had been ignited on the path before him. Until he read the next book. When he came across Berl Katznelson's articles he sat at Berl's feet. And from then on he was a tireless proponent of his teachings: a working nation with no class struggle.

Efrati espoused the liberal point of view with the fanaticism of a Jesuit. His greatest opponents were precisely those who held the same beliefs. Only they held them with weak, flabby hands and Efrati with hands of steel.

Although we disagreed on almost every subject, I respected him greatly. And so did the others. When a man is always true to himself, even though he may change his opinions from time to time, it gives him great strength. When other men of letters raised their voices among us, even if they were more erudite than Efrati, everyone remembered that they didn't put in a hard day's work. When Efrati spoke, everyone forgot that he had never held a heavy hammer in his life. His ill health protected him. He was the only one of us who had spent some time in a tuberculosis sanatorium in his youth. In those days we related to this disease with something approaching reverence, as if it conferred spiritual benefits on those who suffered from it. And Efrati never opened his mouth to speak without uttering a series of dry, heart-rending coughs. Everyone waited silently for the fit of coughing to end. When he finally began to speak, everyone breathed a sigh of relief.

His speeches held his audiences spellbound. In a time when consistency was considered a supreme moral imperative, he gained a following among all those who did not know how to give an unequivocal answer to his rhetorical questions.

During a period of bitter controversy, I discovered that he was more cunning than he seemed. Enthusiasm was a tool which he had adapted to his needs. A weak animal that finds itself in the hunting field of stronger and bigger beasts will emit ferocious growls. When the arguments grew more acrimonious, he sharpened his tongue. He discovered the immense power latent in verbal violence. He hurled words at us which a stronger man would not have dared to utter for fear of being beaten. He took shelter behind his well-known physical weakness and pelted us with heavy rocks.

A well-remembered scene: Efrati leaning against the doorpost of the kitchen door, reading a piece of paper. His face is thoughtful, powerfully concentrated. He sees no one. Hears nothing. A thought stuck in his mind has shut him off behind an iron curtain. Two steps away from him, sitting on a vegetable crate, Zina Shaverin is shelling peas. Through the coarse stuff of her dress and the starched kerchief on her head you can see the slender lines of her figure, her vitality and grace. Efrati's poker face amuses her. She whispers, "Hey, you! Where are you?" But he doesn't hear. She throws pea shells at him. They hit his loose trousers—there's a wide gap between the rough cloth and the skinny legs inside them—and fall to the ground. He doesn't even feel them. Then she laughs and begins to pelt him with the peas. The look he gives her! Zina Shaverin's sweet smile does nothing to placate him. He is furious. She has cut the thread of his thought. How dare she! And wasting the peas into the bargain! His anger grows by the minute. Belatedly, he remembers that she is one of "them." And even the handful of peas she threw at him in affectionate amusement is debited to the political struggle. As if she did it on purpose to put a spoke in the enemy's wheel.

When we were drinking tea in his room I asked him if he remembered Zina Shaverin. "Of course," he said. "A nice girl. Borya was head over heels in love with her."

"I think she was a little in love with you."

"Rubbish," he said, but there was a conceited gleam in his eyes. "In her eyes I was the devil incarnate. She worshiped Elkind and followed him blindly."

Third Notebook:
Nimrod

$\mathcal{T}$he meeting with Nimrod did not take place as Vera had predicted.

Perhaps the word "meeting" is inappropriate.

On his way home from the Suez Canal, Nimrod was involved in an accident. He was taken to the hospital with a head wound and I saw him there. A handsome man. Strong features. A fine beard. Straight nose. Clean-cut lips. Unconscious.

With his neat beard and the huge bandage on his head he looked like a sleeping Indian. His still body was attached to the narrow tubes of a feeding and warning system which sustained the dim flicker of life in his body. The only sign of life he gave was the pale zigzagging line on a green-squared screen.

The nurse allowed us, Olga and me, to sit beside him.

"He won't know you," she warned us. In a low but firm voice. It was her duty.

His eyes were open and blank.

After a while a doctor came in. A young, sturdy man with a flat boxer's nose. He asked us to leave. We were tiring the patient. He refused to say anything about the prognosis. The injury was severe. The patient had been unconscious for a long time. It was impossible to tell the extent of the damage. The human brain was a mystery. Everything was still open. They hoped it would be possible to bring him back to a state where he would be capable. . . . It was hard to say exactly what he would be capable of. Simple movements certainly. Perhaps later, in the course of time. . . . Surprises happened . . . A stammering doctor gives rise to anxiety.

When we left the room we met his wife. "There's no

change," said Olga. "Nira," she remembered to add, "this is my father." "I know," said his wife. Her heart wasn't in making new acquaintances. When she came out, her face was grave but her eyes were dry. "He didn't know me," she said.

"Nor me," said Olga consolingly.

The irony of fate. We were all equal in his eyes: his wife, his sister, his father.

In the hospital grounds, on a bench in the shade, we found Vera. When we approached she stood up and fell on my neck. I put my hand on her shaking shoulders. She recovered quickly. "We must talk to the head doctor." She offered us cookies. She knew that he was being fed intravenously but she brought them anyway.

Alone at home. But for the dog. Doing nothing was eating me up. Reading was difficult, I couldn't concentrate. My thoughts kept straying to the man lying motionless between white hospital sheets. All I could do was write. Writing distracted me. In Borodino, Pushkin wrote his best poetry. He was trapped there during a cholera outbreak without anything to do. I went over my first notebook. I wrote a letter to Epstein: the meeting with the family. The visit to Tel Yosef. The accident.

I added a comment which I would never have dared to write to anyone else: Perhaps I was wrong to have challenged fate. I wanted a son. I got him. Like a baby who had to be washed and changed. Nature didn't like being forced. My daughter too was a stranger.

I wrote to Epstein in Hebrew, as he had once asked me to. After sending the letter I regretted it. Perhaps this too was provoking fate. Perhaps it would harm Epstein. Now that he had finally achieved a measure of peace and quiet, I shouldn't have reminded the authorities of his former sins.

A few words about Epstein.

If I've had ten friends in my life, one of them is Epstein. Even five. Even one. And if Epstein isn't a friend then there's no such thing as friendship in the world.

Epstein is a Jewish Talmudist. To my generation this says it all. He could be a revolutionary and a heretic, but in these things too he remained a Jew and a Talmudist. Very Jewish and a typical Talmudist.

If you cast him into a sewer he would find something there to query and debate. When we said "Talmudist" we didn't mean it as a compliment. With Epstein, it was the opposite. He would prove to us that it was his Judaism which protected him from the filth and degradation. He would say that but for the Jewish tradition of suffering and survival, he would have gone mad a long time ago.

I've already spoken of how he spent the first years of his imprisonment conducting research into the torture methods of the interrogators. And in his spare time he was busy "counting" the number of exiles and prisoners throughout Soviet Russia. He added fact to fact, rumor to rumor, he even studied government statistics and transport reports. The computer in his head came up with a number not very far from the one claimed by Western intelligence agencies who had tools at their disposal a thousand times more sophisticated than his.

Many prisoners, myself included, became addicted to this drug. Amateur research projects helped us to overcome the long stretches of boredom which were enough to drive anyone insane. As the sand of our lives trickled slowly away, it grew into mountains. For a long period in Norilsk I conducted an investigation into hunger. I wrote down a detailed, clinical record of the changes taking place in our bodies, our minds, and our behavior during the great famine. (I investigated myself mainly, but also the others. For a time I worked in the clinic, which gave me a certain advantage over my friends. In exchange for a few drams of alcohol I was able to obtain stale bread, which I would share with Epstein to save him from starving.) I wrote down everything, from the external changes to the impoverishment of our vocabularies. While my companions rotted slowly on bunks swarming with lice, I hid in the clinic and wrote. The act of writing itself was a kind of struggle, a clinging to reality. A stubborn optimism. You're going to die and you try to be of some use to someone. I really and truly believed then that my research was important. The conditions we were living in would presumably not be repeated. And human beings were not rats, to be starved for the purpose of experimentation. The suffering of these people should not be wasted in vain.

I wrote my research in Hebrew, in Latin characters, on the clinic forms. I hoped that I would be able to smuggle it out in the guise of lists of medical stocks. But there was a Jew among the prison guards and he succeeded in deciphering the manuscript after it was discovered. My "research" was destroyed and I was punished. To this day I'm not certain that my work was of no scientific value.

I was obliged to write my research down. Epstein never wrote anything down. "I'll never succeed in getting a single piece of paper out of here," he would say. "I haven't got what it takes to be a smuggler." And he developed a system of memorizing. He was capable of memorizing long columns of figures and doing complicated calculations without having to look at them. "I've got it all in my head," he assured me. "And when the day comes, I'll get it all out. If I live."

We tried to keep him alive: he was the repository of our suffering; all the facts were in his head and nobody would be able to sweep them under the rug. Whatever was recorded in his prodigious memory would survive forever.

He attributed his memory, rightly, to his Jewish education. In the yeshiva, someone who had known him from childhood told me, he was considered a genius. The lazy ones among them would never open a book to resolve a dispute. They simply asked Epstein.

When he wasn't too exhausted, he would give courses to the inmates in all kinds of subjects: mathematics, biology, French, medieval history, Talmud, international law, philosophy, Marxism.

Once he gave a lecture to the Jews among us about the Israeli economy. It was the fruit of a careful study he made of a

Bank of Israel report which had somehow come into his hands.

Epstein himself attached no importance to any of his "research" except for his counting of the prisoners. He would say dismissively that it was nothing but mental exercise, to keep vital organs from degenerating. In prison, he told me, when they weren't taken out to work and boredom threatened his sanity, he would make up detective stories or solve chess problems in his head. A means to cheat time. By the time you've solved the problem the evening porridge has arrived. . . .

But others did not agree. They believed that the prodigious labors of his mind would one day yield a work of genius which would astound Russia. It seems to me that if a man as weak and feeble as Epstein survived what he did in a number of the worst prison camps our times have known, it was only because there was always a nucleus of prisoners who were determined to save him so that he would remember what their dimming minds were no longer capable of holding. As if he himself was a forbidden manuscript passed secretly from hand to hand, to keep it from falling into the hands of the authorities.

We met five times, by chance. Epstein said to me: "Whoever has taken the place of Divine Providence up there seems to be arranging things so that we meet again."

The first time was in Vladimir in 1938. The door of the cell opened and a tiny creature, beaten and bruised and scared to death, was thrown inside. I saw immediately that he was a Jew and began to talk to him. But since my face was smooth and untouched he refused to talk to me. He was sure that I had been planted in his cell to inform on him. He had no secrets to tell. He was arrested for a joke. The joke he told ("Once upon a time a peasant was walking next to a river; he saw a man drowning and saved him; the man said to him, 'I'm Stalin: tell me your wish and I'll see that it's done'; the peasant replied, 'Don't tell anyone that I saved your life' ") was common currency at the time, but someone keen to usurp his place at the Philosophical Institute had taken care that it reach the ears of the man whose word was

law. Epstein was afraid that in his anguish he might add insult
to injury by making some sarcastic remark in my presence which
would increase his punishment. He was painfully ridiculous in
his efforts to defend his torturers to me ("There's no alternative
but to take the strictest measures. Our class enemies are many
and cunning. They may make a mistake sometimes as they did
with me, but it's better for us to accept our suffering with understanding than to let the criminals escape their just punishment"
and all the other well-worn formulas). That was the extent of his
mistrust of me. Even when we were transferred to a cell packed
with thirty-eight prisoners he tried to keep out of my way. The
bullies in the cell tried to push him onto the bunk next to the
lavatory pail and I attempted, without any success, to introduce
a rule that newcomers would begin there and be moved as soon
as someone new arrived, but as long as Epstein remained in the
cell the arrangement didn't work: the newcomers would take one
look at the wizened creature lying on the end bunk and immediately grab the one that had just been vacated for themselves.
When I stuck up for him it only increased his suspicions. He was
sure that I was defending him in order to win his confidence and
cunningly extort an admission from him which he would later
regret.

The second time we met was in 1939, near Riabov. A new
camp was being set up there and the work was backbreaking. We
had to chop down the trees, transport them on rafts to the camp,
and put up the cabins by ourselves. We found it very difficult to
meet the quota that entitled us to enough bread and soup to
keep body and soul together, since the timber was always being
stolen and sold in the adjacent town. We made a tremendous
effort to get the camp up before winter. In winter, woodcutters
died like flies. Epstein was attached to a brigade of weaklings
where the mortality rate was very high. When one of the men in
the brigade I led was wounded I attached Epstein to it in the
teeth of the opposition of the other men, who did not want to
weaken our brigade, which was one of the strongest in the camp.
(When I reach the world which is all good, if it turns out that

there really is a God, the scales will surely be tipped in my favor—I saved Epstein's life.)

Epstein stayed with us for three weeks. There was a considerable drop in the efficiency of the brigade. His productivity was really low and sometimes we even had to carry him home on our backs from the forest, with the last vestiges of our strength. I was faced with a tough problem. I was told that if I didn't find a way to get rid of the "parasite" they would kill him themselves. If we all died of hunger and exhaustion he would die too anyway. But if he was sent somewhere else in time the rest of us would have a better chance of survival. Luckily for me, a commission of inquiry turned up at just this time, and warned the camp commandant that if he didn't start keeping proper accounts he would be punished. I recommended Epstein for the job although I knew that his field was philosophy, not bookkeeping. By the time they found out he wasn't an accountant, I thought, he would have a few days' rest, recover his strength, and maybe in the meantime another job might be found for him in the stores, whose building had yet been completed. But Epstein sat down at the desk and turned himself into an accountant.

At that time we were already friends. In a manner of speaking. In a manner of speaking, because the relations between the giver and the receiver can never be a real friendship. In any case, by this time I had already gained his confidence. Then he told me that for a time he had been a Communist, not out of opportunism, the post he aspired to in exchange for a Party card, but in good faith. In his youth he had traveled a long road from the yeshiva to communism by way of Herzen, Kropotkin, and Rosa Luxemburg. In his eyes communism stood for a classless society and a noncompetitive life. With all his heart he detested competition ("*Nu*, you tell me, could I take part in a race with legs like mine?" he would say). While he was still in the yeshiva, before he lost his faith, he was repelled by the argument for the sake of winning a point, the parading of erudition, the contempt shown for the less brilliant. He believed that the aim of the revolution was to enable people like him, who were prepared to throw their modest wisdom into the common pot to stew there with other ingredients and turn into an active, saving force, to free themselves once and for all from the struggle for survival and the need to measure themselves in terms of success and failure. It was an irony of fate that the only "pure commune" he ever saw in the Soviet Union was in the prison camps. There the laborer was worthy of his hire and the bread was shared equally among the comrades. But in this "commune of scarcity," which lacked the basic necessities of human life, the prisoners did the work of the guards. They helped them to get rid of those who ate without working. The solidarity that existed there was the worst kind of all—the solidarity of the strong against the weak.

For my part, I felt a qualified affection for Epstein. I admired his prodigious erudition and sharp tongue, but I wasn't completely comfortable with his friendship, which had a hint of obsequiousness about it. Epstein did not set too much store by his "poor man's wisdom," which came to him so easily, and abased himself before strong men who could work with their hands, ride a horse, breast stormy seas, and lay heavy hands on a woman's buttocks. He had the sad humor of the cripple which is directed first and foremost against his own deformities, a kind of insurance against being hurt by the cruelty of others. It upset me to see him making these tireless efforts to please "the people." Whenever a group of prisoners got together in the hut, the workshop, or at some "social event" (we had parties there too, and celebrations, and anniversaries of the revolution, and plays and concerts), he would try to make them laugh at his expense, telling jokes about his weakness and his laziness, as if he was trying to protect himself from physical violence by allowing them to sting him with words.

The third meeting took place in Norilsk, and the fourth in 1947 in Kuznetsk. By then we were already bosom friends. Over there my status was such that it enabled me to ensure his survival. When he saw me he fell on my neck and burst into tears. He told me that he been freed at the end of 1944 and remained in the camp. He didn't have the strength to begin a new life somewhere else. He went on working there as an accountant for a salary, married, and led a quiet life for two or three years. And all of a sudden he was arrested again. Without knowing why. When they brought him to Kuznetsk he was sure that his end had come. But the moment he set eyes on me he understood that Providence had decided otherwise.

The meeting in 1957 took me completely by surprise. On the last night of the old year I went out for a walk with a woman friend. We went to Red Square to wait for the ringing of the bells at midnight. In that year, at the height of the struggle against the cult of the personality, new hopes had awakened: there seemed some point in looking forward to the morrow. We stood in the square in an anonymous crowd, gray shadows in long furs, "to listen to the throbbing of time," as a young poet wrote that year. The moment the bells stopped ringing we fell on each others' necks. There was a strong smell of vodka in the air. We broke into song. A man in a high hat and silver-knobbed cane in the old style, a curious figure who looked as if he had stepped straight out of a story by Gogol, wrote eight numbers in the snow with his cane—the outgoing year and the incoming year. A fellow in a dark-green tunic with its collar cut crosswise, who may have been a soldier or a civilian, swayed drunkenly up to the numbers written in the snow and urinated on them. A warm steam rose from the melting figures and everyone, including the women, laughed—a strange, unseemly laugh. Even a militiaman, standing to one side and observing the scene, laughed. Suddenly I overheard a conversation behind my back. I recognized one of the voices but I couldn't place it. They were talking about *The Thaw* by Ilya Ehrenburg, which had just come out. The moment the voice said, "He makes more sense than Ehrenburg. This snow won't thaw until people piss on it," I knew it was Epstein.

I nearly crushed his ribs in my embrace.

And then he said to me: "Whoever has taken the place of Divine Providence up there must be doing it on purpose. Five coincidences are no longer a coincidence."

I remember our conversation word for word.

I scolded him for not guarding his tongue and telling dangerous jokes again. He said, "You're warning me! You who hide your writing in every hollow tree trunk you pass . . ." He pointed to the dirty snow and advised me to use this ink and this paper, which would leave no traces or incriminating documents. We told each other what had happened to us during the years we had been separated, and Epstein, although he was more skeptical than I was about the anticipated thaw, said that he hoped at least that in the new age time would be treated with the respect it deserved. That we would stop falsifying the past, that we would no longer be compelled to relinquish the present for the sake of the future. And so on and so forth for hours, the way we used to talk in Kuznetsk, in prisoners' code, with passionate irony.

In Moscow, Epstein lived from hand to mouth. He had no steady employment and took any odd jobs that he was strong enough to do. He spent most of his time in a small publisher's retyping manuscripts which had been cut by the censor. When people asked him why he was wasting his time on other people's manuscripts instead of writing something of his own, he replied: "A man who quotes his sources may not bring salvation to the world, as the sages had it, but at least he saves one Jewish soul from Hell." His only way of fighting "them" was humble hackwork. The moment you consented to accept a ribbon or a medal or a star, or an extra plate of soup, from their hands you were part of the system. The private who consents to have one stripe sewn onto his sleeve places the marshal's baton in the tyrant's hand. Men of conscience could only be privates.

(I reminded him that in Kuznetsk he himself had only been saved from death because I had consented to be "part of the system" and do "the devil's work." He did not defend his theory overzealously. "A question of life and death is another matter," he said. And he really didn't understand my passion to increase the productivity of the mine when everyone was stealing whatever they could lay their hands on. I tried to explain to him that in my opinion, doing a decent job of work was a matter between myself and my own conscience. But he thought that I was giving a noble interpretation to the simple wish to maintain my privileged position and please the camp commandant. He thought it, but he didn't say it. In order not to insult me. His eyes said it for him. In Moscow I could already read him like an open book. After we had both been hammered into shape on the anvil of the labor camp, words were no longer necessary between us. In any case, they had become mere embellishments, decorations, a little color perhaps. The gist we could already convey by looking into each other's eyes. There was no chance that Epstein would ever understand my attitude to work, work pure and simple. His life history lacked the chapter of the Labor Brigade in Eretz Israel, where my basic values had been shaped. A great many theories and beliefs and revisions had clung to me over the course of the years, and also dropped away from me one by one—but the belief in the sanctity of labor never left me. I said to myself: I'll be a good worker even if a thousand parasites are standing on my back, one on top of the other, and eating the fruits of my labor. Epstein thought I was a fool, an utter fool—the kind who makes it possible for a tyrannical regime to last more than a single day. You hit him and he works like a donkey, like a soldier who cannot break his oath of allegiance to king and country. But perhaps it was because of this that he loved me.)

A few years ago Epstein was reinstated and appointed editor of the philosophy section of a learned journal. He married again, the widow of a prisoner ten years younger than himself, and became a solid citizen. He started dressing smartly and even bought a gleaming, brightly painted new car. I kept away from his house. I was engaged in the dissemination of underground literature and didn't want to harm him. When we met by chance at a concert he was deeply wounded when I told him the reason for my estrangement. He said to me, "I have no other friends apart from you and Kurakin."

One day I went to listen to him giving a lecture at the Philosophical Institute. He spoke to a large audience of red-cheeked boys and girls about the concept of freedom in the writings of Spinoza. "Only a man who never needs anyone else can be truly free," he said. "If the caveman had not surrendered his freedom because he needed to join up with others in order to hunt animals and defend his territory, perhaps we would still be living in the same cave today—or else we would be extinct." "The very use of abstract words is a relinquishment of natural freedom," he philosophized. And I blushed for him. I considered his words a betrayal, and accused him of self-deception and of trying to find excuses for the denial of freedom.

I wrote him a letter inviting him to meet me in the university cafeteria. He said to me, "You didn't understand what I was saying. I was speaking against the camps." I said to him, "I understood the opposite. You're repaying the one who sewed the stripe on your sleeve and offering him the marshal's baton." He looked at me sadly. "Can't you forgive me for having a roof over my head and a table and clean sheets on my bed?" I said, "Half my life I've listened to you laying down the law on how people should behave, and it's hard for me to believe that you didn't believe in your own teachings." He said to me, "I'm a sick, tired old man."

I couldn't be angry with Epstein, but I stayed out of his way. I wanted to keep him in my memory as he used to be. A wise, wizened little man with a tremendous life force stored in his weak body, an enlightened human being who purposely refrained from displaying his erudition so as not to make anyone else feel inferior. He left the yeshiva, so he once told me, on the eve of his rabbinical ordination. He was repelled by the idea of making the Torah a spade to dig with. And the same applied to philosophy, anthropology, mathematics, and cybernetics. His modesty became even more profound when he turned it into an instrument of protest against tyranny. And now his maturity was disgracing his youth. They had cleared his name, offered him an "extra bowl of soup," and he had suddenly discovered that "freedom is the understanding of social necessity" (too fastidious to repeat the usual quotation in all its banality, he hid behind the skirts of Spinoza and found something in his writings too which would serve his purpose).

When I was informed that I was about to go to Israel, I

called him up. This time we met in his apartment, next to the University Institute in Herzen Street. His wife served refreshments on silver plates. Epstein welcomed me with exaggerated heartiness and stood on tiptoe to give me a paternal pat on the shoulder.

"Going to Israel is a bad mistake," he said.

He was not an anti-Zionist. On the contrary: in advising me not to go to Israel he was expressing his concern for the future of the state. Israel required strong young people capable of working—peasants or soldiers, not people like us: "old Marxists who can thread a bear through the eye of a needle," he concluded humorously in order to soften the harsh impression of his first words. "People like us," he added, as if I were asking him to come with me, "can only be a burden to them."

I told him that I had not given up hope of finding some respectable work to do. "And anyway," I added, "I'm not going there to help them to defend themselves or give them good advice. I'm simply going to get to know my family."

"Why don't you go for a visit and then come back?" he suggested.

"Will you arrange it for me?" I asked mockingly.

"I could try," he said. His eyes expressed the quiet pride of a man making a promise that he had it in his power to keep.

"Thank you," I said, "but I think I'll buy a one-way ticket nevertheless."

He accompanied me to the door with a joke that was typical of him: "Old people in previous generations used to go to Eretz Israel to be gathered to their fathers, and you're going to be gathered to your sons."

As we parted he asked me to write to him.

"Are you sure it won't harm you?" I asked.

"Nonsense," he said, "those days are a thing of the past."

I didn't know if he was being ironic or hypocritical.

I see Nimrod's wife often. We pass each other in the corridor, next to his bed, at the hospital gates. Sometimes we stop. I look into her eyes. Big black eyes which evade my look. We don't talk much. Hello, good morning, good afternoon, what's the time?—that's all. We have nothing to say. I'm sorry for it. And even what I can't say to her.

We don't talk about his condition. There's no improvement. And it's worrying. What can we say? What do we feel? After all, we can't say anything encouraging.

We pass each other without touching.

One day the head doctor came into the ward. I waited on one side until he was free and then I approached him. He talked to me as he walked. Asked me who I was. What right I had to know. I told him I was the father. At the same moment Nira came up and overheard. A strange glint appeared in her eyes. As if I was parading under false colors.

The doctor smiled at her, put his hand on her shoulder, and said that there were encouraging signs. I saw that she believed him. Even though he did not say what the signs were or what they meant. I did not believe him. I don't like doctors who permit themselves to throw out irresponsible remarks and expect their words to be taken as gospel just because they are in a position of authority, as if they were the rulers and we the ignorant masses.

She was in a good mood that day and I could say more than one word to her. I told her that I felt in a very strange position. Standing next to the bed of my son whom I did not even know. She said nothing and passed her hand over his brow.

And then I made a bad mistake. I asked her if she had anything written by Nimrod which I could read. I didn't mean what she took me to mean. But with my own eyes I could see her hatred budding.

She didn't reply to my question right away. First she said, "He wasn't much of a writer." And then, after a pause to consider what she wanted to say, she added, "There are some things that I can't show you without permission."

Like the stab of a knife: you've already buried him.

I went back to my desk but my heart wasn't in it. I didn't see any reason to sit and write. I had no more illusions. A page written by me wasn't going to wipe out a single page in the Lenin

Library. In my heart of hearts I suppose I had hoped that one day my son would read my notebooks. Now I couldn't be sure of that either.

I would have to learn to write a letter to a stranger.

I suppose real writers must feel the same way in front of a blank page. Sometimes it whets their appetite. Sometimes perhaps they shrink from the weight of the responsibility.

At moments like these I prefer to do something else. Translation. There the borders are clear. You empty one vessel into another, as they say. One empties out and the other fills up. I feel grateful to the official of the Jewish Agency who found me this work to do for a Russian journal that comes out here at regular intervals. Perhaps in order to disabuse me of the idea that I would ever be able to get work here in my own profession.

Olga found me some letters that Nimrod had written to her many years ago. During her military service and for a while afterward they corresponded. In recent years they had not written except when one of them was abroad. Postcards, mainly. But these she had not kept.

She had not known of his existence until she was fifteen years old, she told me. She had found out about it completely by chance. Her mother was a woman who kept her secrets to herself, she said. Perhaps she didn't want her to get involved with them. She didn't know. Had her mother been truly affected by her husband's faith, or was she perhaps like one of Chekhov's Moabite women: Where thou goest I shall go—one step ahead of you? Her stepfather was strictly Orthodox. Presumably he wouldn't have wanted Olga to have any contact with people who might dismiss her religious beliefs as a lot of nonsense. He didn't trust the firmness of her religious convictions, and he was right. She was an obstinate, rebellious girl. And perhaps he too knew nothing about the past. In any case, her mother did not see fit to tell her that she had a brother. And but for the sting of a scorpion in the Judean hills she might not have known to this day.

The scorpion strung her during a school hike. They rushed

her to the clinic at Kibbutz Ramat Rachel. The nurse who wrote her name down on the form said in surprise, "That name reminds me of someone."

I interrupted her story.

"What name?"

"Berkov."

"Your mother used the name 'Berkov'?"

"Not mother, me."

"And she let you?"

"Like hell she did!"

Olga smiled. It was a kind of battle, she said. She was a "very naughty" girl and made her mother's life a misery. Today she could guess the reason: a protest. She couldn't stand the way her mother had changed right in front of her eyes. As if the man was kneading her into another shape. As if everything she had been up to then was "null and void." Everything that had been permitted in Germany was suddenly a sin. In any case, on official documents her name was Zilberstein, her mother's name after her marriage to her stepfather, but in Ramat Rachel, in her mother's absence, she said "Berkov." When the nurse said what she said, Olga did not know that she was on the verge of an astounding discovery. She just asked, "Who?" And the nurse said, "It was a long time ago." But nevertheless she answered her question. Someone who had been in the country many years before, and then returned to Russia and disappeared. And then she said, "My father was here too, and then he went back to Russia." At that moment a middle-aged member of the kibbutz came into the clinic to get an injection and the nurse said to him, "Listen to something interesting." And the man said, "Very interesting, but there could be more than one Berkov, you know. If anyone knows anything, it'll be Vera." The nurse explained that Vera was a woman from Tel Yosef who had once been Berkov's girlfriend. "She's got a son there too, if I'm not mistaken," said the man.

To this day Olga couldn't understand how she had dared to do it. Perhaps it was the mystery which attracted her. Perhaps it too was a part of her protest. She wrote a letter to "Vera, Kibbutz

Tel Yosef." "My name is Olga Berkov," she wrote, and gave a short summary of the events of her life. As much as she knew. Was there any kind of connection between them? The letter reached its destination and the reply was not long in coming: "There may be. But I'm not sure. Why don't you come to Tel Yosef and we'll have a chat." Together with a timetable of buses from Tel Aviv and Afula. Vera had always been a practical woman. And in a P.S. she asked why Olga had requested her to write care of a friend. Didn't her parents know that she had written? Why not? It wasn't a good idea to hide such things from one's parents.

Olga wrote another letter to Vera. No, her parents didn't know, and there was no reason why they should know. It was impossible for her to come to Tel Yosef. She would never be allowed to go to a place where they didn't keep kosher. But when she grew up and was independent she would come. Vera wrote back that they had a special kitchen for the old folks where they kept everything strictly kosher. But if Olga couldn't come, she would understand. Whenever she came, she would be a welcome guest.

But she never went. She had plenty of nerve, but not enough for that. In the meantime the War of Independence broke out and Jerusalem was besieged. During the war she volunteered to work in a hospital, and there she again met freethinking people: the wounded, the invalids, and their friends who came to visit them. She fell madly in love with a certain boy from the Palmach who died a long-drawn-out death. She saw it as a sign from on high: he was a member of Tel Yosef; he knew Vera; he was a close friend of her brother's.

One Sunday she went out to fetch water and she was caught in the shelling. She ran into a house and went down to the shelter with the people who lived there. That was how she met the girl who became her closest friend, Rachel. The daughter of a well-known Jerusalem family, her father was a lecturer in zoology. Sympathetic to the labor movement. He too had a brother in Tel Yosef. All the roads led to Rome.

She became a frequent visitor to their home, although her

parents disapproved. After the war she took part secretly in youth-movement activities. She was obliged to tell lies, to pretend, and in the end she declared an open revolt. Her mother reproached her and tried to frighten her, but her stepfather allowed her to go her own way. He was not a man to fight lost wars. All he wanted was peace and quiet. He had recently been appointed director of a well-known yeshiva and his only concern was to keep it from getting out that he was nourishing a wayward daughter in the bosom of his family. For some time there was a state of truce between them. When the members of the youth-movement group went out to a work camp before joining the army, she went with them. Her parents did not try to stop her. They knew that it was beyond their power to do so. When the time came she would go into the army too, with enthusiasm, with ardent commitment, keeping faith with the soldier who had died before her eyes.

The work camp was at Tel Yosef. She needed no more signs: it was fate. For one evening she controlled herself but the next day, after work, she could hold back no longer. She asked for Vera, and with trembling knees she stood on the threshold of Vera's room and knocked at the door. Vera gazed at her with overflowing love and said, "I knew that you would come." A conversation of ten minutes was enough. It was clear that the father of this girl was also the father of her son. But Nimrod was no longer at Tel Yosef. A few weeks before, he had left with a group of others and gone to live on another kibbutz. Vera wanted to take her there immediately. But Olga hesitated. She wanted to see him from a "safe distance" first, before she made herself known to him. Young people born in Israel, and especially those born on the kibbutzim, made her feel obscurely afraid. On Saturday she got up and made her way alone to Nimrod's kibbutz, "incognito."

When she arrived there the whole thing seemed idiotic. She wanted to go straight back to Tel Yosef and send him a letter. But she was so conspicuous in her strangeness that someone immediately rushed to her aid. When they asked her who she was looking for, she was obliged to answer. And so she found herself standing in front of Nimrod's room. She wanted to escape the minute the man who brought her there left, but before she could move away from the front of the hut, "where an exhibition of colored bathing trunks was flapping on the clothesline," a young woman pushing a pram came up. She was stuck between the hut and the pram, with no way out. The young woman was her brother's wife. "Can I help you?" she asked. Olga mumbled something, the gist of which was that she was "just going for a walk." She had walked down to the main road from Tel Yosef and hitched a ride with the first car that passed, which had dropped her off here. Nira, with "newfound missionary zeal" and a "certain feeling of obligation toward anything that came from Tel Yosef," invited the anonymous young woman into the room. And although she was busy with the baby, who chose that exact moment to start screaming, she even washed a bunch of grapes for her and offered her a plate of cookies.

Until Nimrod arrived, a strange conversation took place between them. Nira seemed to her a "fanatical kibbutznik," upset by any hint of criticism. (She hadn't intended to criticize at all; her only offense was to ask, "What happens if relations from outside bring you a present?"—because she wanted to bring her brother a gift after examining their room to see what was missing.) Nira was apparently determined to persuade this stranger—especially after discovering that she had received a religious education—that kibbutz life was preferable to any other way of life in the world. Olga was embarrassed and tried to gobble down the grapes as quickly as she could, in the hope of getting away before her brother came. But just as she was saying goodbye to Nira, Nimrod arrived in clean working clothes.

"We have a visitor," said Nira with the childish glee of a Girl Scout who has completed her quota of good deeds for the day. Nimrod held out a big rough hand which crushed his sister's hand in a hard grip, and the smile of a man who was "well aware of his success with the opposite sex" crossed his face when he saw her wince. After assessing her feminine charms with one insulting glance, he went out to work in the garden, "leaving the women to gossip. . . ."

Olga did not make herself known to her brother. She went back to Tel Yosef and wrote him a letter. A few days later he arrived, on horseback. "Let's have a closer look at you," he said when he dismounted, "excited but trying to pretend that it was all a big joke." After that they walked shyly side by side, stammering like a pair of bashful lovers. "Nira knew at once that you hadn't turned up at our place by accident," he told her.

After she joined the army they corresponded. Olga wrote him long letters, whereas his grew shorter and shorter. In the end she took pity on him and stopped writing. And after that they never wrote to each other except when they had news to convey or something particular they wanted to ask. These businesslike letters, she said, were simple, honest, and full of charm. Ever since her marriage they had visited each other regularly, mainly on occasions of family celebrations or troubles. But sometimes simply when they felt like it, on a fine winter's day . . .

"Vera hadn't told him anything?" I asked.

"She did tell him, but he had forgotten all about it."

"What do you mean, 'forgotten'? From the day you wrote to her until the day you went to Tel Yosef he managed to forget?"

"She told him when he was a child. And he forgot. He had a sister in Russia, so what? Russia was very far away. On another planet. In another time."

My astonishment must have been written all over my face. Olga, who was very perceptive, needed no more than one quick glance to guess my thoughts. How did Vera know that I had a daughter? I never wrote and told her. Olga was surprised that I should have kept such an important fact of my life a secret from Vera. "But why?" she asked indignantly. "After all, you wrote to each other. What reason could you possibly have had for keeping it a secret?" I didn't know the answer myself. Thirty-three years later it did seem silly. Or at least odd. Perhaps I didn't want to hurt her feelings. Perhaps I was intent in those days on cutting the last threads that tied me to Eretz Israel. Two separate worlds which never touched. So who was it who had seen fit to "inform" on me?

"And she didn't tell him when you wrote from Jerusalem?"

"No, she wasn't sure yet that I was your daughter. She wanted to make certain that it wasn't a mistake before she told him. And when I came to Tel Yosef with the youth-movement camp and turned up on her doorstep by surprise, I asked her not to tell him anything. I wanted to take him by surprise too. I was very fond of playing games in those days."

"Did your mother know? Was she pleased that you were making contact with . . . the other family?"

"They weren't pleased that I had chosen another way of life. But they gradually came to accept it. I always went home to Jerusalem when I got leave from the army. All they expected of me was not to embarrass them in front of their friends." After a moment's thought she added: "Mother had more than one reason for not being pleased, I imagine."

Recollections for which she found no expression in words flitted across her face. I didn't trouble her with questions. Any attempt at cross-examination would only have made her withdraw from me. For the most part she refrained from speaking about her mother and her stepfather, but the empty gaps in the mosaic were being filled in little by little nevertheless. I only slipped in one question: "Your mother tried to obliterate me, didn't she?" "Obliterate is too strong a word," said Olga, and a momentary sadness crossed her face. "She tried to forget the hard life she had in Russia. She couldn't have been happy to see me suddenly making contact with a man who in her opinion and that of her husband could only have a bad influence on me. Although Nimrod and I never tried to trace you—people said that you were dead but it was impossible to check if it was really true—nevertheless the thing we both had in common was you. Mother had never gone out of her way to remind me that her husband wasn't my father. And now Nimrod's entry into my life naturally brought you back too."

"Did you ever talk about me?"

"Who? Mother and I?"

"No. You and Nimrod."

"Of course we did. We even asked ourselves what kind of person you were, but we never tried to dig up past history. The picture Vera showed us—it was rather blurred, you must know it—of you mounted on a horse was enough for us. Actually Vera would have been quite willing to talk, if we had agreed to listen. But we felt uncomfortable whenever she talked about the past. She tried so hard to idealize things that she made us feel there was no lie she would shrink from to enable us to be proud of you. Don't forget that as far as she was concerned, you were already dead."

In Kuznetsk when each of us lay on his own bunk, staring at the ceiling or the planks of the bunk above him, we would talk far into the night. Heavy, brooding conversations which touched on all kinds of curious subjects and went on until there was no one left awake to listen. We would lie on our backs and address stories, thoughts, snatches of ideas, to the hut at large. Whoever heard heard, and whoever felt the wish to respond responded, or opened a new subject, as if he was talking to himself. And whoever fell asleep fell asleep, retiring into his dreams while the others went on spinning out their thoughts. At first loudly and then in lowered voices. The last two in a whisper. If they were situated far apart they would sometimes climb down from their bunks and huddle in the aisle, talking passionately without making a sound. I don't remember who began it, maybe it was the eternal student, Kurakin, who was trying to trace the presence of God in the elements of chemistry. In any event, one night there was a discussion—in a place which could not have been less worthy of the subject—about the immortality of the soul. Kurakin insisted that it was impossible for a man to disappear without a trace. First of all, he went on existing in the thoughts of those who remembered him. Things he had made or written existed somewhere too. And after he was dead and buried, his body broke up into its elements and took part in the natural process. A plant was nourished by his decomposition and rot, and an animal ate the plant, and a man ate the animal, and so on and so forth, to infinity. In any case, no one ever disappeared completely. Someone said sarcastically, "That's really a thought to warm a man's heart: you thought you were dead and gone when all of a sudden you wake up again, happy and contented, in the shit of some Chekist who ate the meat of a calf that grazed on the grass growing on your grave." And his friends joined in: "A prisoner never disappears: his file is preserved in perpetuity" (as a matter of fact the inspiring message "Never to be destroyed" was indeed written on the files of the "white-hands," or political prisoners) "and the investigation continues after the resurrection of the dead." Others were happy to discuss the subject seriously. Even the sworn believers in a harsh rationalism had a secret hankering for the transcendental. "For a true Communist," someone said then, "the very fact that he is willing to sacrifice his life and renounce all wordly goods in order to build a better world for others gives him a stake in the hereafter." In those days we wanted desperately to believe that somewhere out there, in the world outside the camp, where "true Communists" had been incarcerated together with false Communists, opportunists, and just plain criminals—murderers, rapists, forgers, and thieves—there was a firm nucleus of fearless Communists who did not yet know what the Cheka was doing. When they found out, we believed they would mount the barricades and purge the government offices of the dregs of humanity who had taken control of the bureaucracy.

In the end only the two of us were left, Epstein and I. Epstein, who loved Kurakin, smiled at his "proofs." "We'd better leave chemistry to the chemists," he said. "But it really is inconceivable for a man to disappear without leaving a trace. I can't prove the immortality of the soul. I simply refuse to believe that it doesn't exist. And the immortality of my own soul lies precisely in my refusal to believe in its extinction.

"And yet," he added in the end, "I myself will probably

disappear completely in spite of what I believe. As if I'd never existed. You'll remain . . . you've produced offspring."

"Offspring?" I said. "I don't know them and they don't know me. As far as they're concerned, I'm a ghost from another world. Children you didn't bring up yourself are no better than chemistry."

Who knows, perhaps at that very moment, far away in a distant country, a young man dismounted from his horse and looked closely into the face of his sister.

*T*hat night I read Nimrod's letters to Olga.

She had not kept all his letters. Some had been lost in moving. And she could not find all those she had kept either. One bundle was buried somewhere in an attic or a box full of old things.

"One accumulates so much stuff over the years," she said. "Ornaments, knickknacks, toys, souvenirs, letters, notes, lists. Until you take the time to sort them out and throw away the rubbish, they have already become part of your life and it's impossible to throw them out. And when you need them, you've forgotten where you put them."

Most of the letters were from the years 1952 to 1956. (The Kuznetsk period; in other words, when the discussion about the immortality of the soul took place.) They were written in a lightly humorous style and it was only rarely that a serious note was struck, or a thought capable of casting light on the personality of the writer. A certain embarrassment was evident. The way a young man writes when writing does not come easily to him and he has not yet decided on the right style to adopt in corresponding with a younger sister he hardly knows. Many of the letters were invitations to holidays or family events, ending with the promise that next time he would write at length. There was no way of knowing if he kept his promise, since he hardly ever bothered to write the date at the top of his letters. Sometimes he mentioned the day of the week, or the fact that it was the eve of a holiday, or the Sabbath. Occasionally his humor was warm, genial, affectionate, like the way he informed her of the birth of his second son ("our second daughter is a son, too"). And occasionally it was smart-alecky, empty, and irritating ("we don't eat nonkosher girls here"). The form of address was brusque, lacking in any term of endearment ("Shalom, Olga." Or: "To Olga, shalom." Or simply: "Shalom." And sometimes with no form of address at all. On the top line: "Tel Yosef," with the date or without it, and on the line after that the beginning of the letter itself). Only once did I come across "My dear sister"—and that was when he was angry. She had written something that he didn't like. From the letter itself it was impossible to know what it was. He wrote only that he didn't agree with her ("not on any account"), but that he would tell her his reasons when he saw her. In conclusion, he never wrote "Yours." He wrote "So long." Or "Awaiting your reply." Only once did he write about any conflicts of his own. It was hard for him to decide, he wrote, whether to insist on going to study at the Technion, despite the objections of the kibbutz secretariat, or to content himself with a short course at the agricultural college ("The degree doesn't interest me at all," he wrote. "But the question is if I'll be allowed to direct a project by myself, or if I'll have to look for some engineer to sign for me"). The year—1954. the most serious letter addressed the question of hired labor on the kibbutz. Presumably in response to some critical remark of Olga's. Why did the kibbutzim refuse to employ workers from the development towns which were suffering from unemployment? The letter, which claimed the right for the kibbutz to "preserve its framework and values" even when there was "a certain amount of hardship" which it was "the job of the state to take care of," since there was no point in "destroying the most important achievement of the country simply in order to provide a partial solution to a temporary problem," testified to his unqualified loyalty to the movement dogmas.

I wondered if he lacked any aptitude at all for the expression of feeling—apart from those humorous passages which conveyed both affection and a sincere attempt to amuse his correspondant—or whether perhaps, in all these years, he had not succeeded in finding the right "tone." I wanted to believe that the letters to the women he loved contained more tenderness, without the cynical, arrogant shell of a boy who refuses to grow up.

One letter was rather different from the others. In it he suddenly took a stand with regard to a highly personal question. And did so with all the sense of responsibility of an elder brother.

It was a particularly long letter, full of question marks and short, blunt sentences ("What's all this about getting engaged? Who gets engaged here? I've never even heard of it. You'd better make sure that he's not up to some funny business. Don't be shy to ask him straight out if he's already divorced from his wife. Don't take a step like this without thinking about it first.") And so on and so forth—unequivocal interference in a matter of the greatest intimacy. He himself feels that he has gone too far and in a postscript he apologizes: "I hope you're not cross with me. I don't really know the man. I met him once or twice in the army. But I've heard all kinds of stories about him. And I want you to know that I worry about you. You're so naive, you trust everybody."

Although I read these letters with an avidity stemming from simple curiosity as well as a certain voyeuristic pleasure, I was gradually overcome by a growing sense of disappointment, which settled on me as slowly and imperceptibly as the dust falling on the head of a man working in a quarry: my name was mentioned in the letters only once! I had imagined, and Olga herself had confirmed ("We never tried to trace you . . . to dig up past history"), that they had not wasted many words on me. But nevertheless, when I read one letter after the other without coming across a single passage expressing some kind of interest in their common origins, in the man who had given both of them life and disappeared—I was hurt. I told myself that I had no right to expect it, but nevertheless . . . As if it was evidence of some kind of insensitivity, or of the cutting off of one generation from another (an irrefutable argument against "the immortality of the soul according to Epstein"). Consequently, I was overcome by joy when the words "our father" appeared in one of the letters. (Although, on further consideration, the form he used struck me as rather chilling, especially as this kind of formality was so far removed from his usual usage.)

In the letter in question he wrote that one day he had gone to visit his mother. When he went into her room there was "someone called Efrati" sitting there. Efrati was considered worthy of one and a half lines ("If you read *Davar*, he writes articles about culture and society there. I've never read them. Maybe now I'll try. When you know the person it's different"). Although he had known Efrati since he was a child, he wrote, he had never actually talked to him. The man, who had been "driven around the bend by the split in the kibbutz movement," began to attack him because of the "orientation toward the 'Brave New World' " which the Kibbutz Hameuhad movement had "received as a dowry from Hashomer Hatzair." (He was so impressed by Efrati's language that he quoted a whole sentence word for word with a kind of wonder, marveling at the members of a generation who still spoke in that kind of rhetoric: "They're lifting their eyes to the north again, to see if a candle may have been lit there. . . .") An argument flared up which Vera, who can't stand political arguments, tried to cut short: "What do you want of him? You still haven't finished settling accounts with Vitya." And thus the conversation turned to me ("and then he suddenly began to talk about our father, and Ma couldn't stop him"). He spoke with passionate denunciation about the Yevsektsia, which had "ruined our culture" and "destroyed everything good in Russia" and about the Communist Fraktzia in Eretz Israel, which had "finished off the Labor Brigade and collaborated with the Mufti," and he did not calm down until Vera shouted that if he didn't stop at once she would have to ask him to leave her room. A few days later a letter arrived from Efrati. He apologized for hurting Nimrod's feelings. In the heat of the argument he had forgotten that he had been speaking of a man close to him ("although he had sinned, he was still close to him") and wanted to correct any false impression he might have made. He had not meant to call Nimrod's father an "enemy of Israel." To appease him, he sent him a more faithful description of the man "who was our comrade and was led astray by false lights."

"I'm sending you Efrati's letter," Nimrod added at the bottom of the page. "Maybe it will interest you." And sideways, in the margin—since there was no space left at the bottom—in tiny scrawled letters: "I never answered his letter. But when I met him at the bus station in Afula I told him that he didn't hurt my feelings at all. I don't know our father and I don't care what anyone says about him."

In another letter I found: "Maybe 'don't care' isn't the right way to put it. I care about a lot of things. And I always want to know. But I don't exactly attach too much importance to it all. . . ."

I desperately wanted these words to have been written in reply to Olga's question ("Don't you really care?"), but there was no way of knowing if they were or not. Because the letter in question had no date. And he may have been reacting to something else entirely.

Efrati's letter gave me a peculiar satisfaction. It isn't often that a man is privileged to hear his own obituary. Efrati's letter, as he himself described it, was a "portrait" painted from memory. It was not my own face that I found in it, however, but the group portrait of a generation.

The period, wrote Efrati, was one of "upheaval and radical reform." People believed that the millennium was at hand. The revolution awoke dormant hopes, and, but for the anti-Semitism which "raised its head" and reminded the young Jew that "if he did not take his destiny into his own hands, he would be lost," that entire generation, "at least its younger members," would have been "sacrificed on the altar of the world revolution," happy in the thought that they had been able to "oil the wheels of the revolution." "The pioneers of the nation" who immigrated to Eretz Israel were torn between two faiths. The Labor

Brigade was by way of being a "saving solution for spiritual and physical distress" at one and the same time. But reality woke them rudely from their dreams. The "general commune of the workers of Eretz Israel" was a utopia impossible to realize, despite "all the enthusiasm and devotion which characterized the members of that generation." A few, because they became disillusioned with the Brigade and their comrades and the possibility of a life full of "ecstasy and inspiration," became disillusioned, too, with Eretz Israel. They returned to Russia in the belief that the "pure commune," a "task force" (an expression he may have used in an attempt to impress a young army officer to whom the phrases of those times meant nothing) dedicated to the realization of lofty ideals, could be established only in a country where the regime itself held the communal ideal in high esteem.

After this introduction he devoted a few lines to me, too. "Your father was a strong lad," he wrote, "usually high-spirited but tending to moodiness; lonely, since he was not a member of a big and well-established group, but had joined the Brigade together with three or four friends, one of whom committed suicide while the others scattered to the four winds." He had a "powerful ambition" to prove himself in action, anything that anyone else could do he could do "as well if not better," and he therefore ran from one job to another and learned a number of trades within the space of a couple of years. In the "political sphere" he had no "particular ambitions" and he was "quite passive" in the first years; perhaps if he had not learned Arabic during the period when "he got it into his head that a person couldn't be a shepherd without learning the customs of the Bedouin" he would not have been "carried away to the extreme left and beyond."

Here there was a general remark: The "soul hunters" of the Communist Party (the Fraktsia, the Socialist Workers Party, the Palestine Communist Party—"the same dish with a different dressing") had made the ability to expose the weak points of their "victims" into a "fine art." "With your father this was the Arab question." And since "a scappy knowledge of Arabic" was sufficient to convince him that he "saw the situation correctly" whereas others "completely ignored the problem" from the "moral" as well as the political point of view, these missionaries succeeded in "pushing him to the wall" until he was obliged to admit that they possessed the "philosopher's stone—the universally just solution." And since he was "a young man with a conscience" as well as being "a little mixed up," he found himself in honor bound to throw in his lot with them "to the bitter end." (As for "collaboration with the Mufti"—I was given the benefit of the doubt. Efrati wrote that my connections with the members of the Shomer, and my activities in the Haganah, before I "was led astray," presumably held me back on the "brink of that abyss.")

There was even an attempt to defend me: "You have to understand," Efrati wrote, "the enormous power which Marxism gave simple people."

With a true writer's pen Efrati described in detail the Jewish youths from Polish and Russian villages who traveled to the big cities and great seaports to study the Torah. All this was only to explain the source of the "weakness for Marxism of the semieducated." It gave him "an apparent key to every riddle," a simple formula by means of which he was able to stand up to the truly learned, absolved him of the need to examine "a complex reality," and liberated him from the duty of "looking into his own soul" and discovering there "mercy and compassion" and the other human weaknesses which "slow down the wheels of the machine a little but make human life worth living."

"The weakness of the semieducated"—how furious I was with Efrati when I read those words. The arrogance of the fully educated! He'd read one book more than you and that was the end of your right to have an opinion of your own. And what about the total idiots who agreed with him? But I forgave him. He had taken the trouble to write six closely written pages in order to retract a few words of abuse. I remembered the way we had talked at Tel Yosef as friends from youth. Whom did we have but those who spoke our language, those who remembered these dry bones when they were still clothed in flesh and sinews? At the end of fifty years all our quarrels were transformed into lovers' tiffs.

My learned friend was mistaken in me. During that period I never read Marxist literature at all. All my ideas came from my guts. Like the prophet Jeremiah, my bowels cried out and I was pained at the very heart. I made my way like a dog sniffing his path through the territory of bigger and bolder dogs. It never occurred to me to envy those whose learning was superior to mine. They had read one book, I had read another. They looked into encyclopedias, I looked into the faces of my friends. (For anyone who did not practice what he preached I had nothing but contempt. At the very most I envied those better at riding a horse than I was, but I outgrew that too.) To call me a Marxist! A mistake of that order could only be made by a man who could not see a butterfly in a field without sticking a pin in it. If he had called me importunate, a utopian too impatient for heaven on earth to wait for the coming of the Messiah, he would not have been too far off the mark. But a Marxist! In those days!

The amateur philosophers of the Kuznetsk *beit midrash*—our hut could lay claim to this proud title as long as Kurakin and Epstein were with us—indulged in a little "Marxism" too on their beds at night, when they were not discussing other weighty matters, such as the immortality of the soul already mentioned, or the more pressing question of what to do when the thin soup was dished out in order to arrive at the vat at exactly the moment when the barley began to float to the top. There Marxism had sworn enemies even more obdurate than Efrati. Some said that it was all stuff and nonsense, opium for the masses, a bait for fools, and the like; others treated it with more respect. If luminaries in the West, who were at liberty to shake this loathsome object off the hem of their garments with impunity, wrote learned dissertations about it and gave it a place in their universities, there must be a core of truth in it. And it was only in our country, as usual, that the wheat was separated from the chaff and ground: the flour was hoarded in the government store-houses and the chaff was dished out to the masses. There was also a Trotskyite there, who took up arms in passionate defense of Marxism. Marx's contribution was incomparable. But when his teachings were taken over by idiots, they vulgarized it. Human history was paved with lofty ideas polluted by coarse hands. Kurakin argued characteristically that Marxism had failed because it had no answers to transcendental questions. It was the irony of fate that foolish disciples, who needed something to believe in, read it like a prayerbook. Epstein said it was like a manna that allowed everyone to taste in it what he wished. Some adhered to it because it was clear and lucid; others, because it seemed to them cruel and manly. It treated people as they deserved, like frogs swollen with pride who imagined that they had created the swamp with their croaking. And from this point of view the Soviet government was faithful to its method. If thirty-five years after the revolution they had to keep Kurakin and myself in prison, then they really didn't have any faith in human beings; the conditions of production were intended solely to protect people from the wickedness of their own hearts and make sure that they were in the right place at the right time. In any case, the late Marx, of sainted memory, would turn over in his grave if he could see this brand of communism, which in skipping the stage of capitalism, in taking a shortcut from feudalism to socialism, had resorted to prefeudal methods in order to industrialize, electrify, and arm the first motherland in which the proletariat, unluckily for it, had gained a dictatorship.

For a time we also had with us the well-known physicist Kaplan, who was later released and appointed the head of a scientific institute at Leningrad University. He did not take part in the general debate. But when the three of us, Epstein, Kaplan, and I, were alone together, he said: "I'm not well up in it. The little I have read seems to me clear and enlightened. Of one thing I'm sure—if it's a tool in *their* hands, it can't be a science. They can't bend physics and mathematics to their wills." And then Epstein coined his anti-Marxist battle cry: "Socialism must be returned from science to utopia."

* * *

The next day Olga asked me what I thought of the letters. She said that letters revealed only a tiny fraction of the writer. She was sorry that she had given me Efrati's letter to read. I reassured her. Efrati's letter had not upset me at all. If my own personality was not reflected in it, Efrati's was. A thinker of his kind fails to see important details. He forgot to mention that for two whole years I went barefoot.

This was not the first time that I went through the literary remains of a son, in a hopeless attempt to conjure up his image from letters and notes, I said to Olga, and told her about Yefim. After his death his stepfather sent me a little suitcase with the things he had left behind. In it I found a few souvenirs, letters from girls, decorations, and pieces he had written for the Komsomol paper. I read these pieces over and over again, and instead of becoming clearer, his image grew increasingly blurred. The pieces were shallow, naive, full of clichés, without any individual style, as if they were newspaper clippings pasted in the notebook of a hero-worshiping adolescent. Such bombastic phrases were put into the mouths of their heroes by the worst of the Socialist Realist writers during the darkest Soviet periods. Nevertheless, after I had thought it over again and again, I managed to draw a certain encouragement from these articles. If a person as pure-hearted as Yefim, a simple, noble youth, had believed in all these well-worn, banal phrases, there must be a core of truth in them. Perhaps there was still hope. Perhaps reform was still possible. For in this immense nation there were vast spiritual resources waiting to be discovered, waiting for a new beginning. Perhaps men would fall on the necks of their neighbors again, innocent as children, ready to destroy everything and rebuild it all from scratch.

Olga listened in silence, and when I had finished she said in a quiet, hurt voice:

"You use words incorrectly. Try not to say 'remains.'"

"As long as he's alive," said Olga, "we mustn't lose hope."

I was ashamed. She was right. Perhaps in the depths of his vegetable existence, detached from us, processes beyond our comprehension might be taking place. Perhaps there was a light on in some cellar in the building shrouded in darkness.

The story about Yefim disturbed Olga. She made a calculation and found that he was born when she was six years old. In other words, he had been conceived in the period immediately prior to my arrest. Which meant that Galina Nikolayevna was not the friend of a prisoner far from home, the succorer of a human wreck, but a Moscow mistress right in the middle of the time which seemed to her, on looking back, like the family's golden age. She was surprised at herself for not remembering domestic quarrels, and she was even more surprised when I said that she couldn't possibly have remembered anything of the sort, since there were no quarrels to remember. Not even one.

"In other words, mother didn't suspect anything?"

"I suppose not," I said.

I was sure that if she had suspected anything, Nina would not have held her peace. She had made a fuss over far more subtle things, things as insubstantial as the morning mist. Even before there were words to express them, they were already on the agenda. Often I couldn't even understand what it was that had disturbed her. The most fleeting shade of feeling would be examined as seriously as if our lives depended on knowing what we had felt, and why, and if we had told each other all that had been felt, in the right words, and at the proper time, and not hidden anything—out of fear, carelessness, or inarticulateness. She always urged me to define what I felt toward her. Always. "You can trust me. I'd rather hear something disagreeable than think that you lied to me to spare me pain. I, for example, trust you completely. And I never hide anything from you. For example, last night, when I felt revolted, I told you. Didn't I tell you? I would never lie to you. And you knew how to appreciate it. And you knew, too, that it was nothing to get excited ab out. A woman is a very, very complex creature. One day she feels revulsion, the next day the opposite."

Olga agreed with me. She was only a little girl, of course, five years old. But if there was tension in the house she would surely have sensed it. Small children see things. See and remember. Even if they only understand years later what they saw.

But afterward a doubt crept into her heart. She recalled how Nina had "rubbed me out" after my arrest, as if I had never existed.

"Did she say anything, anything that might imply . . ." I groped.

"No," said Olga. "But not all my questions were answered."

"Was she angry?"

"No, firm."

Children can take a hint, she explained. She didn't understand why, but she understood that it would be better not to ask a lot of questions. She wouldn't be answered. And there would be unpleasantness. And so she soon stopped asking. When she was a little older, she interpreted her mother's silence as a sign of the times. In the homes of her friends it was the same. The moment the father was arrested, they stopped talking about him. As if he had never existed. Many did not shrink from outright lies: daddy's dead, mommy's divorced, daddy ran away with another woman, to another town; sometimes there was no better way to protect the children from upsetting questions at school or in the new neighborhood they had moved to.

Olga had never discussed the subject with her mother. She decided that she understood her motives and respected her silence. In any case, she, too, never spoke about me. Only once she was obliged to lie. At her new school the teacher insisted that she write a curriculum vitae. Olga wrote that I had died a few years earlier of a fatal disease. Nobody asked any questions. After a time she was no longer sure that it wasn't the truth. She convinced herself that she hadn't lied at all. It was the middle of the war, and she was already eleven years old. She asked her mother if she knew what had become of her father. And her mother said: No, nothing is known. We can only hope that the worst hasn't happened.

"And she didn't show you my letters?"

"Letters? What letters?"

"I wrote to your mother. And I always added a line or two to you as well, in whatever space was left."

"We never received any letters."

"How can that be possible? Your mother even answered some of my letters."

After a moment's thought I corrected myself: maybe she didn't actually answer them. She wrote letters and sent them through the appropriate authorities. I couldn't remember if they had contained any reference to my own letters or not.

I asked her if she had ever heard the expression "enemy of the people." Olga was surprised that I should even ask such a question. Of course. That was what they called every second person that was arrested. Me, too. But she hadn't believed it. When she was five years old, of course, she didn't know what it meant. She only knew that it was a term of abuse, a swear word. But when she was ten, and able to understand the meaning of the concept, she refused to believe that her father was really one of them. Why? Because he was her father. And could she understand the reason today? In any case, she remembered that she hadn't believed it. But perhaps she was confusing the dates. At the time in question she was probably already sure that her father was dead.

And then I asked her if she remembered my visit, after the war broke out.

"What visit?"

"To the crèche."

I was surprised that she didn't remember.

"You remember so many details, and precisely that visit, a short, unhappy, tense visit . . . precisely that you don't remember . . ."

She definitely didn't remember. A total blank.

"I was on my way from jail to my army induction, somewhere near Leningrad. I had a four-hour leave, to see my family. It took me two hours to find your mother. Then we went to the crèche. I was wearing a green military tunic and I had a gun. . . . Now do you remember?"

Olga narrowed her eyelids. A flicker appeared in her eyes.
But she said nothing.

"I tried to pick you up in my arms, but you wouldn't let me
. . . I suppose I must have stunk terribly. . . . Four weeks traveling,
without washing, without changing my clothes. . . . Afterward we
wanted to leave, your mother and I, and you held on to your
mother's dress and didn't want to let her go. . . . You cried
dreadfully . . . not like a child . . . a grown-up crying . . . like a
hysterical young girl. Forgive me, I remember how hurt I was by
that weeping. As if God knows what this terrible man was going
to do to your mother if she went with him. . . ."

Olga said: "Just a minute. I can remember only one visit to
the crèche. Of course I remember. It was the only time mother
came in the middle of the day. She came with some relation of
the family—then all relations were called 'uncle' . . . and he fell
on me with kisses . . ."

"Uncle!"

"Uncle. Mother came in and said: 'Here's a soldier-uncle
who wants to see you. Say hello nicely and then he'll go away.' "

"And still, you wouldn't let us go."

"I hardly saw mother in those days."

"And you didn't know me."

"No. It didn't occur to me for a second that that man was
my father."

I made a rapid calculation. She was about five when I was
arrested. A baby. When I came back she was ten. A girl. And I
must have changed, too, during my imprisonment. I tried to
remember details. Did she say "father"? Did I say, "Come to me,
daughter"? Did Nina say anything? This probing in the chaos of
my mind failed to produce results. I only remembered that she
was reserved, withdrawn, and at parting—actually hostile. And
that I was insulted. But I wasn't angry with her. I was angry with
others, with those who had incited her against me. It wasn't only
my wish to be alone with Nina that had pressed me to cut the
meeting short. I couldn't stand the glassy way the child was
looking at me.

"I can't believe that your mother would be capable of it."

"What?"

"Pretending that I was a stranger . . ."

"She probably wanted to spare me the shock. A sudden meeting, and then a long separation again, and even . . ."

And she had no fears that the child would know me? Apparently not. I remembered my face: bearded, thin, tortured, the eyes burning with a strange fire. I even looked peculiar to myself. And afterward she even had the nerve to rebuke me for considering my lust more important than the child's happiness.

"And didn't you ask who this uncle was? Why he came? And where he suddenly disappeared to? And why you had to see him in the middle of the day? And why he fell on you with kisses?"

"As far as I remember—no. We never mentioned the meeting again. I was a well-trained little girl. I knew that life was full of secrets and that it was better not to ask questions which had no answers. In the end all the riddles would be solved. All you needed was a good memory, that's all."

*L*ast night Nina called. She asked for me. Her voice was calm. As if we had spoken to each other only the day before and there was something she had forgotten to say. The Polish accent was still there. And the melody too. Only the beat, it seemed, was slower. She said she had heard about Nimrod's accident. And she felt the need to say a few words. She knew of similar cases in which people had recovered completely. Afterward she asked after my health and how I was bearing up under the heat. Small talk. And then I asked her if we could meet. Nina paused. As if she was waiting for the sound of my voice to die away. Then she said: Why not? I'll try to come to Tel Aviv. And she asked for Olga again. And Olga said yes, yes, yes a few times. I didn't dare ask what had been arranged. I, too, am a well-trained Soviet citizen. If I'm not told, I don't ask.

I go over and over her words in my head, like a boy after a first lovers' meeting. Every word with its secret signals. What she really wanted to say. What had prevented her from saying it. What she wanted to hear. Perhaps she was trying to hint at something. It was hard for me to imagine her in her world. It would have been easier to see myself in her position, returning to the faith of our fathers. My parents had believed in it, unquestioningly. What they had received from their own parents, they had tried to pass on to their children. They were simple Jews. With God in their hearts. My mother wouldn't have been able to live for a single day without God. She would have gone mad with fear. My father's God was a benevolent Jew. He didn't mind if people didn't believe in Him. Sooner or later they would need Him. My father did not impose his beliefs on us. He only pitied us for being godless in a world so full of cruelties. But Nina! She had been brought up with her mother's milk to hate the benighted "deniers of the light." Her father was proud of his enlightened atheism. He held religious rituals in contempt, mocked priests and rabbis, waged a sacred war on superstition. And she, how she had worshiped that handsome man, with the lion's mane crowning his sculptured head!

For Nina to have thrown in her lot with a crowd of intolerant fanatics, who regarded women as inferior creatures, and damned anyone who thought differently from themselves . . .

I couldn't imagine this sensuous woman, who smiled to herself in secret when she caught anyone looking at her, who loved wearing fine clothes—even in Via Nova, where the cultivation of external appearances was regarded with a certain severity, she had managed to give her rags a fanciful air, as if she were dressed up for a Purim party—covering the crowning glory of her hair with a wig, and hiding her elegant body behind their widow's weeds.

From Olga's stories it appeared that she was strictly observant, in small matters as in great. Was it for love of this man of hers, who despised himself for needing her body? Or was it the security of coming to anchor in a safe harbor at last? I wouldn't be surprised. How much suffering she had known. How frail she must have become over the course of the years. Those who have endured much need a code to conform to. With God or without Him. As long as they are not left to their own devices and obliged to find the answers in their own hearts. They need someone who has the answer to every question. A wise man who knows what is permitted and what is forbidden. Where the borderline lies between good and bad. How to cleanse what has been polluted.

About her stepfather Olga said hardly a word. Perhaps her sense of honor stopped her. My curiosity had to be satisfied with a few meager crumbs. Although she made a nuisance of herself, he treated her with exemplary fairness. He never denied her anything. He tried to make her happy. When they lived in Bnei Brak his presence in the house was hardly felt. He spent all day with his students, in another place. In Jerusalem he had a study in the apartment, lined with books from floor to ceiling. But she rarely crossed its threshold. Except when she helped her mother to dust the precious books. When she was at the girls' boarding school, she hardly ever came home. Then he would sit her down in his study, on the other side of the book- and paper-laden desk, and ask her about her studies. But he never showed much interest in her replies. In any case, it was a matter of no importance to him. He had firm opinions about the kinds of things a woman should know. He never kissed her or stroked her hair, and he seemed to go out of his way to avoid touching her. She had never heard him raise his voice. Not to her or to Nina. He never needed to. A look was enough. Like Rabbi Shimon ben Zakkai, his eyes consumed and annihilated. And her mother obeyed.

One thing astonished me. The man was not a Zionist, and in Germany he had applied for a visa to America. They had come to Israel because their application had been turned down. Not because of him, but because of Nina. Olga couldn't explain why they had been so strict with them. Other rabbis had been granted visas. "Maybe it was because the name Minkovsky was known to them," she surmised.

"Minkovsky?"

"Yes. That was the name mother wrote on her D.P. identity card."

"But why?"

"It never occurred to me to ask," said Olga. "I thought that that was how she was registered in the documents."

Was her need to wipe out all traces of me so overpowering? Or perhaps she wanted to pull the wool over her husband's eyes.

"Perhaps she told him that you were born out of wedlock?" I wondered aloud.

"Why should she have?"

"So that he wouldn't worry about whether I was dead or alive."

"Mother was sure that you had been killed," said Olga.

The man, Zilberstein, also had a son from a previous marriage. Already grown up then, and today the rabbi of a small congregation in Pennsylvania. There were no children of their own. There had been. Two. A boy and a girl. The first had died a few hours after birth and the second a few weeks after. "There's a curse on us," said Nina. And to Olga this was proof that her mother was honestly and truly following in the footsteps of the man she had married.

Today I began to "build my house": I found a drawing table in the basement, Olga bought me drawing instruments and a good pocket computer for a present, and in my spare time, when I'm not busy working on the translations that bring in a few pennies and give me my freedom of movement, I go down to the basement and draw designs.

"All you have to do now is buy a plot of land," said Walter.

It's apparently not considered in poor taste here to mock the poor.

There's a Chinese proverb which says that the minute a man stops building his house, he begins to dig his grave.

A wreath on the grave of the Chinaman, from whom I heard this proverb. He had no house, nor did anyone dig him a grave. He was an old Communist. A member of the Central Committee. He was sent to Moscow to take part in a leadership seminar and accused of espionage. He arrived among us broken and bruised, but full of pride. He had not confessed. To what? Nobody was interested. The rebellion against tyranny had already taken on abstract dimensions.

In Moscow he was a Marxist. In Siberia he reverted to being a Chinaman. He would sit for hours motionlessly contemplating a stone or a bush. As if he could reconstruct his motherland from a single branch, like the Chinese artist practicing painting a feather all his life long, so that when he reaches the evening of his days he will be able to paint a rooster.

His eyes would freeze, as if he had stopped time. His whole life in this one minute. All the storms of time contained within his silence. The whole of the vegetable and animal kingdom in a single blade of grass.

The Chinese believe that a single stone contains the cosmos, just as the Jews believe that a single individual contains the world and the fullness thereof. Another proverb that he liked quoting was: "Whatever you have learned is not yours until you have taught it to others." The lesson of his life. He believed that one day he would return to China to teach others what he had seen on the way from Canton to Norilsk.

He dropped by the wayside, and soft snowflakes fell on his face. No one stopped. Somebody hesitated, and a shot was fired over his head. We went on marching with slow and heavy steps. "One Chinaman less," someone said. "At this very minute another ten thousand are being born." A rough joke instead of a tear. Because the Chinaman was well liked.

Walter glanced at my sketches and admired them. I had taught myself draftsmanship, I told him. In the camp library you could find all kinds of obsolete textbooks. In this way I had learned architecture, structural engineering, draftsmanship, and the history of music. One thing we never lacked there was time, although we worked long hours.

"You're wasting your talents here," Zina Shaverin once said to me in the kitchen at Tel Yosef.

The girls used to cook soup in a huge pot on a wood-fired

stove. Whenever they had to fill the pot with water, they would stand it under the tap next to the stove, and when it was full they would go out to look for two strong men to lift it up and put it on the stove. One day I was summoned to perform this task. I poured the water out of the pot, went to the cowshed and fetched a rubber pipe, attached it to the tap, lifted the empty pot onto the stove, inserted the mouth of the pipe into the pot, and the days of hard labor were over.

Zina Shaverin looked at me admiringly.

"You'll be an engineer one day," she said.

"I'm just lazy," I retorted.

At the same time, however, I was reinforced in the conviction that I had found my vocation. A number of years were to pass before I succeeded in enrolling in a formal course of study, but the school that taught me the most was my incurable tendency to claim to know things that I actually did not know.

Once burned, twice shy. After enduring an initial period of "general labor"—chopping down trees, digging canals, moving earth, etc.; exhausting hard labor which few of those unfortunate enough to spend long periods at survived—I did everything in my power to get out of it. I wasn't exactly proud of the tricks to which I sometimes had to resort to land up in the clinic, or next to the engineers' desk, or in the spare-parts stores instead, but no better way of staying alive was available to me. I can console myself with the thought that I took care of others too. It was not only myself that I saved from the giant mill of "general labor." However, this method—taking on tasks that I was not qualified to perform—often entailed the laborious acquisition of knowledge not easy to come by in the conditions of the camp. Luckily for me, I never got into trouble.

I remember one incident when I was nearly caught red-handed. A diesel engine broke down and there was no mechanic available. I volunteered to fix it. I was then working in timber felling, and I would have been prepared to endure solitary confinement for the chance to take a few days' rest. I had only the dimmest of notions of the workings of a diesel engine. I went

over to it, with the camp commander at my heels. I looked the
machine over with an expert eye while my heart quailed within
me. An obsolete model, I stated. Nobody makes them anymore.
Perhaps we can find some old manual lying around. The order
was given and soon I was in possession of a detailed instruction
manual. Within the space of few hours I had learned, the hard
way, all I needed to know. I was given an assistant, too, a chap
whose knowledge of diesel engines exceeded mine by far, but
who was afraid of being punished if he didn't succeed in getting
it back into working order.

In the same way I learned mining engineering and bridge
construction. Who knows, perhaps at this very moment, somewhere in one of the camps, a work by a contemporary Dostoevsky
is brewing, with a gambler like me for a hero, a man who risks
his life at an engineer's drawing table. In any case, from those
days on I have been possessed by a lust for learning. I study
everything that I can lay my hands on. I have never wiped myself
before reading the piece of paper on both sides.

As soon as I have the time, I intend learning electronics. My
ignorance in this field makes me feel that I'm fifty years behind
the times. I found a thick volume in English here. Which leaves
me no alternative but to polish up the English I learned from the
British spy in the Vladimir jail.

Nina kept her promise. A few days after her call she came to Tel
Aviv.

There is something I have to confess. The details of my
conversation with Nina are recorded on a magnetic tape. Without her knowledge I recorded them. So that I would be able to
listen to them later. I wasn't sure that she would come again.

It took a lot of cunning; I had to find excuses to change the
tape twice during the course of the conversation. But she didn't
notice anything.

The preoccupation with a side issue, worrying about the
hidden tape recorder, stealthy glances at the hand on the dial to
check if the volume was right—all this helped me to maintain

some sort of pretense at composure. Later on, when I played the tapes back, I did not find much of interest in them. Nothing of significance was said. But there was great power in what was left unsaid. And the voice, of course, that deep, melodious voice, which even the cheap tape could not flatten.

Nina did not have to make an effort to maintain her composure. I admire her self-control. She looked right into my eyes without batting an eyelash. As if prompted by some sudden curiosity. Her eyes were as big and astonishingly beautiful as ever. But there was a new firmness in them. As if she wanted to warn me not to make a fool of myself. The flesh of her face was a little puffy, but there were no deep lines in it. Her figure too was remarkably well preserved. I was glad to see that she had seen fit to dress up as elegantly as if she were going to the opera in my honor. But Olga said that she always dressed up when she went out. Like a fashionable matron from some other time and place. Her blue-gray hair fitted her head as closely as a helmet. Maybe it was her own hair.

My outstretched hand was left empty. A strange man. I hadn't forgotten. But I thought that God would have forgiven her if she had let herself go and allowed herself to touch the past.

Olga stayed with us for a few minutes and then left the room. With her departure a chill descended. The words that came out of Nina's mouth were emptier than silence. She asked about Nimrod, with an appropriately mournful expression on her face. She asked about my health and said we should thank the Good Lord that we were alive. In other words, she didn't want to hear any complaints. She asked if there was anything I needed, and when I said I didn't need anything, an expression of genuine happiness crossed her face, for the first and only time. She looked radiant with health and serenity. What she wanted to say was conveyed in the tone of her voice. Her voice, as musical as a tender Russian melody, succeeded in transmitting one clear, unequivocal message: as far as she was concerned, I was buried outside the cemetery fence.

I could only admire the way in which she gave me to understand that she was not interested in hearing about what I had been through without her, and that she would be grateful if I did not ask her any questions about her own life either. She said: Lately one hears so many stories from people coming back from Siberia, and they're all the same.

I could not forgive her for refusing the refreshments offered her by Olga—fresh fruit, tea, and cake—because they were served in china dishes rather than glass. Her own daughter's dishes unclean? But I imagined that she was being so scrupulous in order to underline her message. The mountain looming between us towered to great and terrible heights. We were separated not only by time and distance, but by customs and mores, prohibitions and taboos, pile upon pile of punctilious religious observances. A whole culture.

(I remembered my father and mother. They too were observant Jews. But without false pride and arrogance, without anger against the "lawless." Only sorrow. They too tried to observe as many of the 613 mitzvahs in the Torah as possible. But the concept of "mitzvah," although it came from the same root as "command," was applied by them only to such precepts as were not compulsory. And it seems to me that this is so in popular usage too. Only what is beyond the strict line of the law is a mitzvah. All the rest is compulsory, and taken for granted. In any case, even though the rules of kashrut had a certain priority over the other positive mitzvahs, their God would surely have given them to understand that they were permitted to eat an apple offered them by their daughter.)

Without noticing, we began to talk Russian. The Russian language introduced a certain gentleness into her words. Even the expression on her face changed. The pursed lips, the lips of an offended child, softened. Her Russian was old-fashioned. The suffixes were too soft. She sounded as if she was reciting.

How everything has changed, I thought. Us, the world, even the words. As if they were bowed down by the burden of memories which are no longer shared.

In the middle of the conversation, Olga's son suddenly

came into the room, our soldier grandson. He greeted us politely and went out again. Nina said, "What a charming gentleman." And for a few minutes I was aglow with fatuous joy. I thought that she used the word "gentleman" because of the associations it had for both of us. There was a certain polite monkey in the Izmailovi Zoo that we used to call "the gentleman" in reference to some lines of Chodasevicz that we were fond of reciting:

> I have shaken the hands of beautiful women and poets
> And leaders of the nation; not one of them
> Was as aristocratic in every line!
> Not one of them touched my palm
> With so brotherly a touch! And God's my witness,
> No human being into my eyes
> Looked thus, so wisely and profoundly,
> A look into the fathomless depths of the soul.

We would stop at "fathomless depths of the soul" and look into each other's eyes with limitless love. This foreign word, "gentleman," in a heavy Russian accent, was like the seal of a secret pact. Sometimes we rolled it on our tongues in the company of strangers, referring to our love, of which they were ignorant. . . . But this time, it seemed, the word had slipped out of Nina's mouth without any intention of the kind. She thought it in poor taste for me to bring up the Izmailovi Zoo. What could I be thinking of?!

Afterward she told me that she had been so shocked by her father's execution that she could not speak for a month. It was then that she had made up her mind to return to Poland. It was in 1944, and everyone predicted that after the war Poland would be under Russian influence. She hoped that they would open the borders and allow her to return to the land of her birth.

I found it strange that she should see fit to tell me this. It amounted, after all, to an admission that she had had no intention of waiting for me. I said nothing. What did it matter now exactly when she had decided to break off relations with me? Suddenly she asked me about Galina Nikolayevna and Yefim. I was very surprised. I had no idea that she knew about the episode in question. The miserable meeting on my way to the front took on a new meaning. The revenge of a woman with a grudge. She had not hesitated to take her revenge on me, even though I was on my way from Siberia to the western front. She had not even thought that I deserved to know what I was being punished for. And she still had the nerve to blame me for not taking the child's feelings into account.

I said nothing. I adopted her own superior attitude toward sins made obsolete by the law of limitations. She spoke about Galina Nikolayevna and Yefim as if they were characters in a story that had nothing to do with her. They were mentioned only in passing, in order to clarify a point: why she had considered that she was entitled to plan her return to Poland without taking me into account. There was a relaxed expression on her face, but she couldn't fool me. The tension was apparent in her fingers which were tightly locked together. She was pleased with the way the meeting had gone. She had expected worse. I had not been aggressive, or made the slightest attempt at emotional blackmail, except for the remark about the monkey in the Moscow zoo, which seemed to her completely out of context. Nina saw that she could rely on me. There was no danger of anonymous letters to her husband from my quarter. Nor did my occupation pose a threat. A translator from Hebrew into Russian was not likely to make a lot of enemies. And nevertheless there was a feeling of unfinished business in the air. The meeting had not solved anything. We had seen each other, learned what had changed, and what had not changed. And so? We were still tied together by an indissoluble bond.

In a moment of goodwill, after we had spoken kindly of departed friends, I asked her: "And now, what?" For a moment she thought that I wanted to set a date for another meeting. She embarked on a long explanation of all the difficulties in which this would involve her. I cut her short. This was not what I had

had in mind. The question was: How could I set her free of me entirely? As far as I was concerned, I said, this formality did not bother me in the least. But in her world, among the people she knew . . .

Nina looked at me coldly.

"Our marriage is not valid," she said. "And there is thus no need for a divorce."

For a moment I was full of rage. "What do you mean, not valid? Because we never got married according to the Law of Moses and Israel?"

"Yes."

"In other words, from their point of view you are permitted even to a Cohen . . . and I simply never existed at all?"

My irony made no impression on her. But when I added, "In that case, why was it necessary to sweep me under the rug?" she tensed, although she held her tongue.

"Until you learned the laws you must have entangled yourself in a pretty web of lies," I said.

She looked at me with an expression that grew more indifferent from one moment to the next. "And why should I have lied?"

"So that people would think you were a widow. To avoid complications. To be on the safe side."

"I never lied. I was *certain* that you had been executed," she said calmly.

"You were *certain*? . . ."

"I even saw a certificate confirming it."

"A certificate? Who could have shown you any such certificate?"

"Leopold."

"The Pole?"

I never succeeded in getting to the bottom of Leopold Sherrer.

He was the editor of a Polish journal. A tall, frail man with sparse hair and skinny arms, and exceptionally refined manners. Interested in Yiddish literature, he would visit the editorial office, rummage about in the archives, and engage in polemics with the poets. Once he came down to the printing press to look for something. Since we had already met at Minkovsy's, we got into conversation. After that he made it into a habit to drop in to visit me. We became friends—to the extent that it was possible to make friends with a stranger in those suspicious days. He flattered me, calling me "the philosopher of the lead cauldron." And this was nothing to be sneezed at, for he himself was a graduate of the Institute of Philosophy. The Polish-speakers were lavish in their praises: his essays on aesthetics were philosophical gems.

In the course of time he fell into the habit of accompanying me home. He would kiss Nina's hand, pat Olga on the head, and take his leave. Nina was truly lovely in those days. Blooming, gay, always excited. If she heard a concert, read a book, saw something in the street—she had to share her experiences with others. Leopold Sherrer would listen to her and nod his head. He never flirted with her. He never gave her admiring looks, made ambiguous remarks, or showed her any special deference. The wife of a friend.

Sometimes he made us little gifts. He was an inexhaustible font of smoked sausages, rare cheeses, Polish vodka, and theater tickets. But his great love was music. Nina and "the Pole," as they called him at the paper, found a common language. He always succeeded in obtaining tickets to popular concerts which we could never have afforded on our own. Here the nobility of the man made itself apparent. He made a point of inviting us both, turn by turn. Since he was a bachelor, he always had an extra ticket.

I was not naive. I suspected that he was in love with Nina. And that he only invited me as a cover for his true feelings. But I had no fears on his score. Nina, who respected his knowledge and enjoyed his company, could never have fallen in love with someone like him. He was too smooth and smarmy, and he talked too much, she said. But as an escort to a concert, he was a walking music lesson. I imagined that Nina was an open book to me. Her integrity and her arrogance would never allow her to become involved in a trivial love affair with a conceited peacock. I noted, too, that he always took care to bring her home straight after the concert. They never stayed out to eat. He would bring the delicacies back with him and the three of us would feast together. The two of us, actually. He would lecture, analyze the performance, the music, its period, etc.—and we would guzzle.

My musical knowledge was extremely limited. But there was no other form of entertainment available. Perhaps I also did it to annoy—I never once gave up my turn. He would escort me in style to Tchaikovsky Hall, where he had countless acquaintances, to whom he would always introduce me as the best of his friends. He included me in their learned conversations as if I were one of them.

I was repelled by his sentimentality and the highfalutin tone of his speech. But this was a punishment to which I willingly submitted. Sometimes he would waste his most brilliant ideas on my deaf ears. I imagined that he expounded them to Nina, too. I was presumably the audience for the dress rehearsal.

I remember, once he took me to a chamber concert. A Schubert quintet. The music was exquisite—there's no denying that. Quiet and moving, filling the soul with good intentions. But I could see no cause for tears. In Moscow, in 1936, there were plenty of good reasons to weep. Anyone who had survived that crossing with dry eyes had no right to blubber over Schubert. But Leopold Sherrer wept like an insulted child. In the intermission he actually sobbed on my shoulder. How noble! How divine! And how immoral!

"Immoral!" I exclaimed.

Not that it made any difference to me. But I had to give him an opening. I imagined that he was busy hatching some original idea. And politeness obliged me to help my benefactor put his thoughts in order.

With a martyred expression on his face he pointed an accusing finger at the musicians:

"How is it possible—at a time like this! In Central Asia,

children are dying of starvation. Destitute peasants are roaming the roads. In Siberia, old women are freezing to death. And they sit there and produce otherwordly sounds from their violins. Look at them! White-breasted ravens. In their black suits, white waistcoats, bow ties. People without a conscience taking pleasure in a strong vibrato, a fine passage. It's a disgrace!"

And then, as if alarmed at his own words:

"The kulaks have only themselves to blame. How is it possible to stop progress!"

But he suffered anyway.

"And them with their Stradivarii. Taking bows. Happy. Shame on them!"

"You know what?" I said to him. "Next time let's go to the circus."

He patted my shoulder affectionately. "Now I understand why Nina loves you."

In his eyes I was the People, the popular wisdom of the Jew, the philosophy hidden in the lead before it was set into letters.

Sometimes I was afraid for him. He talked too much for his own good. To hint at the fate of the kulaks took real boldness. I wouldn't have dared. But he came out of all the purges unscathed. As far as I know, his journal was the only one in Moscow whose editor remained unchanged for twelve years. He always had money, too, and nobody knew where it came from. Flawlessly dressed, a flower in his buttonhole, his feet shod in two-tone black-and-white shoes from abroad, gleaming like the onion domes of St. Basil's Church on a sunny day.

He was a past master at the art of organizing the impossible. He slithered like a worm through the cracks in the bureaucracy and succeeded in penetrating everywhere. He had all kinds of connections: government officials, clergy, artists, Gypsies, spiritualists, stamp collectors. And presumably, in the secret police too. But the latter was not a sufficient reason for cutting off contact with him. I was obliged to resign myself to his leech-like friendship. The inevitable fate of a man with a beautiful wife.

In any case, if he was close to the authorities, it didn't do us any harm. His connections were usually exploited to help his friends. Including us. Not only that—once he saved me from real trouble.

One evening Swersky, a comrade from the Via Nova commune, pounced on me in the street, next to the printing press. He was wild-eyed, disheveled, and confused. He seized me by the arm, with unnecessary force—although I had no intention of avoiding him—and pulled me into a dark alley. The stupid tricks of a greenhorn. If a policeman had seen us, he would have arrested us both on the spot, without asking any questions.

"Is there anywhere where we can talk?" he whispered in a voice frantic with agitation.

"Anywhere at all."

Swersky was appalled by my composure. He pricked up his ears. He tried to decipher the hidden notes in my voice. Was it simply the complacency of a fool? They hadn't touched me and so I imagined that everything around me was normal. Or perhaps I was one of them myself? The loud answer was a kind of threat. In another moment the label would be waved in my face, and then the handcuffs: a spreader of slanders.

In those days I really and truly believed that all this was exaggerated. The police were tough—so what? Were we to allow lawless elements to endanger a historical opportunity? I knew courteous policemen. Minkovsky's neighbor in the apartment house was a high-up officer, an exemplary family man, discreet and tactful. I had seen a moving film about the beneficial work of the police among homeless youths. I accepted this too—that if the job was necessary and I could not do it myself, it was my duty at least to respect those who did. I thought that Swersky was putting on an act of persecuted innocence in order to make me feel sorry for him. I imagined that he lacked a pass and was presumably about to ask me for shelter.

I felt harassed and embarrassed. I couldn't take him home to our apartment. We were living three in a room. With another family behind the screen. We shared a kitchen with three other families. The caretaker was strict and suspicious. And all the residents had agreed not to bring in guests without a general consensus.

But I couldn't abandon him to his fate either. My conscience would not allow me to reject a man in trouble. Never mind a comrade from Via Nova.

"Can we go inside?"

Swersky's eyes darted about. He bowed his head. He looked over my shoulder and pressed up to me. Like an underground fighter in an old-fashioned Soviet film. With dramatic, heroic gestures.

The kiosk was open. I bought him a bottle of buttermilk and an egg sandwich. I poured myself a glass of tea. I wiped the damp oilcloth on an unoccupied table, not too near or too far from the counter. I sat him down with a flourish, like a man offering hospitality to a welcome guest. I tried to wipe out the conspiratorial impression with which he had opened our encounter. I hoped that he would not make himself too conspicuous. I tried to create the impression that he was a poor, unknown poet from some remote province, with a friend in the printing press who had promised to help him get his poems published in the paper. But Swersky was too frightened to take any notice of my hints.

"And here—can we talk?"

He leaned over the table so that his words would reach my ears alone, but his voice came out in a loud, shrill whistle. Luckily for me there were only four or five people in the kiosk, and none of them turned to look at us.

"Out with it, for God's sake! I don't remember you as a man who was afraid of his own shadow."

"My own shadow . . ." He gave me a reproachful look. "Wait until you hear what I have to say."

What he had to say did, indeed, give me a nasty shock.

After they had forced the Tatars and Ukrainians on Via Nova, and the commune was no longer what it had been, he had decided to leave. He had wandered from one town to another, doing all kinds of odd jobs and escaping when his lack of papers was discovered. In the end he got sick and tired of this way of life

and decided to infiltrate into Moscow, where he had a number
of old friends from Via Nova. He was sure to find a refuge with
one of them until he could obtain the necessary papers. But he
was wrong. None of them dared to take him in. For a few days
he roamed the streets, sleeping in all kinds of strange places, a
toy shop storeroom among the woolen bears, movie theaters, a
wine cellar, the zoo—until the police caught up with him. He
thought that the worst that could happen would be some form
of punishment and deportation back to where he had come
from. But things turned out differently. After a week in solitary
confinement, he was summoned to an interrogation. Opposite
him sat a crude, sharp-tongued brute, who knew Hebrew and
Yiddish, and who offered him a deal: in return for helping
them to convict Elkind he would be given permission to stay in
Moscow.

"Convict him! How?"

"Nothing could be easier," said Swersky.

"And did you agree?"

"What a question!"

"And you're not ashamed?"

Swersky gave me a half-contemptuous, half-pitying look.

"What do you think?"

"What can I think?"

"And what do you think I've come to ask you for? Elkind's
address?"

"I don't know."

"Neither do I."

The whole thing was a mystery to me. But it appeared that
they hadn't given him Elkind's address. They were afraid that if
he turned up out of the blue at a confidential address it would
make Elkind suspicious. They were planning an apparently
chance encounter. The next day they were going to take him to
a point nearby soon before the hour that Elkind usually left the
house. In the meantime they had given him a twenty-four-hour
pass and a bed in a hostel for the night. Presumably in order to
persuade him that they kept their promises.

"And how can I help you?"

"I don't want to go back to the hostel."

Swersky was looking for a place to sleep for one night. And he also asked me to help him escape from Moscow at dawn.

"How? On foot? By train?"

"I don't know yet. I've come to ask your advice."

At that moment I saw the Pole. He was sitting at the other end of the kiosk and reading a manuscript. He did not appear to have seen us at all. But the minute I recognized him, he caught my eye. He got up and came to stand next to our table.

"You need help, I see."

It wasn't a question. It was a statement. Swersky's shoulders shook. I indicated to him that he could trust the man. But he was not required to repeat his story. Leopold Sherrer did not show the least interest in Swersky. From a distance he had seen that *I* was upset, and he had come to help *me*.

"You go home," he said to me. "Nina will be waiting for you. I'll look after your friend."

I was beside myself with gratitude.

"Friends help one another," he said to me in Polish, of which I knew only a few words.

The plan was for Swersky to spend the night at Sherrer's place, and the next morning the latter would take him in a friend's car to the Prioberzhanski Market, and from there he would be smuggled out of the city in one of the trucks that had unloaded its produce, and transported to a place where nobody knew him.

Two days later I met Leopold Sherrer.

"Is everything all right?"

He made a circle with his thumb and forefinger. In other words: plain sailing. He intimated that I shouldn't inquire about the details. The less I knew, the better it would be for me.

Swersky never bothered me again. I told Nina that the Pole was a true friend, without going into details. What Sherrer had said applied to her too. Nina agreed with me. In times like these, she said, there weren't many people to whom you could entrust a secret without fear of betrayal. I would have been happier if she hadn't said it. But that was the price I paid for my chivalrous remark.

What an idiot I was! I still didn't understand that I had given myself into his hands, for better or for worse. You have to be a real simpleton, a trusting fool, to involve yourself in a conspiracy with a man who lusts after your wife.

Even during my interrogation, when I was suddenly asked about Swersky, I still didn't suspect Leopold Sherrer. The police had many ways of finding out what they wanted to know. I couldn't believe that he had handed him over to the authorities and then come to me for my thanks. There was no room in my photograph album yet for characters of such duplicity. I thought that if Swersky had been caught because of him, he would presumably have kept out of my way. And in any case, a man who cried at concerts was incapable of doing anything so wicked.

Today I know better. Nina's story cleared up the episode at the printing press. And not only that. Many mysteries were illuminated.

A new light was shed on acts, gestures, words. And everything connected up into one web.

The man who was capable of producing a death certificate for someone who was still alive had presumably had no hesitations about clearing his path to her of lower obstacles. Her conscience, for example.

When I try to understand how Nina knew about my love affair with Galina Nikolayevna, I can only assume that here too Leopold Sherrer played a part.

We were so careful that even Galina's closest friends knew nothing about me. Not because of any prudishness on Galina's part. She was a free woman and had no reason to hide anything. It was purely out of scrupulousness and respect for Nina's honor that Galina agreed to the underground conditions which weighed heavily on her heart. I too shared her distress, but I could not make up my mind—up to now Nina, and from now on

Galina. In my heart of hearts I knew that this was not the kind of abyss into which a man casts himself with his eyes closed. More than this love existing in its own right, it was a cure for a wound. A scratch that Nina's nail had unknowingly made in my soul. One day I would be cured and I would have no further need of it.

Galina was modest in her expectations and content with the fact that the man she loved bestowed his favors on her. It is reasonable to assume that she did not boast of this poor gift. There was every reason to believe that our secret was well kept.

And nevertheless, there was someone who knew.

Someone who had access to confidential documents read gossip in them too. Detectives never dismiss even the smallest crumb of information. Affairs of the heart, too, are conscientiously filed away. You can never know when they might come in useful. In the absence of weightier evidence, the prosecution could always argue that a man who betrayed his wife was likely to betray his country as well.

One night, after a concert, Sherrer forced an intimate conversation on me. He usually avoided this. A minefield. A man who is in love with your wife does not chatter about women or use obscenities in your presence. This time, however, under the cover of the darkness, he saw fit to warn me. Rumors of relations with a girl who worked in a toy shop had come to the ears of the Party. Although it was none of the Party's business, of course, it would be wise to be careful. Flighty characters were not to be trusted. And if I had any ambitions—it might do me harm. A friendly word of advice.

He spoke like a civilized man of the world. Without a trace of self-righteous reproach, without any cant about "taking advantage of an innocent girl" or similar clichés. He spoke politely and matter-of-factly. He remarked that he could understand me— a man who was married to "the perfect woman" was liable to feel a "primal urge" for the society of an "ordinary mortal," to see if he was capable of "giving, too, and not only receiving. . . ." But nevertheless. We had to remember that "society judged us in its own terms . . . It did not pardon what a man pardoned himself. . . ." And similar enlightened remarks. I was surprised at the time that he said nothing about the insult to Nina. As if to imply that a superior creature like Nina could not be hurt by a nonentity like me. Just as God is not insulted if people don't believe in Him. He worshiped her to such an extent!

Now that I recall that conversation, I understand its purpose. Clearly, he had no intention of "warning" me so that I would mend my ways. I could have drowned in a bog for all he cared. But in his scenario there was no room for inconsequential events. The philosopher in him was delighted to see how one thing led to another, with not even a single gesture made in vain.

He knew that I would soon be arrested. He intended telling Nina that I had another woman. The timing too was shrewdly chosen. A few days after the arrest, as something which had been disclosed during the course of interrogation. By then it was no secret that he had connections in those quarters. If Nina took it hard and sent angry letters to me in jail—I would not suspect him of giving me away. He had specifically said that "rumors had reached the Party." In other words, people knew and there was gossip. As for the man who had taken the trouble to warn me in confidence—he would be the last one I would suspect of betraying my secret to my wife.

Why should it have mattered to him if I trusted him or not? People come back from jail. And what if they failed to convict me of espionage? He might need my friendship one day. In the Russia of those days no one made enemies if he could help it. You never could tell. Fortunes were liable to change overnight.

If Nina reacted in the way he expected—in other words, realized that her scruples were unjustified and felt that she was no longer bound to a convict who was unworthy of her—so much the better. His warning would only reflect credit on him. He had given me a chance, like the chivalrous gentleman he was, to mend my ways. He had tried to save a family from ruin and I had not taken his advice.

After he had given it, there was a long silence.

"If you're angry with me for interfering in your affairs, I apologize. Forget everything I've said," said Sherrer and put his hand placatingly on my shoulder.

"I'm not in the least angry," I said. "On the contrary, I thank you for your frankness. But what can I do? I don't think I can break off relations brutally, from one day to the next. Love affairs of this kind usually come to an end of their own accord as soon as some obstacle crops up . . ."

"Love that collapses the moment it encounters an obstacle," said Sherrer, mimicking my voice, "is not love."

I did not realize then that it was himself he was talking about.

The next day I brought the subject up in conversation with Olga.

"Where did you live after your grandfather was executed?" I asked her.

"I think I've already told you. All over the place—a week here, a month somewhere else. Until we received the permit to go to Poland we didn't have a permanent place to stay."

"And the permit—did you obtain it without difficulty?"

"Without difficulty? Nothing was done without difficulty in those days. You had to beg and plead, run around, look for influential friends to plead your case for you . . ."

"After they shot your grandfather you still had influential friends? I'm surprised to hear it."

And then Olga remembered the Pole. She couldn't remember his name. But it was enough for me.

"Yes, there was some Pole who helped us a lot."

As she spoke she remembered that for a while they had even lived in his apartment. And when they went to Poland, he accompanied them to the border.

Olga was displeased when I asked her "what kind of friendship" had existed between her mother and "the Pole." How should she know? She was a child of twelve, and if there had been any intimate connection they must have done all they could to conceal it from her. Girls of that age can be very spiteful. Although she hadn't been in the least inquisitive then. She was glad to have a roof over her head and food to eat, and she hadn't troubled herself about where they came from.

"They didn't take me into their confidence," she said with a trace of irony. "As far as I remember they didn't behave like a married couple. They hardly ever went out together. And when there were visitors, mother (you know her) behaved as if the apartment belonged to us and he was some kind of servant or janitor . . ."

But after a moment she remembered that the man had not "accompanied them to the border," as she had previously stated, but had intended coming with them to Warsaw.

"And why didn't he?"

"I don't know. Everything was so strange. At the border station two policemen entered the carriage. After glancing at our papers, they asked him to come with them. A formality, he would be right back, they said to mother. They were very polite. But he didn't come back. The train left without him. His luggage remained with us."

"And mother? How did she react when he didn't come back?"

"The questions you ask!" said Olga. "How do you expect me to remember? I was occupied with myself. With leaving Russia. With escaping from the people who had killed grandfather and caused grandma's death. I couldn't wait to be in Warsaw, which mother had described as a paradise on earth. If you could have seen that paradise!"

For a moment she was overwhelmed by her memories.

"Funny that I don't remember mother's reaction at all. Do you think that he was her lover? In any case, if the sudden, mysterious disappearance of the Pole affected her, she must have done her best to prevent me from sensing anything. You know what she's like. She can be soft and gentle. But in moments of crisis she's as hard as flint."

How strange to think that so large a part in the events that overwhelmed our lives in those years was played by the schemes of one man, who coveted my wife.

But when I think of his sweet smile, of the sly twinkle in his sharp eyes, which were always fixed on some imaginary spot at the top of your forehead, I believe that he was capable of it. He was clever, elusive, cunning as a devil, and he enjoyed fishing in deep waters He was in love with dramatic gestures and with plotting true-life dramas in the role of a character acting behind the scenes. The Polish journal was only a cover. He had a secret role that enabled him to play whatever part he wished in other people's lives.

History provided him with a period perfectly adapted to his character and his talents. The era in question has been given many names. Some have characterized it as chaos, some as a time of Sturm und Drang, and others as the beginning of a bureaucratic hardening of the arteries. The "cult of the personality" was blamed. As opposed to these, there were some who saw it as the crashing of utopia on the rocks of reality. In either event, necessary evil and natural evil found a wide scope for their activities in it. And in any case, it was a time which prepared the ground for people like him to grow and flourish.

A belated pain pierced my mind as it suddenly occurred to me that perhaps they had only remained in their seats in Tchaikovsky Hall until the intermission. . . . And they had heard the other half of the concert in his room, over the radio, in one another's arms. . . . They had dressed themselves hastily to the sounds of the final chords, put on their shoes during the applause, and arrived at our apartment a few minutes after the end of the concert. And afterward he would sit modestly at the little table in the hall, drinking glass after glass of tea, and speak with great knowledge and profound emotion about music, orchestras, conductors. . . . With the finest, most delicate distinctions. He could speak for two hours at a stretch about the popular motifs in baroque music without repeating the same idea once. . . .

What made me so sure that she was incapable of loving a man like him? Because he was frail and soft? Perhaps that was what attracted her. He was sensitive, intelligent, and refined. She already had a he-man in bed. What she presumably lacked were caressing words, enchanting, lubricating words, intimate words that touched the heart. All I could talk about were things that you could design and construct. I must have bored her to tears.

I remember the bored look she gave me when I boasted to her of refusing the post in the Comintern which her father had made such efforts to obtain for me. "I didn't return to Russia to sit in an office," I said to her. "I want to be a worker. To build socialism with my own hands."

"You're studying engineering," she said, "and that's a kind of office job too."

The closest things to poetry that I ever said were said then. In passionate words I described to her the feelings of a man who draws something on a piece of paper and a few years later walks over it to cross a seething river. The most beautiful thing in the world, in my eyes, was a suspension bridge. At that moment she almost loved me.

I never brought her flowers, as he did, except on the day that Olga was born. I couldn't drop the names, as he did, of musicians, actors, poets, and ballet dancers met the night before at the theater, or lunched with at a restaurant. . . .

My hands clench into fists of their own accord when I think that on the day of my arrest, when all our friends and acquaintances shunned our home as if we had the plague, he was the only one who came to sympathize and console. His courage did not go unappreciated. The Polish language should erase with loathing from its vocabulary the hypocritical words he said to her then, his hand resting, with affection and respect, on her shoulder. I suppose he was careful not to touch her breast, this time, out of respect for her sorrow. . . .

As long as I was in jail in Moscow, when she came to the prison on Thursdays, the day appointed for her visits, Leopold Sherrer accompanied her, our guardian angel. . . . He wrote our tragedy, and he was constantly there on location when it was filmed. He took the shots, directed, edited, and added a soundtrack of his own.

Better not to dwell on it. Astonishment and rage at the holy innocence of a decent woman. He brought her a forged death certificate; she didn't ask any questions. She glanced at it, passed the back of her hand over the corner of her eye, and moved into his apartment. Maybe she needed comfort. A few weeks earlier her father had made an impassioned protest. The Red Army was standing by while the Germans slaughtered the Poles rising up against them in Warsaw. They gave him a quick trial. A veteran Communist, a candidate for the leadership, was taken out and shot like a common crook. Her mother killed herself soon after. Perhaps Nina needed to weep in her mother tongue.

I was an unimportant bit player in the drama of her life. A death certificate wiped me out. Her sins were washed white as snow. The man who had stood by her side at the worst moments of her life deserved a reward for his devotion. Her past weaknesses received a post factum justification in the light of his exalted virtues. What may once have seemed an ignoble surrender to her baser instincts was now transformed into a profound moral alliance, more valid and enduring than any marriage certificate signed by a rabbi, priest, or judge.

It is not completely out of the question that Leopold Sherrer had a hand in the fall of old Minkovsky too. Thus he ensured her dependence on him. There is no proof, however. And there never will be.

"Shakespeare could never have written a Soviet tragedy," Larissa Verchinsky once wrote me. "It would have been beyond the power of his imagination." She was referring to something else, of course, something private. And she never knew Leopold Sherrer. But she must have come across someone like him in the course of her experience. The power which the Soviet regime bestowed on those who walked in darkness sharpened in their dark souls the kind of cunning and talent for survival required by the intriguing princes of a medieval court.

The end of Leopold Sherrer is a chapter in socialist realism. A knave may play a positive role. But he may not be rewarded. He too was only a supporting character in the story of others. His role was over and his hour had come. Poetic justice was done. This far, devil, and no farther! You satisfied your lust. But there are no happy endings for devils. Politely he was requested to get off the train. The end of the story for you, Comrade Sherrer. A peaceful life in the city of your birth with the woman you love is not written in your stars.

In the train, with her daughter, who does not notice anything, Nina makes her exit from Leopold Sherrer's story with dry eyes.

But perhaps I judge her too harshly. Perhaps she was afraid to cry. Poland, too, was ruled by the people who had executed her father. She dared to cry only when she reached Germany. And then she chose to lean on the shoulder of a man who could promise her peace of mind. The peace of waking up in the morning with the taste of foulness in her mouth and saying, "Blessed is He who made me according to His will."

She would have to bathe in a ritual bath of boiling water in order to purify herself of the foulness which clung to her when she coupled with the devil.

*I*t won't be long before I have to leave my daughter's home and stand on my own feet. I am waiting for a one-room apartment to fall vacant in Finesod House, where, for some reason or other, I have been promised a roof over my head. The Jewish Agency official, Perlmutter, is not forthcoming about the reasons for my good fortune. Finesod House is an old-age home, but only for those still capable of taking care of their own needs. "Fall vacant" is a euphemism. Someone will presumably have to die in order for me to obtain a place of my own.

I wish him a good, long life. But I am already becoming impatient. And not because I am not well treated in my daughter's home. They treat me very well. My mother used to say: "Grandma to stay—jam every day;/Grandpa to stay—fights night and day." But we are civilized people and we never fight. Olga suffers all my eccentricities with forbearance. She never says That's not how we do things here. But I always know when she's thinking it. The young people ignore my existence. I can't complain of their manners. It would be unreasonable to expect them to fall in love with me. They don't understand my language. My accent amuses them and it is to their credit that they don't burst out laughing in my face. My stories are of no interest to them. They are too young to understand that my trials and tribulations are the history of their lives. Up to the age of twenty a person wants to escape his father's fate. At the age of forty he understands that his son's life is bound up with his father's. At the age of seventy he begins to take an interest in his grandfather. If I could afford to buy them presents, perhaps they would feel obliged to listen to my stories in return. But there's nothing I can give them. Their parents have spoiled them and they lack for nothing.

I can't complain about Walter either. He behaves toward me now with greater civility. Even the irony that used to infest his voice like a kind of chronic hoarseness sometimes disappears. This too is a mark of civilized behavior—to show respect for the sorrow of others. The kinds of sorrow which I suffered in the past are apparently not considered worthy of respect. Perhaps he is incapable of understanding the sorrow of a man whose spiritual world caves in around him. Perhaps he considers that all the calamities that fell to my lot in Russia were only what I deserved. The just deserves of the wicked. As if to say: What right does a disillusioned Communist have to demand sympathy from us, who were never infected by that bug?

In any case, recently he even strikes up a conversation with me from time to time. And one day, when Olga was away, he even took me out to have dinner in a restaurant. He spent a vast sum on me, presumably on his expense account. He was in a boisterous, jolly mood. He told the waiters off. Ordered drinks and sent them back. He even talked to himself when he was already a little drunk. I looked at him while he was eating. He raised the plate from the table and shoveled the food into his mouth with quick, short movements. His fork collected all the scraps, scooped them into a lump, and thrust it into his mouth with the deft, careful movement of a surgeon. I asked him if he had ever been in jail. He gave me an approving look. As if he was suddenly seeing me in a new light. You've got a perceptive eye, he said. He had been in jail for a short time, during the British Mandate. But his experience of hunger came from a poor kibbutz where he had stayed as a boy, as a ward of Youth Aliyah.

I thought that I could now understand why he would be glad when I moved out of my room. He had built it like that on purpose—isolated, shut off. A corner of his own. A place where he could seclude himself even from his own family, a kind of shrine where Walter Shaefer could do homage to Evyatar Sheffer, remember the days of his poverty, and celebrate his success.

Walter was the second son of a Hamburg property owner. In his youth he was apparently recalcitrant. His father did not consider him fit to inherit an economic empire and intended it for his elder brother. There was some kind of quarrel at home and he was sent to Palestine with Youth Aliyah, as if into banishment, to endure hardships, improve his character, and then come back and know how to appreciate his advantages. At that time they were still under the impression that Hitler was a passing phenomenon. In the end nothing was left of the family property. His parents and brother emigrated to the United States, where fortune did not smile on them. Walter left the kibbutz resolved to make money. It was his dream to support his father. But in the meantime the War of Independence broke out. And after it was over he stayed on in the regular army. He did well there, but he could not afford to help his father, who was eking out a living as a janitor in a community center. By the time he had left the army and made a fortune, there was no one of his family left to help.

On the kibbutz the youths from Youth Aliyah lived four to a room—a wooden hut under a blazing tin roof. I could understand the longing for privacy which came into being there. Like my own. In a different place. When I left, his dream would come true. And the sooner the better.

With all the sympathy I can feel for him, the less opportunity we have to rub each other up the wrong way, the better. He may think that disillusionment with the Soviet Union has shown me up as an empty vessel, and that I have forfeited the right to hold any opinions of my own. But what can I do if I am still stubborn enough to insist on voicing an opinion once in a while—whether he likes it or not? Not only that, there are some things which are simply beyond my comprehension. I cannot comprehend, for example, how an intelligent person like him, who even reads an occasional book, can believe today, at the beginning of the last quarter of the twentieth century, that the rich are rich by the grace of God.

I quickly lose patience when I meet a man who thinks that the status quo is right. When he prattles on about free enterprise and the laws of the market, a shiver runs down my spine. All the sacrifices of my generation were in vain. If I were to tell him that I am not at all sure that every penny in his bank account got there by honest means, even if he did not break the law, he would think that I had taken leave of my senses. That I had neither forgotten anything, nor learned anything.

I hold my tongue. The silence of a man who eats the bread of charity. As if I were obliged to choose between my views and my family. When I have a place of my own, I will be able to hold on to both.

A visit to Tel Aviv. On the way, between the university and the historical museum, among the plastered and whitewashed new-looking brick houses, the greenish wall of an old Arab house suddenly peeped out. A house with arched windows and a big veranda overlooking the Yarkon River. A kind of greeting from the time when I used to walk here barefoot.

Sheikh Munis has been obliterated by the new buildings, and not a trace remains of its hedges, its vineyards and orchards. Here, not far from the place where the dome of the museum looms now, stood a sabra patch and a solitary cypress tree, next to which my clandestine meetings with Anton took place.

Anton was a Christian Arab, a recent convert to communism, our liaison with the "revolutionary cell" in the district from Summeil to Abu Kishk. He was a university graduate who had studied law in Beirut and visited Moscow twice. His devotion to the Party was beyond question, but in his narrow mustache, his European clothes which underlined his foreignness in the Arab villages, there was a dandyishness unsuited to a professional revolutionary. His attitude to the Jewish comrades in the Party was not free of a certain ambivalence. He admired the way in which they allowed their heads to rule their hearts, but after we had become friends he admitted to me that he did not know if he himself would be able to be a member of a Party which did not recognize the national rights of his people. These words gave rise to painful feelings in me, as if he were accusing me of being a traitor to my people.

I went to Efros and he put me right. There was no contradiction, he explained to me, between national sentiments and Communist vocation. On the contrary, when we opposed the "Zionist adventure" we were concerned first and foremost with the welfare of our own people. The revolution would solve the problem of the Jews—a people dispersed among the nations of the world—but until the revolution reached the Middle East and until the Arabs joined the family of enlightened nations, this tiny Jewish community, which did not shrink from dispossessing the toiling Arab masses of their land, would be the first victim of the chaos to come. It was well known, said Efros, that the Arabs were savages. . . .

I walked about the north of the city like a complete foreigner. I looked at the faces of the people hurrying through the streets and it seemed to me that they were staring at me because of my peculiar clothes. It began to rain and I went into Walter's office. A whole floor in an office building. Walter welcomed me with demonstrative politeness and introduced me to his staff. Since he himself was busy, he asked one of the staff to show me the modern office equipment. The young man, graduate of an American university, treated me like a provincial relation on a visit to the big city. He expected me to be full of admiration for all I saw. He showed me the terminal of a computer and was disappointed when I failed to stare at it openmouthed. Since Russian technology lagged behind the West, I was treated with a certain contempt as if I, too, was an inferior product of Soviet manufacture. In the end I could not restrain myself and said: "How, in your opinion, do they manage to send spaceships into space there? By a court order?"

When the rain stopped I took a bus to Hess Street. I could still recognize a few of the buildings there, and for the first time I felt like a person who has come home. With heartfelt emotion, I stood outside a building that I had built with my own hands. Built and not finished. When the contractors found out who I was, they fired me on the spot. No one protested and no one was even indignant. Working-class solidarity did not apply to Communists.

The building looked as if it had not been touched since then, and was in need of urgent renovations. Here and there the plaster was peeling, and the balcony railings were rusty. The shutters were closed and the plants in the rectangular concrete planters next to the railings on the third floor were dry and dusty. Thin reddish-yellow stems like copper wire dangled from the planters and waved in the wind. It seemed that the people who lived there no longer went out to the balcony to look at the sea and the casino. On the left-hand balcony on the third floor there was a pile of junk covered with a gray cloth.

When I fell from that balcony I landed on a pile of sand and was only slightly bruised. Daniel learned every possible lesson from this incident. First, we were at war with the contractors who were prepared to risk the lives of their workers to make a profit; second, the Labor Federation was not prepared to protect the working class—building the country was more important to them than the interests of the worker.

I went into the lobby. Dilapidated mailboxes, their doors hanging open. Nameplates of lawyers. A dentist. A notary. I went up to the third floor. A lawyers' office. The door opened, and a stylishly dressed girl peered at me with a look of alarm.

"Are you looking for us, sir?"

I was covered with confusion. "I built this building," I said.

She retreated, closing the door softly behind her.

"Some weirdo," she said in a stage whisper.

A man came out. He impaled me with a sharp look, decided that I wasn't dangerous, and returned to the office.

I walked back along Bialik Street. Here, next to Bialik's house, I once met the poet Hoffstein, who was working as a clerk in the Tel Aviv municipality. He spoke about Bialik with respect and suppressed hatred. "When Bialik takes to the street and wants to say something from the heart, he talks Yiddish, but when he goes inside that bourgeois house of his, he cooks up his dishes in the Holy Tongue. . . ."

He told me that he was thinking of returning to Russia. He was a poet and he couldn't survive without language. There was no hope for Yiddish in Eretz Israel. Fanatical Zionists and writers eaten up with hatred would not allow us to develop an original, popular culture, he complained. No one was stoned here yet; but in order to stone a poet to death, there was no need for stones— all you needed was words.

Afterward I went to Olga's gallery. I don't recall whether I've mentioned that, together with a friend of hers, she runs an art gallery. I assume that she doesn't do it for money. She enjoys it. It gives her some kind of independence, even though Walter, it seems to me, is generous. Even to others.

I wandered around the gallery without enjoyment. Perhaps we Russians lack artistic discrimination. Perhaps. If there is anyone who can really and truly enjoy this kind of thing, I envy him. He has extended the horizons of his world. Speaking for myself, I cannot pretend that these scribbles mean anything to me. I wouldn't express myself in the words of Khrushchev, of course. He was a crude character, and selected only the pithiest of popular expressions. From Olga's partner I heard all kinds of illuminating explanations. They were more interesting and gripping than the works of art they were supposed to explain. The only thing that irritated me was her habit of asking from time to time: Aren't I right? For a minute I wanted to say to her:

My dear girl, these boys are leading you by the nose. But on second thought, I changed my mind. They may well have been perfectly serious. And I, for my part, want no more to do with dogmatic theories. Today I can only agree with Besskind. Even if their paintings were scribbles, we should fight for their right to exhibit their scribbles and sell them to the highest bidder. Nevertheless, however, I felt bad. It was not freedom of expression that was at stake here, but a kind of compulsion. There was terrific competition, and no way of attracting attention but by some kind of scandal. I thought about young people who wanted to create something beautiful and did not dare. They were afraid that no one would take any notice of them, if they did not find a way of shocking the public.

I was sorry to hear a false note in Olga's voice. She spoke confidently, and I felt that she was not confident at all. Some authority had spoken, and she copied his words like a parrot. In different circumstances I would probably have made some sarcastic remark. I don't want to hurt Olga. But my heart contracted. People here are at liberty to choose to be completely free. There is no guiding theory, no obligation to adhere to the conventions, no official lies which cannot be denounced in a newspaper article. On the face of it. But even in matters of feeling and taste, people put their hands into silken fetters.

Last night, on television, I met an old acquaintance. He was wearing a skullcap and he had shaved his beard, and I did not therefore recognize him at first sight. I had not seen him for almost forty years.

It was a talk program about "totalitarian regimes." There were a moderator, a professor of philosophy, and two or three participants I did not know. My man was introduced as a sinologist, and for a moment I thought that I must be mistaken. But as soon as he opened his mouth I knew: it was him, Efros.

Only his name had changed. Now he was Professor Efrat. But in the eyes, which now had tiny crow's feet at their corners, the same consuming fire burned. The gleaming bald pate, now covered with a skullcap, had spread over the entire skull, from ear to ear. Bald men do not change much over the course of the years; they only shrivel and their pates lose a little of their shine.

When he spoke, Efros kept his hands in his lap in an effort to check their flight, but the fingers of his right hand danced nervously on the fist of his left, like a musician listening to a tune being played in his head. He spoke Hebrew in a melodious Russian accent, astonishingly tender and caressing, but at the same time he had adopted strikingly Anglo-Saxon mannerisms. Even the structure of his sentences in Hebrew was modeled on English.

He spoke with irritating modesty. Yes, he was a sinologist, as the esteemed moderator had said, and he had spent a few years at Oxford "reading Chinese texts," but he would not "call himself anything so exalted as an expert," certainly not "an expert on totalitarian regimes"—unless they were referring to the kind of expertise acquired by personal experience of Soviet labor camps; but this expertise too should be regarded with caution, since it was in danger of being colored by excessive subjectivity. . . . After this he made a few remarks about the struggles for power in the Chinese power elite, struggles whose secrecy, according to him, derived from the nature of a totalitarian regime, which could not flex its muscles without an ideological pretext. Since the masses were never asked anyway, and in their opinion every decision of the leadership was historically inevitable, the leadership was obliged to appear as one united body until the moment when one group overpowered the other. The rest of the proceedings took place in the courts. The rival group was accused of betraying the ideology common to both groups. Nobody believed these accusations. Nevertheless, they were accepted by all parties as the most practical means of arriving at a settlement between victors and vanquished. Thus in England, he concluded, although in an incomparably more humane manner, when the political leadership wanted to get rid of a monarch too sympathetic to Hitler, they allowed him to abdicate for love. The British public was not supposed to know that there were disagreements between the political leadership and the monarchy.

The moderator shot a provocative question at Efros: When he observed the precepts of his religion without asking any questions, was he not himself embracing a "total ideology"? Although it was opposed to the one he had embraced when he was the head of the Middle Eastern department of the Comintern, it, too, was total. "My learned friend," Efros eagerly took up the challenge, "we must make a distinction between intellectual totality and emotional totality." He had accepted the imperative of religious observance precisely because he sensed a kind of "totality of experience," or, which was a better way of putting it, "the unity of creation," or "cosmic sense," an awareness profoundly steeped in emotional connotations, which had also taught him that his espousal of the revolution—a Jew incapable of killing a fly—stemmed from the attempt of a lapsed yeshiva scholar to live in a world without God. . . . "Intellectual totality" was the opposite of this. It was intended to bestow "total justification" on coercion.

*K*urakin, too, I remembered, believed that the root of all evil was to be found in human attempts to live without God. But he said it with real humility. Whereas the skullcap flaunted by Efros had something arrogant about it—the conceit of a man who thought himself under an obligation to hold perfect beliefs.

Kurakin peeped through the window and was astonished that we did not see what he saw: that God was in everything, in the snow, the frozen skeletons of the trees, even the watchtowers; a benevolent God, who loved all his creatures. Efros's God was militant, jealous and vengeful, intolerant.

To me, Efros's way of talking seemed dishonest. He talked like a fanatic. And his eyes flashed. He ground his liberal opponent to dust. Stalin would never have succeeded in introducing such evil into millions of hearts but for the liberals who preceded him and uprooted God, he said. The slayers of God had permitted men to slay one another. I remembered how he had mocked Besskind. Then, too, he had hated the liberals more than our opponents on the right.

I remembered the only argument I had ever had with Larissa. She admired a certain priest whose great soul was capable of embracing all the vileness of the world. He was one of those who "understood" both Hitler and Stalin. What did we want of them? They were only mediocre people who found themselves in possession of power. Cleverer men than them told them that there was no God, and they concluded that everything was permitted.

I could not endure this preaching. I saw it as appalling arrogance and madness. We of little faith, who wanted to know how and why, and how to prevent terrible things—we were the root of evil? And he had transcended common humanity and was on a par with God? Since he himself had suffered from the regime, it was impossible to accuse him of defending the wicked. He knew that it was man who had failed, and that his only hope was to return to God. All the rest, in other words, all of human history, was insignificant.

Larissa believed that he was a saint. How they had tortured him! And he had refused to abandon his faith. I hurt her by saying that in my opinion he was an ignorant fool who enjoyed suffering and thought himself superior to ordinary mortals who contended with men, whether great or small.

Efros, too, reminded me of this priest. I did not believe in his ostentatious humility, his show of piety. Nor did I like the way in which he drew attention to his sufferings in Russia. Closing his eyes, as if in a sudden seizure of pain.

I must examine myself. I have certain accounts with God. Once I did not mind pronouncing his name. The language is full of his symbols, and they symbolize things which have no name. Sometimes you need a word to express indignation against things in general. But ever since my meeting with Nina, He has given me no peace. All my life I have maintained that He does not exist and behaved as if He does. And all too often, I meet people who say that He exists and behave as if He doesn't. But I was never particularly fond of Efros. Am I jealous of his success? Perhaps. When the moderator mentioned his books, saying that they were highly thought of by scholars, and he smiled with an expression that was dismissive and complacent at once—I almost jumped out of my chair with fury.

Larissa Verchinsky, too, believed in God. Her God was an old Russian writer who dearly loved the people and roamed the countryside in soft felt shoes. He pitied his long-suffering creatures and had a wonderful surprise in store for them in the last chapter.

We met in Solikamsk, shortly before they separated the men from the women. The first meeting was short, strange, and even ugly. I was sitting on a bench in the clinic, with a wound on my leg that had become infected. The medical orderly's assistant, a crude, ignorant fellow, sprayed a stinging liquid onto the wound. A hefty woman, whose face I could not see, was sweeping up the dirty bandages he threw onto the floor. Bending down and walking backward, she came slowly closer, confronting us with a large backside in a shapeless dress, beneath which peeped two thick ankles in torn felt leggings. Suddenly the medical assistant had a bright idea: he turned the syringe from my leg to the woman's buttocks and squirted a jet of the stinking liquid onto her dress, right opposite her vagina. A damp patch appeared, and he roared with laughter. The woman straightened up and stared at him. And there was something in her look that silenced him as effectively as if she had lashed him on the face with a whip.

She was a girl from a peasant family who had somehow landed up in Leningrad in the years immediately following the revolution, and had studied literature there. Her parents were devout Orthodox Christians, and after they had been banished from their village and disappeared into the northern wastes, she had kept faith with their beliefs as a kind of commitment to preserve their memory. Her religion was abstract and intimate and she avoided talking about it. In Leningrad she had met a Jewish doctor and married him. He was an amateur student of culture and folklore and a collector of old icons, which at that time could be bought for next to nothing. They were not allowed to live together for more than a short time. She was arrested after her adored priest. Not long afterward her husband was arrested too. He was accused of trying to smuggle art treasures out of the country.

Everything about her was broad and very typically Russian. Her Slavic features, her sturdy shoulders, her strong arms, her hefty thighs. She also loved in the way of Russian women who have read a lot of books. With absolute loyalty, with utter self-forgetfulness. When she came into possession of a rotten potato, I found two-thirds of it under my mattress. I never touched her. I was afraid that she would faint. Another woman would have lifted her skirts for me among the filthy clothes in the laundry.

We wrote love letters to each other. Her handwriting was exquisite, like a Chinese painting. In the course of time we developed a code. Even if our letters were seized, their content would not be understood. On the surface they resembled notes smuggled to each other by literature students during an examination. Larissa's knowledge of Russian literature was so vast that she could write whatever she wanted to by a series of references to the heroes of the classical novels. Their virtues, their deeds, their travels, their bons mots, were reliable signposts to information of every kind—experiences, opinions, addresses. Even setting a time and a place for a meeting.

We went on writing to each other after we were separated too. And also after we were set free. She went to the far north ("with my own eyes I saw Frishvin's ram"), traveling all the way to Archangel in her search for her parents. She found only two brothers, younger than herself, in the vicinity of Vologda. They had succeeded in establishing a farm in a district where the kolkhoz system was not very strict. Larissa joined them and invited me to come and live with her. There in Vologda, she wrote me, was the real Russia. The feudal lords had never reached those parts, and consequently the revolution went there on tiptoe. There were no kulaks to prosper on the bread of poverty which the peasants extracted from the frozen land. There was no one to covet their mite. There you could find pure Russian popular culture. "We have everything, even matches," she quoted a saying she had heard in Samarkand, in times of great poverty.

"I am an urban creature," I wrote in reply, "and the Russian peasants slaughtered my forefathers."

For a time I lived in the suburbs of Zagorsk. From there I could slip into Moscow on a tram and back. I had no residence permit. I stayed in the house of a widow, a guard at the railway crossing, and grew vegetables in the backyard. I described my life in a letter to Larissa. She replied in a letter which alluded to her wishes: "If Lavretsky has decided to return to the land after all, the air in Vologda is purer."

The railway guard found the letter. She was a good-looking, aggressive mischief maker, and she wanted to keep me there on a permanent basis. Although I told her from the start that I did not intend staying there long, she was jealous of every woman I spoke to. She was jealous of my books and notebooks too, and of any written word she found on my bed. Of the latter, because she was illiterate. Unluckily for me, she was overcome with curiosity to know what was hidden in the elegant curls of Larissa's script. She showed the letter to a literate railway worker. He understood from Larissa's letter that my papers were forged. Lavretsky was my real name, and not the name which I had given. The woman got into a panic and ran to the police. I escaped before the police agents arrived to arrest Lavretsky. At that time there was presumably a lack of manpower in Novosibirsk and the police were always raiding the little towns crowded with freed convicts within the periphery of a hundred versts around Moscow.

Thus I lost Larissa's letters and "Northern Snows," a manuscript describing my experiences in Norilsk, Solikamsk, and Kaluga. I imagine that manuscript is now lying in the file of one Lavretsky, still at large, unless it had happened to come into the hands of an educated investigator who had read Turgenev in his youth. But if Larissa's letters had fallen into the hands of some ignorant fellow, it was not beyond the bounds of possibility that files had been opened also against Grigboyedov, Pichurin, Labyedkin, and Myshkin, and the ignoramus in question would not be satisfied until they were caught.

I have not written much lately. Life has fallen into a routine. No surprises are to be expected. The freshness of the first impressions has faded, and with it the excitement, and the melancholy at the sight of all the changes that have taken place. There is a good chance that tomorrow will be like today. I have let things slide. I no longer fear forgetting tomorrow what I have neglected to write down today. Whatever I forget tomorrow, I shall remember the day after. And if not, it means that it made no impression on me. The memory of an old man is willing to let go of the new. It prefers the old, and clings to the oldest of all.

I must let time pass, and the apartment I am so eagerly awaiting will come in its own good time. As if it were being constructed from my patience. Every hour in which I am able to ignore its existence lays another brick.

The members of my family have grown accustomed to my existence. Even Nimrod's wife sometimes speaks to me. And I have seen her sons too. Sturdy, handsome boys. I shall never know what they are really like. My lot is to gaze at them from afar. Like Moses and the Promised Land. The maid, Nadya, has learned to cook borscht.

Nina has disappeared. She gives no sign. I seem to have put her mind at rest. I have no demands. And she is not troubled by the fact that I exist somewhere or other, beyond the pale.

I make enough from the translations to keep myself in dignity. Let no one be misled by the last word. I am still not able to give my grandchildren the presents I would like to give them. But at least I am no longer in the position I was in some time ago. When I got onto the bus and sat down and opened my wallet, only to discover that I did not have a penny in it. I was not obliged to get off again—a kind woman paid my fare. But the driver said, They always pull the same trick, and nobody said a word. I wonder, was he referring to the old, or to the Russians?

In my spare time I build my house. I have decided to add on another floor, for my grandchildren and visitors from out of town. I am also learning electronics in English. It is not as complicated as I feared. I listen to Arabic lessons over the radio. And I try not to miss "A Moment of Hebrew" either. Once a week I go out. I registered myself at the center for volunteers. From time to time they call me and ask me if I can help some old man who is unable to take care of his own needs. I am glad to do it. Usually, I am asked to do something simple. Like washing them. Not a very difficult job. They are usually not heavy. I enjoy it. First of all, because it's a mitzvah. They're grateful and it gives me satisfaction. But also because every time I leave the house it's an excursion, and I get my bus fares back. And if I have to travel far, I also get expenses. It's nice to be a busy man, who needs eight days to the week.

Today was a great occasion for us. Nimrod regained consciousness.

I must be precise in my use of words. Perhaps I should keep "great" for some other time. He regained consciousness—but he doesn't know anybody. He can perceive objects, figures, but he can't talk.

The doctors say that he will have to be taught everything all over again. As if a baby had been born into the family.

They won't allow me to see him, in order not to disturb him. Perhaps they think he should get used to the people whose pictures he carries somewhere in his brain first, and only then to strangers.

Nevertheless, I was very excited by the news. Hope is like a stimulating and dangerous drug. And how much the more so, when a window is suddenly opened. I realize that I had resigned myself to my fate. I thought that we would never meet. I was the only one to give up. Perhaps because the others had a real person, and I had only an abstraction. They knew whom they were were waiting for. A painful lesson.

I went outside. It was midday. The road is lined with an avenue of ficus trees whose branches touch overhead. It was very still, like in a forest. I experienced a marvelous sensation of recall, as if something that had happened many years before were happening again: the same silence, the same warbling birds, the same mood.

It was in Moscow, in 1919, in the Izmailovi Park. The sound of shooting had stopped. Everything suddenly looked as if it were going to go on forever: a high sky with motionless clouds. A Sabbath world. "We have come into the world only to see the face of the sun." Every movement is a sign from on high. Does a twig fall? A sign that a bird has come from southern lands.

In the afternoon I went to cool my fevered brain at "Zilberstein's." That is not his real name. A nickname I call him to myself. He is an Orthodox Jew, and for some reason I have chosen to believe that Nina's husband resembles him. An idea not lacking in a certain malice. The secret spite of the soul gossiping to itself. I imagine Nina in the arms of this man, whose flabby, helpless body is like a rag in my hands. I can feel a pity full of gloating for him. One day I shall have to ask his pardon.

Naked in the lukewarm water of the bath, he rests his shriveled head in my hand and closes his eyes in enjoyment. In his dried-up body forgotten sensations revive. I soap his smooth chest, and the movement of my hand pulls the flabby skin down over his ribs. A rinse in warm water and the smile of a baby blooms on the dry old lips. I feel proud of my health and my strong hands, and carry him to his bed like a little child. He holds out his legs and arms to be dressed with a sacrificial gesture. Gradually he disappears into his clothes. The head remains. Like a bird of prey whose eyes are wise.

This time, after breathing in the smell of the clean sheets, he held out his matchstick-thin fingers to me. With great pity I gathered them into my hard, big hand, making an effort not to squeeze them.

He promised me that I would go to Heaven.

If you say so.

He insisted. In a cracked voice, as he was entitled to speak for them.

He is strict in religious observance. When the female social worker comes into his room, he looks at the ceiling and addresses her in the third person. He needs a nurse to look after him, but he refuses to let a woman touch him. And there are no male nurses available. Since he can take a few steps from time to time, from his bed to the kerosene ring on which he cooks his meals, there is no place for him in a nursing home. In the meantime he can make do with my help. I bathe him once a week and change his sheets once a fortnight. No trouble at all.

When you see him in his wretched room in a slummy neighborhood in the south of the city, poring over pious old books and soundlessly saying his prayers with his crooked neck trembling, you would think that he had grown old here together with the ancient house and the huge, gnarled eucalyptus tree in the courtyard. But the truth is that he is a man of the world, and the eyelids drooping over the little letters, as if they were muttering together with his lips, veil many sights in distant lands.

Before the Second World War he was the rabbi of a medium-sized town in Hungary. He was in the famous train from Bergen-Belsen. He spent a few years in Sweden and there too he served as a rabbi. He went to the United States and headed an Orthodox yeshiva there in Brooklyn. He was never a Zionist. But after his wife passed away and his daughter was raped and murdered by a Negro, he left America and came to his relations in Israel. He had no idea how poor they were. They died soon after his arrival in the country and he was left alone. He was living on his savings, but he was very careful with his money, in case he still had a long time to live. He is sorry for my irreligious state and he prays for me, too. He says that if only I knew how sweet it was to pray from the heart, I would not miss a single prayer. After I bathe him, he says to me: "You pray with your big strong hands, the hands of a Jewish peasant." He says this every time as if he had just this minute coined the phrase.

He said that he finds it difficult to believe that "after all I have been through," I have not returned to God. Precisely for that reason, I replied. If I had been allowed to live my life in peaceful contemplation, like a boy lying in the forest next to the lake, listening to the splashing of the water and looking at the treetops swaying in the breeze beneath the infinitely high sky—perhaps I would have had a revelation. The sense of the infinity of the universe would have filled me with a kind of reverence. But I was not prepared to learn of the existence of God from suffering. I told him that in the camps, whenever a new wave of prisoners arrives, there are always some who experience a religious revival—Jewish, Christian, Moslem, or Brahmin as the case may be. I have seen old Communists who had lost their faith in the possibility of ordering human existence according to reason, and had sought a refuge from the chaos in their hearts in the bosom of religion. A new prisoner, when he is brought face to face with the cruel laws of the camps, at first grows confused and refuses to believe the evidence of his eyes. The relations between men, even between prisoners, seem to him the absolute evil, or the absolute lie. His outraged soul seeks to hold on to something which will justify in its eyes the will to live. He looks to the opposite pole for the absolute good, the perfect truth, the divine order. And thus the new prisoners find their way to some rabbi or priest, whose consoling words are like balm to their souls. But as they gradually become acquainted with the way of life in the camp, they realize that a resourceful man can somehow get along if he knows how to fix himself up in the clinic, or assisting the kitchen workers to unload the flour from the wagons. And then they begin to rely on themselves again. And the priest and the rabbi go out to look for new victims.

My words distressed him. He consoled himself with the thought that "my actions spoke louder than my words." He believed that there was God in my heart. But I denied Him in order not to have to admit that I had been wrong.

These visits have opened a peephole into remote corners for me. They are teaching me many curious things about human lives and also about the history of Eretz Israel.

From time to time I take care of a man who is confined to a wheelchair. A hopeless case of muscular degeneration. He boasted to me that he used to be as strong as an ox. And he hinted that he, personally, could take the credit for certain heroic but unmentionable exploits. He had been a member of an extreme right-wing nationalist organization during the thirties; he was arrested, escaped, was caught, exiled to Eritrea, escaped, and was caught again; even after the establishment of the State of Israel he had been a member of some underground organization.

I feel sorry for him. He would like to point an accusing finger at the Labor Party he hates so much, but his hand refuses to obey him. He talks to me as if I were his ally. If I listen to him, presumably I must agree with what he says: the workers' strikes are destroying the country; and one day we will have to pay for the fact that we are not treating the Arabs in the only way they understand—i.e., with an iron fist.

He almost had a fit when I told him that I had been in the Socialist Workers Party in the old days. But he soon recovered. We had already been given what we deserved in the Red motherland.

In an old-age home for the incurably ill and incapacitated, the social worker sent me to a paralyzed man of about my own age, whom I visit once a fortnight and for whom I do various trifling errands. Usually, he asks me to write letters to the newspapers for him.

He is a handsome man who once had a certain role to play in the Haganah. In the distant days of his youth he was so full of confidence in the importance of the tasks which fell to his lot that he gave up a normal family life for their sake and never had any children. He showed me snapshots of himself with an expression of grim heroism on his face, wearing the riding breeches which indicated to the initiated the clandestine nature of his role. The day the Israeli Defense Forces were established, his world fell to pieces. Ben-Gurion, his sworn enemy—for political reasons, as he explained to me, since he was a member of the left wing of the labor movement—awarded him the rank of major, which wounded his pride. All his friends and admirers were under the impression that he was one of the pillars of Haganah, and now it transpired that for thirty years he had been perpetrating an empty boast. He became a bitter, quarrelsome man and spent his time attacking the defense forces in letters full of hints to the initiated and words to the wise. Friends exerted their influence on his behalf, and he retired from the army with the rank of lieutenant colonel. Late in life he married the widow of a friend, who was unable to bear children. After she died, he became paralyzed. Friends, with sympathetic expressions on their faces which he found hard to bear, came to visit him rarely, as if according to a duty roster arranged among them on the telephone. They brought him all the newspapers, and whenever there was an article about the history of Eretz Israel, especially military matters, he would dictate a letter to the editor to me. Most of these letters begin: "In the ——— number of your newspaper, in the section "Once Upon a Time" (or Episodes From the Past, or Today Forty Years Ago, and so on) you published an article by ——— about ———. As one who then served as ——— and was responsible for ——— in my capacity as ———, I regard it as my duty to put the record straight." I am a sympathetic audience, and in the lack of information from any other quarter I agree with everything he tells me and encourage him to pile on the details. The social worker says that every visit of mine is worth a week of physiotherapy, which does no good either.

A short visit to my son. His beard has been shaved off, and there is a white cap on his head, something like the turbans which our mothers used to wear. His eyes are open, following moving objects, but their expression is frighteningly blank. They look right through you without stopping.

I remembered: Vladimir. The interrogation. I went into the room. Opposite me sat a pockmarked Asian. With the same expression in his eyes. For the first time I was terrified before they touched me. A primeval terror. Like the sudden awakening from a nightmare. Beware of the man without a soul.

I seek in vain for traces of myself in my son's face. Not a single feature. Not the nose, not the chin, not the jaws. The eyes are black. Vera's features, too, are missing. As if he fell into our lives out of nowhere. A lost soul. The embodiment of a wish. Not flesh of our flesh.

Vera was with me too. She bent over his bed and tried to get him to repeat the sounds "Dad-dy." A sad, pathetic sight. But Vera was not the woman to be deterred. When she did not succeed, she came back to me with an apologetic look. Never mind. Another time. She dragged me to the bed, made me stand closer, to engrave my image on his brain. A disturbing thought: Had all the memories, the knowledge he had accumulated, been wiped out? One blow and you were no longer yourself. And you had to begin again from the beginning. How could I help him? Better not to think about it. The accident had made me into a father. Perhaps I would be needed. My son, it seemed, was now in the twilight of a new birth.

The Passover Seder at Tel Yosef. A great crowd. Among the flood of guests, your strangeness stands out. Laid tables. A stage. A choir, an orchestra, dancers. A bit of tradition and a bit of contemporary poetry. A solemn ceremony, still somewhat artificial. Forty years like yesterday. I too was given a verse from a poem by Alterman to read. I got mixed up and a small child laughed.

I remembered the festival in the days of the Brigade. A bit of reading and a lot of dumplings. A choir sang Russian songs and a Hasidic song, too. To remind us. Once, in Ein Harod, I was God. My voice was heard from the mountaintop. I knew the answers to all the questions. In Jerusalem we went out after the Seder to the Orthodox quarter to eat bread in public. We were beaten up and came back happy. We had fought the good fight.

I sat with Vera among people I did not know. Two soldiers without families, a couple of new immigrants who knew no Hebrew, a boy who had quarreled with his parents, and a middle-aged man who had arrived at the last minute and couldn't find a place next to his family. I thought of Vera's loneliness. Some of our generation were sitting at tables crowded with their offspring, three generations.

During the singing after the meal we spoke about Nimrod. The middle-aged man turned out to be a member of Nimrod's peer group. He called him "Tiger." But that was evidently the nickname given to all the reserve officers who volunteered to command outposts on the Suez Canal. He had amusing anecdotes to tell. They had turkeys in their little menagerie. They laid eggs and hatched them. Nimrod was too impatient to wait. He lit a primus stove under an upside-down tub and put the eggs inside it. From time to time he would remove an egg and crack it, to see if there was already a chick inside it. We laughed. I felt a strange happiness stirring in me: my traces in my son. If not a physical resemblance, one characteristic at least, this impatience. In the room there was a surprise waiting for me: a bundle of papers belonging to Nimrod. Letters, articles in the kibbutz paper, school essays. Olga's letters weren't there.

Like rummaging in an empty drawer. The articles about the economic affairs of the kibbutz lacked all individuality. When he worked in the dairy branch, he demanded increased investment in it. When he worked in the garage, he claimed its due. When he was the kibbutz treasurer, he demanded a cut in expenditure. Some of the articles were obituaries for comrades fallen in the War of Independence. They too did not illuminate a personality. Everything fitted everybody: we were stunned, impossible to accept it. And it did not suit the young man in question to be dead; how could he be dead—he loved life so much. Only in one of them did he state a fact, which leaped out of the verbiage like lightning: a boy who chased a foal all the way to the Bedouin tents next to the Sahne pool had a face of his own.

Only one of the articles showed any traces of individuality—a handwritten piece for the wall newspaper at school.

In 1940, at the age of fourteen, he set out with a group of boys on a forbidden expedition to Sarta, near Nablus. They walked all night, hid during the day, and walked back the next night. On their return, they were hauled over the coals. Lectured for risking their lives for nothing. His reply was somewhat crude, but strong. If they weren't prepared to endanger themselves to learn the byways of the motherland, how would they know if they would be ready to risk their lives when it was really necessary? In the spirit of the times.

My traces, I rejoiced. In my spirit. A portrait of myself as a young man.

Moscow. The Hehalutz training farm. Waiting impatiently for immigration papers. Hearing the footsteps of the Messiah. And suddenly a rumor: in the Borochov Club in Lubianski Proyezd, an emissary from Eretz Israel. There were two of us. Impetuous, precipitate. We decided to find out if there were secret ways as well. By the time the papers arrived—perhaps the messianic era would dawn without us. We pressed up to him, our eyes burning. Expecting an encouraging pat on the back. He gave us a patronizing smile, full of pity. God forbid that we should try. The roads were dangerous. And there was no point in risking our lives unnecessarily. He poured cold water on us: Life in Eretz Israel was very hard, the heat was unbearable, there was no shade, the mosquitoes sucked your blood, and snakes and scorpions lurked under every stone; experienced workers collapsed. And you? You've gathered a few potatoes? Chopped a bit of wood? That does not qualify you to be workers in Eretz Israel. A land which devours its inhabitants. It will break you, he warned us. You'll come home beaten. For work, even hard work, in the clear, cool air of Russia bears no resemblance to the back-breaking labor which awaits you in Eretz Israel, a scorching land where even the tap water comes out boiling.

We took his words literally. If this was the situation, we would have to strengthen our bodies and toughen our characters before arriving in Eretz Israel. Since Hehalutz was in the doldrums and it was not at all clear whether any immigration groups would be organized in the immediate future, and the attitude of the authorities, too, was not clear, we decided to set out without waiting for our papers.

We reached Odessa when Petlyura's men were in charge. The corpses were still lying in the streets and a British ship was anchored in the harbor and firing its cannons. We ran through the deserted streets and found refuge in Rabbi Glicksberg's synagogue, rejoicing at our good fortune and the opportunity of preparing ourselves for what lay ahead by participating in a real battle. (Actually, the battleship was not firing at the town at all, but only asserting its presence, while the corpses had been hit some days earlier, and Petlyura, who had already taken steps to restore order and issued instructions to open the theaters and dance halls, saw no urgency in removing them as long as they could strike terror into the hearts of his enemies. But we could not know this.) The next day we presented ourselves at the Hehalutz offices and agreed to work on the agricultural farm run by the agronomist Zussman, who fertilized the vegetable beds with sewage water which gave off an appalling stench. We were glad that our noses, too, were being subjected to trials which would prepare us for living among camels and donkeys. Not content with this, we would tread barefoot on the uncultivated land on the outskirts of the forest, in order to accustom our feet to snakebites, and once we even pushed our hands into a beehive in order to immunize ourselves to the pain of a scorpion sting. The water we washed in was cold, and the water we drank was hot. We heated it up on the oil burner before putting it to our lips, so that it would be as hot and tasteless as the water that came out of the taps in Eretz Israel. When we received our first wages, we went to the dirtiest quarter in Odessa, and there, in a tavern where Babel's heroes caroused, and no respectable Jew set foot, we ordered bloody pork chops and large tumblers of undiluted alcohol, in order to accustom ourselves to overcome fear and revulsion.

We set sail exhausted and satisfied with ourselves. Many

trials and tribulations still awaited us at sea and in the ports of
Turkey, but we welcomed them all gladly. On the Jaffa shore,
soaked to the marrow of our bones by an unseasonable cloud-
burst, we stood in the pouring rain, indifferent to the cold and
wind, like red-necked Siberian peasants, taking advantage of this
unexpected natural disaster for a last-minute immunization
before plunging into the risks and dangers of real life, where all
our deeds would be necessary, and no longer exercises in immunization.

*T*he last day in my daughter's home. From tomorrow—an
independent man. By a curious coincidence, today is Independence Day.

Last night, on Memorial Day, I thought: This generation of
Jews too is better at mourning than rejoicing. Pain joins, joy
separates them. The holiday itself is nothing but noise. Panic-
stricken celebrations, as if they were trying to cheat fate. If they
pretend to be happy, perhaps they will be spared. Thus a Jew
walks past a dog, whistling a merry tune. The dog is not deceived:
the Jew is afraid.

My private celebration, too, is steeped in sadness. The sorrow of parting. There are moments when I am almost certain
that I have a family. I am leaving just when my grandchildren
have grown accustomed to me. I helped my granddaughter with
her geometry homework and she smiled at me when I suggested
a way of solving a complicated problem to her. This morning she
hit me with a plastic hammer in order to include me in the
holiday fun.

The young soldier has begun to call me Grandpa. True, he
pronounces it with a certain amusement, as if there were something comic about my belated arrival in the bosom of the family,
but even this sound is music to my ears. A simple friendship is
beginning to come into being. The strangest thing of all is that
the background to it is ideological. We are evidently, in some
sense incomprehensible to me, allies. He holds extreme left-

wing opinions, and honors me for the early days. The early days only. Everything that came later he dismisses, as if I had in some way disgraced myself. It is difficult for me to follow his line of reasoning. He seems sadly confused. Or perhaps it is I who am confused. The members of his generation, he believes, have learned from the mistakes of the past. They will do things differently. Humanely. Perhaps they'll learn how in universities.

There is something a little fashionable about his radicalism. It commits him to nothing. Leaving home to dedicate himself to the cause in some other part of the world does not occur to him. Terrorism and civil war are both out of the question. A more agreeable revolution I cannot imagine.

He is ready to listen to my stories about the days of the revolution, but he does not want to hear about the Labor Brigade. It is anachronistic and irrelevant. And boring, too.

As for me, from day to day I come closer to the conclusion that the only days in my life when I was really happy were the first days of the Brigade. I was a happy-go-lucky barefoot ragamuffin, displaying his bare feet a little too prominently, perhaps, but not so as to give anyone offense. We were anarchists full of pride, with a passion for organizing. What confusion! And how happy we were in our poverty. "I have a loaf, / I have no loaf, / What difference does it make to me?" we sang. Every man did what his heart told him. Without order, system, or theory.

I still have a little sense of adventure left. I welcome change in my life. I am setting out for a new place with the joy of youth, if I may be permitted a note of irony: a man who still has his curiosity is not yet altogether lost. A man of my age who is still ready to try new experiences is not yet altogether old.

Only Olga's friend Rachel is sorry to see me go. She is about to complete her essay on the left in the Labor Brigade and she needs my comments.

Surprising, completely unexpected news. Epstein has received an exit permit and he will be arriving in Israel soon. There are no details in his letter. What made him change his mind? Or perhaps he was forced to leave? And is he coming alone, or with his wife? Where will he live? Does he have any relations in the country? Is my assistance required? Has he received an appointment at the university? I am concerned about him. The life he has been leading in Moscow recently! Perhaps the shock will be too much for him.

But in my heart of hearts a strange joy stirs. Like a beginner at writing whose first book has gone to the printer's.

I will be able to let him look at my notebooks. He won't be hurt when he comes across my surprise at the things he said to me before parting. The wounds of love carry conviction.

Perlmutter told me that there is someone who knows me at the old-age home and who is glad that I am coming to live there too. Efros. The circles are closing.

Fourth Notebook: A New Leaf

A new place. In the corridors, the smell of old age: disinfectant, medicines, the breath of people afraid of drafts. Through the window I can see the sea.

The sea is a vivid blue, and from here it seems steeped in an eternal calm. This is the way it looked from the window of my aunt's apartment in Odessa. When I look at the sea, I remember my father.

How he loved the sea! He walked on the soft, warm sand and there was an expression in his eyes which I had never seen before. They shone with a gleam of such childish joy that it awoke a tremor of anxiety in my eleven-year-old heart. My hand was clasped in his, and nevertheless I felt as if he had abandoned me and escaped to his own childhood, where I did not exist.

His flat feet left prints hardly deeper than mine in the damp sand next to the water line. His legs, white and thin and smooth, shivered with cold. His hand closed over mine pulsed with a rhythmic beat, as if in response to some soundless song. We walked a fair distance before entering the sea—to isolate ourselves from the crowd, but not at a dangerous distance from them. The moment we went in, a soft, high sound escaped his lips, a kind of whoop, perhaps a cry of joy, perhaps an exclamation of surprise at the coldness of the water. But when he saw me staring at him, he stopped at once. His face took on its usual stern and serious expression. The gleam in his eyes died down, and he gave me a paternal look, full of responsibility and all the authority of the head of a family who would never dream of indulging in frivolity or empty pleasures. His next steps were executed with a kind of gravity, without evident pleasure, as if in obedience to doctor's orders.

*   *   *

The man whose room I inherited was a judge in Gomulka's courts. He had family in Haifa, wealthy people who took no interest in his few possessions. Some of them were given to charity. I inherited his table, his reading lamp, a chair, a few dictionaries—Polish-Russian, Polish-French, and French-Hebrew—and a huge pile of letters in Polish, arranged in files according to subject and date.

I put them away in the built-in cupboard, and they take up a considerable amount of its space. I need the shelves myself, but I cannot bring myself to throw away letters. Human lives are folded up in them. I phoned the organization of immigrants from Radom, his native city, but they said they could not help me. Reading the letters alone would take weeks or even months. A wearisome and thankless task.

I pulled out a few letters at random and glanced at them. The Polish I had acquired in the Minkovsky family was enough to read simple language. I wasn't bored, even though I did not know the man and had never seen him in my life. He had bombarded public figures and institutions with his letters and filed away every missive he sent and received. His reverence for written and signed documents extended even to laconic replies from government offices. I even found a letter from one of Gomulka's secretaries. It said that he would receive an answer to his questions after the case had been examined.

The personality of my predecessor aroused my curiosity. I asked the older residents about him, and now I am studying his life history, from the end to the beginning.

His name was Aronovitch, and he was only fifty-nine years old when he died. His room was unoccupied for four and a half months. He suffered a stroke and was taken to the hospital. When he came out he was paralyzed and unable to care for his needs. He was transferred to a rehabilitation center where he died three months later.

Although they knew he would not return, they did not give his room to a new resident. Despite the shortage of rooms, they behaved with humanity. But perhaps Perlmutter had a hand in it. As long as Walter did not press him, he did not care if the room intended for me was standing empty.

As long as Aronovitch was alive nobody took any interest in him. His family in Haifa, so I learned from speaking to the residents, were glad when he passed away and freed them from their guilt. He had written letters to them, too. Their answers were few and far between. I read one of them. It said, in a shamelessly offensive and revolting polite style, that when they themselves had arrived in the country the conditions were far harder and they had not complained. I reconstruct his figure like an archeologist who has dug up a broken jar.

I could have lived the rest of my life without ever knowing that he had existed. And yet, now that I am breathing his loneliness into my lungs, I cannot banish him from my room.

Epstein used to say that old age brings back to consciousness myths that reason has banished from it. I am beginning to believe, without actually believing it, that there are no chance meetings. It was necessary to someone for me and Aronovitch to meet. A little sooner or a little later—it makes no difference. We are already inextricably involved with one another. He is already part of my life history. I will die in the room where he looked for the last time at the sea.

This "belief," I know, will not stand up under scutiny, but it suits me nevertheless. It removes a little of the anarchy and saves the world from chaos.

In the administration they don't know much about him. He arrived on the recommendation of the examining committee, which found him deserving, since he met the criteria whose exact nature is a mystery to everybody. They said that he was a quiet, self-effacing man with a strict daily routine. Every morning at six he went for a walk. When he came back he made himself breakfast. After that he went back to bed and dozed until eleven, when he went into town. Nobody knew where or why. In the afternoon he played chess with a few of the residents. In the evening he spent an hour in the club and at eight he returned to his room.

He did not possess a television set. Only a radio and an old gramophone with a big pile of records, mostly Polish folk songs, and a few classical pieces—Chopin, Szymanowski, Wieniawski.

The nurse in charge of the clinic said that he was generally speaking a healthy man, but that he suffered from high blood pressure, which rose steeply in times of stress. She found the things that upset him strange: the political situation, verdicts handed down by the Supreme Court, articles in the newspapers, the manners of certain people, an empty mailbox on a day when, according to his calculations, he should have received a letter.

She cannot understand why I am asking all these questions. After all, I never knew the man. Nevertheless, she answered me patiently. My curiosity is one of the diseases which she is supposed to take care of. She has studied geriatrics and learns something useful from every idiotic conversation with an old man.

I never found a photograph of Aronovitch, but gradually a picture built up. I could have drawn his portrait the way the police compose an Identi-Kit picture. I saw him going down in the elevator, preoccupied by the planning of his day, descending the front steps with a deliberate, thoughtful tread, preserving in his memory every gesture of his fellowmen, words said and unsaid, insults open and disguised, secret promises, hidden rivalries, undeclared intentions. I seated him at his desk, his right arm resting on the surface, the pen frozen between his fingers, and his head tilted to the ceiling, straining after some elusive idea or crushing phrase. I stood him next to his cupboard, the door open, his fingers hovering over the files lined up like soldiers on parade, and suddenly, triumphantly, pulling one out, flipping through the documents with marvelous dexterity, and stopping, his hand slipping over the old paper while the index finger points accusingly to the quotation he needs to underpin his argument. I feel sorry for him. This loyalty to documents touches my heart. I can imagine the mental anguish of a man who permitted himself in those stormy days to judge his fellowmen. Only a man whose conscience had not been completely obliterated would have needed to treat these official papers with such tremendous reverence. These documents were his defense. When he arrived at the gates of Heaven he would show them to the angels. True, he had judged, but he had not relied on prima facie or hearsay evidence alone. Without papers written and signed according to the requirements of the law, he had never convicted a soul.

This was the source of his correspondence with public personalities and institutions, to protest injustice, to set the record straight, to create more and more "documentation." The slavery to documents, to adapt a phrase of Lenin's, is the geriatric disease of socialism.

I even found love letters. At first I was surprised at the sight of his letters to his beloved. But it was not his pedantry applied to even the most intimate of matters. He had not kept copies. The letters had been returned to him for security reasons. The woman, married to a colleague, was afraid to conceal them in her home. And they were too precious to her to destroy.

This love seized him when he was forty-eight years old, at the height of his career. I did not put these words into his mouth. They are written, in his slow, neat handwriting, in one of his last letters. He was suddenly struck by lightning, and fell like an oak. Even his immigration to Israel was a consequence of that fall. The woman was not prepared to take the crucial step, and after the disappointment of his hopes, he was no longer capable of living in the same city, the same country, as her.

The woman's letters made me like her. They were written in a simple, pleasant style and testified to her honesty. She wrote that although her feelings for him were deep, she considered it her duty to suppress them. She enjoyed herself in his company, but felt miserable when she came home. They would have to part. When she weighed her desires in the balance against the suffering of others, her instincts told her what her choice must be.

His letters were gentle and angry by turn. Sometimes as sweet and sticky as treacle, and sometimes sarcastic and hurtful,

like an insulted adolescent in love. His language, too, was not to
my taste. Full of inflated phrases, some of which demanded an
effort to understand the intention behind them. It seems that in
a world which is sick of bombast, judges and terrorists are the last
who still stand in need of such high language, as if they were
writing the holy books of our times. (Even in Russia they have
stopped beating the drums with all their might. Polemicists have
learned to sting rather than club their opponents over the head.)

Poor Aronovitch. This late love turned his life upside down.
And for its sake he left his wife and grown-up children and exiled
himself to the land of his fathers, which was far from his heart.

I think of Leopold Sherrer. He too had been struck by the
arrows of love. He was prepared to give his all for it. My all. The
government's all. If he had succeeded in crossing the border into
Poland, perhaps he would have won Nina, and Olga would now
have been a Warsaw matron, and I would never have met Aronovitch. Perhaps the two of them would have met. Aronovitch
would have given Leopold Sherrer a stiff sentence, after the
documents proving he had informed on Minkovsky had arrived
from Moscow.

This week my son was transferred to the rehabilitation center. He
can sit in a wheelchair. They have also taught him to pronounce
a few syllables. When I entered the room he looked at me and
recognized me. That is to say, he knows that I am the man who
was there the day before yesterday and last week.

I go frequently to visit him. With a strange hope in my heart.
Once I saw a documentary film about a characteristic of certain
birds. They attach themselves to the first moving object they see
after they are hatched from their eggs. A man in a white coat led
a flock of little ducks after a broomstick. Sometimes I feel like
that broomstick. I was one of those who moved in front of him
when he emerged from his shell.

The physiotherapy has done wonders for him. He can pronounce words and lift the spoon to his mouth. Sometimes he
misses and my heart contracts. Like a gosling whose feet tread on

each other. But the doctor is full of admiration and we, too, are infected by it. Soon, he said, we will be able to teach him arithmetic. I volunteered to do it, and the doctor promised to tell me how.

A strong, muscular man sunk like a heavy burden in a wheelchair. His right leg stiff as a log of wood. Fate plays tricks on us. What I lost in the distant years of my youth has come back to me in my old age. With hard, happy hands I wipe my son's backside. A helpless baby of forty-five who is afraid of the dark.

Last night I helped the duty orderly to give him a bath. His muscles are firm, his shoulders sturdy, his arms like cables and his belly flat. His limbs have been softened by long bed rest, but they have not lost their strength. Only his male organ is flabby, lying on his heavy testicles like a sleeping lion.

After the bath I took him out onto the porch. He looked straight ahead of him with a blank expression. Suddenly a bird flew from a treetop. It hung in the air and flapped its wings. He glanced at it and laughed.

Hope swept me, like a gust of wind in my face.

On Saturday I met Efros.

The weather was fine and I decided to go to the beach. The walk from the house to the beach and back exhausts me. But nevertheless, I devote my Sabbaths to it. I saunter down a broad street, between high buildings, in a sun-bathed city, and think about my mother and my father. Where does it come from, this ritual which I repeat every week, unless it is too hot and I am afraid of trouble with my breathing? When I cross the sand dune next to the sea on my bare feet, I see my parents' footprints in the soft sand.

For many years I wiped them out of my mind. I left my father's house with no intention of returning. My parents were that "old world" which my generation helped to destroy. Now that I have grandchildren, I am sorry that I did not know my grandfather and grandmother. They were Hasids—and in my eyes, idol worshipers.

This time I never succeeded in leaving the house, because in the passage I was accosted by Efros. He was standing in the doorway to the club, where the religious residents of the house held their services, and watching out for the early risers in order to rope them into the prayer quorum. I should point out that he did not recognize me.

I told him that I was not in the habit of praying. He bowed his head—a movement I well remembered: he would tilt his head to one side, and fix you with his rolling eyes if your replies were not to his liking, or he thought that you were trying to trick him—and said: "Praying never hurt anyone." I enjoyed playing hide-and-seek with him. "What is it good for?" "It cleanses the lungs and the blood." "So does fresh air." "Come on, what do you care? Do a Jew a favor. If God doesn't hear our prayers—what have you lost? And if He hears—it will be marked down in your favor up there, and one day you'll get your reward. . . ." He spoke, and his shrewd eyes were fixed on me all the while, in a kind of playful rebuke, which lacked the modesty of a true believer. "You know what?" I said to him. "If there is a Heaven—they'll let me in. They'll say: Berkov was sure there is no God, and therefore he didn't pray, but sometimes he behaved as if there was a God. But when you arrive they'll say: There's no room for Efros here. He prayed in order to get a reward."

At that moment he recognized me and rose up on his tiptoes in order to embrace me.

I had no option but to pray. "And it doesn't bother you that I'm praying without pious intent?" "No. Lack of intent is transformed into intent." And he added: "During the moments of prayer your mind is purified of empty thoughts."

The melodies touched a chord in my heart. I remembered my father on the Day of Atonement, the prayerbook pressed to his heart, his finger stuck between its pages—he had no need of the book, he remembered the prayers by heart—and the tears pouring from his eyes. This was his true, clear, reassuring, unambivalent figure: a weeping Jew. The opposite of the father at the seashore, who did not look but nevertheless saw the white-skinned girls in their tight-fitting bathing suits.

Efros acted as the leader of his little congregation—rabbi, cantor, and sexton rolled into one. He shot angry looks at anyone who whispered to their neighbors, and prayed aloud, stressing the words, with fervor, with utter abandonment, as if in a bitter dispute with someone who did not believe in his orthodoxy. I remembered Kurakin praying devoutly, with no one watching, alone, lips moving soundlessly, as if he were ashamed of possessing something he could not share with his fellows. As if he were gobbling a potato under his blanket when everyone was sleeping.

In the Party too, Efros was the most faithful of the faithful, flawlessly orthodox. On Saturday night he already knew the official Party line about to be made public on Sunday morning. He did not have any sources of information which were inaccessible to others, such as Daniel, who was superior to him in the Party hierarchy. He was simply endowed with sharp political senses and always guessed the most violent reaction that it was possible to imagine. He "employed the Marxist-Leninist method," he said, which was "as exact as a slide rule," and consequently he had no need to wait for the publication of Moscow's reactions to the events of the day. This very formula contained violence aimed against the leadership of Daniel, who did not dare risk guessing, and preferred to wait for the publication of the official Party line. Everyone knew that Efros was setting a trap for Daniel. Even veteran Marxists, well versed in the fine print too, were sometimes astonished by the strange resolutions of the Central Committee—like the Party line on China, on the permanent revolution, or on the German Communist Party—and were not satisfied until the thorny problem had been explained away. But no one dared disagree with the argument that if the "method" was employed properly, in Eretz Israel as in Russia, the same result would inevitably be obtained, like engineers using the same logarithmic tables. Expressing doubts as to the "scientific" nature of Marxism was in itself blasphemy, to be regarded in the same category as sabotage, subversion, and treachery. Efros's orthodoxy where extreme positions were concerned obliged Daniel to treat him cautiously, and to avoid disagreeing with him in the presence of the comrades. And if Efros made a mistake and in the end Moscow took a softer or more compromising line, it was Daniel and not Efros who was found wanting and accused of a left-wing deviation. The margin of "permissible error" allowed to the leaders was less than that granted those of lower rank; the latter were permitted to exaggerate in "vigilance," like children forgiven for going too far in their enthusiasm to please their parents, but not for naughtiness intended to annoy.

The prayers dragged on, and I had to give up my walk to the beach. I went up with Efros to his room on the third floor and we sat together for a while. We spoke about old friends. I told him about my last meeting with Elkind and a few conversations I had had with Daniel in *Der Emes* offices. He told me about "the Worrier" and Bronstein and about a strange meeting with Loka, who had sat in prison under a Caucasian name, since he was sure that the fate of the Jews was sealed. I told him that I had met Besskind's son, but he did not remember who Besskind was at all. The woman standing next to the ironing board had left no mark on his memory. His mind, which was busy searching for the magic formula with which to tempt Besskind into signing our petition, was not free to snap irrelevant pictures.

Before we parted he invited me to be a permanent guest at his prayer services. He said that a man did not have to believe in every detail of the Holy Writ in order to participate in a ceremony which reminded him where he came from and where he was going to. He quoted the example of Aronovitch, a dyed-in-the-wool aetheist and ignoramus, who until a few years ago had been a judge in the Polish courts, and who nevertheless had agreed to pray with them "for the music" which reminded him of his childhood. He told me that he had done his best to avoid making friends with Aronovitch, even though he was an interesting and cultured man. The trouble was that the moment you won his trust, you were obliged to listen to the same monologue: In Poland there were no show trials or travesties of justice like in Russia. He, Aronovitch, in any case, was always scrupulous about due procedure and clear proof.

I told Efros that I didn't mind making up the quorum once in a while; I wasn't the kind of antireligious fanatic who relished smoking a cigarette in public on the Day of Atonement, but if I made a regular thing out of it, I would be guilty of a lie in the soul. I told him about the answer given by a friend of mine, Antonov, one of the most dedicated activists in the democratic movement in the Soviet Union, to a priest who wanted to bring him back to the bosom of the Church.

Antonov vacillated between Karsnoptchev's group and Yemilianov's group. For a long time he had been under the subtle but firm pressure of a priest with great charm and rare courage, who was out to convert souls to the Church. "We are being punished for our sins," he said to Antonov," and there is thus no hope for Russia unless she returns to the bosom of the good and benevolent God." "But I don't believe in God and Jesus," said Antonov to the priest. "Did I ask you if *you* believed?" replied the priest to Antonov. "I'm asking you if the world can get along without God and the Redeemer." And then Antonov replied: "I joined the democratic movement because I was sick and tired of rulers who seek to sanctify the constantly changing official version of the *Short Course,* and the amendments to the constitution issued by the Central Bureau; and you're asking me now to go back to believing in sacred texts which up to only a few generations ago permitted entire villages with their inhabitants to be bought and sold?"

Efros criticized the democratic movement harshly. What was the reason for its existence? To disseminate a few duplicated articles? What benefits would this bring to humanity? The priest was right and not Antonov. Anyone who didn't understand that there was no hope for Russia until the Russian stopped reforming the world and returned to reforming himself, had learned nothing. If the whip and the Twentieth Congress and the tanks at the gates of Budapest and Prague had not taught him this, then he would presumably die in his stupidity. This stupidity was the Pillar of Hercules, which supported the tyrant who held in his hand the false version of the vain dreams of Marxism.

He said that the heroes of the democratic movement had succeeded in inventing yet another form of exploitation. The famous exploited the nameless. The former could afford to shout from the rooftops, conduct long interviews with foreign correspondents, and pose as martyrs. They smuggled their articles out to the international press, were written about in editorials, and were protected from the authorities by their fame. But the ones who paid a heavy price for their arrogance were naive young men, teachers of mathematics, graduates of psychology courses, bad poets, whose work was not published because it was bad and not because it defied the regime. They were put away in lunatic asylums—the cleverest invention yet in the art of population control. They did not know how to say things which made newspaper headlines, and enlightened public opinion, which was quite capable of resigning its conscience to the murder of small, poor nations, would not go out of its way to extricate them from there. They were no match for the clever doctors of the KGB. Their wretched replies to the brilliantly logical and sophisticated cases made out against them by the medical reception boards really did sound like the nonsensical chatter of madmen. They themselves, even before they were injected with the haloperidol which disturbed the balance of their minds, lost their self-confidence; was it not a little crazy to demand international attention for their pathetic personalities? Was it not insanity to believe that it was possible to bring about a revolution in a vast country by means of a few poems and chapters of prose? Why, the slipperiness of the pilferers and the cunning of the Asian merchants was subverting the regime, without a pretentious fuss and bother, more than all the samizdat literature put together. . . .

Our conversation ended before I had a chance to reply to him. True to form, this time too Efros took up his stand on the side of the exploited. As for me, I was sick and tired of arguing. I promised Efros that I would not give him the slip if he needed me, even for a prayer quorum. To myself I said that if one day I weakened to such an extent that I could not go to sleep without

God at my pillow, it would not be Efros's God that I would call on, but Kurakin's.

When we parted he asked about Nina. I did not know that he knew her. He told me that one day he had gone to visit Minkovsky and we had peeped in for a moment and vanished, like a pair of lovers. I did not remember the incident. In other words, my mind too wiped out simple facts. Efros laughed. "You didn't see anyone, you were so absorbed in that woman of yours."

"I lost track of her," I said.

"A striking woman," said Efros.

And then he added, with a smile not lacking in a hint of malice, that "poor Minkovsky" was crazy about his daughter and believed that fate held something better in store for her than what it had actually provided. In his heart of hearts he cherished the hope, more suited to a petit bourgeois than a Communist leader, that he would be able to consolidate his position in the ruling circles by means of marriage ties with an influential leader, or at least with a cultured man like Leopold Sherrer.

$\mathcal{A}$t twilight we meet in the club and play chess. Efros has organized a competition for the house championship. Someone has managed to get hold of stopwatches, and we wage exhausting battles like true professionals, solemn and tense with secretive expressions on our faces.

Efros frowns when he plays and his hands shake. He fixes his opponent with his lopsided stare, as if he had caught him red-handed. He needs to win in the same way that a politician needs to be loved or feared. He is not pleased with me, and he is glad that we are not living on the same floor. In his eyes I am frivolous, or hypocritical, because losing does not make me angry. He does not avoid me, however. For two reasons. The first is that we have memories in common, and the second, that he beats me at the game. When he wins he is as happy as a child.

At the end of the sessions we sometimes remain behind in

the club and chat. Gossiping about the world and the fullness
thereof and discussing political questions. On every question we
are sharply divided. There are two clearly defined camps here:
the old-timers and the new immigrants. There are also under-
currents of hostility. The former had to wait for years before
getting into the old-age home, and presumably they also pay a
handsome sum for the privilege. The latter are maintained here
at the public expense and pay only a token fee. Only those who
have well-off families, like me, pay the full sum.

The *beit midrash* of Finesod House lacks the intimacy of the
beit midrash of Kuznetsk. There is no resemblance between a
conversation carried on from bunk to bunk, when your eyes are
closing with weariness and you are making an effort to speak in
order to sustain some kind of human contact among the filth, in
both senses of the word, and a conversation struck up out of
boredom, with everyone trying to show off whatever learning he
possesses and make others respect him. Sometimes it seems that
they are talking simply in order to hear the voice coming out of
their throat, like a man singing to himself in the forest, to banish
the fear. In Kuznetsk we would abandon ourselves to heart-to-
heart conversations, and we were not ashamed to philosophize
like boys in the upper grades of high school, in order to overcome by speech the brutalizing influence of back-breaking physical labor. In Finesod House most of the inmates do no work at
all, but try to convey the impression that they have various pressing affairs to attend to. Despite yourself you are obliged to listen
to the encapsulated wisdom of a lifetime in the form of such
truisms as "Everybody looks after number one," or "Politics is a
dirty business," or "Growing old is hell," and other truisms so
universal that their repetition seems completely superfluous,
and you would far rather hear about some exception to the
general rule.

It is pathetic to see how people sometimes tear themselves
away from the warmth of the club and its noisy sociability in
order to shut themselves up in the loneliness of their sad rooms,
simply because at the beginning of the evening, before the de-

bate heated up, they pretended that they could not stay long because they had urgent appointments elsewhere. And afterward they could not retract—there was always someone with a fantastic memory, who might forget that he had already told the same joke twice, but who would never forget to remind them, emphatically and even triumphantly, that they were in a hurry to keep an important appointment. At moments like these, when I see such pure malice digging its claws into some poor wretch who wants only to be allowed to forget his former boast, I, too, sometimes feel the wish to shoot a venomous dart at my interlocutor.

There are more women here than men. They keep to themselves and do not join the company of the men. Only one woman participates in the chess championship. She is three years younger than me and insists that I call her by her first name. It is not a hard name but nevertheless I forget it from time to time, perhaps because I have never before met a sixty-seven-year-old woman called Efrat.

The woman, Efrat Ricklin, is the oldest native of Eretz Israel that I know. She was born in Rishon le Zion and wandered from one colony to another as a young girl. An inexplicable excitement seized hold of me when she told me that for some time she had lived with her parents at Migdal. In the year 1921 we had been one and half kilometers apart and we had never met. She spoke about this fact with real sorrow, as if we had missed something. She forgets that if we had met we would have been sworn enemies. She was a bourgeois and I was a class-conscious worker. We speak to each other in Arabic and astonish the others. As if we had secrets from them. Her Arabic is full of Yiddish, and her low, slightly husky voice brings pictures from those days into my memory.

The separation between men and women is only apparent. In private, cautious gropings take place. And there are already a couple of passionate love affairs. There have been jealous scenes and even one suicide attempt. A desperate appeal to a beloved soul. As long as he is alive, even if he is connected to the world by an infusion tube, there is still room in a man's heart for love and hate.

I feel a cautious affection for Efrat Riklin. She has volunteered to bake me a cake for the Sabbath. In Finesod House this is tantamount to a declaration of love.

I am not troubled by a constant stream of visitors. Up to now two people have visited me: the secretary of the Russian Emigrants Association and Perlmutter. The former came to congratulate me on moving into a place of my own. The latter to enjoy my gratitude. He has hinted several times that but for his influence I would have found myself in Beersheba. Walter thinks the same. Perlmutter is one of those people who have spent their lives in "unmentionable" occupations. I wonder what he told the committee which approved my application to live in Finesod House.

From time to time Olga or Walter comes and picks me up to take me home for a visit. They wait for me in the entrance hall and call me on the house telephone to come down. They have not even taken the trouble to see how I have settled in. "You know that if you need anything, you only have to ask," said Olga.

Once my grandson was sent to fetch me. He arrived in uniform, in an army car. Ever since then the "Elders of Zion," whose privileged status derives from the roles they played in public life during the Mandate, are prepared to include me in their circle. They are willing to efface a deviation that lasted forty years from my biography.

I always beat Efrat Riklin at chess. She plays intelligently, but she uses up all the time allowed for every move, and thus makes mistakes at the last minute. Sometimes she gives me a playful glance, as if to hint that her losses, too, are a gift of love. This annoys me. This old girl is sure that even the most enlightened of men would sulk if he were beaten by a woman.

The best chess player on our floor is a seventy-five-year-old retired doctor and amateur painter, who keeps an empty pipe stuck in his mouth all the time. He hums tunes into it, and even bangs it on the table as if to shake the tobacco out before every move. He is a pleasant, friendly man, but very quiet. He is never seen in the club except during the chess matches. He introduced himself to me with all his names on the eve of the first match, but the pipe swallowed his words. We address each other by our first names, although we have not exchanged even one sentence not connected with chess. Sometimes we take part in nocturnal consultations about deferred games. I respect him for his tact and discretion. He always beats Efros, and guessing the suffering which this causes his opponent, he says to him: "You could have won this time if you hadn't made a mistake." Efros believes him and promises himself aloud that he will never make the same mistake again. The next day he is sure that he actually beat the man. If he had not played strictly by the book, which he does not regret, he would have been able to correct the mistake which spoiled his game.

The man and I speak to each other in Russian, even though he has been in the country for fifteen years, eight of them as a general practitioner in development towns.

We are friends, although I have told him the history of my life and he has told me nothing. All I know is that he was born in Leningrad. I have always believed that the people of Leningrad are different from the rest of the Russians. They are more "Western," refined, precise in their language, and sometimes, it seems, conceited too. In any event, they are colder than us Ukrainians and Byelorussians. They are withdrawn and repelled by emotional outbursts. These are prejudices, of course, but anyone who holds them has a greater chance of approaching a native of Leningrad. If you don't fall on his neck, he may give you his hand.

What happened between us last night exploded all the myths.

The beginning was unpromising. During the game, early in the evening, he asked me if I understood anything about stereo sets. I told him that I was not an expert on the subject, but that I was prepared to take a look. He said that he would not dream of troubling me, and I felt that he was afraid of insulting me—in case I came, pretending expertise, failed to fix anything, and disgraced myself. He said that he had all sorts of tools, including a soldering iron, but he did not know how to use them. I promised him that I would not solder the wrong wires together, and that I would not blush if forced to admit failure.

The fault was quickly mended. The man was full of gratitude. He said that he had received a new record as a gift and he was very keen to hear it, and if I had no objections, he would put it on right away.

The moment the first sounds were heard, the man was transformed. The melancholy that descended on him! As if he had just heard the most appalling news, and by the time the first harmony changed, he had already finished protesting to Heaven and resigned himself to his fate. His handsome face paled and a little muscle twitched in his throat. A bluish mist veiled his eyes and his hands clasped each other as if in prayer. Gradually the tears gathered in his eyes, and when his eyes were full, they trickled down his cheeks drop by drop, one flowing down to his chin while the other waited in the corner of his eye.

Leningrad or no Leningrad, I said to myself—a Russian soul. Full to overflowing!

I, too, was thrilled by the music. The sonorus chords of the choir in Rachmaninoff's "All-Night Vigil" brought to mind snow-covered expanses, a sleigh gliding through the silence and cutting an ever-narrowing path in the snow, the music seemed not to beat against your ears from outside, but to well up quietly inside you, without beginning or end. I allowed the sounds to flood me, and suddenly, unconsciously, a prickling warmth gathered in my eyes, too, as if sand had spilled into them. The look the man gave me when a tear trickled down my cheek too! As if two brothers had met after a long parting . . .

When the music died down, we both sat in silence for a long time. As if he had read my thoughts he suddenly said to me, "In the first year the only thing I missed was the snow." The very words I had written in my diary after the visit to Tel Yosef!

Then he said: "The music old men hear is not the same music that young men hear. . . . All those layers of sorrow and pain, grief and sighing, rebellion and resignation, into which it sinks . . . and the sounds that respond to it from within. . . . It's like the sensitivity of an ailing limb—the slightest change in the weather makes it start itching immediately . . ."

This was the beginning of a night-long session. The tears melted his heart. He spoke like one who had been sentenced to long silence and who had suddenly found an attentive ear. Thus two prisoners open their hearts to one another when they are sure that neither one is an informer. His hands spoke with him, not without restraint, but drawing long, rounded lines in the air.

This music is one of the great enigmas of the soul, he said. As a child he had been taught to avoid their churches and to spit when nobody was looking. His ears had heard nothing but Jewish prayers and Sabbath songs. And nevertheless, when he grew up, and especially after leaving Russia, whenever he heard these pure, clear male and female voices singing to themselves, his own childhood, which had no part in these sounds, came back to him, with its sweet sadnesses and easily appeased wonderings, the childhood of a Jewish boy among Gentiles, attracted and repelled by turn, cherishing in his little heart pride in his distinctiveness and longing to be like everyone else. In Jerusalem, in Gethsemane, he had stood for a long time mesmerized, listening to the monotonous chanting of the prayers, as if all the years he had lived under those high domes he had found there a refuge from his grief. Listening to the velvety sound of the quiet voices of the priests, faith and hope had returned to him. . . .

He had received his love of music from his father, a fiddler who played at weddings and celebrations. As a child he had played the violin. But for the revolution, he would presumably have followed in his father's footsteps. During the war he was a medical orderly on the Prussian front. He had deserted with his unit and returned to Leningrad. After the revolution he had worked for a time in a pharmaceutical factory. A soldier he had met on the front had become an important man, and thus he found his way into medical school. He was not a Communist, but neither was he hostile to the regime. He was nothing. A human being, who loved music, painting, people, and women. If he had not married the woman he married, perhaps nothing would have happened to him. He would have worked for many years in the same hospital, and retired. To fish, and spend his summers on the shores of the Black Sea.

It was because of his wife. Because of her, his life was ruined. Because of her, he had left everything and come to Israel. She was a good woman, he said. Good-looking, decent, and devoted. Russian to the backbone. Generous, admiring, kindhearted, trusting. A true peasant woman, but not ignorant. On the contrary, perhaps a little too well educated. She had studied at the university and remembered what she had learned. You could never tell if what she said came from her heart or from a book. She threw quotations around as if everybody had read everything. From the village she had brought her healthy body, her stubbornness, her childish notion that everybody born in the big city was clever, and her unshakable faith in the Russian Orthodox Church.

Her faith did not prevent her marriage to a Jew, but it was to blame for the fact that she landed in jail. She would go and listen to the sermons of a certain foolish priest, who had the temerity to preach against the Soviet system, and during the period of the struggle against the clergy, she was arrested as a counterrevolutionary.

After her arrest, charges were fabricated against him too. And he, too, spent a few years in the universities of life that Gorky did not know. But it was not the time he spent in prison which upset his mental balance, but rather the days that came after his release. In prison his life was relatively comfortable. He served as a doctor not far from home, and after four years his rights were restored. For fifteen years he waited for his wife and he was faithful to her all that time. When she was released, she did not return to him. I'm sorry, she wrote to him, but I cannot live a lie.

A few years earlier, while she was still in prison, she had written and told him that she had fallen in love with one of the prisoners. He had received the letter eight months after it was written, and decided to ignore its contents. Perhaps she had changed her mind in the meantime. Perhaps the prisoner had been transferred to another camp, or died, or betrayed her. It seemed to him strange, and foolish, and not quite human, that she had found it necessary to write to him about her love affairs. In such circumstances, in any case, everything was forgiven in advance. If her flesh was starved, he was not the man to hold her to sacred vows. She had left him a girl and she would return to him a woman. He remembered how fresh and vital she was, and presumed that she would not abstain from satisfying her appetites. He only hoped that she would not come back with some incurable disease. He wrote her a long letter—she would complete her term, come home, and everything would be as it was before; there was already a house for her to return to, and he had hung pictures on the walls, and put plants in the windows, just as she liked—and he did not even refer to her confessions. Two years later he received another letter. The address was new, and he was delighted. She must have forgotten all about that affair by now. But when he opened it he found that it contained the same message as before. He should find himself another woman—a good man like him would easily find a a woman to love and admire him—because she had no intention of coming back to him even after she was freed. He wrote back immediately: If you love this man that you are living with now so much, I can only bow my head and be silent; but if anything happens to you, if this man leaves you and finds himself another woman, or if you change your mind or discover that you don't love him as you now imagine—and living together can sometimes be disillusioning— you can always come back to me: I will forgive and forget. Her reply arrived quicker than he expected. You are a good man, perhaps too good, but you don't understand, you don't understand at all what I am trying to tell you. I am not living with the man that I love at all and he is not with me and I have not seen him for two and a half years now, but I cannot live with you when I love another.

He gave me a suspicious, apprehensive look: perhaps he had gone too far and I, an insensitive soul, a man toughened in a hard school, would mock him for still thinking, after so many years, of the same childish woman, who read too many books.

That's the Russian soul for you, he continued. Full of childish pride, yearning for a holy life, believing in some cruel, uncompromising consistency, like the early revolutionaries.

She also wrote and told him explicitly that she did not even know if this man loved her, and in any case he was unfaithful to her all the time. He had a wife in Moscow and he was living in a village a hundred versts from there, in the home of a soldier's widow. But she loved him anyway. And she seemed to be hinting that these facts only made her love the purer. It was impossible to shock her. And perhaps the frivolity of this man only strengthened her desire to save his soul and bestow upon him the perfect joy radiating from those who love without expecting to be loved in return, and so on and so forth—emotional extravagances common in Russian literature, which perhaps are not mere flights of fancy after all, since if there is such a demand for them it must mean that people believe in them, or at least wish, with all their hearts, that they existed.

After her release, although she had lost track of her beloved, she did not return home. And then he left Russia and came to the one place in the world where he had family. He was not a Zionist, just as he was not a Communist. But there were people everywhere, and everywhere they fell sick and needed doctors. And there was music everywhere, and there were good orchestras here too. When he arrived in Israel he lived in the home of his relation, who passed away and left him the house. After he retired, he sold the house and moved into Finesod House.

In the first years after his arrival in the country he still played with the idea of marrying again. But whenever he was about to take the plunge, he remembered Larissa and changed his mind.

* * *

I knew that he was recounting a chapter of my life to me even before he mentioned Larissa's name. Once or twice I was nearly tempted to confess, but I held my tongue. I was afraid of his sensitivity. He might marvel like me at our amazing meeting— how strange are the ways of God! I wanted to exclaim: Efrat Riklin and I never met at Migdal, the number of whose inhabitants was less than that of Finesod House, and the husband of Larissa Verchinsky chose me out of all the people in the world to complain to of the sins of the novel and the rotten fruits it produced in the soul of the Russian woman! But I was afraid that he would withdraw from me and regret that he had poured out his heart before me. It did not seem right to listen and nod my head, or make a few comforting remarks, or even quote Push- kin—"To love we learned not from Nature, but from the chap- ters of a bad novel"—and so although I had not intended doing so, I gave him tit for tat. A secret for a secret. And I told him about Nina. How I was holding my peace in order not to ruin the happiness of a woman I loved. And that good man, Verchinsky, clapped his hands and said, with true sympathy and in the clear, musical voice of a priest reciting a prayer: "I am dust beneath your feet."

*A*nother visit to my son. He was tired and troubled. His right hand fluttered before his eyes as if chasing away a fly. He did not have the faintest desire to learn arithmetic. I sat him in the wheelchair and pushed him to the porch. We sat side by side, facing the orange groves dividing the rehabilitation center from the village. I thought about Verchinsky's words: "The green that old people see." What serenity a man like me can derive from the bright color of the citrus trees! I pull it out from beneath the thick layers of snow, as if I had been waiting for it all winter. It seems to me a premonition of change. A proof that time does not run out, but accumulates. But suddenly everything seemed to shrivel. I looked into the eyes of my son: open and shut at one and the same time. I thought: What is the green that is registered on his mind behind that dull steel mask?

When I took him back to his room, for his physiotherapy, he suddenly burst out and shouted at me in a loud voice. The nurse hurried up to separate us. She asked me to leave the room. Something in the look of my face irritates him. There is no way of knowing what it is that he has remembered. In any case, it is best for me to go away and not risk upsetting him.

I asked her if I could come back. She said: "Tomorrow. Don't worry, he won't remember." I went out and stood in the corridor. A limbless young man asked me to wipe his nose. When he blew into the handkerchief in my hand, I could not hold back my tears.

At that moment the nurse pushed Nimrod past. He looked at me and did not see me.

In the cafeteria of the old-age home, sitting with Efrat Riklin, I heard Efros's voice from the next table. He was telling a group of young people—two girls, a slightly older woman, and a dark, long-haired boy with a wild beard—stories from the camps. Since Efrat Riklin was silent, I could hear everything he said. He was speaking about chopping down forests in a temperature of forty below zero. His descriptions were vivid and fascinating. Some of what he said was devoted to the changes which took place in people. His tone was cool, superior, quasi-scientific, as if he were describing the characteristics of liquids or gasses at low temperatures. It was obvious that he obtained tremendous satisfaction from the attention on the faces of his young listeners. From time to time he would shoot a quick, inquiring glance at the youngest girl—an exquisitely beautiful girl with a snub nose and big, shining eyes. She gazed at him worshipfully—those who have never experienced so much as unrequited love in their lives attribute powers not of this world to those who have suffered greatly.

Suddenly he noticed me. He introduced me to the youngsters and said, with a generous gesture, that a man like me could probably tell stories that were no less interesting and even more fascinating than his. They widened their circle at Efros's table and invited me to join them. Although the company of the young people was agreeable, I did not feel at ease. It was an embarrassing, strange, and even rather silly situation. One of the young girls hurried over to our table and moved the two glasses of tea, one of which was already completely empty, to their table, and we had no option but to join them. They all fell silent, as if the moment I sat down I would break into speech. That was what they had invited me for, after all. I was furious with Efros for making a promise in my name which I had no intention of keeping, and not even leaving me a loophole of escape.

"What can I tell you?" I said.

"Come, come," said Efros. "Don't be so modest. I've heard stories about you . . ."

An offended expression momentarily crossed his face, and was immediately replaced by one of anger. He was prepared to share his golden crown of thorns with me and I rejected his offering? I felt that he regarded me as an ingrate. He was prepared to lend me even the admiration of the beautiful young girl, and I disdained him.

We fell into an unpleasant argument. I said that the stories about Siberia were all painfully alike, and in any case they were all well known. After Zibulsky, Herring, Solzhenitsyn, Shalamov, Nadezhda Mandelstam—what was there left to say? There wasn't a single detail that had not already been recorded in Solzhenitsyn's books. Although I did not count myself among his admirers. This wrathful Christian, who tried so hard not to hate the Jews as such, but only one by one, as they deserved—if he had been put into power he would certainly have crushed the criminal prisoners with an iron hand. In his eyes they had not been created in the image of God. Nevertheless, his books deserved to be read. An encyclopedia of suffering. There was nothing left for us lesser beings. And really, what did we have to say? If we dwelled too much on those days, we would still be suspected of wanting to be paid compensation for our suffering, pain, and humiliation.

Efros sniggered. "Berkov, you amaze me. Are you trying to

say that you never speak about it to anyone? Never?" He provoked me.

"I speak about it," I said. "As an example. A parable."

Efros made a gesture of contemptuous dismissal. "All that
tremendous experience. . . . An apocalyptic experience. . . . The
most profound trauma suffered by humanity in the twentieth
century. . . . The rupture which split the globe and tore subterra-
nean currents from the bowels of the earth—all this passed over
your head without your learning or understanding a thing. The
poison fed you in your youth is still seething in your bones.
You're incorrigible. . . ."

He turned away from me to his disciples, and in the tone of
a patient science teacher, a skeleton nailed to its pedestal in the
corner, his stick gliding precisely over the dry bones, he explained, as if I didn't exist: "A classical example of the Bolshevik
mentality. Anything that doesn't bring immediate benefit to the
Party, the regime, the education of the youth, public morale,
discipline, increased production rates, brainwashing—lacks all
importance. It is superfluous and harmful. Any human experience which has no positive lesson of the said kind is simply
gossip, malicious slander. The story is not important. The lesson
is important. Art is instrumental. Writers are the engineers of the
human soul. Poets—kindergarten teachers. Don't moan, was the
slogan after the revolution. It hurts? So what? Keep quiet. Nobody cares about your private stomachache. You see around you
opportunists, crooks, rogues, and sadists, settling quietly into the
bureaucracy, flattering, fawning, doing ugly favors for their superiors, trampling over the weak and denouncing people simply
for being depressed at the prevailing state of affairs—so what?
Perhaps subjectively you are right, these fellows are not particularly sympathetic. But objectively your moans and groans only
serve the enemies of the revolution. When you fire an engine,
your hands get dirty. There were camps in Siberia? Nobody
denies it anymore. But the lesson was learned. The conclusion
was drawn. The cause is known, and so is the remedy: the cult of
the personality. And as everybody knows, it was ruthlessly
crushed. And that's that. It no longer exists. There is a collective

leadership now, and anyone who sat in jail without a trial has been rehabilitated, and the guilty have been punished. In other words, anyone who pipes up about how they trod on his toes too is simply painting monsters on the wall, frightening the Third World, and selling his soul to the devil." Efros sniggered. He threw me a look. As if to make sure that I was still there. "And here you have a man with a parable. He himself is the best example: although he rebelled against them, and amused himself for a while with samizdat and magnetizdat, and God knows what else . . . and played at underground games . . . and probably swore to avenge the tears of the innocent . . . and promised himself and his friends to restore the good old days . . . and to bring back pure communism again—he never learned the essential lesson. . . ."

"All that long speech just because I wasn't in the mood to begin telling stories? I don't have a button that starts playing tunes the minute you press it, you know."

Efros flushed furiously. I was well aware of the reason for his rage. And for a moment I regretted having gone too far. I had cut him to the quick. What did Efros have in the world? He had no family, he didn't even have a child. His trials and sufferings were his treasures. In this he was not so very different from me. And I had allowed myself to speak of them lightly. But I, too, had cause for annoyance. My only crime lay in the fact that I did not feel like showing off my sores in public. And he had bombarded me with heavy cannons. I could not endure the ease with which the loyal dogmatists of the past now heaped scorn on the altar at which they had worshiped. No more than forty years ago, he had shot arrows of scorn at me from his mocking eyes when I dared to question the eternal verities, which he proclaimed as confidently as a man who was in private communication with God. If I didn't clap my hands loudly enough, I was immediately accused of blasphemy. And now he was basking in my disgrace in front of his disciples, like a science teacher who had found a strange frog and was giving it an electric shock to show them how it squirmed.

A silly argument ensued. I took up the cudgels in defense of the democratic movement, and he accused it of hidden anti-Semitism. He dismissed my remarks scornfully: they had no basis in fact, and I spoke as an autodidact, who had never done any serious research into the subject. He spoke as if he were warning his students against superficiality. And he made me so furious that I forgot my resolution not to lose my temper for nothing and reminded him that in the past, too, his opinions had been bolstered by learned authorities, only then he had found them in different books. Nor did I refrain from hinting that his methods of debate themselves derived from the school which he was now denouncing. The argument waxed fast and furious and ranged as far as the Jewish question and the class struggle. We touched on the subject of God and free will and other no less weighty matters. We must have seemed slightly ridiculous to our youthful audience, who listened to us with baffled faces. More than once I wanted to put an end to the heated debate. But every time the irony in his voice provoked me to answer him in the same coin. I could not endure the mocking yelps that escaped his throat while he was listening to me and gathering his forces to jump in and interrupt my words. I even tried to imitate the unintelligible sniffing sounds he himself produced during a chess game, like a kind of warning hum, while he unfolded his arguments. We might have gone on for hours—both of us were presumably deriving some kind of peculiar enjoyment from the skirmish—if Efrat Riklin had not intervened.

She actually tugged at my sleeve. "That's enough for now. If you could only see your faces. Red, flushed. One of you will end up by having a stroke. That's all we need. Like Aronovitch."

The voice of practical wisdom. Like cold water on my feverish brain. I was ready to put an end to the argument there and then. To apologize. What could we do, we were typical of our generation. Passionate arguers. It was too late for us to change. But not Efros. He flared up more vehemently than before. But his fireworks were no longer directed against me, but against Efrat Riklin. He discovered a hidden meaning in her words. An accusation. Worse: a libelous slander.

He pounced on her. It was not the first time he had heard these hints. He rejected them with contempt. He had never argued with Aronovitch at all. Aronovitch spoke and he kept quiet. But the man had worked himself up more and more, until something snapped in his brain. It was wicked even to hint that he had anything to do with the regrettable event, just because he had happened to be among the audience. It was nothing but malicious gossip and slandermongering.

She shrank into her chair. Why was he shouting at her? Nothing was farther from her mind than making any accusations against anybody. She had simply remembered Aronovitch, and that unpleasant evening, after the book about the Polish courts had come out, and Aronovitch had found it necessary to justify himself, and repeated over and over again that his conscience was perfectly clean, and that he had never in his life convicted anybody whose guilt had not been proved. And it was true that Efros had not argued with him and had allowed him to go on and on, but on the other hand you couldn't really say that he had had nothing to do with it at all, because whenever Aronovitch stopped to take a breath and rest before he charged again, Efros would stare at him and say only one word, which was hardly audible, as if he were talking to himself, one Yiddish word with two syllables, "Real-ly," and that was enough. Like cold water on red-hot iron. But perhaps the silence of the others, especially the Poles among them, had hurt even more.

When we left the cafeteria she accused me of treating Efros badly. He had offered me the hand of friendship and I had rejected it. But for this too she found an excuse. Perhaps it was our nature. Not the nature of Russians, but the nature of old men. Educated old men. If we didn't abuse each other, we wouldn't be sure that we existed. Old women, she said, woke up at night every hour and coughed loudly. Perhaps somebody was listening.

Sometimes you feel a longing to wake up at night and hear a groan that does not come from your own body.

* * *

I cannot forget the sight of Efros's face when he got up from the table. Such pallor I have seen only on the faces of people on trial in court. His eyes had gone gray and his forehead seemed to have shrunk. For a moment I felt sorry for him: a Jewish crook. What had gotten into me? He had wanted to make an impression on his youthful disciples: Look, I have friends from over there, brothers who shared my fate. He had wanted to boast of the fraternity of the camps: Look how different we are from each other—I, Efros, a learned man with an academic reputation, and he, a self-educated braggart; and nevertheless, the bowl of soup we ate together has made us brothers.

And what did I do? I humiliated him. I dragged him into a foolish argument about things which no longer have any bearing on our lives. I forced him to insult me, to mock my ignorance, to patronize me—which was not what he wanted. Because it did not suit the role he was trying to play. Furthermore, on my account an accusing finger had been pointed at him: his Yiddish "Real-ly" had blocked an artery in Aronovitch's brain. And who knows, perhaps it was only a Jewish sigh.

Efrat Riklin criticized my behavior: an old man's spite. A soul spitting out its poison. Like the body which no longer controls its functions. But what does a woman like Efrat Ricklin —a girlish old woman from the colonies of Judea, who learned French in the palmy days and shorthand typing in the hour of need—know about the suffering, of the inheritance of two ideal-ists from the twenties, whose bloodstreams were invaded by the revolutionary virus? We would have been prepared to shoot one another in order to ensure the knaves of the next decade a life free from care.

The argument was not a disinterested one. The things that were said were not important at all, they were code words for other objectives—underneath the verbal sword sharpening a deep disagreement seethed with doubts half a century old.

I purify my soul in seven ritual baths before I call the things by name. If Efros were ever to discover the definition which I am about to give here, he would say that the poison had infected the finest of my tissues, the gray cells which break up the picture of the world into words and syllables.

But I will risk it and say: we belong to two different classes.

I can see his clever eyes glinting underneath his elegant spectacles: "Real-ly!"

In remote jungles, in the islands of East Asia, many years after the end of the war, rearguard battles were still being fought by starving Japanese soldiers who did not know that the war was over.

Our war is not over. Efros is a member of the officer class. I am a soldier. We set out to fight a common battle together, but there was no hatred deeper than our hatred for each other. There was no comradeship-in-arms in our forces. In the officers' mess a unique set of relations, full of dangerous arrogance, grew up; and a sad friendship, the comradeship of the persecuted, next to the bare wooden tables of the soldiers. This is a metaphor, of course. Both of us were completely penniless. We ate moldy bread and sticky halvah. I never envied him for being invited to Paris, to meet Comintern representatives, and put up at luxury hotels, for reasons of conspiracy, and coming back full of self-righteous stories about the disgraceful exploitation in the meat market of the Place Pigalle. On the contrary. I knew how hard it would be for him to return to the wretched hut he lived in, in a Tel Aviv slum. When I speak of an officers' mess I mean something far deeper. I am not speaking of people who had accepted high office, and were consequently debarred from making friends with recruits. In this class war things were far more complicated. Among the officers there were true soldiers too.

But Efros was one of those who preached principles to others. I ate from his hand. Perhaps this is the way of the world. There is no army without a hierarchy. And we saw ourselves as the soldiers of the world revolution. But when we were left to our own devices, we fought each other. Like a defeated army: the soldiers shoot the officers; the officers jump into their cars and escape.

A strange, hopeless war. There is no knowing who is for us,

who for our foes. Shall I say that Efros is an opportunist, and therefore we—in other words, the idiots, the innocents, the Communists of Käthe Kollwitz and Franz Masserel—should aim our broken pens against him? Someone will surely be found in our camp to take up the cudgels on his behalf: a mistake in identification, he is one of the best and most honest of the lot, he believed in what he said and was sure he was right; and when he realized his mistake, he had the courage to recant, all the way, without stopping at the roadside to look at the convoys of refugees and throw stones at them.

And nevertheless, my heart tells me that the most tortuous of the class struggles takes place all the time between Efros and his like, who are cleverer than us, more sharp-witted than us, who know what they want and know how to impose it on others, and my poor brothers, the naive and foolish, the pure in heart, who do not even know how to hate properly.

A hopeless struggle. The winner is known in advance. It is difficult to keep it up. Other, more urgent wars are always cropping up in the middle. Efros will blow the trumpet and we will mount our horses and postpone our war to another time.

And when we come home from the war, battle weary, we will be eaten up by doubts. Perhaps Efros is really one of the decent ones. Others are far worse than him. He, at least, possesses the authority of a faith which we lack: he believed in the revolution and was prepared to go to jail; he believes in God and is prepared to be ridiculed and have doubts cast on his sincerity.

Sometimes I envy people who can deceive themselves.

On second thought: I am really an anarchist. And this is why I was so happy in the Labor Brigade, in that first year, before the organizational patterns were set.

It was touching, but at the same time maddening—the way Efros tried to dress himself up in a crown of thorns. Now that the wheel has turned and it is respectable to be at the bottom, he wants to be an officer in the camp of the martyrs too. The extra bowl of porridge, the prize for more perfect misery, is awarded there to those whose teeth were broken too. You suffered? He

suffered twice as much. You were beaten? They didn't pull out
your nails. You are unfortunate? He is Job.

In Verchinsky's opinion it is very foolish of me to make an enemy
of a man like Efros. I smile: he can't harm me anymore. And
Verchinsky retorts: As long as a man lives, even if he is no longer
any use to anybody, he can still do harm.

People leave wicked wills behind them in order to make bad
blood among their relatives, he said. In Leningrad, he told me,
a dying man sent a wicked letter to someone who had been his
wife's lover twenty years before. He copied letters and figures at
random from a record catalogue, and the police arrested the
man for treason on the basis of this message in "code."

This, too, is a kind of immortality of the soul.

"Efros was the man who recruited you into the Party," he
said. "And now you're taking your revenge on him. Isn't it a little
late in the day?"

"It wasn't Efros," I replied. "Two other men influenced me.
The first was Elkind, but at that stage he wasn't even a Party
member himself. On the contrary, he accused Moscow of ignoring the Jewish question. The second was Daniel. And he actually
recruited me. He tempted me, pulled me by the tongue, led me
by the nose, stuck a ring in it, and drove me like a donkey.
. . . And I love both of them with all my heart and soul."

During the period when I was a Party propagandist, I told
Verchinsky, I would fall in love with my victims. "Victims" is of
course a term borrowed from the lexicon of those outside the
faith. For I was convinced that I was a true guide. My only doubts
concerned the right I, Avigdor ben Elimelech Berkov, had to
proselytize intelligent people, hungry for a word of truth, who
trusted me and did not know that I was operating on behalf of
a Party whose conduct revolted them. In any event, I felt the
deepest affection for the unemployed who followed me because
they had been caught in their time of trouble and were angry
with the whole world. I loved the ignorant Arabs who seized
upon the *"imperializm"* which I offered them as the root of all

their troubles, as if I were putting Aladdin's lamp into their hands. I felt profound compassion for the perplexed poets, who wrote didactic verses while at the same time longing both for a nobility not of this world and for a friendly handshake from a Jewish worker with a rough hand and a warm heart. Strangely enough, to this day, after experiencing things fifty times worse, I cannot forget my dismay when I heard Efros refer, with profound contempt, to the "barefoot bourgeoisie," i.e., the leftists of the Labor Brigade, and the "comrades with the Oriental imagination" in Jaffa and Ramleh, and my astonishment when I saw the hostility in his eyes as he said that in Russia the poets who "accompanied us for two or three steps" would have been "sentenced to death" for their "idiotic verses." "They spew out their miserable souls in public and drivel on about proletarian culture, but if the bosses were ever to crown them with the title of National Poet, they would betray the revolution on the spot, without batting an eyelid. . . ."

When Efros used the words "private stomachache" to his disciples, he was quoting himself. I wonder if he remembered. Only then he had used them to cast a stone at the "enemies of the revolution," and now, at someone who did not want to groan with him in a duet.

I remembered something Larissa Verchinsky had once written me:

"Many writers have failed at Socialist Realism. They were sure that they were being required to lie, to paint things in rosy colors. But what they were actually being asked, almost humbly, and without any wicked designs, to do was to give preferance to a humane literature, which speaks to the hearts of simple people who want to know about the world. These people are not interested in what you draw up from the dark depths of your soul. They don't care if you find pearls there or rotten fish. They're not interested in neurotic individuals. They want stories with a clear moral lesson, like a parable or legend. And these too have a right to exist. Such stories can be written honestly and fairly. Without lying. But those who volunteered to lie, in order to obtain apartments and honors, sold their souls to the devil."

There were some writers who loved the Soviet motherland the way parents love a backward child. Pretending that everything is all right in order not to hurt his feelings.

Of the generation of the revolution the only one that Larissa liked was Paustovski. But he too did not escape her barbs: even he sometimes lied out of cowardice. But who are we to judge cowards? "I thought of Lenin and the mighty popular movement at whose head stood this amazingly simple man. . . . I could not understand the reason for my emotion. Perhaps it was the sense of those great days, perhaps the belief in the happiness to come . . ."—a quotation in one of her letters. "Perhaps! A poet should be careful not to flatter even an enlightened ruler, never mind one who advocated terrorism," she added.

"A true poet stands full of wonder before a bird," she wrote. "He does not ask how its wings bear it. He asks why God needed a bird."

I suddenly remembered the bird that stood before my son, and his miraculous laugh.

*A*n unexpected visit. Olga's friend Rachel. She came with a director of documentary films, who wanted to talk to me: perhaps the story of my life could serve as a framework for a movie that he wanted to make.

While she was talking to me the man looked at me. A more impertinent look has never been directed at me since my interrogators tried to expose my lies. As if he were judging me through the camera's eye, for good or for evil. Perhaps he would cast me off like an old shoe if it turned out that my face was uninteresting.

He was still not sure, he said. Still groping. He would meet a few people. Then he would decide.

He was afraid, evidently, of arousing my hopes.

"Why should you want to take pictures of an old pensioner?" I inquired, somewhat provocatively. He was offended. He did not make propaganda movies. He was interested in a story, a full life cycle; it was a rare opportunity to meet someone who was there and left and went back again. But he wasn't promising anything, of course. We had to talk. He spoke for a long time, asking few questions and trying to win my confidence.

What goes on in the Soviet Union is well known, he said. In every detail. And nevertheless—it's an enigma. The people, their behavior. Until you get to know them, you think: rabbits, sheep. Declaiming nonsense with passionate enthusiasm. You wonder: Do they believe it all? Do they believe a little of it? Do they reject it all? Do they send out musical signals to each other, when it's really true, when it's half true, when it's a downright lie? You meet them in the West, face to face, without listening devices, and they repeat the same hollow slogans to you. You're completely at a loss. Are they making fun of you? Don't they trust you? Don't they care if you think them idiots? One day you crack the shell. And to your astonishment you discover intelligent, shrewd, sharp-witted, erudite people. They look down on you, as if anyone who hasn't been through the Soviet forge has no idea what kind of world he's living in. Even our democracy seems fatuous to them. Any businessman can cheat the state. Any trade union can ruin the economy. And so: Where is the truth? Who are the true representatives of Soviet education? How many are in this camp, and how many in that? Why do all the voices of protest coming from Russia sound like the bleating of a lamb?

Five years ago, he was in the Soviet Union to attend some conference on the cinema. He wanted to get an idea: What kinds of lives did people lead? Was there anything in common? What were the Jews like? Was there a younger generation? A study tour. He met a Jewish director. And the latter asked him for books in Hebrew. He asked him: "Aren't you afraid?" The director replied: "I'm sick of being afraid." The next day he brought him a small packet, wrapped up in a Russian newspaper. The man threw away the newspaper and held the books openly under his arm. He asked him: "Is it allowed?" And the man replied: "In Russia nobody knows what's allowed. Not even the police. Only what's forbidden. But not everything that's not forbidden is allowed."

He met an Italian scriptwriter, a Communist. A charming young man. The Italian told him the following story: A party leader, a great man, a writer, a journalist, a philosopher, a resistance fighter, had aroused the wonder of an intellectual. The intellectual asked him: "How can you, a man like you, take orders from the Georgian bully?" "Orders?" replied the Party leader. "If only there were. We would know where we stood. Our lives are impossible precisely because we have to guess at his intentions. That's why we are sometimes more orthodox than the Pope."

He sat and talked to an actor and an actress, Jews with beautiful eyes, sad, pathetic. A husband and wife. They spoke in Yiddish about the cinema, about actors, about movie cameras. All his attempts to turn the conversation to the Jewish question came up against a blank wall: they weren't interested in politics.

After a while the woman went out to make a phone call. The actor immediately leaned over the table and whispered rapidly: "It's terrible, there's no freedom, no honesty, for Jews it's hell." He asked him: "Why did you wait for your wife to leave? Don't you trust her?" "I trust her," replied the man. "But I pity her. What she doesn't hear can't harm her." He said to him: "If you're not sure of me, why did you speak?" The actor said: "Haven't you ever felt the need to go out into the street and shout, and risk everything for one cry from the bottom of your heart?"

They were joined by a dignified, elegant man with white hair and smiling eyes. A civilian suit covered with medals. A colonel. The deputy chairman of the conference. The actor and his wife greeted him with sincere friendliness. With true cordiality. They spoke to him in French. They chatted about movies, gossiped about directors, lamented the taste of the audiences. While they were talking a tall, beautiful woman with deep, sparkling brown eyes approached the table. "Allow me to introduce my wife," said the colonel. When they parted, the actor and his wife wanted to accompany him to his hotel. The colonel said, "Please, there's no need. I'll take him in my car." The colonel's wife went with the actors, and they strolled over to the car park.

The colonel spoke English fluently, like a professor of political science at an American university. Not the language. The style. The liberal spirit, the openness: "Try to understand, there are two million Jews and a hundred million Moslems. The Arabs have oil, power, American bases. What have the Jews got? The Soviet Union cannot afford to make enemies of the Arabs. But you should know: we love you. We admire your army. You are gallant people, and you resemble us."

Then the colonel explained: "I sent the actors home because I couldn't have said these things to you in their presence. The Jews are afraid of their own shadows. They would have been alarmed by my words and we would have felt uncomfortable. But not all the Jews are like that. Only the men. In the bad days, during the time of the personality cult, Jewish women did not deny their husbands. They did not tell their children, Your father is an enemy of the people. They did not sleep around like whores. Did you see my wife?"

"She's Jewish."

"How did you know?"

"It's written in her eyes."

"You Jews are cunning devils." The colonel laughed affectionately.

When they parted the colonel gave him a Russian newspaper in the English language. "Read it on your way home. It will interest you." On the plane he read it. He did not understand. The colonel's article was a stupid collection of empty slogans. Marxist garbage. Denunciations and abuse. Only one question bothered him: Why had the colonel given him this superficial article to read? So that he would know—see, this is how we talk and this is how we write? Or perhaps he really thought it was his masterpiece.

A few years later he met the actor in America. The actor reminded him of their meeting in Moscow, and told him that they had feared for his fate when the KGB man took him off in his car. And then he told the actor what the colonel had said about Jewish women. "Really?" said the actor. "That's interest-

ing. When his wife died, he went to Riga and married her sister."
And suddenly he burst into tears. He asked the actor: "Why are
you crying?" "Maybe all those years the colonel was trying to tell
us something and we didn't understand."

I wrote down what he said. Questions hidden inside stories.
My answers are of no importance here. They are written down in
a notebook over many pages. I spoke for about an hour and a
half. As I spoke he fixed me with a penetrating look, as if he were
recording everything in his brain, recording and filing—what I
said, how, why, when I got carried away, when I skipped things.
A truth machine.

My thoughts have not been so well organized for a long
time. Every detail. Period after period. Many things become clear
to you when you try to explain them to an intelligent person.
They become inextricably entangled when the person in front of
you is a fool. It's the same with books, I think. A writer who thinks
that his reader is an ignoramus gets things confused and talks
nonsense.

Today I understand how I, who lost my temper easily and was
sure of my innocence, came to my detention and interrogation
confident, calculating, clear-headed, and composed. The law of
big numbers. So many people had been arrested, some of them
well known as loyal Communists, modest in their demands and
ready to sacrifice themselves for the sake of the revolution, that
only an utter simpleton could believe that his behavior had any
importance at all. We behaved like the villagers living on the
banks of the great rivers—they saw the water rising and hoped
that the flood would not wash their fields away.

Although they were in the habit of arresting people in the
dead of night, it did not come as a surprise. There were so many
unmistakable signs that when the knock at the door was heard
you actually breathed a sigh of relief. At last. An end to waiting
and suspense. The signs were overt or covert. Overt: you were
summoned to a friendly talk with the authorities and you understood that from now on you would have to pay something for

your freedom. Covert: someone spoke to you too openly about the strains and stresses of the times. Something loathsome had been thrown into your lap. Whether you complained or not, you were in their hands. If he was one of them, the punishment was imminent. If he was an innocent who had unburdened himself of his feelings, it would take longer. In either case, it would be counted against you. Anything you heard without reporting incriminated you. You were guilty of not doing anything, too.

Sometimes even this did not happen. You simply felt it at the tip of your nose—your name was on the blacklist and they were watching you. The caretaker fails to greet you. An opportunist, who knows instinctively when anyone is out of favor, is rude to you. The stupidest member of the cell criticizes your style. Nobody laughs at your jokes. The cultural committee stops asking you to say a few words of greeting. A neighbor passes you on the stairs without raising his eyes.

You wonder how everybody knows that you are out of favor. You ask yourself when they will begin to actually abuse you.

When they throw you out of the Party, you can only count the days. You wait for the raid. You burn whatever seems to you forbidden. You hide whatever seems to you permitted. They come, throw some of your papers into a sack, and leave. If they don't find anything, they'll come again, this time bringing the incriminating material with them.

When they come, despite the rapid step on the stairs, the rude knock on the door, you feel like a sick man who has summoned an ambulance. You wonder why they bother to pull out their pistols. You'll go with them anyway. You'll try to ingratiate yourself with them. You'll behave like a high school pupil taking an examination. You'll chatter, make eyes, show off your knowledge.

If they don't slap you in the face, you'll marvel at their benevolence. You'll be prepared to believe that they arrested you at night so as not to disgrace you before your neighbors. Look, they're not even taking you away in a Black Maria. Written on the van in huge letters is "Bread," or "Meat."

When they take you up to the third floor, you wait curiously to meet your interrogator. "The Cheka dungeons" were what you were expecting. The third floor is something else again.

Between hope and despair a man cannot defend himself. If you are ready, it's a different matter.

Time out of number, I have organized the sequence of events in my mind. I have imagined what they will do, what I will do. What they will say. What I will say.

In the bread van I was tense as a spring, alert, stimulated, ready for what was to come. The third floor did not mislead me. The sensitive, well-cared-for hands, the hands of a violinist, of the interrogator, did not give me any illusions either. I knew: the dungeons were here. These fingers would clench into fists.

"Why were you arrested?" was my interrogators' first question. A battery of three.

A provocative question, when it came from the people who had given the order for your arrest. They were expecting the usual answer—"It must have been a mistake"—with hidden satisfaction. Thus the chemistry teacher enjoys his experiment: he pours phenolphthalein into a base and it turns pink. In other words, you agree with us that others have been justly arrested, and now we will prove to you that it is the same in your case.

"I suppose it must be written in the file in front of you," was my answer.

Our eyes met. A moment of confrontation. Each of us wondering about the other. I: Which of you is bored? Which is an arrogant character who believes in his profession? Which a sadist who would hang cats up by their tails? Which an innocent idealist, who believes that the dirty work, if necessary, should be done by decent people? And what would stop them? Tears? Silent sobbing? Screams? Fainting? Begging?

The thoughts must have been whirling around in their minds too: Is he a floor rag, can we intimidate him and finish him off in time to go and see a matinee? Is he a stubborn character whom we will have to beat black and blue? Is he frightened out of his wits and just pretending, and will the offer of a cigarette be enough? Is he a chatterbox who likes arguing, and who will talk simply in order to prove to us how clever he is?

The toughest interrogator I ever met was an arrogant fellow, a professional who needed to succeed. He didn't have too much time to spare for a case like mine. If he couldn't get a conviction on a serious charge, he would compromise on another. He didn't care if I lived. His reputation was not made on the likes of me. He needed to break an oak. Not the twig of a vine.

He looked at me and concluded: what he needs is a beating. A hard one.

I saw it in his eyes. And when the blows fell, I was not surprised. I took them stubbornly, in silence and without any illusions. I had never cherished any illusions of being able to withstand torture. But I said to myself that from now on I was defending my life. I would not confess to spying for Britain. I would compromise on the fifty-eighth, or any other transgression that did not carry the death sentence. At least I knew why I had to submit to the beatings. One day, two days, three. Until he despised himself for not being able to crack a wretch like me without any effort at all.

And thus I saved my life. With my own hands, back, and head. It was not fate. Not the whim of my jailers which gave me my life. Not chance. I did it myself.

$\mathcal{A}$ few days later the director came again. This time he brought a photographer with him. A skinny fellow with a sharp chin and nose and small, deep-set eyes. He circled us like a bird of prey. "Don't take any notice of me, go ahead and talk."

"Don't take any notice," the director said, too. "Talk." He put a tape recorder on the table. He pressed a button. "That's it. Now. I'm taking a couple of stills. We'll develop them and see what comes out."

I could not take my mind off the severity of the photographer's look. Like a kangaroo court. And the way they talked to each other too. In undertones. As if they had gone out of the room to hold a consultation. "Take them in closeup. Maybe from the side. That's it. Wait for him to talk. Make it natural." The judges. They smoked without stopping. Filling the room with smoke. As if some great responsibility had been incurred here. Weren't they wasting their time on me? What if I was found unworthy? A waste of all their efforts, of the old photoes of Tel Yosef they had brought with them, the notes they had taken in the archives of the labor movement. Serious people. For a moment I seemed to myself a frivolous fellow. I had failed to grasp the full import of the event. Here I was being offered a chance of life after death, of immortality on celluloid, and I was not rising to the occasion, I was not cooperating. "Look over here, just a minute." Click. "That's it. What did you want to say?"

"I can't ignore it," I said. "All these things, the camera, that revolving spool, they confuse me."

They did not realize that I was joking. "Try. You'll get used to it. Here, talk to me." They gave me to understand that if they did not succeed in catching me as I was, they might be obliged to give up the whole idea. A threat. "Even electrons change their behavior under the camera's eye," I said. "Every camera shot is a forgery," I teased them. "Perhaps it takes a lot of getting used to. Me, I can't sit in front of the camera without making faces. And what do you need the tape recorder for, anyway?" I continued provocatively. "If you make a movie, you'll have to do it all over again from the beginning." They hadn't decided yet, the director stammered. In other words, the decision to grant me immortality on celluloid was not up to him. He sounded embarrassed. His boasts were empty. He was not the boss. Someone else was going to look at my face and decide if I was worthy. It is rare indeed for a man to meet the arbiter of his fate in person. Only his emissaries are visible.

It was like an interrogation in every way: my acts, my views, did I have any regrets, what about? Provocations had been perpetrated, bombs had been thrown; and intimate questions too, without any shame.

When I say intimate questions, I am not speaking of sexual

matters. Even though these too were touched on, but in a general way. ("Is it true that there was a certain asceticism, and when they talked about free love they only meant that people lived together without the benefit of a religious ceremony?") I am referring to other questions:

"Do you believe in God?"

"In God? What kind of a question is that?"

"It's important to know."

"For the photographs?"

"It's relevant."

He spoke vehemently. Impatiently. My stubbornness was getting him down. As if it wasn't clear who was asking the questions and who giving the answers here.

"If you really have to know—I don't know if He exists. I believe that He's necessary."

"Necessary? To whom?"

"To the beaters."

"To whom?"

"The beaters. Perhaps they'll think twice before they hit so hard.

"And He's not necessary to the beaten," I added. "On the contrary. They shouldn't believe in Him. They shouldn't believe that the whip is the wrathful rod of the Lord."

A debate in Kuznetsk: one side said the authorities have to believe in God. To give an account of themselves. Others were of the opinion that it was too dangerous. They were cruel already enough when they spoke in the name of historical necessity. We argued with a Russian Orthodox priest: if evil, too, came from God, then Stalin was the embodiment of His will, a punishment for our sins. So what were we complaining about? The pride of the free thinker: he chooses the good every hour of every day. Epstein said: If there was a God in Heaven, he would come down now to kiss the feet of the man who placed himself on the heavy side of the tree trunk we were supposed to carry on our shoulders.

"And why did you go back to Russia?" the director inquired.

"There's a simple answer: for ideological reasons." "I know. But that's not enough. I heard another version. Because of personal conflicts. Is that right?"

"Because of the snow," I said to him.

"The snow?" He laughed. He was sure I was making fun of him.

"Yes, yes. It was hot here, and we were used to a different climate. My skin came out in a rash too. I went back to Russia— and it disappeared."

Other questions were about the Kibbutz and the arms robbery. Was it true that we had sentenced Ben-Gurion to death? He was disappointed at the vagueness of my answers. "I was a member of the Kibbutz," I told him. "I took an oath, I was trained, I trained others, but I don't know if I knew all the secrets of the group. A death sentence against Ben-Gurion? I never heard of it. I had a minor role in the gold robbery. I tailed the money changers in Beirut. I never took part in the robbery itself." The director thought I was holding out on him. He told me that he had questioned a woman on Kibbutz Kfar Giladi, who had been involved in the robbery, and she had refused to testify. "I was sworn to secrecy," she said. "But it's all obsolete now," he said. And she said: "If I get an order, I'll tell everything." He asked: "Who can give you an order now?" And she said: "You see!"

When they realized that I had no sensational stories to tell, they packed up their instruments. But first they asked me again about guilt feelings. I made a gesture of dismissal. I sensed that the director was firmly convinced: I was hiding something that I had no reason to be proud of.

To Rachel, who had recommended me to them, they said that to their regret I had refused to cooperate with them. For some reason or other, I was afraid of the cameras. Presumably I felt a heavy burden of guilt, or so they imagined, and for this reason I wanted to forget the past. . . . They couldn't believe that a man would miss the chance to star in a documentary movie, unless he had something to hide.

* * *

Afterward I mulled things over. Truly, I don't think that my role in the gold robbery deserves to be immortalized. Nor did it give rise to any feelings of guilt. Or to anything more than a few superficial thoughts. I never bothered my head about whether it was right or moral. Our code stated that "expropriations" were permitted. You took from the bourgeoisie and gave to the comon kitty. The loot of the oppressors was returned to the needy. What boy doesn't enjoy underground games? Youthful delinquency receives a moral sanction from historical necessity. For a ragged, half-starved pioneer it was one long fancy-dress party: an opportunity for guzzling and making whoopee. In Beirut, while we were trailing the money changers, we spent a few days in a luxury hotel and emulated, very successfully, the lifestyle of decadent effendis. It would be ridiculous to pretend to a heroic martyr's halo.

And please don't try to impose a guilty conscience on me, either. The joys of Christians: they sin and chew the cud to their confessors. I have cruel memories. And I know that some of the things I did were stupid and naive. And it is too late to mend them. I am not trying to justify myself. I never joined the Communist Party because of all the favors I expected to receive. I sold my shares in the world to come without making any calculations. During the revolution, idealists were murdered in order to ensure a life free of care for knaves. The Communist faction in Eretz Israel was, in my opinion, an insignificant episode, a kind of corridor through which I infiltrated from the future to the past. Unknowingly, I performed a classically Jewish role: the chosen people. The revolution had chosen us to be the Jesus of our times. Although we said "Render unto the revolution what is the revolution's"—they crucified us. To bear its pain. Homeless, cosmopolitan, internationalists, ready to forgo a motherland not theirs in order to make a revolution in China. We were its voice crying from the depths. The bearers of its epistle to the Corinthians, the Prussians, the Negroes, and the Indians. The bearers of ill tidings, massacred for bearing them. Whom would they have hated like us, from the bottom of their hearts, with such a burning hatred, if we had disappeared into Palestine, into the Crimea and Birobidzhan?

We spoke about it once, Rachel and I. She is now doing research on the structure of a revolutionary party. The questions she asks are no longer hangers on which to hang the coats of which her "paper" is sewn. She really and truly wants to know how it happened. What did we think? Were we too blind to see? She needs to know, she needs it so badly that it hurts. Until she met one of us face to face, we were a featureless cliché, haters of Israel, the mental illness of the Jew, ready to sacrifice his Isaac so that others will believe in his belief. Now she knew a member of the Yevsektsia: me. And suddenly all the rest became individuals too.

She wanted to understand: the purges, a project unprecedented in human history, in which hundreds, thousands, hundreds of thousands, maybe millions of people had participated, detectives, policemen, informers, interrogators, judges, executioners—it wasn't a clandestine operation, after all—was it possible that they didn't know that they were extracting from their victims confessions to crimes that had never been committed? How come the earth hadn't shaken under their feet? How could they have looked each other in the eyes? Slept with their wives? Dangled children on their knees?

I restrained myself from placing a hand on her fragile, slender arm, the color of honey. Her earnest love of truth touched my heart, but at the same time it also gave rise in me to a certain suppressed irritation.

I tried to explain: there was no conspiracy here to fabricate a heroic lie together. There were irreconcilable contradictions, with every man's hand against the other. The triumph of one was the downfall of the other. The Komsomol member sent on a punitive expedition to confiscate the peasant's seeds was sure that in so doing he was feeding his poor, starving mother, hundreds of miles away.

Some of the best theatrical artists in Russia, a land of sweeping dramatic gestures—directors, playwrights, scriptwriters, actors—found an outlet for their talents in closed rooms in the presence of a tense, captive audience of one, a forced participant in an explosive drama the likes of which not even the epileptic Feodor saw in his wildest imaginings. What flights of fancy were dreamed up by the bored boys of the secret police! The games of cat and mouse they invented! Did they believe that their victims were guilty? Or perhaps it was only their professional careers that were at stake? Dialectics made it possible for them to dismiss the question of the subjective truth from their consciences. They could always console themselves with the thought that the general tactic was part of the struggle against a hidden enemy, a struggle in which innocent and helpless bystanders, too, were hit by stray bullets. Dialectics alone, however, was not enough. There had to be a human relationship too. Interrogators who began the job as cold-blooded professionals finished it full of powerful emotions: hatred and contempt. Contempt for those who gave in easily, hatred for the stubborn, the brave, the insulted, the convinced of their innocence. Within a day or two the interrogator took no more interest in the charge sheet. The man standing in front of him and fixing him with foolish, heroic looks drove him wild with fury. In the depths of his heart he accused him of a different crime: the man who tries to be a hero is guilty of the sin of false pride and vainglory.

Even the Grand Inquisitor knew that God did not desire a confession extorted by torture. Loving God to save your skin was blasphemy too. But he went on torturing his victims nevertheless, to make them repent of their impertinence and give up their belief that by not causing pain to their fellowmen they would gain the kingdom of Heaven. He could not forgive them for regarding themselves as superior to a man who was prepared to burn a whole town at the stake for the greater glory of God.

The dedicated ex-Komsomol member who had volunteered to do an ugly job would not forgive his victims for believing that by refusing to serve the Cheka or the NKVD or the KGB they were preserving their humanity. With all his might he set out to prove to them just how fragile that humanity was. The minute they despised themselves, they would stop feeling superior to him.

In the end, when she was sure that the friendship between us allowed her to ask even a question like this, Rachel dared to ask—tactfully and gently—how I myself had withstood the cruel ordeal. She asked, and there was an apologetic expression in her eyes, as if she was perfectly willing to withdraw the question if I did not want to answer it.

"I won't cast a stone at anyone who lied," I said to her. "Nor at anyone who informed on his friend."

Like many others—who can count them?—I too, as soon as I had applied to study at the technical college, was asked to present myself at the office building which had once housed the All-Russian Insurance Company.

I was received with smiles and frightening cordiality. On the desk lay two documents: the college application and a recommendation on behalf of Skornik, a friend who had left Via Nova and applied for permission to reside in Moscow. The first of these was laid aside. The second was closely examined. I was scolded like a child: "How could you allow yourself to recommend a man who came back from Palestine? Do you know him? Let's say you were close to each other, even lived in the same room and ate from the same dish—how do you know *why* he came back from Palestine? Who sent him? Who encouraged him to come? Who paid his fare? Whom did he meet before leaving the country? What did he promise the British agents when they let him out of jail? Have you got the means of ascertaining all these things? It's pure frivolity to recommend a man you don't know."

The hint was as heavy as bear's paw: I myself had come back from Palestine. There was room to ask why I had returned. I too had been arrested by the British and released. I understood that I was being asked to "atone for my sins" before they were prepared to discuss my application to go to college. The conversation proceeded as if there were no connection between the two things. They told me that there were malcontents working at the newspaper office, and that their dissatisfaction made them dangerous. They were not satisfied with the state of Jewish culture in the Soviet Union. On the face of things they had done nothing wrong, but who knows what they had in their hearts? The enemy was cunning and wicked and hid his true intentions. If we were not vigilant, "we would wake up one morning and discover that they had stolen the pillow from under our heads . . ."

They sent me away without making me sign anything. My nods were enough for them. Presumably they thought that after I had become entangled in their net, they would get me to sign an undertaking, which they would be able to show my friends, in order to make it easier for them when they were asked to inform on me. I congratulated myself on my success in deceiving them. But I did not sleep well that night.

I said nothing to anybody. Not even to Nina. I was afraid that she would be horrified and run to her father, in whose influence she believed. I did not know if I could trust him. I was afraid that he was too naive, one of the last Mohicans of pure communism. He would talk to whomever he talked to, and his daughter would be taken in on Article 77/1, which said that anyone who called an informer by name was guilty of impeding him in the course of his duties.

For a number of weeks I walked around in a daze. Sometimes I would be filled with a momentary spirit of heroism and make up my mind to go back to that office and announce: "I am not with you." And let come what may. "My feelings rebel and I have no aptitude for the task," I wanted to say to them. "Perhaps I am not worthy of carrying a Party card. Perhaps the process of the ripening of the New Man has been held up in me, due to various atavisms or perhaps due to my Jewish origins— but I cannot be an informer. I cannot find any fault in a man for giving vent to an occasional sigh and hoping for better days."

I was spared this heroic gesture. Divine Providence sent me Kimmelman.

He came to us from Kiev, where he had been working for a factory newspaper, and immediately received a job on the staff. He wrote an economics column—in other words, translated the official handouts into Yiddish. I gave him one look and detested him from the bottom of my heart. The anti-Semite latent in every Jew baptized, however cursorily, at the font of the emancipation stirred into life in me. Nevertheless, I would never have plucked up the courage to inform on him simply because he was a slimy fellow who couldn't keep his hands off the buttons of your coat and breathed right into your nose with an ingratiating smile plastered over his cunning face. But I listened to him several times and heard him spreading malicious gossip in a style that none of the rest of us would have dared to adopt. I allowed him to bait me, too. I listened to him attentively. He whispered into my ear that he was worried by the mass arrests. He blamed Stalin for appointing Yagoda, a man without a conscience, to a responsible post. I said nothing. I thought: This time you've gone too far, Kimmelman. If you wanted to pull me by the tongue, you shouldn't have put such a blunt hook into my mouth. No one can say such things without being arrested.

I no longer had any doubt: he had been planted among us, a bait for fools. But in spite of the attempted cunning of his look, he did not have the wit to play such a role among a group of journalists, each one sharper than the next.

I informed on him. I was careful not to leave any traces. I pretended that I was seriously conforming to underground rules. I had more experience at the game than my employers. Walking in the street, I reported to a liaison man. For a few days I knew no rest, until I caught sight of the portly little man waddling down the steps. A few weeks later I was vindicated. Kimmelman was not arrested. And I received my reward. The gates of the engineering institute opened before me.

I paid a heavy price for my trick: Kimmelman's friendship. Whenever we encountered each other in the corridor, he would send a greasy smile in my direction, like two adulterers meeting in broad daylight. I felt profound revulsion when he patted me on the shoulder as I sat bowed over the typesetter. He would station himself behind my back and shoot out juicy slanders against his colleagues. The idea being that they were all a bunch of hypocrites, and we were the only honest, consistent men around. "Christianity can be understood only after it has been accepted," he quoted Kierkegaard. It appeared that I had not understood him. He did not see himself as someone who had fallen from grace, but on the contrary, as a man of superior morality. Anyone who acknowledged the necessity of the secret police, without which the regime could not exist, and refused to cooperate with them, was in his opinion an immoral man. Like a soldier who uses the field lavatories but refuses to clean them when his turn comes around.

The gates of Hell are crossed with a single step.

Kimmelman's consistent moral code did not make him immune to insult. The hauteur of those who kept their mouths shut cut him to the quick. His need to trip them up stemmed from a deeper source than his loyalty to his masters. It was important to him to recruit them into the ranks of the informers in order not to be in a despised minority. In a society of hunchbacks, the man with a straight back is the odd man out. The only hope for informers is for informing to become the norm. He was not pleased with me. In his eyes I was not sufficiently active. In his opinion I lacked the missionary instinct. Like a man who had found his way through the forest and did not care that others were lost.

I made no attempt to swell the ranks of the informers. I felt no need to enjoy the coziness of company. I hoped to succeed in surviving the dangerous days by adopting a modest silence. I developed methods of defense against frankness. I tried to avoid contact with people. I spoke to strangers only when necessary and about technical matters only. I lived in a private world of silence. An underground of one, without the attractions of underground camaraderie. It wasn't easy, for I enjoyed an oppressive popularity at the newspaper office. I was considered an odd fellow, and they all tried to understand what made me tick. A man who had seen the world, knew a number of languages, and was not interested in writing articles. They could not understand why I insisted on doing work that made my hands dirty.

Everyone wanted to make friends with me: I came from Eretz Israel. Even the sworn enemies of Zionism could not conquer their curiosity and wanted to hear about the pioneers, the Histadrut, Jerusalem, and friends and relations.

Sensitive poets, fastidious men of bourgeois extraction, who tried to purify themselves by "going down to the people" and manifestations of honest affection for members of the working classes, could do so by having a heart-to-heart chat with a simple chap like me, whose fingernails were black. I was obliged to pretend that I was busy, or insensitive. My heart went out to these ragged priests in the temple of a dying culture, but I was determined to keep them at arm's length, for their own protection. Exactly as in some trashy melodrama—I acted the part of the bad guy in order to save the innocents from themselves.

There was no refuge from loneliness even at home. The family nest was not padded with soft feathers. I was afraid of Nina. She lacked any political instincts whatsoever, was sure that she was protected, that she belonged to the social elite by virtue of the fact that she was the daughter of a distinguished Communist leader. Moreover—she was married to a working man and fulfilled all her obligations, even to excess, with certain heroic moments to her credit which anyone could read in her personal file: she had tried to live in a remote kolkhoz, and but for the fact that she had fallen ill, she would still be living there today. Her honesty would not allow her to conceal her criticism, I feared. She would complain to anyone who seemed to her decent and serious.

Before Olga, too, I was obliged to hold my tongue. At the age of two or three, she was already as well trained as a little parrot. She was in love with the good, kind Stalin in the way that convent girls are in love with their Jesus. I was obliged to foster this love in her heart, in order not to upset her mental balance. So that she wouldn't suspect me of despising the nursery school prayerbook.

Well—I thought then—the system has achieved its aim.

Everyone in his restricted sphere has learned to sacrifice the present for the future, to burn this moment in order to warm the next one, to surrender himself for the happiness of the unborn, to the end of time.

Larissa Verchinsky, in her last letter, before she dived into oblivion in the depths of the north, quoted something said by one of the characters in a novel by Romain Rolland: "If we sacrifice truth, honor, and every other human value for the sake of the future, it is as if we are sacrificing the future itself."

At that time I had already emerged from the warm womb of despair. I wrote back to her: "The future? What is the future? I know only hope. And hope is always the present."

Looking back, my resolute silence, my passive struggle against Kimmelman, seemed to me the embodiment of a life full of hope.

I remembered the look on the director's face when I said "The snow." A look of disgust at the antics of an old man trying to be original.

No stranger is capable of understanding the insane love of a Russian for the landscapes of his motherland.

Do the sons of other motherlands too cleave so to the "dewy paths" of their childhood, or is it only the Russians? America, they say, is full of the sons of Rishon le Zion and Gedera—the descendants of the early "Bilu" settlers of the First Aliyah. Is there no melody that pierces their hearts when they hang up their harps on a foreign soil? Englishmen go to America and are happy in American universities built to imitate English models. Germans traveled to south Russia and enjoyed the sunshine, the raspberry bushes, and the fertile soil. Frenchmen settled all over the world. As long as they could talk French, they lacked for nothing. Their language was their motherland. Only we, it seems, are homesick for landscapes eaten up with Russian melancholy; for the wind which sweeps them, sonorous as a male choir. Only we, it seems, believe that the pure voices of our women grew out of the rushes on the banks of the Volga. Only we, it seems, are capable of feeling such love for the brothers we hate, whose fickle souls veer between extremes—"The soul so joyful yesterday/Today is fatefully empty"—leaving them eternally longing for consistency, for stability, and for loyalty with no reservations.

How I loved/hated in my youth the Russian, who falls on your neck with a drunken hiccup, and leaves you guessing to the last minute whether he is about to weep or stick a knife in your heart.

Hundreds of thousands returned after the revolution, only to die. Bukharin, who was living with a young woman in Paris, and whose family, which he had abandoned in Russia, was not in any danger, left the young woman and returned to the motherland, although he was sure—he even said so to his friends—that Stalin would murder him. And did anyone promise Ehrenburg that luck would be on his side?

I went back because the ground was burning beneath my feet, but I was glad to do so. And I was grateful to the Party Central Committee for allowing me to abandon the life of a professional revolutionary in exchange for Russian boredom.

$\mathcal{A}$s I said, I did not join the Party on fire with passionate conviction. I did not reach it like a pilgrim coming to his Holy City. I was swept into it by a whirlpool. Hopes and disappointments, one after the other in dizzying succession, swept me into the eye of the storm.

Faithful to my self-image as a consistent person—consistency was a simile for taking an oath of allegiance—I sat at the feet of those who presented me with riddles for which I had no answer: Elkind, Daniel, Efros, Feitelman, Kopelevitch, Anton.

By the way, when the British Intelligence discovered our meeting place, we fled them, Anton and I, through a field dotted with little vegetable gardens. The vegetables were watered by shallow irrigation canals leading from the Yarkon River. I was barefoot, and ran through the canals. I even enjoyed squelching through the soft, cool mud, while Anton, in his patent leather shoes, jumped from bed to bed and trampled the plants under his feet. At that moment I said to myself: They say that this is not my country. But it isn't Anton's either. The earth belongs only to those who would never trample a seedling underfoot.

For a long time my status was that of a candidate on probation. This was a one-sided test. The applicant was not entitled to change his mind. The Party, however, had the right to reject and humiliate him.

The initiation ceremony was functional and unimpressive. Perhaps precisely because of this, it gave rise in me to an obscure anxiety. This is a serious business, I said to myself. Like signing an irreversible obligation. They needed no rites and rituals. There was no Bible, no pistol, no torch shining into your face.

Efros was waiting for me in the grove of trees in Bograshov Street. We went into a house in the process of construction, jumping over a nailed board. In the yard, in a shed full of building materials, behind an iron-bending table, sat Daniel between two people I did not know. He congratulated me for passing the test, and I placed my last week's wages on the table— my membership dues. That was the end of the ceremony.

"The Party" was an abstraction. I knew very few members. The tasks imposed on me were routine and uninspiring. I handed out leaflets, I gathered out-of-work men around me on street corners and emptied the shallow ideological baggage I knew by heart into their ears, I took part in secret cell discussions. The discussions were superficial and boring. But I was not disappointed. I persuaded myself that these activities were part of something immense. An enthusiastic private peeling potatoes in the camp kitchen consoles himself with the thought that this, too, is part of the war effort. Later I discovered that some of us were taking part in the more secret discussions of a more restricted cell. From that moment on my life was lived in expectation of the day when my right to enter the inner circle would be recognized.

We were few in number, and I personally knew fewer than

thirty people. But among those thirty, it seems, the entire human gallery was to be found: from Noah to Lot, from Stavrogin to Pichurin. Pinchas and Zimri, Shammai and Hillel, Faust and Mephistopheles, Othello and the court jester. And a stammering Trotsky and a local Stalin, whose paranoia applied only to the Left Poalei Zion.

They all prophesied in one tongue. And nevertheless it was hard to distinguish the false from the true prophets. Both were endowed with fervor, authority, and resolution. Even in so small a circle, however, there is an advantage to be gained by the man who understands exactly whom he is dealing with and has no scruples about exploiting the weaknesses of his comrades. Even in a band of paupers you will find people greedy for money, status, and power and also the hidden arrogance of those who aspire to pull strings behind the scenes. The man who offers them a dish of olives, who flatters them, who allows them to insult the less intelligent, and takes them aside for confidential consultations about nothing, is the man to whom they will submit. And once you have eaten from the hand of someone in authority, however humble and insignificant that authority is, you will never admit that you were bought by favors. You are protected by an inner mechanism which teaches you to agree enthusiastically with whoever satisfies your little lusts. Thus people like Efros and Kuperman grew up within our ranks. Until the Party, which was run like a secret army, decided which of them was number one, and which number two. And from that moment on, what was a false prophecy yesterday was a true one today. I was only a boy, but when I grew older too, I never saw a gentle person, or a scrupulous one, gain a position of power in the Party.

On the contrary: humorless braggarts, whose lips had never been touched by a smile of kindness, eager to break all kinds of emotional taboos—they were always the ones to gain the upper hand. And what rare courage was required to ask a question about means! Was it permitted to deceive, to lead astray, and conceal information in order to attract the doubters into our ranks? By the very act of asking the question you showed the infirmity of your purpose and proved your unworthiness to wear a soldier's boots.

On the Druze Mountain, for the first time, I was involved in "high-level politics," serving as an interpreter for a top Comintern agent. I was horrified by the ugly way in which he treated the noble-looking sheikh, leading him up the garden path and flattering him in the most revolting, obsequious way. I was a greenhorn, and posed a hesitant question: Perhaps the man was cleverer than we were, and held his tongue only out of politeness? Perhaps, in fact, he was trying to let us know what he thought of this kind of "diplomacy"? The agent's reaction turned the journey home into a nightmare. He ridiculed me in the rudest terms. "What do you know about the Arabs? An Arab who succeeds in making a fool of a stranger is regarded as a hero. He can't see any reason for telling you the truth. Who are you, his uncle? And if you succeed in tricking him, he is full of admiration for your cunning." He had learned all this in one short course.

I, who already knew a few Arab, both polite and rude, foolish and wise, honest and rogues, cunning Bedouin and poor but dignified fellahin, had already outgrown these and other popular stereotypes, but I did not dare express an opposing view. The hierarchical structure of the Party did not allow me to be cleverer than my superiors.

I was often obliged to parrot empty slogans. Such as the slogans about the "toiling Arab masses" which did not exist. In my picture of the world, things were more complicated. In my capacity as a kind of liaison man with the Arab section of the Party, I had learned to distinguish between the urban and the rural population, between the Bedouin and the simply homeless, between the Egyptians and the Houranis, the natives and the immigrants. But all this knowledge did me no good at all. The program demanded clear, unequivocal definitions. Nobody was interested in "bourgeois" research. Anyone who tried to strip a slogan of its fine feathers was regarded as already having one foot in the enemy camp.

Volkovsky, a Polish writer I met in Moscow during a writers' congress, arrogantly dismissed the argument that superficial slogans brought nothing but harm to the Party. We should not even despise the trial by red-hot iron, he said. Both the liar and the truth teller would be burned, of course, but if they both believed that the red-hot iron would reveal the truth, the truth teller would put his tongue to it unhesitatingly. And the liar would shake with fear. Even false slogans were a means of discovering who was for us and who was against us. The man who did not shrink from spreading lies for the sake of the revolution proved that he was loyal to it. The one who hesitated revealed the ambivalence in his heart.

It was probably my Arabic which sealed my fate. If they had not needed me, I would presumably never have been admitted to the inner circle of the faithful.

I might have sunk anonymously into the wretched ranks of the unemployed, and later managed to fix myself up with a job in some workshop or construction workers co-op, and built myself a house with a porch in a workers' neighborhood. My children would have gone to a labor movement school for the children of workers, and today I would have been a member of the old folks' club affiliated with the Histadrut. And perhaps I would have compromised with the conventional lies of a Zionist workers' party, and perhaps I might have performed some modest role in the government administration. When I say "conventional lies" I do not intend casting a stone at anyone. There is no political party without its conventional lies, which are like the test by red-hot iron. Only history can refute them.

But since we were persecuted, we closed ranks. Even if I had wanted to give free rein to my doubts, I would not have been able to. I would have accused myself of looking for excuses to run away from the danger.

Today it seems strange to me that I was never co-opted into the military arm. After all, I had been a member of the Kibbutz, and I knew how to dismantle and reassemble four different kinds of pistols in the dark. It was probably Loka's perspicacity. He must have sensed that I was not the material of which truly reliable heroes are made. Many are the thoughts in the human heart. And you can never tell which of them will gain the upper hand.

I never liked taking orders. To spare my feelings, Efros pretended to be consulting me. But it was quite clear that I was not supposed to disagree with him, or allowed to doubt his right to judge me. He would smile upon me if I was obedient, be angry if I was impertinent.

The cell meetings were a kind of rite. Like a prayer for rain. I would sit there wishing I was out in the street. Outside, children were playing soccer, housewives were chatting from one balcony to the next, tanned youngsters were going down to the beach, writers and poets were drinking tea on the pavements and renewing the language. The "means of production" and the "forces of production" and the "superstructure" were lifeless. I could have taken a train to Jaffa to enjoy the bustle of the marketplace, gone to the park to see if the trees were in blossom, the flowers in bloom.

Not that I took the Party lightly, God forbid. At that time it was possible to believe that a small group of people who knew what they wanted could act to change the world. How many comrades did Lenin have in Zurich? And what did they do? Exactly the same thing—they sat and argued and wrote pamphlets and made passionate speeches to empty wooden benches.

I accepted the Party axioms with a pose of heroic submission. I agreed that the members of my generation should be regarded with a measure of suspicion. We bore a dangerous heritage of suffering on our backs. All kinds of atavisms, sensibilities from another world, Jewish anxieties. The generation of the wilderness. Only our sons would see the Promised Land. "Forty years long was I grieved with this generation" was not an idea to deter men who had received an Orthodox Jewish education.

For a while I was put in charge of the ideological education of poets and writers. Because I had once met Yesenin and heard Mayakovsky in the Little Theater Hall, I was found worthy to deal with this vacillating group. I could quote a few lines of Anna Akhmatova—"The bread of strangers is only a flame/To warm their souls in the cold"—and that was enough to gain their attention. Some of them sensed at once where I was leading them, and became my sworn enemies. Others were easily seduced. A few of them were captivated by the tunes of the ocarina. Others were simply afraid of being left behind. The chariot of history was galloping forward—how could they fail to jump aboard? There were gentle, fastidious souls, too, who were afraid that the revolution might fall into the hands of hooligans, and wished to refine it by their embarrassed presence. There were angry poets too, full of tremendous contempt, who could not endure the petit bourgeois—who lived in an ugly house, without a picture or a flower, and read trashy books, and believed in every demagogue, and flirted with his ugly neighbors, and cheated his customers, and bought shares in American railroad companies—and the revolution gave them a chance to revenge themselves on him in their dreams. They "stood him against the wall" and shot him, and hurled revolutionary slogans at him to outrage him. There were also some mediocre poets who were saved by the Party from the contempt in which they were generally held. They preferred to think that they were being persecuted for their beliefs.

But I soon wearied of this too. I was glad when I was arrested, twice, and there was no longer any room for me either in Tel Aviv or among the Arabs.

"I'm better at building than destroying," I said to Elkind when I came to Via Nova. "Let others pull the old world down. We Jews should concern ourselves with construction."

I have begun to teach my son arithmetic. Up to now only figures. I tap the fingertips of my left hand with the index finger of my right, and say their numbers aloud. He looks at my lips and choked syllables come out of his throat. I never allow myself to show him that I am disappointed in his progress, lest he stop learning altogether. Indeed, in a short space of time he has made great progress. He is able to add up simple figures, even when he forgets their names. I wonder what light goes on in his mind when he sees me. Perhaps: Here is the arithmetic man. When I enter his room, he makes signs with his fingers and smiles.

Last night he shouted at me. He forgot something he had once known. I was to blame. I remembered my father's words: I shall be your ransom.

Walter likes to pretend cynicism: If he's already blaming others for his mistakes, he must be on the mend.

They are teaching him to "talk" too. They place a board of letters before him and his finger combines them into words. Last night we conducted a short conversation. Suddenly he asked who I was. Your father, I replied. He burst out laughing.

The "class struggle" is an expression which has been eroded by this century. It has been desecrated and emptied of all content. Stalin, who called for vigilance, on the grounds that after the revolution the struggle against the class enemy sharpens, emptied it of all content. He pushed the class struggle outside the borders of Russia. Inside Russia everyone—the receivers of fat salaries, the bureaucracy of the revolution, who drove Ziss and Zim cars, did their shopping at special stores, lived on the fat of the land and the southern shores, and their wretched comrades on the kolkhozes, benighted peasants who stole frozen potatoes from the general stores, and old peasant women who stood up to their knees in sewage water to dig up a burst pipe, the heroines of dumb labor, with their old-fashioned picks—all of them are classical representatives of one class. And all those beyond the borders of Russia and the authority of its leaders—even the poorest of the poor—are members of another class. There is no nation which has tormented its workers as cruelly and protected the privileges of its leaders as harshly as this nation which set out to save the working class from its servitude. The Soviet theater of the absurd was not performed in closed halls. General rehearsals for the opening night took place on every street corner. Every line in the morning newspaper was a replica which bore no resemblance to the original. And if you went and complained, you would lose even your right to be a poor citizen. You would find yourself serving the revolution without expecting a reward in the frozen islands of the north.

But touching rearguard battles take place in my daughter's home too. My grandson received a pocket radio as a gift from his father. He kept it at his girlfriend's. When they parted, he left it there. Walter said: "If you had bought it with money you earned yourself, you wouldn't have been so generous." The boy lost his temper. He took all the money he had in his pockets and threw it onto the table. He counted it and found that a small sum was missing. He asked me for a loan. I told him: "Take it and don't give it back." Walter mocked me: "You're fighting the class struggle in my house."

My grandson's radicalism came from the girl he has now left. An original, passionate, disheveled creature. A class-conscious member of the proletariat, she left her rich parents' home to live in a derelict shed, which she renovated herself. She works in a mental hospital and writes poems which rebel against Hebrew grammar. She has no respect for money or property, or any aspect of the status quo. She wears long Bedouin dresses and her little breasts dance cheekily underneath the coarse material. Her face is small and pale, and there is a wondering, hungry expression in her enormous eyes. Hungry for a truth and a meaning which you and I cannot grasp. It seems to me that she also, quite simply, goes hungry. My grandson abases himself before her. She is living out his secret fantasies.

He did not get his admiration of the revolution from me. It was not from me that he learned this version of protest, with guitars and rock bands and their hoarsely shouted songs. I can imagine how much the lad suffered in his love for her. She is too busy with the permanent revolution to find the time even for the stability of true love. He would be satisfied with one revolution, after which a new order would be inaugurated. And his father imagines that he can go to the girl, with a broken heart, and make the most contemptible of all possible requests: to give him back the property that was his before they lived together in a commune.

*L*ast week Rachel brought me her paper on "The Left in the Labor Brigade." She showed me the quotations in my name. All kinds of random remarks I had made to her. It transpires that she went home and wrote them down.

When the sky reddened, we went out onto the balcony to see the sunset. We stood side by side without talking. The red ball dropped heavily, like a ripe fruit, into the calm, oily sea. Silver stripes danced before our eyes and the last of the sun rays caught the edges of the clouds, which looked as if they were leaning on pillars of light.

On the other balconies there was a stir. The sad excitement of the old. They wanted to let me know that they had seen what was up. Efros's eyes were full of naked envy. Verchinsky silently signaled sympathetic affection. Efrat Riklin did not speak to me for two days.

I read Rachel's essay and I was disappointed. I found in it all the failures of my own essay "The Classless Society." Facts, quotations, it was all correct—but the spirit was lacking. And the people weren't people but representatives of points of view.

Sometimes she added, perhaps in order to introduce a little color, short descriptions of personalities, such as: "impatient," "enthusiastic," "extremist," "under the influence of the Fraktzia," "popular with his comrades," "fearless," "a dreamer, but firm in his views," "an adventurer," and the like. Locks of hair, without the people underneath them.

The ideological controversies, in sharp language but full of foreign phrases, were like leaking balloons. Like flying rags.

And nevertheless, it was hard and bitter to read.

I remember the strong impression made on me by the look on Borya's face when he spilled the pail of milk milked by Zina Shaverin. What a waste! Borya, who never peed except into the basin dug around a plant! The passionate rage on his face! Was it because he loved her? Because he hated everything she stood for? Or perhaps he had been seized by a holy joy: he had proved to himself that the Zionist sentiment was stronger than any other feeling. The fluid of life extracted by Communist fingers from the teat of a cow purchased by the money of the Zionist Federation would never touch our children's lips!

It was weird and strange to me. But I sensed that for Borya at least, ideology was already coursing through his bloodstream. The others were only pretending.

Very possibly, only literature can do justice to obsolete ideas. But she, it seems, avoids them as if her life depended on it, as if they were completely beyond the pale.

Last night I was informed that the idea of the documentary movie had been shelved. My guess was proved right: the director was disappointed by the fact that I had not played an active part in the gold robbery, nor was I prepared to beat my breast in front of the cameras. But I was surprised to hear from Rachel that he had also been disappointed by my answer to his question about whether I believed in God. "The cameras like sharp contradictions, vivid colors, closed circles," she said. I heard the irony in her voice and I thought that she was a woman after my own heart.

"If they want a penitent robber, let them go and take pictures of Efros," I said. "And I shall have to get along without them. It seems that I am doomed to perish with the written word."

She laughed. "Efros has a blank face. As if he had never experienced anything in his life."

I said that maybe it was better this way. If my face had been seen in every house in Israel, it could have harmed Nina. Someone would have seen me and put two and two together and spread the word. But she said that there was no such danger. Those people did not watch television.

* * *

I played chess with Efros. He beat me mercilessly. I wanted to give up, but he insisted that I go on playing. He wanted to draw out the enjoyment of his anticipated victory.

Between one game and the next he said: "I have a story with a moral."

I understood the sting in the "story with a moral," but until the end of the story I did not understand the analogy.

For a number of years the authorities had Landauer, a famous physicist who was later awarded the Lenin Prize, tailed by a little informer: an intelligent, friendly fellow, who had taken a quick course in physics and knew enough to ask learned questions but not enough to understand the answers. He went in and out of Landauer's house, ostensibly for scholarly purposes, but actually in order to remind the famous physicist that the authorities were keeping an eye on him. Landauer realized immediately that the man was not a scientist, surprising him at unexpected hours because of some urgent, burning question, but an inexperienced agent sent to spy on him; nevertheless, he did not throw him out of his house. He preferred to play host to a sympathetic informer, whose intelligence was not dangerous, and to whom he was accustomed, rather than to rack his brains trying to guess the intentions of all kinds of strangers knocking at his door. He assumed that if the NKVD had a reliable source of information inside his house, they would see no need to encircle him with a net of occasional informers.

In the course of the years the informer became an integral part of the household. He would perform all kinds of little services for Landauer's wife, take the children to school, repair the electrical appliances, throw out the garbage, help Landauer with his work, and fix things with the *oprawdom*, or caretaker, also an informer, but of a far lower rank. He was invited to meals and to all the family celebrations.

The young man's absorption into his "foster family" was so successful that it gave rise to conflicts with his wife. She accused him of neglecting her and their children and she was sure that he was hiding some love affair from her. And she was not far wrong. By the time Landauer's eldest daughter grew up, the informer was in love with her. This would not have bothered Landauer, but for the fact that he could see a reciprocal love beginning to stir in the seventeen-year-old girl's heart too. He could not bring himself to wound her tender soul by telling her the truth about "Uncle Vassya." And not in order to spare the honor of the latter. Landauer feared a deeper trauma. He did not dare expose her family's hypocrisy to her.

The Lenin Prize relieved Vassya of his responsibilities, but upset his mental balance. He shared in the family's joy, but at the prize-giving ceremony he fell into a deep depression: the labor of years had been wasted, the mountains of documents he had diligently been preparing, every evening for thirteen years, had failed to produce any fruits.

In the Landauer family they went on affectionately recalling Vassya, who had suddenly disappeared without a trace: from now on they could live without pretense, and the girl, who was told nothing even after his disappearance, could go on believing in the goodness and kindness of the world. When she asked where Vassya had gone, she was told that he had been overcome by a sense of responsibility. Since he had fallen in love with her, he had sentenced himself to exile. He had a wife and children, and he did not want to hurt them. Thus the girl was enabled to remember lovingly the brave, proud, honest man who had sacrificed his love on the altar of decency and the sanctity of marriage. And this unfulfilled youthful love would go on nourishing her feelings all her life.

On no account could I understand what the lesson of this story was. I racked my brains to no avail. Efros refused to give me a clue.

Verchinsky tried his hand at solving the riddle. "Perhaps he wanted to hint to you that not every story has to have a lesson. Life, even the life of a petty informer, is full of surprises, and even someone who never learned any lessons may have had an interesting life."

Then he added: The two of you are waging some kind of

secret war, whose purpose I don't really understand. You're trying to prove that you came out of the upheaval with a lot to show
for it, and he's trying to prove that you were shown up as an
empty vessel."

I corrected him: "I don't want to prove that my hands are
full. All I'm trying to say is that the greatest disappointment of
the twentieth century did not murder our souls, and that the
revolution did not always blow us about like leaves in the wind.
When I examine my life history, I discover that wherever I had
a choice, I chose."

I beat Efros at chess. I wouldn't have found it necessary to
note this down in my diary except that he made such a fuss about
it. He claimed that I had moved a piece while he wasn't looking.
He made a scene and demanded a return match. I refused to
play with him because he had accused me of cheating. He yelled
that I was a liar and threatened that he would get his own back
on me.

Efros cannot accept defeat. But for the fact that I am bigger
and stronger than he is, he would have fallen on me with his fists.
I said that I would not play with him until he apologized. He
screamed that he would never ask the pardon of a man like me.

"Don't upset yourself on account of his outbursts," said
Verchinsky. "He's a sick man."

It transpired that they had locked him up in an insane
asylum and tormented him. I was astonished that he should have
hidden this biographical fact. Verchinsky, who had been summoned to his room when he succumbed to a fit of depression,
knew it but kept it to himself out of respect for Efros. Verchinsky
thought that if Efros boasted of cutting down trees in a temperature of forty degrees beneath zero, and tried to conceal the fact
that for a long period of time they had driven him crazy with
injections of sulfur and amylobarbital, he was not cured and his
privacy should be respected.

"Unintelligible reactions are to be expected," said Verchinsky. "Like in cases of brain damage. They appear to be
cured, and suddenly they break out and you can't understand
why."

* * *

Something is going on around me and I don't know what it is. As if I was being plotted against. If it had happened in Russia, I would have thought that I was about to be arrested. The *opraw-dom* of Finesod House has stopped greeting me. Efrat Riklin avoids my eyes. She said that she had an important question to ask me, but she puts it off from day to day. Residents pass me on the stairs without raising their heads. The waitress in the cafeteria lowers her eyes when she places the glass of tea on my table.

It's as if I were being accused, and I cannot defend myself, since nobody will tell me what it is that I am being accused of.

In the end I managed to get it out of Verchinsky. He winced in pain when he was forced to tell me what it was all about. He hates gossip from the bottom of his heart.

There are rumors abroad that I was an agent of the NKVD.

"Efros!" I exclaimed. "The bastard. I'll break his bones."

Verchinsky cooled my ardor. "You won't be able to prove anything. All you'll achieve is to arouse suspicions that there's truth in the rumors. If he's behind it, he presumably never said anything definite, only hints. Maybe he even said that he didn't believe it himself, but he sowed the seed."

"So what am I supposed to do? Go from room to room and argue my innocence?"

"Don't do anything. In this house people hear all kinds of rumors and forget them."

I put it down to Verchinsky's credit that there was no change in his attitude toward me. Did he believe it? I asked.

"I attached no importance to it whatsoever," he said.

"And if I tell you that I never served them in any capacity whatsoever, will you believe me?"

Verchinsky looked at me sadly. "I believe you. But I suppose, that if the choice was between life and death, it means that there was no choice."

He believed me because there was a tear on my cheek when I listened to an adagio by Rachmanimoff. But this is an unreliable criterion. Leopold Sherrer could cry when he heard an allegro con brio, and nevertheless he was a monster.

I caught Efros at the bottom of the corridor. We were alone and he was quaking in his boots with fear.

"Me!" he cried. "Could I do a thing like that? The rumor reached me too, but I refused to listen to it. Such things are impossible to prove or to refute. In my opinion, it's as if they don't exist."

"Who says such things!" I shouted.

"You don't want us to start informing on each other here, do you? People talk. So what if they talk? They'll talk and they'll stop talking."

A visit from Vera.

In the cafeteria she looked around her. "Only old people. I would go mad."

I indicated that she, too, probably spent most of her time with people of her own age. But she embarked on a passionate defense of the advantages of kibbutz life. In the dining hall she sat at a table and all around her she saw young families, children, youngsters. On holidays and festivals she was part of the general celebration, surrounded by people of all ages. "I can also cross the street, sit in a cafe, and look at young people," I said. "It's not the same thing," she argued. "On the kibbutz people are responsible for each other." Even if young people were not prepared to sit next to her in the dining hall, she did not resent them for it. It was the way of the world. But she knew that if she fell ill and was unable to care for her needs, the kibbutz would look after her.

Proudly she told me that the health committee had ordered a special chair for her so that she could sit and sew. She boasted that her output was no less than that of the young women of forty or fifty. When she failed to meet the quota she had set herself, she would go back after lunch to finish her work.

I inquired about the boredom of doing such monotonous work. She was indignant: she never had the time to be bored. She was far too busy trying not to fall behind.

I could imagine her to myself, bending over her sewing

machine, stealing glances at her neighbors, to make sure that their piles were no higher than hers, abstaining from gossip in order not to distract herself from her work. At the end of the day she probably counted the items, calculated their price, and went home happy in the knowledge that she was earning her keep, in addition to her old-age pension from the National Insurance, which went straight to the kibbutz.

Verchinsky would say: "The work ethics of the old are not like the work ethics of the young . . ."

I gave in. If the socialism enclosed within the borders of the kibbutz were to be tested by its attitude toward the weaker members of society—the old, children, the sick, the mad—the balance would be positive.

I asked her why she tried so hard to prove to me that the kibbutz was such a fine place. Supposing I agreed with her. Had anyone invited me to enjoy life in this utopia?

Vera gave me a look full of meaning.

I would have no respect for myself if I went to lie and groan in her room simply in order to exploit the material advantages of the kibbutz.

I do not think that I would be able to sit in the dining hall, surrounded by young people who were trying all the time to forget that I was living at their expense after turning my back on their parents.

The longest day. The anniversary of the German invasion. I remembered that week. The prisoners celebrated: they were being given a chance to love their motherland again. A few, and not one Jew among them, dared to say: "They made their bed, now let them lie in it." A German Communist, who was saved from extradition to the Gestapo after the Molotov-Ribbentrop pact by his Polish extraction, requested an interview with the camp commandant, and demanded that he be conscripted into the Red Army as an intelligence officer. The old revolutionaries cheered Stalin, as if he had declared war. Many longed for the day when it would be granted them to die for the revolution, to prove their innocence. I wrote to Nina: "From today a new chapter in our lives has opened." I did not explain. But in my heart I decided that when I was freed I would not see Galina Nikolayevna again. There was no reply. Presumably she never even received my letter. For no reason at all, I was suddenly deprived of the right to correspond with my family.

Signs and omens. With the intensity of the old, clinging to any straw of faith, I too tend to believe in omens. This morning I received a phone call from Epstein.

More and more, the circles are closing.

Without losing a moment, I took the "First Notebook" and got onto a bus to Holon. There, in one of the barracklike buildings that were built for the new immigrants after the establishment of the state, in a tiny apartment belonging to distant relatives, in a hallway separated from the rest of the apartment by a wooden partition, on a plain iron bed covered with a faded rug, leaning on an embroidered cushion and listening to a creaking little radio, I found Epstein, in baggy gray trousers, and a yellow shirt whose short sleeves reached his sharp elbows, tinier, it seemed to me, than before, his white hair sparser and his big black eyes more prominent, as if they had popped out of his head in order to widen his field of vision.

His poor little room was in semidarkness, and his eyes were turned to the doorway. I paused there, a silhouette against the light, in order to compose my feelings, and find the right words. But his face showed no signs of recognition. It was only when I spoke that a kind of shudder convulsed his little body and a sound like a whimper escaped his lips.

I could not hold back my tears. From his eyes too, which were fixed on me without moving, the tears flowed.

"Vitya?" he said. "Oh, Vitya, is it you?"

"It's me, it's me."

"Come and sit here on my bed. At the moment there isn't a chair. . . . Not that I have any need of one . . ."

"Come, come!" I exclaimed. "This isn't like you. You always kept your spirits up, even in situations a lot worse than this."

Epstein forced himself to smile. Crooked black-yellow teeth were exposed and immediately covered up, like a rapid blink of the eye.

"All of us reach the threshold of our breaking point, in one way or the other . . ."

"Enough, enough," I said.

(The breaking point—this too was a subject of discussion among the "philosophers of Kuznetsk." And I, with my tendency to find a mathematical expression for every idea, composed a kind of formula: The better the conditions, the lower the threshold of the breaking point. A man deprived of half his bread of affliction will survive. But the man who is accustomed to eating roast goose will be killed by hunger. The very fact that Epstein saw fit to allude to my formula was a gesture of friendship. A well-known philosopher quoting the epigram of a layman. There was an ironic allusion here too, to our old debates on the subject of freedom and well-being. No sooner had he emerged from slavery into freedom than his spirit had been broken.)

"So, you're here too," I said. "I thought you had made up your mind that Israel did not need old Marxists expert at the art of threading a bear through the eye of a needle."

"You remember that I told you the bad days were over and done with? Well, they weren't. You were right. I was wrong."

He told me that a certain young man, "and, unfortunately, a very learned one," had set his sights on his post and informed against him that he was spreading false ideas under the cover of seminars on Spinoza, failing to place sufficient stress on the philosopher's "aetheism," and ignoring the campaign waged against him by the benighted rabbis, and so on and so forth, accusations which were "neither true nor false." He had been hauled over the coals by the university authorities—especially one man of whom everyone was in awe, since he had a direct line to "God himself"—and been forced to sign a humiliating declaration, "which had nothing to do with the teachings of Spinoza," but "touched painfully" on the most elementary questions of ethics. In the end he had been dismissed from his post.

"I made a mistake," he said, "when I undertook to edit the *Philosophical Journal.* If I had been a printer or a proofreader, nobody would have bothered to pull my chair out from under me . . ."

Together with his job, the apartment and car disappeared too. And after that, his wife. I had refrained from asking about her, in order not to give him pain, but he spoke about her quite dryly. He warned me against ambitious women, and quoted the sages to the effect that "Three things satisfy the mind of a man: a handsome house, handsome furniture, and a handsome wife." A handsome woman, he said, wants a handsome house and handsome furniture. And once a man had "satisfied his mind" with the latter, he was sure to find the former as well. But this was cupboard love, he said, and when the cupboard was bare, the love flew out of the window.

"And you should beware of non-Jewish women too," he went on, a sarcastic smile cutting his mouth like a knife. "As long as you have assets, you're a man, a colleague, a comrade, a citizen, a lover; the moment you lose them, you're a Jew. . . . Anti-Semitism may be illegal, but it's not illegal to hate the Jews. . . . And when you're trapped in the same cage, the situation becomes unbearable . . ."

My letter to him had something to do with it too. His wife found the letter and went to consult a friend. "The man is destroying himself," she said, "and dragging me down with him. It isn't enough for him that he's out of favor and under surveillance. He's got the nerve to correspond with Israel."

"But you didn't answer my letter," I said.

"That only made things worse. It proved that I was concealing my connections with the Zionists.

"If your letter hadn't arrived, they would only have invented something worse," he comforted me. "They're a heavy-handed lot. They would have fabricated some document thanking me for the sketches of the Soviet battle order in Khabarovsk, or something of the kind. Black and white, an open-and-shut case, so that even the stupidest lawyer would understand that he should

beg the pardon of the court for undertaking the defense of a
criminal like me. . . ."

After his wife left him—she made things as unpleasant as
she could and then walked out, for which he was not particularly sorry since in any case he had never seen her as a partner
for life, but rather as one of the perks that came with the job—
and he no longer had an apartment worthy of the name, "and
friends even less so"—there was nothing left for him but to
choose one of two things: to kill himself or to join distant relatives in Israel. It never occurred to him that it was possible to
choose both together.

"Enough, enough," I cried. "Here you have both relatives
and friends."

"Thank you," said Epstein. "But let's stop talking about me
and hear something about you. You sound as if the country
belongs to you already . . ."

I told him a little about my doings, sparing him the things
I thought might depress him. You don't lean on a cripple. I told
him about my notebooks.

"You're writing?"

"Like a hungry man who's found a potato and is afraid it
might go rotten . . ."

"What are you writing? 'The Snows of the North' or 'The
Classless Society'?"

"Neither. Whatever the eye sees and the ear hears."

"That's fine for anyone whose eye sees," he said, and I failed
to get the hint.

I told him how glad I was that he had come. I had written
a diary and I couldn't show it to anybody. The urge to write had
prevailed over caution. I was afraid that my relations would be
hurt. And I had resigned myself to regarding my notebooks as a
kind of legacy, the property I would leave to my inheritors. But
now I had been lucky enough to find a reader.

Epstein sighed. "A reader?"

He thought that his blindness was noticeable, and therefore
he had not seen fit to mention it.

"I can only read very big letters. And certainly not handwriting," he said.

*T*here are moments of reconciliation. You say to yourself: What more can I ask for? "It was only to see the face of the sun that I came into the world." And this sky. And these mountains. And the sea, of course. The sea.

How I love to go down to the sea. The soft sand, the water, its slightly burning saltiness, its warmth. A wave falls defeated at your feet. A distant storm subsides in the shallow water. And the people in the water, beautiful bodies, ugly bodies, thin, fat, young, old bodies, side by side, without barriers, undressed, without pride but in what God gave them, their vulnerable nakedness a little sad, but containing the potential for a simple joy. The boys and girls playing with a ball on the wet sand, showing off their sunburned limbs, the old men remembering that all they were and are is contained in this flabby flesh. And the children, their small bodies taut as bowstrings in a reckless race into the unknown, a headlong dive into adventure. The old women shedding their clothes and revealing their modesty, the young girls with their wooden paddles, their limbs quivering with excitement: one bends to pick up her ball and her twin looks as if they were about to plunge to the ground.

On the beach I am part of the crowd. When I enter the water and my thin bony legs stride through the foamy waves—I am alone. I throw myself into the water and it encloses me and takes me out of the world. Only the sky above, and this deep blue. Loving them, for their own sakes. In the water the time is always the present. With the eyes of my father I gaze at the worlds of my sons. And when I close my eyes, I take the pictures with me underneath my lids. In my darkroom I develop them, and see them again in their bright colors. And the circles close.

Truly I want so little. For me the future holds nothing. I am content if tomorrow is like today. I shall call it happiness. I shall take up a book. A well-written passage moves me. A lucid line, a truthful word, the right sadness. I shall listen to Tchaikovsky and let fall a secret tear. I shall speak to Verchinsky. I shall play chess. I shall see the gratitude in the eyes of the old men I lower into the bath. I shall plan the garden around "my house." I shall sleep without nightmares.

But how easy it is to raise my hopes!

Last night Nina called. She wants to meet me. For a moment or two my surprise was such that I could not speak. "Are you there, Vitya?" "I'm here, I'm here, of course I'm here." My whole life flashed through my mind. Thus, they say, a man feels in the moment before his death. "Tell me where and I'll come."

She gave me the address of a little cafe in old Tel Aviv. She would wait for me there. She asked me to be discreet. It was a serious matter. But she refused to go into details. Not over the phone.

The pictures that flashed through my mind! The curls falling onto her brow, her voice whispering in the passage, her passionate kisses, the touch of her hand on my skin.

Everything I had ever held against her was wiped out in a second. I remembered everything for the best. I was prepared to remember even Leopold Sherrer with love. A man loyal to a single lust. And rightly. Wasn't she worth it? And the charity of her youth. The way she followed me into an unknown land. A slender-fingered girl pianist, who chose to love a peasant rather than face the yearly examinations at the conservatory with her heart in her boots. And the heartrending moments by the cradle of a sick little girl.

In my imagination I looked forward to secret meetings, whispered words of love. Holding her hand underneath the table, shamelessly breathing sweet nothings into her ear. . . . Nina, oh, Nina. . . . And I had been prepared to resign myself. And I had not dared to hope. Shame on me! To his last breath a man should be prepared to fight for his own.

But the meeting was bitter. Nina was confused and angry. She was beside herself. She didn't even know why she had asked to meet me. To scold me? To consult me? To ask me for something? Her face was pale, worn. There was an ugly fear in her eyes. Someone had written an anonymous letter to her husband. It said that I was alive and in Israel. There were a lot of details in the letter. Even where I was staying. Her husband showed her the letter. He asked her what she had to say. And she lied and said that she knew nothing about it. But what would happen if he investigated the matter? It was a mess with no way out.

I didn't understand why she was so worried. I apologized: it wasn't my fault, I had done everything in my power to efface myself. I had not mentioned her existence to anyone. Everyone believed that I had had a wife in Russia who had died many years ago. I had even been invited to take part in a television program—I rounded out the facts a little—and I had refused for the same reason. Nor had I asked to be sent to this swarming hive of an old-age home, where everybody poked his nose into his neighbor's business. I wouldn't have minded if they had sent me to some remote development town. But it was a small country, and anyone who wanted to tell tales could do so anywhere. I even wrote my articles in the Russian-language press under a pseudonym, in order not to attract attention to myself. What more could I have done?

Died, I said after a moment. A joke, and in her eyes a tasteless one. She did not understand what it hinted at. How far I was prepared to efface myself for the sake of her happiness.

Afterward she was sorry for her frankness. She said that it wasn't herself she was worried about, she didn't want her husband to be hurt. He was a weak, sickly man. And if he found out that she had lied now, he would be convinced that she had lied then too, when she told him that she had seen my death certificate with her own eyes. And it would give him a terrible shock.

I promised her that he would not find out. But anonymous letter writers are nasty people and they would not spare him. If they discovered anything, he would know it too.

She asked me to find out who had written the anonymous letter. Presumably it was someone who held a grudge against me. I said that I couldn't understand why someone who had a grudge against me would want to hurt her husband, who had never done him any harm. I said that I would try to find the man and put the fear of God into him. But I doubted if he would write another anonymous letter, to deny the first.

I had no intention of becoming a private detective in my old age. I detest investigations and interrogations. I could think of only one man. Efros. But I remembered our conversation. I had been careful and told him that my wife was dead. And he had believed me. He had even taken the opportunity to hurt me by telling me that Minkovsky did not want Nina to marry me.

I also remembered that the only person to whom I had told the truth was Verchinsky, but I was loath to question him—he would think that I was accusing him and I might lose his friendship. Nevertheless, my curiosity gained the upper hand. Very tentatively, discreetly, trying to keep my voice as casual as possible, I told him about the anonymous letter while we were playing chess.

Verchinsky had no hesitations about blaming himself. He was very sorry that he had let it slip. My guess was right. The person he had told it to was Efros. Not intentionally, mind you, but the man had boasted of his magnanimity, and he, although he did not lose his temper easily, could not let him get away with it. You! he said sarcastically, you wouldn't sacrifice a single pawn for anyone else; but I know a man who for the sake of the woman he loves has sacrificed even his name, and signs his translations and his articles with a pseudonym. And then Efros, who guessed immediately whom he was referring to, exclaimed: "Woman? What woman? His wife is dead."

A look that Nina gave me during our meeting has not stopped haunting me. She had the same look in her eyes, the look of a trapped animal, when they came to arrest me.

At first she was afraid that they had come for us both, and she was terrified for the sake of the child. But when it became clear that it was only me they had come to arrest, her face took

on an expression of dignity and disdain. She looked at the young
detectives turning the house upside down with a chilly hauteur,
as if none of it had anything to do with her.

When they broke into the apartment with their revolvers
drawn, my first feeling was one of idiotic pride: they thought me
so dangerous! But I soon realized that this gesture was not aimed
against me. It was a kind of drill which they strictly observed.
Standing orders. They knew very well that I would go like a lamb
to the slaughter, like so many others. I could not even find it in
my heart to be angry with them. They were only instruments in
the hands of others. Furthermore: if I was innocent, I would only
harm my case if I behaved suspiciously. Besides, I couldn't be
angry with them because they were such nice, polite fellows (the
blue uniforms, with all the terror they aroused, were covered by
gray overcoats), and they spoke in lowered voices so as not to
disturb the neighbors.

Later on, however, I discovered that I was mistaken in them.

I had placed the doll, with the sheaf of poems by the poet
who had already been arrested inside it, in Olga's arms before I
opened the door. When they approached her bed I asked them
not to wake her up.

"It's too late to worry about your daughter now," the
younger of the two, a boy with a soft, smooth baby face, said
nastily. "You should have thought of her before."

He spoke of my "crimes" in a tone of utter conviction. I
wondered if he really believed it, or if this too was a kind of drill,
to make his job easier and compensate him for his sleepless
night, to pour his hatred for me into battle slogans, in case he
might be tempted to treat me like a human being.

Stealthily, bowed down under the weight of his shame, hating the whole business with all his heart and soul, Zirkin, a
neighbor from the third floor, sidled into the room. To witness
the arrest. He looked at us with the eyes of a slaughtered calf,
begged for mercy with a nervous blinking of his eyes, and sat
down in a corner.

"I'm sorry that you have been disturbed at an hour like this on my account, Comrade Zirkin," I said.

The older of the two, who had seemed very humane to me, judging by the way in which he carefully returned everything to its place, gave me a sudden slap, insulting in its suddenness, as if it had been latent in his palm all the while, biding its time.

"Shut up! No talking to the witness!"

At the same time the younger detective was struggling with Olga, who yelled with all the power of her lungs.

"Leave her alone," said the older one. "All we need here is a baby screaming."

"Shame on you!" exclaimed Nina at the roughness with which he threw the child and the doll back onto the bed.

He approached her and looked coldly into her eyes. Her gray eyes stared back with an arrogant, haughty look. I wanted to cry out to her to stop this dangerous confrontation, but she could not hide her hatred. And then he jabbed two fingers into her face.

"Open your mouth! I have to see that she's not hiding anything there," he justified his actions to his friend, and a loathsome, lecherous smile made his handsome face ugly as he stuck his fingers into Nina's mouth and poked around in it.

It was then that the look came into her eyes: helpless rage, fear, a recognition of the uselessness of any expression of emotion.

In jail, in the first days, when I closed my eyes, that look pierced me. I remembered how I stood wretchedly by, my eyes downcast, impotent, boiling with rage, paralyzed.

I read the introduction to my diary to Epstein.

He interrupted me in the middle.

"Why do you have to apologize? And if I were you I wouldn't keep on threatening: I'm going to tell the truth in a minute. Ninety-nine out of a hundred liars are sure that that is exactly what they are doing. And only one out of a hundred has got the guts and the self-respect to say to himself that he has seated himself at his desk in order to lie."

Autumn is approaching. An autumn without autumn leaves. Only one tree in the garden of the house across the road is turning yellow. There are heavy clouds in the sky and the sea is a greenish-gray. Finesod House is like a transit camp, the turnover is so great. People die and others come to take their places. I have been here only for a few months, and already I feel as if I have put down roots. I welcome the newcomers with much willingness to pass on my experience to them, just as the veteran immigrants, two weeks in the country, welcomed new immigrants at the Jaffa port in the 1920s.

I am learning to type Braille. But I don't know if I will have the strength to type my book for Epstein. When I visit Olga, I go down to the basement and "plan my house." On what I am earning now, I will need forty-five years to transform it from a drawing to a reality.

Nimrod is learning the multiplication table. He already knows that I am his father, but he calls me Avigdor, a name which he is the only one to use. It is like a code word signifying the closeness between us. I wrote an article and signed it "B. Avigdor." The article is a kind of letter to a son—but I do not know if he will ever be able to read it.

The pains in the foot which was once infected by gangrene have grown worse lately, and it is hard for me to walk. For the most part, I stay at home. But I never know a moment's boredom. I live in the clear knowledge that the coming days will have a surprise in store for me.

I am expecting Nina.

I know that she will come. Not today or tomorrow. Perhaps not in this coming autumn. But she will come. I am certain of it.

I can wait.

Forty days before she was born a voice from Heaven foretold it.

There is no longer anyone to stop her. The day that she met me in the Tel Aviv cafe, Zilberstein was taken to the hospital and he never recovered. A few days ago he died.

She will mourn for as long as her heart and her respect for appearances tell her to, and then she will come. She will take her inheritance, she will even forfeit a little of it in favor of other relations, and she will come. For what else do old people need, besides love?

When she comes I shall say nothing. I shall ask nothing.

An end to questions. I questioned. I was questioned. Enough.

I shall only take her coat off her shoulders and lead her into the room. As if she had come home from a short walk outside. It is cold out there and snowing. And inside there is warmth and light.

Only to myself I shall whisper soundlessly: Welcome, happiness.

As long as a man lives, he still has a chance to turn over a new leaf.